The Midshipman

By

Douglas Hargreaves

ISBN: 1-4107-2617-7 (e-book)
ISBN: 1-4107-3330-0 (Paperback)

This book is printed on acid free paper.

1stBooks - rev. 04/16/03

Doug…sometime in his life has to have been a

gambler.

Who else would dream up a plot in which youngsters 12 to 14 years of age would sell the entire Caribbean Fleet of the British Navy on it's Beams Ends.

Doug's little sailors- Midshipmen and Powder boys get into some incredible situations that nothing short of a miracle could save them.

The author's skillful pen and agile mind, effect a series of rescues that could happen.

However – Dear reader ---- he is also realistic enough in his writing to know that not all the good ones return.

Read it… You'll Like it S. T. R.

CREDITS

Editor: Robert Haugen
Proof Reader: Luke's Mom
Designers: Compuservices
Cover: Stewart Irwin

TABLE OF CONTENTS

CHAPTER ONE

The Earl of Windsor

"I do not intend to return to that pig sty again. I have nothing to learn from that place and I refuse to be associated with those imbeciles who call themselves my classmates. I am being tainted by my very association with them. You cannot make me return to school. I refuse!" the young Earl screamed at his father who was pacing back and forth in the great library of the Windsor estate.

It was obvious that the twelve-year-old Earl of the House of Windsor was in another one of his tantrums and heaven help anyone who got in his way.

"David, you must listen to reason and return. There is no other academy that will take you. You have been expelled from them all and you must complete your education. I will not hear another word of this childishness from you just because someone happened to brush past you without acknowledging you or some other ridiculous occurrence," the Duke said, trying to reason with his son. His patience was at an end as he had been through this scene many times. The headmasters of the many schools the Earl attended referred to him as extremely intelligent but entirely incorrigible, and they felt that there was no help for him without a major change in his attitude. The desire to strangle the little monster was prevalent amongst everyone who knew him. Ordinarily, discipline for bad behavior was a caning by the Headmaster, however, the school was not allowed to discipline the Earl in this manner.

The Duke continued pacing back and forth, still holding the letter he had received from the last Headmaster. The letter stated that the Earl was extremely bright and learned quickly but because of his obnoxious nature and troublesome attitude he could no longer be tolerated in the school and was being expelled. The writer went on to apologize to the Duke but was sure he would understand.

> *"...The boy is entirely devoid of conscience and manners and is bent on destroying everything and everyone with whom he comes in contact. If I might make a suggestion your Lordship, I think you should consider sending the boy to the Navy for a career in that service.*
>
> *We would have suggested corporal punishment with the cane had we thought it would have any deterrent effect on the young*

Earl. We sincerely apologize to your Lordship but we are unable to cope any longer..."

"David, you have finally succeeded in turning every school in the country against you. You are now without further opportunities of an education in the formal system. I am not prepared to go through the same problems we had when we employed tutors for your education. You virtually drove them mad," the Duke admonished.

"Why are you always taking everyone's side against me? Why is it that I am surrounded by dolts?" he screamed at his father.

"You devious excuse for a human being. You have disgraced all of our household as well as the family name. I am not prepared to stand by and see you ruin your life as well as everyone else's. Do you hear me, David?" the Duke shouted. "I have put up with your tantrums and your disgraceful and arrogant behavior for the last time. I have enlisted you in His Royal Majesty's Navy, where perhaps at long last you will learn discipline and further your education. Perhaps one day you may make something of yourself," the Duke announced.

"What in damnation are you saying, Father? Never in ten thousand years or your life time will I join any group of thugs employed by HIS MAJESTY, the drunken idiot!" David screamed. He ran from the room, bumping into the butler who was bringing the

Duke's lunch. Everything went flying, including some valuable china pieces.

"Send a messenger to Admiral Lord Guthery and have him send someone to collect the Earl of Windsor immediately. He is to be their problem forthwith. I want him out of the house by the week's end!" the Duke ranted on to his butler, who was busy cleaning up the remnants of the Duke's lunch. "Never mind, I have a better idea. I'll send the Earl by our own coach and we can be done with this mess sooner," the Duke said, seeming pleased with his decision. The butler was only too happy to be excused. The air was quite alive with fuming and oaths.

"Samuel, fetch the Earl to my study immediately. There is no need to pack. He'll not be requiring any clothing other than what he is wearing. Have the coach brought around. It will be going to London," the Duke ordered.

Samuel, who had been a butler in the house for many years, even before the young Earl had been born, heaved a great sigh of relief as the significance of the Dukes orders registered. *Drat the little monster, he'll get his comeuppance now, so he will*, Samuel smiled to himself. *Great joy at last! Now the household can return to normal.*

Samuel knocked on the door, expecting to receive a tirade of abusive oathing. "Samuel, I am not going to tolerate being disturbed! Do you understand me?" the voice from within screamed.

"Your father requires your presence in the library forthwith m'lord," Samuel instructed.

"I don't want to see him unless he is prepared to talk nicely to me. After all, I am the Earl, his only son. What does he want anyway?" the Earl yelled.

"I'm sure I do not know m'lord, but he sounded impatient, if I may be so bold," Samuel replied.

"You may not be so bold, you dilapidated excuse for a man servant. Inform him I do not intend to disturb my quiet time listening to more lectures on our wonderful education system," the Earl announced, in a most arrogant tone.

"As you wish m'lord," Samuel replied, relieved at not having to address the young tyrant face to face. Samuel returned to the library where the Duke continued to pace back and forth. "Your Lordship. I'm afraid the young Earl is not prepared to see you." Samuel hesitated in using the Earl's exact words.

"Has the coach arrived? I want him bodily removed from his room and placed in the coach with you, Samuel, as a guard to ensure his safe arrival. I do not want him escaping. Tell him he is going to visit his great Aunt. He sometimes tolerates her as she is of the same disgusting nature. They deserve each other's company," the Duke concluded.

* * * *

The coachmen proceeded to the Earl's room with much trepidation and knocked out of courtesy and custom.

The Earl yelled that he was not seeing his father under any circumstances. Samuel nodded to the two coachmen to enter the room. They had been looking forward to the day when they might thrash this insolent waif. They carried the yelling and screaming Earl out into the carriage. The Duke could not bring himself to watch or say farewell to the boy. Even if it was his own son he was sending away, he was happy to be rid of the menace. Now he would be the Navy's problem and he was certain they would handle the matter as they saw fit. Young David, Earl of Windsor, fifth in line to the Windsor fortunes and all its estates and holdings, fought and screamed as the coach drew out of sight. The Earl of Windsor was about to commence a stage of his life he would never forget.

Samuel was subjected to every insult the Earl could express with threats of dismissal and even death if the Earl was not released immediately and returned home. Samuel maintained a solid determination that the Earl was to be delivered as planned. David would be out of his life and all the other members of the Windsor Estate, hopefully forever.

* * * *

"Why are we drawing up to this building, my Aunt doesn't live here? Am I to meet her here? What's going on may I ask?" the Earl proceeded to give his guards a difficult time.

The coachmen secured the horses and entered the coach. They removed the young Earl, carrying him as he screamed all sorts of demeaning obscenities.

A Naval Lieutenant opened the door to receive the undignified newest member to His Majesty's Royal Navy.

"Ah, I see you have brought his Lordship, the Earl of Windsor, or should I say our newest Midshipman, David Clements to be indoctrinated into the service. Gentlemen, you may leave the body in my care. I will have him properly attended to forthwith," the young Lieutenant said, as he bid farewell to Samuel and the coachmen.

"Damn you Samuel, I'll see you burning in hell before this fiasco is finished! You may take my word on that you treacherous misfit!" the young Earl screamed after the departing men.

The Lieutenant was not impressed and called for assistance when the young Earl started making for the door.

"I'll see you all burn and your ship sunk!" he screamed at the two guards sent to attend to him.

Master David Clements, Midshipman, was being attached to His Majesty's Ship, *Subdue,* which was a very appropriate name for the ship that would carry the responsibility of turning the Earl into a seaman and an officer.

"You will no longer be addressed as your Lordship but by your new title, Midshipman David Clements. You are about to become a Naval Officer. Stand at attention when I am talking to you," the Admiral shouted, trying to control his temper.

"You have no right to do this despicable and certainly treasonable act upon me. I'm sure my father will have you demoted for this scandalous act. I'll see to it myself you old goat. Do you know who I am?" the Earl demanded.

"Confound it Lieutenant, shut this magpie up or I'll have him before the mast before he's even sworn," declared the Admiral.

The First Lieutenant placed his hand upon David's shoulder, who shrugged it off and shouted, "I demand to see my Father at once, you hear?"

"Lieutenant, there is no point carrying on further discussion with this popinjay. Get him out of my sight! Get him into a uniform and have his belongings sent over to the *Subdue* as soon as you can. I will send a letter of explanation and apology to Captain Willoughby, who I am afraid will have to deal with this." The Admiral turned to David and with disdain in his voice continued. "Young man, I'm sure you will be 'standing to the mast' more than you will be performing ship's duties unless you change that attitude of yours. Now get away with you!"

"I'll see you reduced to nothing, you old goat!" the Earl yelled as he was being led away.

"Lieutenant, see that instructions are written to accompany this boy to his new Captain. I want him to receive a warm welcome in front of the mast before all the crew to witness! Perhaps that will tone down this arrogant little puppy. He is too dumb to be cited for insubordination," said the Admiral, with a wave of his hand in dismissal.

CHAPTER TWO

A Warm Welcome

Aboard the ship, *Subdue*, the Captain was conversing with his Lieutenant. "Mr. Wright, I suppose you have heard that we are being saddled with another of the Admiral's political mis-adventures. This time he is sending us the Earl of Windsor, a twelve-year-old terror on two legs. A despicable and incorrigible brat of a child we are expected to tame and mold into a King's Officer." The Captain breathed out a deep sigh. "I am giving you this wretched assignment as you seem to have a way with the young gentlemen. I don't know what spell you have over them but whatever it is it keeps the young people in line. I expect a progress report and you may take whatever steps you see fit in this endeavor. He is to be afforded no extra considerations or privileges. He is just another Midshipman and will be expected to study and perform like the others. Mr. Wright I'd say you have your hands full this time. Good luck. I am leaving the ship for a short time. On my return I expect to hoist anchor and leave on the tide," the Captain said, making his way to the entry port.

Captain Willoughby normally left the every day routine matters of running the ship to his First Officer, while he spent much of his time lounging in his cabin consuming copious quantities of wines from his private collection. He was often in a complete state of inebriation, as he dreamed of accumulating great sums of money from prizes yet to be taken.

Back at the Admiralty Offices, the Admiral's staff Lieutenant had given up trying to get a uniform on the Earl. He determined it was an impossible task, so he bundled the uniform into a parcel and sent it to the jetty where a boatman was waiting to take the Midshipman to the *Subdue.*

The Admiral's Lieutenant and the boatman, literally carried the struggling and screaming Earl down to the boat where he promptly fell in an undignified heap into the bilge. Like most harbor transports, foul bilge water and other materials lay inches deep in the bottom. He was soaking wet and covered in grime when he stood up, shouting and screaming at the boatman and the Lieutenant in his humiliation.

"You will rue the day you ever set eyes on me, you pig! Let me out of this filthy wreck immediately!" the Earl yelled looking up at the ship's entry port.

Mr. Wright smiled as he looked down at the screaming Earl and thought of how he was going to enjoy taming this young hellion. He wondered how anyone so young could have succeeded in being so obnoxious. The young man was being sent aboard the right vessel to change his attitude.

The boat had been rowed with great haste to the ship anchored a short distance from the Jetty. All aboard the *Subdue*, as well as most every ship in the harbor, could hear the shouting and screaming threats of the struggling Earl. The Midshipmen of the *Subdue* were gathered along the railing by the entry port enjoying the diversion from their duties grinning and looking at one another as they shook their heads. They knew what lay ahead for their new shipmate.

They wondered if this could be the new Midshipman they had been expecting. The one who was a member of the aristocracy, an Earl or something of that sort. This fighting bantam rooster surely could not be the Earl of Windsor.

There was no doubt in anyone's mind, that severe disciplinary measures would be taken upon the Earl. Aristocracy or not, the lad was in for a very difficult time unless he changed his arrogant attitude.

The *Subdue* was an efficient ship, but the crew worked under bullying Bos'n's, with the First Officer and the Second Lieutenant ruling the Midshipmen.

The *Subdue* had gained a reputation for being one of the most savage and cruelly disciplined ships in the fleet and obviously one to be avoided at all cost – not that the crews had any choice in the matter.

The Captain turned a blind eye to the punishment meted out to the crew, which in many cases was unjust. Even the smallest infraction of rules would result in a flogging. The Midshipmen lived in utter fear living in squalor and unable to bathe or maintain cleanliness. Their appearance resembled that of the disheveled powder boys. None were excluded from the cruel punishments even though they held temporary King's commissions aboard *HMS Subdue*.

Most ships were crewed by hapless men, pressed or removed from the city streets or local goals for service. They were badly treated, and had little to lose other than the skin off their backs, by stealing and committing other acts of disobedience.

Subdue's Master, Will Kenting, knew about the devious behavior of First Officer Wright and his cohort Senior Midshipman Colin Breckenridge. They were sadistic and voracious pederasts, and preyed upon the younger men and boys of the crew. He had, on several occasions, reported his observations to the Captain who shrugged the Master's claims, as minor mischief and it was to be expected aboard ships that were long time at sea. The Captain would not hear another word of such claims.

David Clements, Earl of Windsor, was a handsome boy and the Ship's Master knew it would only be a matter of time before the young upstart would succumb to the humiliation and physical abuse.

All aboard knew what was in store for the young Earl as a result of his behavior and attitude. The commotion he created upon boarding the vessel provided a great deal of entertainment for the crew. It was unfortunate for the new Midshipman that the Captain had still not returned, and it would be the First Officer who would be dealing with him.

The ship's Midshipmen felt some degree of anguish for the Earl. Twelve year old Kenneth Walters, who until now had been the junior Midshipman, knew only too well what lay ahead for the Earl, but was thankful he would no longer be the Junior Officer having to cater to the whims and fancies of the Senior and other Senior Midshipmen.

The Earl was shoved unceremoniously through the entry port, sitting and looking around at all the staring crew members, especially the other Midshipmen. His eyes stared at them with utter hate that seemed to penetrate their souls.

"What are you all staring at, you nincompoops? I demand to see the Captain immediately! Do you hear me? Right this instant I tell you!" the Earl ordered. The Midshipmen looked at each other and shrugged. They knew it was already too late for the Earl. It would be the Mast for sure. He would 'Kiss the

Gunner's Daughter' – the old Naval expression for the whipping young boys took while bent over the barrel of a gun.

Discipline aboard naval vessels was essential for strong effective war ships, and at times, punishment for rule breakers was harsh but effective. Seamen who disregarded the rules or orders were tied to a grating and flogged. This punishment was witnessed by the crew as a deterrent against similar behavior.

Aboard the *Subdue,* the young Officers were disciplined with a rattan cane or a sword scabbard upon their buttocks while held across a gun barrel. Their punishment was the most humiliating because it was witnessed by the men they commanded.

"I am First Lieutenant Aubrey Wright and you will stand at attention when you address me, do you understand English?" directing his question to David.

He motioned the two Senior Midshipmen to take the Earl below and outfit him in his uniform. "I'll not have you stand punishment in civilian clothing and as filthy as you are." He questioned the boatman as to whether or not this was the right lad assigned as Midshipman.

The Boatman replied, "Oh yes indeed Sir, and a mighty handful he was too," shaking his head as he replied.

"Mr. Roberts, assemble the crew to witness punishment," the First ordered the Second Officer. The ship's crew was gathered on the deck and knew exactly what lay ahead for the newest member of the crew. *There is nothing that tames the wild and unruly ones like the cane,* they thought. *The boy would learn something by the time this punishment was through.*

The Earl was returned to the quarter deck struggling and screaming as he attempted to remove his uniform.

"Mr. David Clements, you are being called to account for your insubordination and despicable behavior. The Admiral has written that you are to be punished before all gathered here as witnesses to an Officer's punishment. You will received six strokes."

The Earl feeling a little uneasy, realized that his bluff was being called, and that if he were to ever save face he must take the offensive and call them to face his own charges.

"I don't quite know what you plan for my so-called punishment, but all who take part in this, will rot in hell when my Father hears of this terrible indignity wrought on a member of the House of Windsor!" the Earl yelled. Cheers could be heard from crews aboard other ships anchored in close proximity to the *Subdue.* The Earl's screaming could be heard throughout the anchorage.

It wasn't until the Earl was bent over the gun barrel that he realized he was about to be caned and to suffer the indignity and humiliation in front of the crew. He started to shake and scream even more obscenities. When the first stroke of the scabbard struck, he screamed at the top of his lungs, cursing all in attendance especially the First Lieutenant. The next strokes were one after another and by the time the last one was completed, the young Earl was a howling and screaming demon. He was escorted to the Midshipman's berth in the gun room where he was assigned a locker and a berth.

He remained standing, sobbing quietly and seething inside. He was trying to sort out his feelings and think of some way he could retaliate against those in authority. He had never felt the cane before. It was a new experience for him and one he did not wish to repeat.

Midshipman Kenneth Walters entered the berth and introduced himself. He tried to comfort and befriend the Earl but was brushed aside. Walters knew too well that David Clements was doomed. He recalled when the First Officer and the Senior Midshipman had ordered the boys from the powder room to their cabins. He had been told what took place under the guise of disciplinary action. Kenneth had protested on behalf of the boys, only to be horribly thrashed and then sent to the First's cabin where he was then abused. He knew it was worth his life to interfere again.

"I don't require assistance from anyone," David stumbled around the gun room selecting a berth he preferred over the upper hammock he had been assigned.

"Boy?" directing his orders to Walters, "get that fellow's gear off my berth immediately, I am taking that hammock. Throw his things on someone else's berth!" David ordered.

"I'm not allowed to touch anything that belongings to the Senior. They'll have me to the mast or even worse just like you were," Kenneth warned.

"Do as I say, or I'll do it myself, and I'll blame you for it. NOW!! Do it this instant!" David continued to raise his voice.

The Midshipman stood silently in the doorway, knowing he couldn't be a party to this blatant act of mischief.

"You will be disciplined and subjected to terrible punishment when my Father finds out what happened to me," the Earl warned.

"You're not really an Earl are you?" Walters asked.

"Yes I am, and you and everyone aboard this ship will pay for this day. When my Father the Duke hears of this, you will all wish you were dead."

Midshipman Walters quickly departed the gun room and reluctantly reported to the Senior the happenings below. He did not want to be involved in the trouble the Earl was in already. As much as he hated to inform on the Earl, he knew the terrible consequences he would face if he didn't. The Senior quickly departed to search for the Earl.

"So you little snot, you are still at it. You have still not learned your lesson. The caning wasn't enough. Well better prepare your backside, for you're about to get another. I hope you have some meat on your rear end, or else you will have your bones fractured," the Senior warned, enjoying the distress reflected in the Earl's face. David realized he had gone too far, and there was no turning back. The Senior left and returned a short time later with the First Officer.

"I see you have been at work on the Senior's belongings," he said. "Fine my lad, if this is the way you want it, then so be it. The mast for him and remove his britches," the First ordered.

Once again the Crew was assembled while the Earl was given six more canings. There appeared no end to the laughter as the men pointed to the Earl's reddened and bruised posterior. He was left weeping quietly to himself embarrassed and humiliated beyond anything he had ever experienced.

"Now Mr. Clements. You will return to the berth and return everything to its original place, and you will take whatever berth is assigned you. Is that clear?" the

First ordered. David sneered through his tears at the First.

"I repeat! Do you understand my instructions?" the First asked. David made a face. "What are we ever to do with you my lad?" He smiled at David's insubordination, knowing he was in charge of handing out punishment. "Senior, I wish this upstart to be given twelve additional strokes immediately, and then you will personally take charge of this little monster.

Any further problems, and we will have every inch of fat pounded off his little posterior and have him hanging by his heels from the yard," the First Officer threatened as he walked away.

Once again the Midshipman was bent over the gun barrel, his breaches down around his ankles and twelve additional strokes were applied until the Earl lost consciousness. He was carried to his berth where the ship's doctor examined him, and in spite of his terrible injuries, approved the Earl for active duty.

"Hear that your stinkin' little Lordship? Get to work now and replace all my belongings and get this locker looking the cleanest it has ever been," the Senior ordered. Turning to Kenneth Walters, he continued, "See that he obeys every detail, or you know what's in store for you."

The threat had a profound effect on Kenneth as he looked away and blinked hard to hide tears that were forming in the corner of his eyes. He knew he couldn't let anyone see this weakness in an Officer, even is he was just a boy. He begged the Earl to cooperate.

The Earl laid on the deck unable to stand. Walters commenced cleaning up the mess, and restoring everything to their original places. David watched the Midshipman carry out his detail. His pain was unbearable, and he found himself unable to speak. Kenneth completed the cleaning up and helped David onto the upper berth.

"Your Lordship, please don't fight them. You can't win, and we are about to be put to sea. They have to discipline you to save face. It will go on your record, and you will never get a promotion. You will end up a powder boy or something terrible like that. Please listen to me, I know what I'm talking about," Kenneth warned.

"What's your name?" David asked through his sobbing, holding his arrogance under control.

"My name is Kenneth Walters and I'm twelve. I was the Junior Midshipman till you came aboard. I've been aboard six months. This will be my second voyage."

"Kenneth, why do you stay in this terrible place?" the Earl asked.

"Because I can't get off the ship. I would like to have escaped many times, but there is no way. If you're caught, you are hung for desertion. You'll get used to it after awhile. Just beware of the First and the Senior, they are always looking for ways to have you punished. They put you on report making some excuse to get you caned or even worse," he said bowing his head and looking around to see if anyone might have overheard his conversation. David wondered what could ever be worse. Unfortunately, someone had overheard their conversation.

"Well Mr. Walters, filling in our new Midshipman with all the formalities of the ship are we?" the Senior asked as he stood in the doorway.

"Oh no Sir, just telling his Lordship that he had best follow orders or be prepared to be punished," he replied, shaking from fright.

"You will be happy to know that because of your helpful little talk to this royal pain in the neck here, you are about to share a position over the gun barrel with him – or would you rather be summoned to the First's cabin? You knew that all Officers and Midshipmen were not allowed to converse with this misfit!" the Senior smirked.

"Please, Senior, Sir. I never meant any harm by warning the Earl about orders and other things," the Midshipman begged. "Sir! I really don't wish to be punished."

"Oh you don't wish to? Did I hear you correctly Walters? You do not wish to obey an order?" the Senior taunted Kenneth. "Too bad. The First

Lieutenant will be happy to see you after your watch is over. Understood Walters?" he ordered as he left the boys.

Kenneth, with a look of utter despair, blinked his eyes to hide his tears and replied, "Yes Sir, I'll be there."

"Why are you being summoned to the First's cabin and why are you crying?" David asked.

"I can't tell you, and I can't talk to you any more or I will be in more trouble," he said as he was departing.

"Thank you. I shan't forget I assure you," David replied as Kenneth left the quarters without saying a word.

A short time later the Senior ordered the Earl from his berth to begin his instruction on how he was to stand his watch. Kenneth was not sure whether he should be happy or greatly distressed upon hearing that the Earl was being assigned to him to teach and tame. David made up his mind to go along with the orders, and not provide the Officers with an opportunity to have him punished again. He would wait until the right opportunity to escape presented itself. He would get even.

The Captain returned to the ship and immediately ordered the ship to weigh anchor. All hands were busy as the ship prepared to sail. Kenneth and David were working near each other as the ship was preparing to sail.

"It's my duty to assure that all lines are secure aboard, and that every man is accounted for. Seamen try to escape the ship at times like this when there is a lot of commotion and activity," Kenneth advised David.

"Your Lordship—er, I mean David. I am asking you not to engage me in any conversation other than questions about the ship. I will be severely punished if I disobey those orders," Kenneth confided while looking over his shoulder for anyone who might overhear.

The procedure of weighing anchor was complete, and the ship's huge sails began tumbling down from the yards. For anyone not seeing the event before, it was an impressive sight and the Earl watched in fascination, awestruck by the beauty of filling sails. He thought about trying to swim ashore, but knew a long-boat would catch up to him and return him to the ship.

He decided it would be best to pretend he had finally been beaten into submission and would wait for his opportunity to escape.

The ship was slowly moving past the quay, and David thought of one last attempt at escaping this nightmare. The crew had just secured the lower main sheets, and there seemed to be a lot of strain on the lines. It had taken several men to pull them in. David took his dirk, and slowly walked along the rail to the nearest sheet. Looking around and finding everyone busy about their duties, he decided on a course of action that would cause great confusion. He would cut the sheets. Unfortunately, David was observed by the Master, who was sympathetic to the young Earl's plight, but could not allow him to endanger the ship.

David reasoned that everyone would be busy determining what had happened, while he made his escape over the side.

The Master watched David walk uncertainly to the main sheets and realized what the young Earl was about to do. He caught the Earl's hand holding the dirk. Ship's Master Will Kenting knew the dangers that lay ahead for the Earl without his being involved in another act of treachery. He was afraid for the life of the boy.

The *Subdue*, the Master knew, was different. It was not the seamen who preyed on the young people, but the Officers. They were untouchable and would, without hesitation, bring a young Midshipman up on prefabricated charges, to be in the position to save them from severe canings, expecting the exchange of personal favors. The Master knew that the young Earl would suffer horrible indignities at the hands of the Senior Officers.

"Your Lordship, stop what you are planning because you cannot escape. You could be put to death for what you have in mind. Walk away now as though you have never spoken to me," the Master pleaded.

David restored his dirk to his belt, but not before the First Officer observed the Master's interception and immediately dispatched the Second Officer to secure David in the ship's brig until he could be dealt with.

"What have you to say for yourself Kenting? As Master of this ship why would you wish to become involved with that little thug? I missed you on deck where you should have been, and found you conversing with the Earl. It was fortunate that you caught the little villain in time.

You are getting soft old man, and I don't think it will gain you much to be making up to his bloody Lordship. He'll not do you any good, I'll be bound," the First Officer snarled.

The Master's heart and his prayers were going out to the young Earl. He knew the boy was in very serious trouble.

David was shivering as he sat in the small cold compartment known as the brig. On the walls, were markings etched into the wooden bulkheads by men who had been there before him. *Where are they now?* he wondered. He couldn't control his shaking, as he realized that soon he would suffer yet another beating. He would not allow them to see him snivel or cry for mercy, after all, he was the Earl of Windsor. *My honor is at stake, but then, so is my bottom,* he thought.

Kenting approached the Captain, asking for special consideration for the new Midshipmen. "Captain he is new to all this. It is completely foreign to him, and it is obvious he is here against his wishes. I'm sure in time he will come around and become a good seaman. He comes from good stock and is very intelligent."

"Well at least someone sees some hope for him, however I do not, at least not at this moment. He could be a terrible threat to the ship and the crew. I'm afraid he will have to suffer through his temper tantrums as any other Midshipmen would do. I have turned him over to the First. We shall see what he can do with him. The Earl will learn or he will be dead in a fortnight," the Captain concluded, dismissing Kenting.

"Your getting soft in your old age Kenting, you have to be hard to impress the law of the sea on these youngsters. Eventually they'll learn even if they die in the process," the First Lieutenant said after overhearing the Master's plea on David's behalf. The Master knew there was nothing further he could do.

"Kenting! Stay clear of the Midshipman unless he is being instructed, and do not contact him in any manner. Now I think I will have two crew to watch," the First yelled after Kenting's departing figure. Kenting disliked the First Lieutenant with a passion, and would cherish the opportunity of dispatching the same beatings upon him, as he did to his Midshipmen.

David's worst fears were realized as once again he was taken to the mast where the crew were formed to witness punishment. It was strange for them to have to be present for the caning of royalty. He was still a young boy who one day would be an Officer, and from whom they would take orders. Most turned away as the caning took place. Earl did not cry this time, he only whimpered as he collapsed on the deck unable to stand. He was carried to his berth, where the physician once again examined him.

"He'll heal. He is healthy enough for light duty," the Doctor announced.

The ship was sailing in a moderate breeze and the gurgling of water past the ship's hull tended to lull David to sleep. He slept for several hours before being awakened and advised he was required to stand his watch. It was two hours into the evening watch (2200 hrs) and the sky was beautifully clear when he arrived on deck.

The Second Officer, motioned David to stand by the port quarterdeck rail and assume lookout duties. Anything that was strange, must be reported immediately.

David used the rail to support himself. Despite his terribly aching body, he was impressed by the beauty of the evening. The sky was beautiful with the moon playing on the light fluffy clouds floating above the sea.

His watch ended uneventfully, and David headed down to his berth. He was exhausted from standing in the one position all night. As he was entering the Midshipmen's berth, the First Officer intercepted him and ordered him to his cabin. David stood in front of the First, with a look of defiance in his eyes, but refrained from speaking.

"You will never attempt to put this ship in danger again, otherwise I assure you, you will hang by your bloody aristocratic neck until you are dead. Earl of Windsor, you belong body and soul to us. You hear me your bloody Lordship?" the First continued lecturing and badgering David.

David continued to stare silently at the First.

"Say, 'Yes Sir, I understand Sir'!", the First barked.

"Yes Sir, I understand Sir," David mouthed in a hardly audible whisper.

"You cross me one more time or disobey any of my orders, no matter what they might be, and you will pray for the day you can die, hear me Earl?"

"Yes Sir," David was not prepared to tangle with this man any longer, at least until he was well enough.

Being dismissed, he trudged sadly back to his berth in the Mid's quarters. He couldn't see what was so terrible about going to the First's cabin. He wondered why Kenneth had been so upset about having to go there.

The Senior and Kenneth appeared to be sleeping in their respective berths. Kenneth looked bedraggled and appeared to have been crying. He did not open his eyes. Kenneth tried not to awaken the sleeping Midshipmen. In spite of his efforts to be quiet, the two Midshipmen awoke and jumped out of their berths to stand in front of him.

"Well look who's here, the little snot himself. Had enough at last, have yuh?" the Senior snarled. David was about to say something, but Kenneth standing behind the Senior shook his head, as he grasped for David's intentions.

"You're not going to get any sleep this day. The Master is ready on deck for the Mids to get instruction. Today it is navigation. This will sort the men from the children," the Senior said looking at Kenneth. "Quit your sniveling or you can expect another meeting with me or the First, understand?" he smirked with a warning look on his face.

Kenneth did not speak as he secured his dirk and ducked out of the cabin. The Senior followed him out leaving David alone.

* * * *

David proceeded up to the deck, finding his way to where the Master was teaching class.

"Ah your Lordship, it is good to have you in my class. Today is navigation, and I am prepared to assist any of you who are having trouble with your sums," the old Master said smiling at the four boys. The Senior was also in attendance and the Master dreaded the thought of having to spend so much time with this dolt. He was a slow learner, and the Master thought there would never be a time when the Senior would be ready for his Lieutenant's examination. At eighteen, the Midshipman had the most seniority, and regardless of his ability, he ruled the young men's berth. The next boy in line was Philip Frothingham. He was fifteen and was next in seniority. He was bright and handled the Master's quizzes with ease.

"Gentlemen. If I am sailing a course of 240 degrees North, what is the reciprocal course I would steer to retrace my previous leg? Who can answer?"

The Senior held up his hand but answered incorrectly. Kenneth did not understand what reciprocal meant and had to ask the Master, who obligingly answered. David sitting by himself, mumbled the correct answer. Everyone looked at him.

"What did you say? Speak up, Lad," the Master smiled, feeling a moment of triumph for young David.

"The original course would be South not North, and the reciprocal course would be 060 degrees East North East true," David replied. The Master's shocked look, drew the attention of the Captain who had been listening to the instruction. He too was surprised by David's answer. He looked away quickly as the Master glanced his way.

"That is correct. You caught me fair and square on that one. I was just testing to see if anyone would pick me up on it. Bless my soul so I was." The Master smiled at David's quick mindedness. He proceeded to instruct on various other navigational problems, however David refrained from answering any further questions, even though he knew the answers.

He is going to be one clever one if only he holds his temper, the Master thought to himself. He hoped the Captain had overheard David's astute reply.

CHAPTER THREE

Scapegoat

David found that being left alone and ostracized was not to his liking. He knew that he didn't have to associate with the others, but at the same time there was a loneliness he had never felt before. He was certain the Officers had been ordered to stay clear of him unless on duty, and there was no way to avoid conversing with him.

On several occasions he tried to make conversation with Kenneth, the third Midshipman, but was ignored. Kenneth, coming off duty one morning, passed him in the companionway but looked away.

"There is no one around Kenneth, you can at least say hello," David said.

"I'll only get punished, so don't talk to me please," Kenneth said while passing.

The Earl had no one to converse with other than the old Master, Will Kenting, but even this was only possible during classes. At times he would lay in his berth wondering how he was ever going to survive his dilemma.

Until now he had never found anyone who wanted to make friends with him nor anyone he wanted as a friend. He enjoyed intimidating the others and only liked Kenneth and the Master. His only joy was the challenge of outperforming the other Mids in the instruction periods. That, at least, provided some satisfaction.

"David, the Senior wants you to report to the First Officer," Kenneth informed him with a look of distress and sadness.

"I'm sorry David, but it should all turn out for the best," he added, as he left the berth.

David couldn't think of any reason why he should be called in for another lecture by the First and wondered at Kenneth's statement of concern.

* * * *

"Well now your Lordship," the First said mockingly as the Senior looked on with a smirk on his face. "I have a report from the Senior that you have been pilfering in the Mid's lockers. What do you say to that?" the First asked.

"That is not true, Sir. I have done no such thing," he replied. But David suddenly realized what he had just said and to whom he had said it.

"You're calling the Senior a liar? You are telling me that he is wrong?" the First leered, enjoying the look of panic on David's face.

"I was beginning to think we were making some progress with you but it would appear I was wrong. You seem to have quickly forgotten your lessons at the mast. I believe a refresher is in order on two counts. First, for pilfering in the Mid's lockers and second, for insubordination to a Senior Officer. How do you plead yourself?"

David remembered the 'Sir' in addressing an Officer. "Sir, I would like to ask the Senior when the pilfering took place and what was taken, if I may Sir," David requested. He tried to sound confident but his legs were like rubber and he knew the odds were against him. He hoped the Senior would cross himself up with his own lies because he was so stupid.

"Lieutenant, I don't mind answering those questions. I am only doing my duty. While walking towards the powder room to complete my watch inspection I passed between the Midshipmen's hammocks and noticed the Earl feigning sleep. He quickly turned away as I was passing. I didn't like the way he was laying so I thought I had best take a look. The Earl was not expecting me to return so I caught him red handed with belongings from the other

Midshipmen's lockers. He tried to cover up his actions but his performance was dismal at best," the Senior reported.

"What say you to these details of your treachery Mr. Midshipman Clements?" the First questioned.

"Sir, may I ask the Senior at what time of the night this occurred?" David replied.

"It was fifteen minutes to midnight, Sir. I was just ending my watch, Sir," the Senior replied, looking uneasy. He wished he was elsewhere because he didn't trust this smart snob one little bit.

"Sir, I was standing my watch at that time. Second Officer Roberts will confirm the time," David replied, confident he had bettered the Senior. The Senior realized how stupid he had been not to remember they had been on the same watch together, and that David had signed in on the log directly below his own signature.

"Roberts, was the Midshipman on deck with you at fifteen to midnight?" the First questioned, turning to the Second Officer. David caught the eye signal between the two men.

"I don't believe so, Sir. No, I think not," Roberts replied and quickly looked away. He couldn't stand the look of contempt on David's face, but he knew what would happen to him if he didn't try to cover for the Senior. He was ashamed of his cowardice.

"So now we have a confirmed liar as well. What did you expect to gain by involving an innocent Officer in your wild story? Surely you knew we would check your story," the First stated smugly.

"Sir, I don't know why Mr. Roberts denies I was on duty with him. The log will show I was there at that time," David answered.

Mr. Roberts realizing that he had just perjured himself, having not thought about the log book. *Why did I have to get put into the middle of this?* he thought. He worried about what the First would do to him after this interrogation was over.

"Sir, perhaps I was mistaken regarding the time," Roberts replied, looking at the log book, trying to cover for himself. "The log does show Mr. Clements having signed in on his watch. My apologies, Sir," the Second Officer offered, excusing himself to leave.

"Clements, you will stand to the mast this very moment. Take him away Senior Breckenridge. One day Master Lordship you will learn, albeit the hard way," the First ordered.

"I have been proven innocent of your charges, Sir. Why am I to be punished for something I didn't do? Why would you make up such a story against me?" David sobbed knowing full well why.

He hung his head as tears slowly filled his eyes. He wondered how he was going to endure another caning and the pain it inflicted. He wondered why anyone would tell such lies just to have him punished, but it was evident by the way he was being treated just how much he was hated and despised. He thought back to the day he arrived aboard *Subdue* and how he had behaved. No wonder he was disliked so much. However, he would remember every one of them until the day he died. He wondered how long before that became a reality because he couldn't take much more of this.

CHAPTER FOUR

Sail Ho!

The *Subdue* was enjoying a relatively quiet and easy voyage as the weather had been ideal and the winds most favorable. Guadalupe was only three days hence and the seamen were anticipating a few day's of leisurely rest while in port.

The Captain's table was laden with a variety of luxurious foods and the invited ship's Officers and Midshipmen, with the exception of David, were enjoying the sumptuous meal to the fullest. Knowing they were so close to their destination, the Captain felt he could afford the additional food rations.

"We don't hear much from the renegade these days. I wonder if we have actually got through to him, albeit through his backside," the Captain chuckled.

"That will be another day, Sir. I'm sure he is busy conniving some other act of treachery. I swear the Duke must have been at his wit's end and desperate to rid himself of his monster offspring," the First added. Everyone laughed, as it had turned into a bit of a game, wondering what act of violence the Earl would commit next.

"He won't get away with much. Everyone is keeping their eyes on the little sod," the Second Officer added.

"For certain he stands for all his meals as he can't sit these days. I hear he's suffering a little malnutrition due to there being very little left for him by the time the others have been fed. This can do nothing but demean and humble the little bastard, if I might be so bold, Sir," the First commented to the Captain.

"Kenting, you seem to be the only one who can tolerate the lad. How are you finding him in his studies? Don't suppose he is opening his brain to anything we tell him."

"As a matter of fact gentlemen, the Earl is head and shoulders ahead of any of the other Mids," the Master replied, looking at the others. "He is a virtual genius with figures and has a memory like an elephant," he continued with some pride at being able to come to young David's defense.

"Well, at least he does something well, besides destroying everything," the Captain acknowledged, touching his lips with his napkin. "I think the Senior deserves a good deal of the credit for taming the shrew," the Captain added with a chuckle.

"You're all aware that it is the Senior's responsibility to get the Earl into shape," the First added, with a look of triumph on his face.

"Hummph, well at least there is something the Senior can do and hasn't bungled," the Master added in rebuttal.

The Senior, who a moment before was basking in the compliment given him by the First, suddenly turned pale at the Master's remarks.

"Sir, I've heard that privateers are rampant in these waters. Are we apt to see or engage any?" the Second Officer asked, endeavoring to change the subject.

"There's a slight chance. However, I feel they will not venture this close to Guadalupe.

They will be after merchantmen and thankfully there are none around us at this time," the Captain replied. He wanted no part of an engagement when he was so close to port.

"We'll have to keep a sharp lookout. Impress upon all duty watches that they are to keep alert for strange sails," the Captain said as he stood to dismiss the diners.

Meanwhile, below decks, David and Kenneth looked at each other across their berths and a small smile appeared on David's face. He wanted Kenneth to know that he understood what was happening and that he wasn't blaming him. Kenneth received the unspoken message and looked around before smiling back.

Slowly a bond was developing between the two boys. David appreciated the danger Kenneth was in by talking or associating with him. The other Officers had been instructed to let the little beast simmer in his own misfortune. His behavior, when first presented aboard, would not soon be forgotten as no one had escaped the Earl's wrath that day. Captain Willoughby and the First Officer felt the isolation, plus his beatings, were a way to tame the boy. They knew he would soon learn how much he depended on the rest of the crew to survive.

It seemed that only Kenneth and the ship's Master knew of David's utter despair and loneliness. They wanted badly to help but knew they would have to wait for an opportunity when they could converse with and encourage David without the fear of detection.

The crew, who had been witness to most of the Earl's demeaning punishments, were somewhat sympathetic to David's plight and tried to pass on signs of support. They felt he did not deserve this isolation and had served his time.

"Midshipman Walters! Report immediately to the First Officer's cabin," the Senior shouted from the doorway. The smile quickly left Kenneth's face and turned into a look of fright and despair, the likes of which David had not witnessed in any of the other crew members.

"Yes Sir," Kenneth answered as he reluctantly got up from his hammock, adjusted his clothes while giving David a sorrowful nod, then left the berth. David thought for some time before he came to the conclusion that Kenneth was about to be punished. Perhaps he was being assigned special duties by the First such as boot cleaning or some other menial task. David was thankful he had not yet been assigned chores, although he suspected it was only a matter of time.

* * * *

"Sail Ho!" shouted the lookout in the crow's nest. His voice could be heard throughout the ship.

"Where away you dolt?" the Captain shouted.

"Tops'l just visible on the horizon off the port bow Sir," came the reply. "It appears to be closing rapidly," the lookout went on.

"Where is the First?" the Captain shouted. "You, Clements, fetch the First immediately."

David ran down the companionway and knocked on the First's door.

"Get the hell away from that door whoever you are," shouted a voice from within.

David also heard a boy weeping quietly. Then he heard someone say, "Shut up you sniveling little turd or I'll give you something to really weep about."

"The Captain requests your presence on deck immediately, Sir. We have spotted another sail," David informed the First as he pushed open the door. Kenneth was sitting on the edge of the cot wrapped in a blanket, his uniform on the floor. The First charged the door and knocked David to the floor.

"How dare you enter an Officer's quarters without permission! You're to the mast when this sail matter is resolved," the First said as he darted up the ladder, kicking David aside.

"What are you doing Kenneth? Why are you here like this? Kenneth, did he beat you badly – and why not at the mast?" David asked, confused at the situation.

"Get out of here before the First returns," Kenneth spoke firmly.

"Kenneth, I don't know what's happened but, believe me, I want to be your friend," David assured the weeping Midshipman. "You're to report on deck for your watch," he added as he left Kenneth to dress.

* * * *

The strange ship was closing faster than anyone had anticipated and the Captain ordered battle stations just as a precaution. The First Officer confirmed from high atop the lookout that it was a merchant vessel, obviously in great haste.

"Sail Ho!" the call from the lookout went out again. From the deck no other sail could be seen but the lookout could see another ship overtaking the merchantmen.

"Hullooo on deck," the lookout called. "It looks as if the merchantmen is running for protection from a Frenchy what's chasing 'em Sir."

It seemed inevitable that the *Subdue* was in for some excitement and possibly some action.

CHAPTER FIVE

The Battle

The call to battle caused seamen to run in every direction making for their assigned battle stations. The younger Midshipmen were frightened at the thought of the impending action. Only the two Senior Mids had been in battle before and now it was once again time to stand to the enemy.

As Kenneth headed for his gun station he ran past David without saying a word. The Marine drummers beat a roll and the ship was now in fighting trim for the impending action. The French frigate cut sharply across *Subdue's* bow, firing as each gun came to bear. The Frenchman's first salvo of grape shot was a lucky one, scoring several hits on *Subdue*, ripping her fors'l to shreds and tearing into the upper yards which tumbled to the deck. The screams of the injured could be heard over the sound of the French onslaught. The Frenchman crossed over, leaving his stern to *Subdue's* broadside but the French target was too small and only a few hits were made.

"Full starboard! We'll wheel and chase the bugger!" the Captain shouted to the helmsmen.

Subdue answered her helm and swung in pursuit of the frigate which had altered course in an attempt to turn inside the closing *Subdue*.

"We've the weather gage Sir, we'll soon have the advantage if the wind doesn't veer," the Master shouted to the Captain. The fallen yard had already been removed, leaving the decks clear again.

"First, I am going to swing to port and we'll be on his inside. He can't come about as fast as we can so be ready to broadside the beggar and be prepared with the grapples in the event we come around and overtake him on his turn." The Captain was excited at the prospects of outwitting his opponent.

Subdue turned easily inside the frigate, came up behind and fired her bow carronades while still turning.

"Prepare to board. We're going to drive the bowsprit right through the bugger," the First yelled.

The two hulls crashed together and miraculously the masts survived the impact of the collision. "Clements! Go down to the gun deck and tell gunner

Edwards to hold his fire until I give the signal," the Captain ordered.

David ran down the ladder but was intercepted by the Senior who took hold of David's jacket and held the boy.

"The Captain has changed his mind and wants you to go to his cabin and fetch the chart that's on his desk."

"But I have a message for the gun captain," David explained.

"Tell me and I'll pass it on and be quick about it," the Senior advised impatiently. As David departed down the companion ladder he couldn't understand why the Captain had changed his mind so quickly but he turned and made his way to the Captain's quarters. The sound of the battle raging in the waist was overwhelming as was the excitement of going into battle for the first time.

David was repulsed at the sight of several seamen being taken past him on their way to the Orlop. This was where the surgeon would perform his mending. David wished he could be on deck and engage the enemy as the others were doing.

Subdue's marksmen had been lucky in that their targets had been the Officers and Commanders of the ship, and there were only two left in charge. The battle sounds of swords and muskets was slowly fading away as *Subdue's* Marines proceeded to clean up the remaining defenders of the French frigate. Her Captain reluctantly surrendered his sword just as a stray musket shot brought him down. The only surviving French Officer moved to the fantail to remove the colours after being wounded himself and realizing there was no hope. They had lost the engagement. The dead and wounded lay everywhere and blood flowed in the scuppers to the sea.

Captain Willoughby was jubilant as he surveyed the prize and ordered the First to evaluate the losses and damage to each ship. He was delighted that his counter maneuver had completely surprised and fooled the enemy Captain who now lay dead on his own quarter deck. They had fought bravely. This was a great victory for the *Subdue* which had been the proposed victim. The crew yelled and danced in celebration as they started the clean up.

A Marine guard, passing the Captain's cabin, noticed the door ajar and discovered David searching for the supposed charts. "What are you doing in the Captain's quarters?" he shouted, surprising David.

"I was sent to collect the charts from the Captain's desk but I can't find them," David explained.

"A likely story and by whose orders? We know all about you – you miserable, arrogant, little coward, hanging out here to avoid the battle topside. To the Captain with you," he shouted as he pushed David ahead of him and up the ladder to the deck.

"Sir! I found this Midshipman in your cabin, supposedly searching for some charts you requested. More like hiding if I may be permitted, Sir," the guard informed the Captain.

"What were you doing in my cabin? Did you deliver the message for the gun captain as I ordered? What were you up to you treacherous little demon?" The Captain was furious. "To the brig with the spineless trollop! I'll deal with him later! In the meantime we shall bask in the moment of victory. We caught the French and we caught a coward," he chuckled, rubbing his hands together.

"Sir, I was sent by the Senior to obtain the charts from your cabin. He told me he would deliver the message to the gunner in my stead, and that these orders came from you, Sir," David shouted in his own defense, above the din of the repair crews.

"Senior! This trollop of a Midshipman has spun me a yarn that you ordered him to my cabin for some charts. Is this correct?" the Captain asked.

"Captain, I know nothing of any such orders. I haven't seen him since we started boarding the Frenchy," the Senior lied. David could hardly believe his ears as the Senior out and out misinformed the Captain.

"You know young man, you can be hung by your scrawny little neck for the treasonable act of cowardice you have committed this day. How are we ever to get through that thick skull of yours that you belong to the Navy, and we will do whatever is necessary to prevent you from endangering your fellow crew members?" the Captain said, enjoying each moment of David's distress.

"But, Sir, it is true! The Senior must have forgotten," David continued trying to vindicate himself.

The Master, who had been standing by the wheel, overheard the conversation and David's high pitched voice as he tried to defend himself.

"Begging your pardon Captain, but may I have a word? I would like to put something straight if I may. I saw with my own eyes the Senior intercept the Midshipman as he was heading for the gun captain. They talked for a few moments, then the Earl departed in the opposite direction. I overheard the Senior deny that he ever saw the Earl. That is not true. He did encounter the Midshipman and gave him another order presumably to go to your cabin, or I'll miss my guess. He has had it in for the lad ever since he has been aboard," the Master concluded.

"Senior, what have you to say to these charges? Are you involved as well in some treachery? Did you indeed conjure up this fabrication in order to entrap Mr. Clements?" the Captain asked. The Senior became flustered and altered his story, confessing that he had intercepted the Earl with other orders concerning charts he thought the Captain might desire. The First Officer stood by silently looking on.

"I will be needing you both to assist in manning the prize. It would not seem appropriate to have you punished in front of your prize crew, so we will attend to it in my cabin," the Captain said, seeming to enjoy the distress of the two Midshipmen.

"Mr. Roberts, secure Mr. Clements in the brig and Senior, I'll deal with you later. Carry on," the Captain ordered.

"Sir, why am I being sent to the brig when I was cleared of the charges?" David asked nervously.

"You, my lad, for disobeying orders, and the Senior for his lying – and both of you for behaviour unbecoming an Officer in the time of battle!" the Captain chortled, disgusted with being questioned of his decision by a Midshipman.

David knew he had been vindicated and wondered why the Captain had ordered him held in the brig, a small cramped space next to the Orlop. He plugged his ears to the cries and screams of the wounded seamen as the surgeon cut, sewed and sawed. For the first time in his life David started to weep uncontrollably in his utter despair. No matter how he was trying to reform his ways they were not going to allow him to change. They wouldn't be satisfied until he was dead.

It was getting close to dusk when the Captain advised everyone that he wanted the prize underway before nightfall.

"Bos'n, fetch the Midshipman and have the Senior brought to my quarters along with your baton. They shall enjoy each other's misery when they feel the stave. Perhaps we will make some headway with this chap, eh Master? The Midshipman seems to be quite docile, don't you think?" the Captain said, knowing the Master's concern for the Earl.

"Mr. Wright, attend to the punishment then ship them over to the prize. They will answer to you for the rest of the voyage. We'll see how you handle your first prize and your new Officers," he snarled.

David felt the terrible pain of the club and wept to himself as each stroke seemed to reach his very soul. He prayed the beating would stop before he fainted. The Senior yelled and screamed obscenities at David as he was marched away from his caning. David knew the Senior would somehow, someday, seek to retaliate for this evening's humiliation.

CHAPTER SIX

The Prize

"Welcome aboard the prize ship *Toulon.* I expect you two will make interesting shipmates as we continue our journey. Let me warn you, your mighty Lordship, that you will wish you could be rotting in hell before this trip is concluded." The First Lieutenant spat out the Earl's title as he greeted the two Midshipmen with a snarl.

"You, Midshipman Breckenridge, have the dubious honour of acting Second Lieutenant aboard the *Toulon.* Third Officer Wolsley will be my First Officer. I'll be watching you and best you make your mark on this ship or any chances of promotion that may be forthcoming, will be set aside permanently. Understand me?" he questioned Breckenridge.

"First Officer, I want us under way immediately," the acting Commander barked at Bull Wolsley. He was called Bull because of his deep voice and his huge size. He was a very large man and was grossly overweight. No one dared comment or make humour at his expense.

"Aye, aye, Sir," he acknowledged as he shouted orders to the crew to set the sails. The two ships separated and were now sailing apart as the sails caught the evening breeze. The crews would have their hands full minding enemy prisoners as well as manning the ship when they were so short handed.

Back aboard the *Subdue*, the Master paced the quarterdeck, deeply concerned for the well being of young David. He was certain that no good could come from this present arrangement. He knew that the Senior, in his acting appointment, would engage the Earl in some sort of skulduggery that could only end in disaster for the young Midshipman.

Toulon's acting First Officer, enjoyed assigning the most demeaning assignments to David. He was confined below decks and made to clean the Orlop of all its gory mess, along with Mr. Wright's cabin which was in complete disarray.

David was filthy from all the grimy work he had been assigned and desperately wished he could wash and change his clothing. He knew this was not likely to happen and in his torment he anguished away at his tasks. He had never been one to show his deep heart-felt emotions but his tears expressed his deep agony and unhappiness. There appeared to be no end to this torment. He had not only been separated from his friend but had even lost track of time.

"Sail Ho," the lookout shouted, pointing to a spot on the horizon. The *Subdue,* sailing a few miles astern, also noticed the strange sail.

"Two sails in view, Sir," the lookout shouted again.

David was ordered on deck as more lookouts and messengers were required. It was almost dusk and it was evident to Captain Willoughby aboard *Subdue* that their earliest contact with the strange vessels would be after dark and he wasn't about to do that. They would meet the next morning as neither ship would want a meeting at night which could endanger them both.

"Signal from the *Subdue,* Sir." Breckenridge hesitated as he desperately struggled to interpret the coded signal. Aware that the Commander was growing impatient, he made up a fictitious signal rather than suffer the embarrassment of being unable to read the message.

"We are required to investigate the strange sail, Sir," he reported, trying to bluff through his failure. David read the signal correctly. "Lay back and form on *Subdue*," he whispered to himself. David was afraid to bring himself to speak to Mr. Wright and come under the First Officer's wrath, so he kept his discovery to himself. He wondered if, because of the great differences in the messages, he should speak up and give the correct signal.

"Get sail on her and let's try and close the strangers as much as possible before nightfall," the First Lieutenant ordered. More signals from the *Sundue* were ignored by Breckenridge as he continued to flounder with the flag codes and his deception in his new role.

"Ahoy the deck, looks like a merchantman being pursued by what appears to be a large sloop which is gaining fast," the lookout shouted to the deck. Darkness overtook the vessels as they raced towards each other through the night.

"The bastards will shorten sail soon and we'd best be prepared for an engagement at first light," Mr. Wright advised Bull Wolsley.

"Should we not shorten sails, Sir? It will be dangerous to continue as we are," the Second Lieutenant advised.

"Stay full and bye for another half hour, then shorten and we'll be closer to the vessels when dawn breaks," the Commander advised. His arrogant and over confident nature was taking command of his better judgement and all caution seemed to be going by the way.

"Your 'Mighty-Ship' is requested to attend Lieutenant Wright in his cabin immediately," Breckenridge ordered with a smirk as he gave David his orders. David feared punishment or perhaps another lecture or even more demeaning duties to be assigned him. "You'll come off your high and mighty ways when Mr. Wright gets done with you matey," Breckenridge said, continuing to badger David.

With some apprehension, David went to the First's cabin and knocked on the door. "Who is there?" the gruff voice from inside shouted.

"It's Midshipman Clements reporting as requested, Sir," David announced himself as he opened the Officer's door. He found it difficult to keep his body from shaking and wondered what he had done now to invoke the displeasure of the acting Commander.

"What a filth you are," the Officer said. "I'm told you have been slacking off in the performance of your duties. Look at you. You are a disgrace to the uniform. You stink and your clothes are falling off you! Surely this is not the Earl of Windsor standing before me? I am going to give you a chance to reinstate yourself of these accusations of non-performance of your duties, but first remove those stinking garments you call a uniform and go up on deck. I'll arrange for the pump to be brought up and you'll stand under it until you are clean, you pig!" he ordered. David was stunned by the request and hesitatingly removed his clothes, embarrassed at his nakedness in front of an Officer – particularly Mr. Wright.

"On deck with you now and when you are done return to my cabin. I'll have a fresh uniform for you," he said, starting to shout.

The seamen on the quarter deck overheard the First's orders through the skylight and glanced knowingly at one another. The men on the helm, who were closest to the skylight, overheard the conversation from below and even though they had little sympathy for the Earl they all felt that he didn't deserve this. The seamen rigged the pump on the deck and, after some priming, soon had a steady, powerful stream of water pouring out. The Earl was thankful for the darkness that was engulfing the ship. It would hide his embarrassment as he stepped onto the deck. He was surprised to discover he was not the only one having to stand before the pump hoses. Three powder boys were also about to get a bath. Several of the crew laughed when the boys stood under the chilling waters of the pump. The pressure was so great it sent them flying across the deck and nearly over the railings and smashed them into the scuppers, much to the amusement of the crew. It was savage treatment reserved only for the younger crew members.

"Man Overboard!" one of the crew shouted. The pumping crew and a few others rushed to the railing but there was no sight of the poor child who had just been washed overboard by the high pressure pump. David could not believe what was happening and the callous, indifferent way the crew and officers accepted the loss.

"Get a line over the stern now," David screeched.

"Belay that! Get back to your duties or you'll feel another rope on your own sterns!" the First shouted.

The crew quickly returned to finishing their assignment of bathing the Earl and the remaining boys who, at that time, were shivering under the chilled waters. They were being battered and bruised and the water stung terribly.

The crew felt the Earl was finally getting what was coming to him and it should have been him who had gone over the rail rather than the poor little bastard powder boy. They were also aware of the Commander's devious punishments of the young boys of the ship. It had occurred many times before and they knew what lay ahead for the Earl. His royal connections could not help him now.

The Earl was shaking from the bruising he had taken and the coldness of his bath. He had a terrible sense of foreboding as he descended the steps to the First's cabin. He knocked timidly on the door and was beckoned to enter, closing the door behind him. David noticed a new uniform laying on the berth and walked hastily toward it, wanting to dry off and get dressed.

"You're not done yet 'Your Highness'," the Officer commanded.

"Please Sir, I don't want to be punished again," David begged. Gone was his aggressive attitude and bravado.

"This punishment is just between us, your Lordship, and remember, no one will believe you if you use your mouth, so be mindful of that. Your next step could be a court-martial, which will see you imprisoned or even hung, so let's get on with it shall we?" The Officer approached David with an evil smile on his face.

* * * *

"May I dress now, Sir?" David questioned, with sarcasm dripping off the word 'Sir'.

"Yes, be quick about it and let this be a lesson to you," the Officer said. David was completely at a loss and at the end of his endurance. He realized that any further aggression on his part would only see him dead. Never in his entire life had he been subjected to such depths of humiliation.

The First advised David to mend his ways and keep his nose clean. He could not help but see the fire of hatred and loathing in David's eyes as though it was burning deep within his heart.

"You set the pace of your own misfortune lad when you arrived aboard the *Subdue.* Now it seems we are finally making some headway. Getting to the bottom of your problem – so to speak." He let out an evil little laugh. "We intend to change your attitude for all time. Is that not true, your Lordship?" the Commander bowed mockingly. David determined he would not allow himself to grovel or beg, nor allow the Officer the satisfaction of knowing the depth of his personal despair.

The sound of gunfire and shouting surprised the Commander, and he quickly adjusted his uniform and darted towards the stairway shouting at David to get dressed and report on deck.

David heard a tremendous crash as if *Youlon* had hit something. He was knocked off balance and fell to the deck as he struggled to get his clothes on.

He was startled when he heard a voice announcing, "This ship is now under the control of *The Black Eagle*. Drop your weapons or die on the spot. Any resistance will be futile and will only see you dead. You are so stupid to have fallen for the oldest trick in the book, a night boarding. Take these Officers and chain them aboard the *Despicable* and divide the prisoners between the two vessels. Search this vessel from top to bottom. I want us to get under way and get some distance between *Subdue* and ourselves before dawn," the leader shouted. He was delighted with his new prize, which added to the two he had already captured would make a tidy sum in their purses when reaching port.

David realized their ship had been taken in a surprise boarding, but couldn't understand how this could have happened in such a short time without hardly any resistance being offered. True they were very shorthanded and had no Marines, but there seemed to have been no resistance on the part of *Toulon's* crew.

David heard the boarders coming down the ladder from the quarter deck to the companionway. They would find him in a moment. He lifted the lid of the trunk and quickly climbed in, pulling its contents over him. He knew he wouldn't suffocate but wondered how long he would have to hide.

* * * *

Morning found the *Subdue* rolling in moderate seas and entirely alone, with no sails in sight. Captain Willoughby was frantic and in a terrible state.

"What in bloody hell inspired that damned fool to take off in pursuit of those ships? Can't he read his codes? Damnation, what do we do now? Where are the bastards anyway?" He ranted more to himself that anyone else. The lookouts reported no ships in sight.

Kenting, the Master, approached and expressed his deep concern for the crew of the *Toulon*. "The privateers along these shores have no mercy on Naval Ships. Heaven only knows what they'll do if they have captured *Toulon*. Mr. Wright has no experience in such fighting. If they were caught, they'll all be dead by now, I'll be bound," he said, wringing his hands behind his back. He was really more concerned for the

Earl than of any of the others. He silently prayed for David's safety wondering which would be worse, to be in the hands of the enemy, or in the hands of the ship's Officers.

"Oh Davey, I wished I might have helped you laddie," he mumbled to himself.

"Your concern for the *Toulon* and her crew is very touching Master, however, I suspect your real concern is for the monster, that rancorous misfit of a nobleman. Is that not true Master? You've been endeavouring to ingratiate yourself in hopes of some compensation or favour down the line. Correct Master? I know you Kenting," the Captain snarled. "I've watched you with the boy, I know what's going on in that tattered old brain of yours."

The Master winced under the reproach.

* * * *

On board the *Toulon* David remained hidden in the sea chest for what seemed like several hours, until he heard the anchor let go and heard the crew leaving the ship and men being assigned to stand guard.

"You three stay aboard the frigate until you are relieved. You can find food on board for certain," the seaman in charge ordered sarcastically.

So there are only three guards and they do not know I am aboard, he thought. Perhaps he might at least have a fighting chance of escape. His first thoughts were of deserting the Navy by jumping over the side but what then? Where would he go and what would he do when he got there? As much as he wanted to escape the ship and the tyrants who ran her, he knew he couldn't survive on his own. He needed the crew.

His thoughts turned towards a plan to outfox the three guards. He recalled the ship's brig was forward near the powder room. If he could somehow lure the three guards into entering the brig he would have a chance. Finally he had a plan set in his mind and although there was great risk, it was nothing to what he had been through.

When he could hear no further movement, he climbed out of the trunk and made his way forward. He found the key to the brig hanging on a peg outside the barred door and crawled in behind the compartment. He could hear the guards rummaging about in the galley searching for food. He remembered seeing some seaman's clothing in one of the berths while he was making his way forward. Returning down the passageway he gathered the garments together making a perfect dummy. It almost looked real from a distance. He hoped it would appear realistic enough to mislead the guards.

David carried it to the brig and laid it facing away from the door in a prone position. He threw a blanket of sail cloth over the dummy and stood back to admire his work. *That should fool them*, he thought as he prepared to bait his trap. He made certain the door was open and the key was in the lock and that it worked.

Assuring himself that everything was in readiness he crawled in behind the brig, out of sight, laid flat on the deck and commenced making a long moaning sound in the deepest voice he could generate.

"What the hell was that? Did you hear somethin'? Sounds like a woman," one guard commented as he went out into the companionway. The other two followed as they filled their mouths with salt pork and bread.

They crept quietly along the companionway listening for more sounds. Again they heard the moaning sound. "It sounds like it's coming from the powder room or the brig. By God, the dogs must have had a woman on board. Look there, someone's in the brig, lying on the deck."

David was happy to see all three guards crowded into the brig around the dummy seaman, as he swung the door shut, turning the key as he did so. The seamen rushed to the door, drawing their weapons as they endeavoured to locate their adversary. They had been caught entirely off guard and were now quite secure for the present, shouting and banging on the bulkheads.

David smiled at the success of his ruse as he hastily ducked out of sight. Knowing they were armed, he ran down the companionway out of danger. He wasn't about to take any chances at being shot at.

He ran along the companionway and up the ladder to the deck. It was dark and difficult to see but after a quick search he determined he was alone. He could hear the muffled yelling from the guards but was sure the sounds would not carry beyond the ship herself.

He was hungry and decided that if he was going to be of any help in saving himself and the crew he had best get some food. The galley had plenty and was well stocked. He ate until he was satisfied. He felt full for the first time since leaving port. He wondered what time of day it was. He knew it was very dark with a few stars appearing through low broken clouds. The moon was trying hard to shine through, occasionally casting its bright beams upon the water and the other ship anchored nearby. It was disturbing to realize all the ship's boats were gone but upon giving more thought to the matter he decided it would be better to swim, as using a boat would be too noisy and alert the pirate's lookouts who were on the shore.

A French frigate lay between the *Toulon* and the shore. He recognized the vessel as French by her lines. The Master had instilled ship recognition into all his charges. He reasoned he could swim to the frigate and rest, then continue on to the shore. He noticed also that there were other vessels in the inlet. A merchantman lay anchored close to the opposite shore from the *Toulon* and also a 'Sloop of War' which he presumed to be the privateer's vessel. All the ships were in darkness and he could hear no voices to indicate there were guards aboard.

He removed his shoes and jacket and forced himself out the stern windows and into the water. He had braced himself for the shock of cold water but, to his great relief, the water was warm and ideal for swimming. Quietly he made for the frigate gasping for air as he reached up and pulled himself clear of the water. It was farther than he had anticipated as he pulled himself up onto the frigate's rudder pintles.

He waited a few minutes until he had rested, then slid back into the water. His swim to the shore was much easier and he touched the bottom and quietly waded out onto the heavily grassed beach. Time was important to him, although he had no idea what time it was, but judged it to be just after midnight as he looked at the moon directly overhead.

He made his way though the underbrush, staying clear of the open areas. There were sure to be guards on duty, although from the noise and celebrating that was taking place inland, he felt certain everyone was participating in the celebration.

He made his way on his hands and knees to the edge of the main clearing where the activities were taking place. He was close to the only building on the site. There were two guards sitting on either side of the front door apparently guarding the structure. David wondered if this was where the crew were imprisoned.

The building appeared to have one door and no windows, at least as far as he could see, and it was facing the huge campfire. He was surprised to see all three of the *Toulon's* Officers tied to a post and sitting on the ground. There was no way they could escape. *Good, this would serve the scoundrels right*, he thought, silently wishing they would be tortured until they died. His hate for the three Officers smouldered deep within him.

The Officers, at the same time, were wondering how they were ever going to survive. *Where had the Earl disappeared to?* They hadn't seen him amongst the crew being forced into the building. *Probably hiding away when the ship was taken over. Just like the little coward to think of saving his own skin.* They came to the conclusion their captors were murderers and privateers and there was no question in the Mr. Wright's mind that their time was limited. He thought perhaps death at the hands of these renegades might be easier to face than the court-martial that lay ahead for them. There was no way to contact any of the crew as they were locked away elsewhere.

The successful capture of the *Toulon* and the other vessels gave the pirates great satisfaction and a reason to celebrate with casks of liquor in ample supply. They were slowly getting so intoxicated as to be incapable of movement and gradually fell asleep in drunken stupors.

David determined that if he could some way rescue the crew, they stood a good chance of escaping. He wondered what would happen when the crew were finally released. *Surely they would be grateful and help him. Would there be a court-martial for the Officers?* All these things he pondered as he endeavoured to work out a plan. He would certainly enjoy testifying against his abusers and smiled at the thought of the Senior being humiliated just as he had been.

David's confidence was returning and he was starting to feel like himself again. He felt he was free and in control of the situation and that was the way he liked it. Even the terrible things that had occurred aboard ship were not so important as the situation ahead of him. He remembered how his father had always called him cocky and blatantly sure of himself to a fault. *We shall see Father,* David thought.

He wondered what his father would say if he could see him at this moment. He realized he had the opportunity to make things right and truly earn the title as the Earl. He also thought that, in spite of all his harassment and bullying, he felt good about himself and how he had survived and not given in. He recalled the times he had thought of jumping overboard and letting the sharks finish him off. He would then at least be free of these felons, especially that imbecile, Senior Midshipman Breckenridge. For once in his life, David truly wanted to succeed.

He crawled quietly to the rear of the building to discover that there was another door at the opposite end. It was chained and locked so he had to somehow find the keys.

The guards at the front were laying against the building and to David's relief, were nodding and falling off to sleep in their drunkenness. Other activities were still going on around the fire which was slowly dying out. No one seemed interested in keeping the fire going. The burning embers cast frightening shadows amongst the trees, like fingers trying to entangle him.

He crawled until he was beside the building, farthest away from the frolickers. David was not certain if they were truly asleep and wondered if they would awaken and catch him as he was trying to locate the keys.

He melted into the shadows moving back to the front of the building where the guards were sleeping. He found what he was looking for in plain view. A set of keys was laying in the lap of the guard on the far side of the door. He would have to go back around the log building and come up the other side. This was the most visible and dangerous side as it was in open view of the clearing.

He lay flat on the ground as he crawled along the edge mingling with the dancing shadows from the fire. His heart was pounding so heavily he felt it would jump out of his body. He reached the corner of the building and suddenly realized his white body must create an easy target if someone happened to look his way. The party appeared to be losing momentum as one by one the leaders around the fire drifted off into a deep sleep.

David reached for the keys, retrieving them easily, and crawled backwards to the rear of the building hoping he had the right keys for the back entrance. Success or failure depended on one key on the ring.

He froze in his tracks as a seaman staggered past close enough to touch him and urinated into the bushes inches from David's hiding place. He closed his eyes and held his breath at the close encounter and heaved a sigh of relief when he discovered he had not been wet upon nor seen.

He found a key that appeared to be one made for the lock and put it quietly into the lock. He was afraid of alarming the crew and giving his position away. He'd not soon have another chance.

He turned the key and to his surprise the latch turned and the lock fell off. He gingerly removed the chain. Someone on the inside close to the door, heard the chain being removed and warned his fellow prisoners. The door started to swing open and the crew were about to rush the door when they recognized the Midshipman who motioned them to silence. Luckily they identified him immediately.

David informed them which way to go to avoid detection and they should position themselves around the perimeter of the camp and wait for a signal to attack.

"Sir," the Bos'n whispered. "I'll take over from here. This is where the need for muscle comes in if it meets with your approval." He ordered the crew to secure as many weapons as they could find without giving away their positions.

David informed the Bos'n of his plan to release the Officers. "Let them rot in hell Davey, they don't deserve to live. Serves them bloody well right. They are the ones who got us into this here mess," the Bos'n said. "David. It is too risky. You have done enough this night. Why don't you go back to where you swam ashore and we'll be along shortly after cleaning up here," he continued.

The Bos'n admitted, jokingly, to David, that being small had its advantages as in this case. David smiled as he put on a shirt given to him to cover his upper body and disappeared into the shrubbery.

The seamen were excited and having been able to find several abandoned weapons were prepared to take care of the privateers. In their condition they would never know what was happening, nor would they care.

David crawled behind the huge trees and blended in with the shadows until he came to a point close to where the Officers were tied. They appeared to have been secured with rope lashings with their arms tied behind their backs and around the post. The First

Lieutenant was the closest to the edge of the clearing. He was shocked into almost shouting and giving the whole affair away when he saw David crawling with a dirk in his hand. The ropes were cut and David pointed the direction the Officers should take to escape. He completed freeing the other two and they quickly disappeared into the surrounding brush.

David crawled through the bushes until he came up behind the leader who was sleeping against a post. He noticed some brass snare wire around the neck of some luckless animal and quickly untied it, placing it like a garotte around the leader's neck and around the post. He never awakened and David was sure he would not move far until the crew found him.

He crawled away into the trees and told the Bos'n what he had done. The Bos'n outlined his plan of attack and quickly hustled David back from the line of fire.

"Your Lordship, Davey, you've done your part this night, now your work is finished. We'll see to the rest. We'll catch you up by dawn. Away with you now and don't turn back for any reason, you hear?" the Bos'n said, patting David on the shoulder.

David disappeared into the forest before the three Officers joined the Bos'n. He was completely exhausted as he made his way back through the bushes to the edge of the water. The Bos'n had said he should return to the ship so, leaving the shirt on shore, he slipped into the water and retraced his earlier course to the two vessels.

Reaching the *Toulon* he pulled himself back in through the opened stern windows. He made his way to his berth, crawled onto it and immediately fell asleep in spite of the howling of the guards still locked in the brig. The excitement and physical exertion had drained him. That was where First Officer Wright found him upon returning to the ship.

CHAPTER SEVEN

The Betrayal

"Gentlemen, I cannot tell you how serious our position is. Our whole future lies in the hands of that child. He was very lucky to have been able to pull this coup but now we must take action, otherwise our careers are done. If word gets to the Admiral about this catastrophe, we are all finished and will possibly face a court-martial. Each of us is in this together. My suggestion is to turn the events around and make a plan to somehow lay the blame of the misreading of the codes and our subsequent seizure onto the Midshipman." Wright spat the word out as if he had eaten something disagreeable.

"An excellent scapegoat, Sir. I will be only too happy to testify at a court hearing that it was the fault of the Midshipman," the Second Officer voiced his cooperation. The First nodded in agreement. Nothing would suit them better than to see David Clements get his full comeuppance, especially after this amazing rescue of his. Not for a minute did they feel indebted to the Earl.

The credit for this venture would go to the Earl and they would be in disgrace. "It is imperative that we get underway immediately. I would like to take the frigate with us and locate the *Subdue*. We'll barely have enough crew to bring both vessels out and I hate leaving the schooner and the merchantman but there is no other way for it. We are only a day and a half sailing from Guadalupe, where prize crews can be rounded up to bring in the other two. That should place us on the honour list." The First was feeling confident.

"The privateers were badly mauled in the surprise attack by *Toulon's* crew so we have nothing to fear from that quarter. Split the crew and take along any of the prisoners who wish to defect. We'll need them. We have barely the minimum number to handle the frigates as it is. Mr. Wolsley, you will have command of the frigate and take Mr. Breckenridge as your First. The Bosun and I will sail ahead and you will take station off our stern quarter. Keep close. We will have to sail as best we can until we meet *Subdue*. If I know Willoughby, he'll be ranting and raving somewhere nearby, if he's sober that is."

"Now you must all remember that I am charging the Earl with dereliction of duty and cowardice in the face of the enemy. He provided us with an incorrect code which resulted in our leaving to pursue the Privateers. You all remember when we were overtaken by the privateer that the Midshipman was missing from his watch while he hid below in my cabin. Correct? Then away with you and let's get under way," he ordered. "Oh yes, throw Clements into the brig on half rations. No sense in wasting good food on the likes of him," Wright ordered.

* * * *

David awakened when the Bos'n shook him. "What time is it Chief?" David asked.

"I am ordered to place you under arrest and lock you in the brig. I'm sorry about this Sir but Mr. Wright has ordered it, what am I to do?" he whispered.

David couldn't believe what he was hearing and was shocked by the turn of events. *How could he be under arrest when it was he who had saved the entire crew? What was happening? How could it be possible?* he thought, trying to control the tears that were forming.

"Chief, you know it was I who released you all. You know it was I who made possible your escape. Why then are you treating me this way?" David asked.

"Sir, it ain't fair but it is not of our doing. The First has ordered it. I am sure it is part of a conspiracy to take the credit for himself and his Officers. My heart bleeds for you lad," the Chief responded to David's question.

David thought about the Chief's words and suddenly it became clear to him that Mr. Wright was conspiring to turn his defeat into a victory for himself. He wondered how anyone could do such a terrible thing.

Later in the day the British frigate was sighted and signal flags were hoisted, advising the *Subdue* of their presence. The *Toulon* and her prize had sailed to intercept *Subdue* having left the privateer's schooner and the captured merchantman behind in the cove.

Captain Willoughby was delighted with the captures and not at all surprised to hear of the Earl's latest treachery. He had him brought over to *Subdue* to be lodged in the brig until a decision was made as to what to do with him.

Throughout the night, David was visited by several members of the crew who told him they knew what was taking place and would somehow make things right. The Master, who had been forbidden to have any contact with the Midshipman, found an opportunity to visit. He confirmed the Officer's intentions to have David discredited and court-martialed, making him take the blame and claiming the glory of victory for themselves.

"They'll not succeed David. Everyone knows of the conspiracy and the crew have a special hatred for those Officers. They'll come through for you laddie," the Master said. "David, I also will testify of the abuse you and Walters suffered under Breckenridge and Mr.

Wright. You will never have to suffer that indignity again."

David felt ashamed that anyone knew of his ordeal with the Officers. The Master and several crew members continued to provide David with food and assured him that they would watch over him from then on. David was somewhat comforted by the reassuring words of the Master but still felt a degree of uncertainty. He knew only too well the desperation Mr. Wright and Senior Breckenridge were experiencing and knew also they would stop at nothing to dispose of him before he could testify against them.

CHAPTER EIGHT

The Conspiracy

The three Officers discussed a plan of action, and decided that if they played their hands right, they could swing this catastrophe to their own advantage. They would blame David for the false interpretation of the code.

He would be blamed for desertion while the rest of the crew had fought gallantly to save their vessel from capture. As lookout, he failed to observe the forthcoming collision with the Privateer and the subsequent loss of their vessel to the renegades. The reason he had not been captured was that he was in hiding below. They had a neat package to hand over to Captain Willoughby, if and when they eventually caught up to him.

The ultimate glory would come with the display of the three prizes two, of which were behind in the island cove. What glory they would enjoy.

“Gentlemen, our very lives depend on us keeping our stories straight. It could be a rough time, but we can only come out of this as heroes, and we’ll get rid of the Earl at the same time.

They laughed at the last remark. Getting rid of the Earl was a prime concern, for he was the only one who really knew the truth. He would never have the opportunity to tell it.

“Take the Earl to the brig, and see he is kept away from the crew. We can’t have any slip ups, or it means the end for us.”

The Senior informed David that he was under arrest for treason, and would be locked in the brig until they caught up to the *Subdue*. “Your going to hang, you little bastard. you hear. Your going to hang by that scrawny little neck until you stop kicking. Ha! That will be a sight to behold. Your aristocratic little body swinging in the breeze,” the Senior mocked as David was being taken to the brig.

“How can you do this? I just saved your life, how can you charge me with treason. If anyone should be charged it should be you and the First!” David shouted in utter despair. One of the seamen guards taking David to the brig, gave him a wink, and whispered in his ear that all would be well and to just bide his time and not provoke the Officers. For the first time David felt hope that he would get through this horrible ordeal in spite of his grave misgivings.

The following morning the *Subdue* was spotted heading in their direction just above the horizon. The lookouts were happy to see the parent vessel. They had reason to be thankful this voyage was about to come to a happy conclusion.

"Shorten sail, we'll be meeting within half an hour," the First shouted.

In spite of the fact the three Officers felt they had concocted a foolproof tale of their exploits, there was a good deal of apprehension among them. It wasn't over yet. As the vessels stood into wind, several crewmen unlocked the door to the brig and removed the Midshipman. They hid him in the powder locker where the Officer's would be less apt to search. They would be frantic to discover David's whereabouts after his escape.

Aboard the *Subdue*, the Captain paced back and forth appraising the story told by the three Officers. He had to believe them as they were the King's Officers, but something seemed amiss in the telling of the story. The story was too pat, and almost unbelievable.

"Bring the Midshipman. I want to formerly charge him with his last bit of treachery," the Captain stated.

Kenting had been informed of the crews' plan for David, and heard the story of his heroism. The Master regained his happy smile as he went about his duties.

A seaman came running to the Captain, informing him that the Midshipman was not in the cell. He had escaped.

"That can't be! He could never get out of the brig, without outside help. You Master, what do you know about this? No doubt you are involved in this treachery!" the First Officer shouted frantically realizing the implications of the Earl's escape.

"Captain, with your permission, the crew and I would like to put straight the matter of our missing Midshipman and the contemptible story contrived by these Officers," the Master spoke. The seamen started to move towards the quarter-deck.

"What's the meaning of this mutinous act? Back to your stations all of you," ordered the Captain.

"Sir! With all due respect, justice may never be done unless you hear the other side of the charges?" the Bos'n ventured.

"Sir, there is another side to this story which you have not heard and which will have a great bearing on the truth of these charges," the Master continued.

"These men are all in league with the Master. Everyone knows what's going on here," the First shouted. The Senior and the Second Officer were beginning to feel the stress of their situation and wished they were elsewhere.

"What other story? What is their left to tell? I have heard the charges and I concur, the Midshipman has been justifiably found chargeable under the rule of the sea. The deserter has no recourse," the Captain admonished the Bos'n.

"Captain Sir, we were there. We were held captive until the Midshipman at great risk of being captured himself, secured our release. Further Sir, the Midshipman cut the bonds that held the Officers in captivity. Tied to a post on the edge of the clearing, they were. And as for Breckenridge, Sir, it was not Mr. Clements who misread the coded signal from you, Sir, it was the Senior making up a false message to save face in front of the other officers," the Bos'n went on.

"How do you know all this?" inquired the Captain, feeling a little insecure in his initial judgment.

"Sir we were there!" he replied firmly.

"Some crew were able to read the signal, and it didn't correspond to the one interpreted by the Senior. It was the opposite to what had actually been sent, Sir! We feel that the wrong person is being accused here. We cannot stand by and see the Earl, who single-handedly was responsible for the capture of the prize ships and the release of the crews, be accused. I personally watched him tie a wire garrote around the leader's neck securing him to a tree. He couldn't move or he would have cut his own throat. These are not the actions of a treacherous Officer. They are the actions of a brave and probably frightened young boy, Sir. The Earl has won the admiration of each one of us, and it is our duty to speak up for him," the Bos'n finished.

"Do you have the Midshipman?" the Captain asked.

"Yes Sir we do."

"I am prepared to hear the Midshipman speak for himself on these charges. Until I have done that, the three Officers are relieved of their duties until I am convinced that the truth has been heard, is that understood?" The Captain turned to the Officers. "If you are found to have distorted the truth in any way regarding this act of treason, you will be bound over for court-Marshall as soon as we reach Guadalupe. Please bring the Earl to my cabin," the Captain requested. The Master nodded approval from his position by the helm.

David was brought to the Captain's cabin and was greeted by the use of his title. "Midshipman Clements, your Lordship, the Master and crew have presented an entirely different story of the events dealing with the capture and subsequent rescue of the *Toulon*. I somehow have found it hard to follow that you are the same Midshipman that shipped aboard the *Subdue* several months ago, and that you alone are responsible for this act of bravery. Would you be so kind as to relate the sequence of events as you remember them, starting with the horrible acts of indecency upon you, by the First and the Senior Midshipman?" the Captain requested.

David related the story, including all details of his and the other young men's punishment at the hands of the First Officer. The rest of the story unfolded making it evident to the Captain, that the story was true, and that he had been duped by his Senior Officers.

"Summon the First Officer to my cabin. I want him to explain his way out of this. I have every reason to suspect that the Midshipman is telling the truth," the Captain concluded.

CHAPTER NINE

The Prizes

His Majesty's Frigate *Subdue* slowly plied her way over brilliant blue seas. The moderate breezes carried her towards Guadalupe and the end of an extremely eventful and profitable voyage, considering the prizes they possessed and the subsequent funds which would wind up in each man's pockets.

She was accompanied by the three captured vessels. Captain Willoughby had thought better of leaving the two remaining prizes in the cove and had split his own crew to bring the vessels out. There would not be sufficient crew to man the guns if they were forced to battle.

The privateer's sloop, *Despicable,* along with the captured frigate *Selome* and the merchantmen, followed in tight formation with *Subdue,* while *Toulon* brought up the rear. All together they presented a formidable force even though the ships there could not have fought their way through a fishing fleet. The perception of a major task force belied the actual condition of the formation. Signal guns fired their welcome, as they sailed proudly into port.

Captain Willoughby looked happy as he gazed at the vessels following in his wake. He envisioned a triumphant return to Guadalupe sailing at the head of his convoy of captured prizes. The Admiral's squadron and their respective Captains stood open mouthed as they watched the spectacular entrance.

Captain Willoughby felt this accomplishment should surely see him promoted to post rank or even further. Thoughts of the disciplinary action he was about to take on his Senior Officers, were pushed into the back of his mind by visions of the awaiting hero's welcome.

Admittedly, the captures had been a fluke of good fortune in which he had played little part. He reluctantly conceded that most of his good fortune could be attributed to that monstrously treacherous Midshipman, the Earl of Windsor. He pondered the matter over and over in his mind. *If word of this got out to the Admiral his future would wind up in front of a court-martial. He also worried about the charges of treason and conduct unbecoming an Officer that he should lay against his two Senior Officers. How would he ever explain that to the Admiral? That confounded insolent opportunist Midshipman Breckenridge has created a headache as well.* He felt his problems were much too great for one man to bear and opened his liquor chest to relieve the tension.

It was his intention to glean all the credit for himself and he wondered how he was going to be able to drum these misfits out of the service so as to not cast any aspersions on his own performance.

Perhaps he could bargain with the two Senior Officers to go along with any plan he might have to save their worthless hides, and his. He could save their positions and make them completely subservient but what ever was he to do with the Earl?

He knew he would retret the day his newist addition joined the crew. *He has spelled trouble right from the beginning with his disgusting behavior and high and mighty aristocratic attitude of deserving better than anyone else.* The Captain chuckled inwardly as he realized that the Earl had indeed received more attention than anyone else, albeit, across his britches. Willoughby felt he may have suppressed the Midshipman in body but he knew he was far from taming the boy's spirit.

He thought he could not be questioned concerning the discipline of the young men if David Clements had the misfortune to succumb during one of the punishment sessions. *He was simply performing his duty as Captain.* The more he considered the matter the more he liked the idea of being able to eliminate the pompous brat. *Yes, that would certainly work. How could he be faulted by carrying out the letter of the law? Dereliction of duty in the face of the enemy was treason. Punishment at the mast would prove fatal and he'd be rid of the only uncontrollable witness to all the events.* He could handle the three Officers.

"Perhaps I can be more subtle. Perhaps I can leave the demise of the boy to the First Lieutenant and his favorite Midshipman, Breckenridge," the Captain spoke aloud as he continued pondering the matter. *Midshipman Walters could be included as he had already spent several occasions of punishment at the mast and in the First's cabin. Yes, this should settle the matter.*

He wanted the entire problem put ship shape so that there would be no complications when he boarded the Admiral's ship in the harbor. *Now was the time to act. The ship would be dropping anchor in a short time. Best he get on with his plan.*

* * * *

The First Officer sat uneasily in a chair across from the Captain.

"Lieutenant Wright, you realize you are facing serious charges, any one of which will send your career into oblivion. The whole mess is very complicated and I have no sympathy for your devious and disgusting behavior. However, I think I have a plan by which you and that idiot.

Breckenridge can reinstate yourselves and perhaps even stay the charges against you. I'm sure you realize you have no recourse but to accept any suggestions I might make," he said with a smug look of contempt on his face.

"Sir, I realize there were extenuating circumstances surrounding the events and, in view of your perception of the situation, I will certainly agree to any plan that will benefit my case," the First replied, smiling inwardly for the first time since being confronted by the Master.

"I know of your devious punishments of the young men aboard this ship and I am suggesting you and your compatriot enjoy one last visit at the expense of your two worst nemeses. I want you to somehow let the Earl escape so that it appears he accomplished this on his own. I want Walters to be involved in a rescue attempt of Clements. At that point you will have maneuvered the two to your cabin where they will meet their untimely demise – if you get my meaning? They may even end up overboard, if you wish. It will appear as a failed attempt at escape while at the same time, my dear Lieutenant, I will have you exactly where I want should you attempt to deceive me and betray my confidence. Do you understand the seriousness of this situation? My career is also at stake and I shall not have any subordinate ruin it. Now get on with your plans. We only have a short time to complete the task," the Captain ordered.

The First Officer withdrew to the main deck where he paced back and forth as he hatched his plan. He would not only look after the two Midshipmen but Breckenridge as well, who could make trouble and then be blamed in the event matters turned sour. An ace in the hole so to speak.

"Mr. Roberts, I want to see you in my cabin immediately," the First Officer ordered. He wanted to share his plan with the Second officer.

"Sir, you wanted to see me?" Roberts said, speaking to the closed door.

"Enter. I don't think I have to remind you of the dilemma we're in and it'll require our mutual understanding of the problem."

"You and I are under ship's arrest due to the big mouth of the Master who spilled his entire innards to the Captain. This has created such a degree of uncertainty in the Captain's mind that he doesn't quite know whom to believe. Thank goodness he hasn't had that wretched little monster in for an interview yet. He has subtly suggested that a mishap befall Mr. Clements and Mr. Walters. The Captain, fortunately, does not put much credence in anything Clements has to say. He is under the impression neither Walters nor Clements are aware of any plans to dispose of them. Little does he know how much they were involved. That is where you come in," he whispered, not wanting to be overheard.

“The Captain has the Earl locked in the brig. He is not under guard which will make this next request easy. I want you to release the prisoner, making it look like a conspiracy on the part of his friends, whatever you choose to do. He must be kept out of sight of the crew and the Master at all costs. That shouldn’t be too difficult if you wait ‘til the next watch change after dark. Bring him to the Midshipman’s berth. Tell him to wait until young Walters returns. He will then be told what to do in order to make good an escape, understand? That should be simple enough, even for you,” the First directed with considerable contempt.

Darkness overtook the squadron and all seemed quiet and serene. The Captain had retired to his quarters to drink himself into a stupor, leaving the First in command. Midshipman Breckenridge was staying as far away from the Officers as he could. Anything to avoid another confrontation with them as he had been humiliated enough in front of his peers. No more. He’d get even with the Earl sooner or later. The Earl was the source of all his misfortunes. A smile crossed his lips as he thought of how he had deflowered the monster. *That brought him down off his lofty snobbish perch,* he thought to himself.

“Mr. Breckenridge, the First requires Midshipman Walters to his quarters now!” the Second Officer ordered.

Ha! Back to his old tricks again. I suppose he figures this will be his last chance with the boys, Mr. Roberts thought to himself. *He should quit while he’s ahead! Doesn't he realize he's been discovered for this deviant behavior and is facing possible court-martial?* Roberts couldn't believe how careless and arrogant the First was, in spite of the circumstances.

Midshipman Walters bowed his head as he heard the request. He knew what lay ahead but had hoped that all the commotion aboard ship would have lessened his chances of punishment. *What have I done now, other than talk to David?* Kenneth thought.

The Midshipman knocked and was told to enter.

"Well Mr. Walters, we meet again. I presume you thought that you were going to get away with all this treachery without any consequences, hmmm? Well, I am going to punish you but also offer you a chance to escape. There will be a boat tied under the stern plates. We are only a short distance from the harbor entrance and it is an easy row to shore. You can simply disappear and that will be the end of it. Am I not being a benevolent benefactor?" he smirked.

* * * *

The Master was walking past the skylight when he heard Kenneth moaning. He realized he was too late to help. *How could the Captain have allowed Mr. Wright to remain as watch Officer in view of all that had happened?* The Master was furious with the Captain for this!

"Get a haste on Mr. Walters and prepare to get into the boat. I have opened the stern windows for you. Remember you are not to implicate me in any way or you will be arrested and hung, understand me?" Wright instructed.

"Yes Sir," Kenneth whimpered, wiping his tearful eyes. This was not how he expected to end his Naval career. It had been his parents' plan for him to make his future in the service of the King. *Now what is going to become of me?* he anguished to himself.

* * * *

"Sir, I have Midshipman Clements to see you," the Senior announced. He had been ordered to escort the Earl to the First's cabin. David entered with grave foreboding. He knew he was going to be punished, but crying or protesting were not going to help, so he simply braced himself against the humiliating experience.

"I'm letting you free your Lordship, after you have been punished. You may join Midshipman Walters in a boat I have located at the stern window. You can make good your escape and that will have done with it," the First cooed confidently. "Prepare yourself for punishment you rotten little swine," he ordered.

The Bos'n and two crew members had been waiting until dark to attempt to release David, however they observed from various vantage points David being released into the hands of the Senior Midshipman.

They heard his orders to escort David to the First's cabin and immediately set about making a plan whereby the entire crew would take over the ship. It was a mutiny.

The Master secured the Captain's door from the outside without arousing the sleeper. The plan was to prevent bloodshed and take over before the Captain realized that things were not as they should be.

David cried and openly begged the First to spare him this last humiliation. There was a knock at the door and the First pushed David aside and told him to be quiet or he would kill him.

"Yes, what it is?" the First asked.

"Sir, it is the Master, and I wish to converse with you on deck. It seems there are other vessels in the immediate area, Sir," he said, convincingly.

"I'll be there as soon as I attend to some unfinished business," was the reply. The Master and three crewmen then opened the door and took the First without a word being spoken. David rushed out, trying to hide his embarrassment.

"He'll never harm you again laddie, never," the Master spat as he ordered the First to be locked in the brig.

"Chief, keep him quiet," the Master ordered and a rag was put in his mouth to maintain silence. The crew had already captured Breckenridge and locked him in the cordage locker away from the First. The Senior knew there was no way out for him. He knew his future was at an end.

"Where is Walters?" the Chief asked.

"He's in a boat at the stern Sir, waiting for me," David replied. He ran to the stern windows and beckoned Kenneth to get back aboard.

"Kenneth, you're safe now."

"David! I was afraid we were both going to be cut adrift to die out here," Kenneth wept. Both boys tried to compose themselves as Naval Officers should, but they had been through a very traumatic time and no one blamed them for their boyish behavior.

On deck the Master was guiding the *Subdue* and her consorts to an anchorage just beyond the Admiral's ship. Anchors were set and the four vessels rode easily in the current as the tide changed.

The Master and Bos'n entered the Captain's cabin awakening him from his drunken sleep and told them the ship was at anchor.

"Why wasn't I awakened? Who is responsible? Mr. Wright?" he shouted, dressing as he jumped around his cabin. Something must have gone wrong with their plan he thought.

"The devil's teeth," he cursed to himself.

"Sir, the crew has taken command of the *Subdue*," the Master said.

"You'll all swing for this bit of treachery," the Captain shouted.

"Then you will swing with us, Sir," the Master replied.

"Sir, your First Officer and Second Officer and Midshipman Breckenridge are being held under ship's arrest. They are willing to testify before your court-martial that it was the young Earl who saved your precious ships and released the crew. They are prepared to tell all. When this news breaks you will be summarily court-martialed and cashiered out of the service. You were going to claim the victory as your own which you know was not true. If you go ahead with your mutiny charges the entire crew and officers are prepared to sink your testimony. On the other hand, if you will place the credit where it is justly due, issue your report on the behavior of your Officers and forget this mutiny ever occurred, then we will go along with that and take our rewards in terms of the prize money. Oh yes, and you will decline the Captain's share of the privateer's ships. That prize money goes to the crew. Those are the conditions Captain. I'm sure you will find them more than fair and certainly more than you deserve," the Master completed his conditions.

"It would appear I have no choice. Yes, I will go along with your terms and the young Earl will receive an apology and a berth on this ship if he so desires. There is no doubt he will be mentioned in the *GAZETTE* after all the folderol settles down. He will be a national hero. And what of you Mr. Kenting? What is your plan?"

"I'll seek another vessel if that is possible. If not I shall retain my position here," the Master said.

"Well, so be it. I should fair reasonably well, after all I am the Captain," Willoughby announced smugly.

"The Admiral, Sir Charles Willingham, requires your presence aboard the *Vengeance* at your earliest convenience, Sir," Midshipman Walters said, informing the Captain.

Kenneth realized how different it was aboard ship with the First and Senior in the brig. It was a happy day for him and some of the other young boys aboard when they realized they would no longer be subjected to his abuse. He wondered, *What is going to happen to them, and what about the Earl? What was going to happen to him? He was the real hero.*

* * * *

"Good to see you again Captain Willoughby, I see you have managed a major victory in our area. Come sit down and join me in a Claret while you give me a verbal report. I expect you will have a written one ready soon?" the Admiral said, all smiles as he thought of the prize money he would be sharing.

Captain Willoughby relayed the contents of his report almost word for word leaving out anything. The Admiral interrupted several times asking that the details be reconfirmed by the Captain.

"You mean to tell me the young Earl is responsible for this huge victory? Tell me Willoughby, how could he have been so abused while under your control?"

"Sir, the lad had a very poor attitude and his behavior was most unbecoming an Officer. He was establishing a bad code of behavior for the crew, and I had to make an example of him to curb his mutinous ways. He was taken to the mast on several occasions, few of which had any effect on his behavior. I believe that through the continued punishment and embarrassment he suffered, he finally realized the error of his ways and started to act like a seaman. His academic progress has been nothing short of outstanding, and he could make an exceptional leader in time," the Captain concluded, reluctantly.

"And what about your Senior Officer? You realize there will have to be a court-martial? Your First Officer and the Senior Midshipman will have to face severe charges. This will be a tremendous embarrassment to the Navy even if those two hadn't involved the Earl. Once his Father hears of this there is no telling who will be affected by the Earl's testimony. Captain, your future as well as mine may rest in the hands of this young lad. How do you propose to handle it?"

Willoughby looked bewildered as he attempted to calm the situation. As he started to speak, the Admiral interrupted with a bellow.

"Good heavens Willoughby, how could you not be aware of what was happening to the Midshipmen? Surely you had some inkling of things not being right? Come on, out with it man!" the Admiral shouted impatiently.

The Captain shifted nervously in his chair, trying to think of something to say to calm the Admiral. "Sir, will you meet with the Earl? Perhaps he may be able to solve our problem if he is treated with some respect, especially from you in person," he offered.

"Yes, yes, that sounds reasonable. Perhaps we may find a chink in his armor whereby we can settle matters amiably. Perhaps salvage the entire affair to our mutual satisfaction, eh?" the Admiral replied, hoisting his huge bulbous frame from his chair.

"Willoughby, send for the boy – ahmmm, I mean the Earl now, and we'll get things under way. I am afraid my temper is at its limits in this matter, and better I act before I am at a complete loss of my senses by your actions – or I should say, lack thereof. You expected to claim the victory as your own, didn't you Willoughby? What changed your mind? Was it the Master who seems to have asserted a lot of influence on the outcome of this affair? I will also want to interview those two damnable perverts, Willoughby. What part of their exploitation did you play? Did you condone these atrocities?" The Admiral's face reddened as he grew more angry.

Willoughby remained silent, sinking deeper in his chair, wondering how long this verbal beating would continue.

"I'll convene their court-martial after I have heard their story," the Admiral said, dismissing the Captain with a wave of his large hand. Captain Willoughby departed, only too happy to be away from the Admiral's cross examination.

* * * *

"Mr. Walters, will you fetch Midshipman Clements to the Admiral's cabin immediately? Be quick about it, you're not in the clear yet, you know," Captain Willoughby cautioned the Midshipman.

"David! David! The Admiral wants to see you in his cabin right away," Kenneth yelled excitedly as he relayed the Captain's orders.

The Earl was standing off to himself deep in thought about what lay ahead and what he was going to do. It would all depend on the Admiral and what he had to say. No use trying to second guess what the Admiral had been told about the affair. He would just have to take each day one at a time. He hoped the

Master was right and that all would work out in the end.

CHAPTER TEN

New Beginnings

"Come in and sit down lad and we'll start, shall I say, at the beginning," the Admiral motioned David to a chair in front of his desk. "Smithers, I'll require your presence both as a witness and to take notes," he instructed his steward.

"The story I have heard about this entire affair defies believability I'm sorry to say. The crew has performed in a mutinous way, as have several of the ship's Officers. I intend to get to the bottom of it, and I want you to confirm the story as I relate it. Do you mean to tell me all you know about his hand in this business?" he asked as he shifted to a more comfortable position. David felt this was going to be a long drawn out affair. Until coming aboard the *Subdue* David had never been intimidated in his life. As a matter of fact he made it a rule to be the intimidator. He felt very uneasy under these circumstances.

"Sir, I was not present at the time of the meeting of the crew with Captain Willoughby nor do I know of the Master's part in the affair. I was in the brig Sir!" David related. "The Bos'n, and some of the crew, unlocked my cell and informed me that I was being released and moved to another location. I was to remain silent, making no sounds. They said it was for my own safety. I was placed in the powder room with two powder boys who were to watch over me. I wasn't sure what was taking place. I was just happy to be out of the brig," David said, relating the first part of the story.

"Then when did you know that a mutiny was taking place?" the Admiral questioned.

"Sir, I was never aware a mutiny had occurred. I was brought to Captain Willoughby's cabin where he questioned me with allegations of my treachery and deceit. He asked me many questions about what had occurred in the First's cabin with Kenneth Walters and myself. I confirmed what he had been told." David was perspiring under the piercing eyes of the Admiral. He was sure the Admiral was trying to intimidate him with his staring.

"Tell me what it was that took place in the First Lieutenant's cabin."

David shifted uncomfortably in his seat, looking down at the deck. "Sir, I was called to the First's cabin where he informed my that I was to be punished and that I was to disrobe. He called me a dirty little pig and that I was to go on deck and stand under the pump and be hosed down. I was dirty, Sir, and I had not been able to bathe since arriving on board."

"When I returned there was a new uniform laying on the berth. When I went to put it on, I was ordered to wait. The Senior came in and the First left, leaving me with the Senior."

"Were you still naked at this point?" the Admiral interjected.

"Yes Sir," David replied.

"I'll save you the embarrassment of relating the details of your assault, carry on. Did you see the doctor aboard?" the Admiral questioned.

"No sir, I was afraid I would be punished again. I was all right."

"Hrumfff" the Admiral growled. "You realize how serious these charges are?" he said, pacing back and forth, wringing his hands behind him. "Did you realize your ship had been captured?" the Admiral continued.

"I had just finished dressing when I heard gunshots and fighting on the main deck. Everyone was rushing about. I was going to go on deck when I heard a strange voice ordering the crew to surrender or die. I went back into the First's cabin looking for a way to hide or escape. Men were yelling and running through the ship. I could hear them coming down the ladder to the cabins. I knew I couldn't get out so I climbed into the sea chest and hid under the clothing. I heard them rummaging around the cabin, they even lifted the lid to the chest but then closed it again, leaving to search in other places."

David sat up in his seat and leaned forward, continuing his story.

"I heard, through the skylight, that three guards were being left aboard to guard the ship, while the crew and Officers were taken to some camp on shore. I played a prank on the guards, luring them into the brig to look at a dummy I had prepared. When they came to investigate the noises I was making, I locked them in, and left before they could use their weapons. I searched the ship for anyone else but found no one. I was very hungry so I went to the galley to find some food. I hadn't eaten for two days as I was being disciplined."

"It seems you were always being disciplined." the Admiral interrupted. "I understand from the log that you were before the mast on five different occasions. It states further that you were incorrigible and nothing could be done with you. You were insulting and most abusive, to say the least. You were most disrespectful of the Senior Officers. Are these allegations correct, and if so, why did you behave this way?" the Admiral asked.

David hung his head. "Sir, I was being sent away against my wishes. My father decided that I was going to sea. I admit causing him much grief," he explained, staring at the deck.

"So you were broken. The discipline had its proper effect and you have now altered your behavior, is this correct?" the Admiral continued questioning.

David decided that he would not tell the Admiral of his desire to desert.

"It seems entirely possible that you have concocted this disgusting story to retaliate against those Officers who punished you. Am I not correct, Mr. Clements?" The Admiral had seized on this course of questioning. *Perhaps I can break the boy's story*, he thought to himself.

"Sir, that is not true. Several besides myself were punished in the First's cabin," David replied sadly at the Admiral's suggestion.

"Carry on with your story." The Admiral waved his hand at David.

"I decided to swim ashore and determine what I might do to help the crew. The privateers did not suspect anyone had escaped."

"There's no need to go through the rest of the details, I've heard them several times before. I cannot see you being clever enough to have made up such a yarn unless you had experienced it yourself, and surely your family name required your deep concern for your honor, even if your initial behavior did not," the Admiral said, for the first time acknowledging the Earl's background. "Are the tales of your imprisonment after you had rescued the crew and her Officers true?"

David looked up at the Admiral, looking directly into the Admiral's questioning eyes.

"Yes Sir, it was their plan to discredit me, blaming me for the whole happening," David went on.

"The details of your story are cause for the greatest concern. There is no question that the Officers involved were going to take credit for the rescue and the capture of the prizes for themselves. It appears that Captain Willoughby also saw the opportunity to go along with the Officers, in order to enhance his own situation and cover up the whole fiasco."

The Admiral continued to slowly pace back and forth in front of David as if he were contemplating the story over and over again in his head.

"These accusations are most disturbing. I am inclined to believe you and I'm sure that, under cross examination, these Officers will melt like lard. It is obvious the Master and the entire crew of the *Subdue* insist on verifying your story and, through their feeling of indebtedness to you, they took the drastic measures of disobeying the ship's Officers. You have strong allies Mr. Clements," the Admiral said, waving his steward to his desk.

He approached his desk and leaned over it, placing his hands down sharply in front of the steward. The steward jumped to attention.

"I want a court of inquiry assembled for tomorrow morning. Signal the three other Captains to repair aboard at their earliest convenience," the Admiral ordered. He turned and looked at David. "Until further notice Mr. Clements, you will have no duties to perform. One last thing. Was the other Midshipman, what's his name, Walters, subjected to the same, er – punishment by the two Officers?" he asked.

"I believe several times, Sir. Kenneth was often called to report to the First's cabin for punishment. He never told me what the punishment was. He and the other Midshipmen were forbidden to talk to me," David said, confirming the Admiral's worst fears.

"Do you know that these Officers could be hung for their offenses? On top of their treachery, the disgrace these men bring to the Navy, is indescribable. I cannot recall, in all my days in the service, hearing of such abominable acts," the Admiral explained to David.

"Sir, I do not wish to testify against the two Officers. It would be too embarrassing for me and for the Navy, as well as all the other young Officers aboard. I would not like to be the cause of their dismissal. It is over with. They will have suffered enough by the time everything is completed," David sighed.

"You mean you would forget the terrible degradation they imposed on you?" the Admiral spoke with a sign of relief in his voice. He had wondered if he should presume on the young Midshipmen to reconsider this most serious charge against the Officers. It would reflect badly for the Admiral and his command. The disgrace would take years to live down.

"If Kenneth and the others will, then I will," David replied.

"Would you be kind enough to have a word with Midshipman Walters regarding the matter? I would like you and Mr. Walters to report to the fleet surgeon for an examination to make certain you were not injured," the Admiral instructed.

David tried to assure the Admiral that everyone was fine and didn't require an examination, however, the Admiral wanted to have his conscience clear that he had done all he could for the boys.

"You are a very brave and indeed a clever young man and a credit to the Navy and, of course, your family. You will certainly be mentioned in the *GAZETTE*. A most prestigious beginning for you, young man," the Admiral said.

* * * *

Kenneth and David were sitting on deck while the Master proceeded to outline some assignments in navigation. "Is everything all right? Things have worked out to your satisfaction?" the Master asked.

David turned to his friend. "Kenneth, I know how terribly you were treated. It is no longer a secret. We were not the only ones to suffer, under those two. I want you to know the Admiral is very upset. I told him I would not press charges against the Officers if you and the other boys agreed not to as well. The Officers might well be severely punished for what they did," David said.

Kenneth looked at David then to the Master. "David, if you can, so can I. I will try to forget it."

"Kenneth, why didn't you speak to the Captain or to the Master? I heard you being summoned to the First's cabin many times, and you wouldn't tell me about it. I want to be your friend. I have changed from when I first came aboard. I see things differently and you were the only one who tried to help me. You are my friend," David said, smiling at Kenneth.

The two boys nudged each other as the Master gave them his stare. He too had a sparkle in his eyes as he proceeded to lecture.

"Mr. Walters, the Admiral would like to see you in his cabin immediately," the steward yelled. Kenneth looked at David with a knowing look.

The inquiry was a short affair, with the Officers pleading guilty. They knew that the evidence against them was too conclusive and that they had best not contest. They had no other choice. They had been condemned by their own treachery.

Captain Willoughby was given a severe reprimand but not relieved of his command. It would be a long time before he saw any further promotion. The First Officer and the Senior were demoted and reassigned to other vessels. A full court-martial would have drawn attention to the situation and the Admiral's command would have come under severe criticism, plus there would have been embarrassment for the entire Navy. The Admiral felt pleased with himself that he had made the best of a terrible situation and warded off what could have seen his career ended.

* * * *

David and Kenneth were reassigned to *HMS Halcyon* Sloop of War, as was Mr. Kenting, the Master from the *Subdue*. It was a new ship and a new start for the heir to the house of Windsor.

David was given a hero's send off as he climbed down the *Subdue's* side into the awaiting barge. "Three cheers for his Lordship! Hurrah! Hurrah!! Hurrah!!!" they shouted. David was embarrassed as nothing like this had ever occurred in his life before. David and Kenneth were transported to their new assignment aboard the sloop of war and the newest addition to the fleet. The barge came alongside the sloop and the Midshipmen were wondering why the rails were lined with seamen. David looked around to see if there was another barge pulling alongside. The Bos'n's pipe sung out as the boys climbed aboard. Everyone seemed to be looking at them as though they had two heads.

"Captain's compliments, your Grace and he would like you to report to his cabin immediately," the Officer of the watch instructed. David wondered at the sudden use of his title.

Something was going on and he was feeling apprehensive.

"Midshipmen Clements and Walters reporting, Sir," David said as confidently as he could, after knocking several times on the door.

"Enter!" Captain Fulton Tate called. David entered first, with Kenneth following.

"Gentlemen, I wish to welcome you aboard. You will find life considerably different from the one you have just left. On this ship we work. You may have enjoyed some degree of notoriety and been treated like heroes aboard the *Subdue* but here you are just two ordinary Midshipmen. Learn well and you shall be rewarded. Fail to learn or attend to your assignments, then you will be rewarded in another way. I understand, Mr. Clements, you have already enjoyed several trips to the mast. Well, there will be none of that here unless it is absolutely necessary. I trust it will not. There are only myself and two other Officers aboard. You two, along with Midshipman Gerrard, make up the remaining Officers. Mr. Clements, you are just another crew member aboard the *Halcyon*, see that it remains that way. No special privileges here unless they are earned. We have some formidable tasks ahead of us and I hope you are up to the challenge. That's all," the Captain dismissed the boys. Outside, they looked at each other wondering what they had got themselves into.

They were in the process of berthing in, when a familiar booming voice startled them into whirling about. The Master from *Subdue* was standing in the entrance way.

"Greetings my fine young gentlemen, I have also been reassigned to this sloop of war. I trust you will be prepared for some tough lessons," Kenting smiled.

Both boys looked at each other, hardly believing their friend had joined their ship. They all shook hands. Somehow the occasion called for a more personal welcome for the only person who stood up for them throughout the ordeal. David could not restrain himself and with tears fogging his eyes he put his arms around the burly Master. Kenting likewise embraced David. Then it was Kenneth's turn. The two Midshipmen could not have been happier with this turn of events.

"Highly irregular behavior, your Grace," Kenting said, trying to sound gruff.

"We're alone and I don't care," David announced with a belligerent look on his face.

"Up anchor," came the Bos'n's call. The three headed up on deck.

CHAPTER ELEVEN

HMS Halcyon

It was a clear, bright, sunny day that saw *Halcyon* raising her anchor and catching the first breezes that would take her neatly out of the harbor. Everyone was pleased to be away from the stinking mess that was Guadalupe. They were all happy to be getting about the business of patrolling. The little ship was like a feather on a breeze, the way she responded to the helm with hardly any turns taken upon the wheel. The crew seemed happy as they went about the chores of getting underway. David assumed the Captain must be a good man, even if his first impressions were of a strong disciplinarian who stood for no nonsense.

The acting First Lieutenant had not made his appearance when the boys departed the quarter deck for their berths below. A good First officer often was able to act as a buffer between a tough Captain and the crew. David hoped so.

The ship sailed out past the Bench with its cannon barricades pointed menacingly down upon them. This would be a difficult fortress to penetrate if the need ever arose.

David and Kenneth reported to the Master for their assignments.

"Midshipman Clements reporting for duty, Sir." David saluted smartly.

The Master could not help but be impressed by the tremendous change that had occurred in the young Earl's behavior. David Clements was a ship's Officer at last, and his entire attitude was now in tune with the best traditions of the Navy. However, there was a dark cloud looming on the quarter-deck which caused the Master to shift his eyes in a signaling manner of recognition. David followed the Master's eyes as he too took in the two figures standing together in conversation.

David's heart stopped momentarily as he recognized the Officer talking to the Captain. He could not make his mind comprehend the meaning of this Officer's presence on board.

"Kenneth, don't look, just glance at the quarter-deck and tell me what you see," David whispered to his shipmate.

"Davey, it's Lt. Wright. What's he doing here? Oh God, I hope we are mistaken. If it's him Davey, we're in for it good," Kenneth remarked, tears and fright showing in his eyes.

David had seen that look on Kenneth's face many times before as he awaited punishment at the hands of the First. What was to happen to them now that their old nemesis was aboard as First Officer?

The Master was ordered to the helm but as he was leaving he whispered, "I'll do what I can for you lads, I promise."

David could not fathom how this Officer would be allowed to sail having on his staff two of the young Midshipmen who had destroyed his career. *How could the Navy do such a terrible thing to us? He'll kill us if he gets the chance,* David thought. David strained to hear what was being said between the Captain and Mr. Wright.

"I'll talk to the three Midshipmen now. Have them come to my cabin and I wish you to be there as well First," Captain Fulton-Tate ordered. "The young gentlemen are comparatively new to the service and one of them I hear tell was a true red neck renegade but has since been tamed. He has, in fact, established himself as a bit of a hero through some outstanding action aboard his previous ship. You may recall the name, David Clements. He is the heir apparent to the House of Windsor, I understand. Well, it won't cut any ice on my ship. No special privileges and we must make sure they learn that quickly. The Master can look after that part. You will be in general charge of the military aspect of their training and discipline. I understand from your background that you handle the young gentlemen very well," he concluded.

The First wondered where the Captain had heard such endorsements. *Well, all the better to attend to Master David Clements,* he thought.

David and Kenneth, along with their shipmate Remus Tulliver, were ushered into the Captain's cabin. David and Kenneth avoided the staring eyes of Lt. Wright.

"Midshipman Clements reporting, Sir."

"Midshipman Kenneth Walters reporting, Sir."

"Midshipman Remus Tulliver reporting, Sir," the three announced themselves. Their salutes were returned.

"I am Captain Fulton-Tate, and this is First Officer Wright." The Captain made a gesture towards the First as an introduction. "Lt. Wright will be responsible for your seamanship training as well as your discipline, while the Master will attend to your academics."

Shuffling through records on his desk, the Captain continued. "I see here that Mr. Clements and Mr. Walters have served under you on your last ship, Lieutenant. At least you are familiar with each other's ways and that's good."

David and Kenneth exchanges glances, wondering what could be good about this situation.

"Mr. Tulliver, you have just come aboard as a volunteer. Might I ask how you came to be here in Guadalupe?" the Captain continued.

"My parents were owners of a large plantation here. The plantation had just been sold and my parents, brother, and I were traveling to England on a merchant vessel. Our ship was captured by privateers a day and half out, and my parents and my brother were killed." Remus hung his head, trying to hold back his emotions, remembering the ordeal of his loss.

"Your records show you are just thirteen, and also that you were pressed into the service when you were picked up by one of our vessels. Is this true?" the Captain asked.

"I was kidnapped against my will. It was not my desire to enter the service. I just want to return to my grandparents in England," Remus replied.

"Were you able to save any of your fortune?" the Captain inquired.

Remus informed the Captain that the entire sum had been forwarded by a company ship several weeks before. It would be held in trust until he returned to claim it. "I do not wish to be a part of this crew and I demand to be placed aboard any ship heading for

England," Remus informed the Captain, with some force.

"Well my lad, whether you like it or not, you are a member of this crew, even if you are only a volunteer. You will remain a volunteer until you learn to act as a Naval Officer. Is that clear? You do not even qualify as a Midshipman yet. You are still a volunteer at this point."

"Yes Sir," Remus replied, with deep hatred and sadness in his eyes.

David and Kenneth stood spellbound throughout Remus' story, concerns for their own safety partially forgotten. Remus was just a few months older than they.

"Mr. Walters, you will assume the Senior's duties as you are the most experienced. Mr. Clements, you will familiarize Tulliver with the ship, its workings and protocol," the Captain ordered.

David glanced at the First and at once turned away as those penetrating eyes revealed just how dangerous this voyage could be. He wondered if he should tell the Captain of the situation but felt it was his word against the First's. He couldn't understand why Mr. Wright had been assigned to their ship after the court of inquiry. *Why had he been sent aboard the Halcyon after what had occurred on board the Subdue?* The boys left the Captain's cabin each full of foreboding,

David and Kenneth for one reason, and Remus for another.

"You, new boy, I wish to see you in my quarters immediately," the First said, catching up to the retreating Midshipmen.

"Sir, the Master is expecting us at this moment," David tried intervening.

"You little snot, you mind your tongue! You and I have a lot of settling up to do. So bear that in mind whenever I give you an order. Do you hear me Mr. Clements?" the First rebuked David.

David stared at the First, hatred seething through his eyes.

"Mr. Clements, come with me. We have some charts to assemble for the Master before our next session," Kenneth ordered David. The boys retreated down the companionway to their berth.

"David, what are we going to do? How are we going to help Remus? What's going to become of us?" Kenneth questioned plaintively. He hung his head and started to locate the necessary equipment required for their navigation lesson.

They both wondered what was being said in the First's cabin.

"Come in Mr. Tulliver. I just wanted to make you welcome and to give you a few precautions regarding the discipline aboard this ship, and to warn you as well. I cannot stress too strongly my concern over the two Midshipmen you have the misfortune of associating with. They are trouble makers and misfits. They will attempt anything to discredit the ship's crew and Officers and I can only warn you against any association with them. They are liars of the worst kind. Heed nothing of what they tell you and you'll get along fine. Remember, I can make you or break you, depending on how you perform. Is that clear? You're new aboard a King's ship, so mark well my warnings or you'll never see England. I'm only telling you this for your own good. Alright? Have I made myself clear? Oh yes, you will have certain duties here in my quarters from time to time. You may leave now."

Remus left the First's quarters confused and bewildered and headed to the deck where the Master was starting his class with the Midshipmen. Both David and Kenneth searched the new Midshipman's face for any signs of stress. There didn't appear to be any, but Remus avoided looking in their direction.

"Welcome Mr. Tulliver, I am Mr. Kenting, Master of the *Halcyon*. I am in charge of your navigation classes. I trust you will find them interesting. Pay attention and you'll benefit immensely. Now, shall we carry on?" the Master said, taking up his chalk board.

The two Midshipmen looked at one another wondering what the First Officer had said or done to Remus, who sat by himself listening intently to the Master.

CHAPTER TWELVE

Old Terrors

HMS Halcyon was making good speed as she headed northward. The south wind on her tail was causing an unpleasant corkscrewing action which normally left even the most stalwart seamen in a state of wretching. David wondered how much longer the ship would be on this heading. *Surely it must be about time for the Captain to open his sealed orders from the Admiral in Guadalupe.* Three days ago they had been anchored placidly in the great harbor, sweltering under the mid-summer heat and even at sea there seemed to be little relief from the penetrating rays of the sun.

Midshipman Clements, not wanting to be seen as a seasick urchin, stayed close to the railing where he could lean over and vomit clear of the decks and not be observed by other crew members. He felt terrible and had not eaten for two days. He hoped for a course change which would see the ship beating on the wind instead of making this sickly motion. He looked about him to see if anyone else was experiencing the same misery. He was alone as he waited for the next bout of heaving and reflected on the events of the last few days since weighing anchor. Kenneth was too busy with the ship's inventory duties and his gun crew to spend any leisure time with David. Remus was conspicuous by his absence at any duty or activity where David or Kenneth were involved. Even in passing, Remus avoided looking at them. It was only too obvious to David that the First had issued orders for him to stay clear of the two Midshipmen. He thought back to his own treatment by the ship's Officers of the *Subdue*. He could understand the crew's feelings towards him at the time when he first joined the ship and he did deserve most of his punishments. He realized that now but there was no such situation at present to justify the treatment he was receiving aboard the *Halcyon.*

"First! I want all hands gathered on deck. I wish to have a word with them," Captain Fulton-Tate directed the First Officer. It seemed obvious to all within earshot that he had opened his orders and was about to reveal their destination and duty to the crew. David and Kenneth ran forward along the starboard railing almost colliding with Remus heading in the same direction. "Sorry Remus," Kenneth apologized. Remus didn't acknowledge the apology but continued across to the port side. He couldn't have made it any clearer that he did not want to be near the young Officers.

"The First has gotten to him, David," Kenneth whispered. "I am afraid for him and I don't know of anything I can do to change things. Please watch yourself Davey, he is going to make trouble for both of us, I just feel it," Kenneth said, turning and giving his full attention to the Captain's words.

"I am hereby directed to sail amongst the islands in as inconspicuous a manner as possible in an endeavor to rout out privateers who may be hiding on any one of the islands. There are many sheltered coves to hide a vessel. The *Subdue* will be searching the easterly side of the islands. Night foraging by the privateers must be stopped by any means at our disposal. It is hoped that, at this time, we will make quick work of them. Lookout is the key word for the venture as we pass close by the islands, and be alert for anything that looks irregular and out of place. We will search everywhere. I caution you against any undue noise while we are in close proximity to the islands. Silence will be most precious. I will be sending patrol launches to check the coves. That is all," the Captain concluded.

He turned and walked over to the helmsmen, while the First descended the stairs to the main deck directly in front of David and Kenneth.

"Well, my young cabin companions, what is it to be? Hell on earth, or friendly cooperation huh?" He smirked at the sight of the two Midshipmen as they stood petrified at the First's remarks. They had been expecting something.

Turning to Kenneth he said, "Senior, take the purser and inventory all the small arms on the vessel and, mind you, refrain from the temptation of taking one for yourself. Sooner or later you'll be at the mast as before and then, my good man—well you understand, I'm sure," he laughed menacingly.

Without a word to David, Kenneth departed for his assignment with the purser. He tried to keep his emotions under control but this threat was devastating to him. He had rejoiced with David at being free of the tyranny aboard the *Subdue* and now this. *How could this be happening?* He wanted to talk to the Master but knew he would be placing Mr. Kenting in an untenable position. His despair was almost more than he could handle as he went about his duties below decks in the ship's armory. He hadn't had a chance to talk to David, and wondered if he would ever find the opportunity to escape, with the First now looking for any reason to discipline them. The Bos'n's rattan on the buttocks was a terrible thing to endure, and sometimes left the victim a writhing, screaming mass on the deck. No one would dare venture to come to his aid. Kenneth thought his only way out of the dilemma was to desert ship at the first opportunity. Anything would be better than what lay ahead for both he and David at the whim of the First Officer.

David was assigned to boat drill, emphasizing the skills pertaining to launching the long boat silently from its chalks and then boarding and rowing away unheard. He had been assigned twelve seamen, all of whom were experienced, and were a help to David who had never before commanded a boat of any sort. His identity was still unknown aboard *Halcyon*, which suited him just fine. It saved him from ridicule and embarrassment. He was trying to make it on his own merits as opposed to being the Duke of Windsor's son. The aristocracy was not always well received in England and certainly not aboard a King's ship. There was too great an economic spread between the very rich and the very poor. David had proven that he was intelligent and had the makings of a good ship's Officer. He would do well when the time came for him to write his Lieutenant's examinations. For once in his life he was living his life without the stigma of his title. Now that he had achieved honorable mention for his bravery, he was acclaimed a hero by his shipmates. All that too was behind him, for on board the *Halcyon* he was just another Junior Midshipman, another snotty.

Captain Fulton-Tate was watching David work his boat crew and was impressed with the excellent drill. This crew was ready for night operations and he felt that the boy had promise, knowing little of the weighty matters which constantly haunted the youngster. He knew nothing about the terrible threats that the First Officer had directed to the young men of the ship.

The drill finished and the boat secured, David reported to the First Officer that he had completed the exercise. He was satisfied that they had performed well and were ready for action as he dismissed the boatmen.

"It appears your crew members have done well and I agree they are ready. Now, Mr. Earl, are YOU ready for action?" the First asked sarcastically. "Report to my cabin at the end of your watch and present your report on this afternoon's drill," he said, walking away.

David knew that no pleading on his part would forestall the inevitable. He wanted to scream the truth so everyone could hear what the First was really like, but knew it would be classed as a treasonable act and he would be the only one to suffer. He, like Kenneth, knew that they had to escape, perhaps to one of the islands during the night.

"Mr. Wright, please brief Midshipman Clements on his operations for this night. Make certain he understands exactly what he is to do. I'm counting on a satisfactory mission," the Captain explained to the First.

"I have it scheduled already, Sir. He'll be well briefed, I assure you," the First replied, enjoying the little game he was having with David. He laughed to himself as he thought of the different terms used for his gross activities with the Midshipmen. *Now it was called 'briefing'. What humor*, he thought.

"I am having Remus Tulliver attend the – er – briefing to acquaint him with the operation," the First said, continuing his little game.

"Good idea Mr. Wright, you certainly have a way with the young gentlemen," the Captain laughed.

The Master overheard the conversation and knew the First was at it again. *What could he do to save the boys?* There was nothing he could do. He too was new aboard the *Halcyon.*

Stand firm and hold on David. You'll survive and overcome this ordeal, the Master thought to himself.

"Mr. Clements, the First requires your presence now. He is about to discuss the briefing with us," Remus advised looking sheepishly at David. These were the first words he had spoken for the past several days. A ray of hope seeded itself in David's mind that perhaps it was only going to be a briefing, as Remus was being included. He was trembling just the same as he made his way down to the First's quarters.

"Mr. Clements and Mr. Tulliver reporting as requested, Sir," David announced, saluting the Officer.

"Good, good. Well, Mr. Clements, I've missed you – and our little get togethers; however, we'll make up for that, won't we?" the First chuckled. "I've asked you here, Mr. Tulliver, in order that you might observe the briefing, and will naturally be more prepared when it is your turn. Have you prepared your report Mr. Clements?" he asked turning his attention to David.

"Yes Sir," David replied, the report shaking in his hand as he presented it to the First.

"Why are you so nervous, Mr. Clements? You've been briefed before. There is nothing to be nervous about now, is there? Of course there isn't. This isn't your first ummm, briefing. You know what to do, now get at it," he ordered.

"Sir, I must inform you that upon the decision of the court of inquiry, I wrote a letter to the Admiral with a copy to my father. The letter stated plainly what and who you are, along with Breckenridge. I also advised that Walters and I had not testified to your sadistic behavior to save the Navy the terrible embarrassment you have caused them. Sir, your days of abuse are done. Neither Remus nor any of the powder boys will ever attend to your cabin again," David announced.

The First Officer stood with his mouth wide open and a seething hatred boiling within. "You'll pay for this you little snot. One way or another," he shouted.

David looked questioningly at the First. "Are you planning to draw more attention to your presence and your behavior by having us punished? Mr. Wright, my letter has doomed your career," David smiled as he motioned Remus to the door.

"Don't you dare leave without my permission!" the First screamed hysterically.

David and a bewildered Remus left without further words. They were standing by the number one gun deck when the Captain called to David. "Mr. Clements! On deck immediately!" he shouted.

David froze. *What now?* It was getting dark and the ship was almost in position for dispatching the long boat and its load of investigators.

"Mr. Wright's compliments, Mr. Clements. You are to report to your boat station and prepare to launch as soon as convenient," Kenneth spoke quietly.

CHAPTER THIRTEEN
Another Prize

The night seemed particularly dark and only the outline of the leadsman in the bow could be seen. It would be another two hours before the moon rose, which would be enough time to get to at least half the coves on the small island. There wasn't a name for the island, but it lay off the northern point of Martinique. David stood quietly in the stern, his hand guiding the tiller, contemplating his plan.

"Quiet there, we're getting closer to the point, in a minute we'll be around and into the cove," David whispered, reprimanding the sailor with the noisy oarlock.

"Bos'n, we'll take a look, and if we see anything that requires investigating, we'll put ashore just around the point and trek on land the rest of the way around," David explained quietly.

The cove was a small one, but still had enough depth to take a schooner or even a small frigate. There was little sea room to maneuver though. David decided to waste no time in the cove and seeing nothing, they rowed across the entrance to the opposite shore. Once again the same procedure was followed. They would approach the point of the cove, then creep around and look inside. This cove, according to the charts, was larger and would afford excellent concealment for a privateer. His heart was beating rapidly as he strained his eyes to picture a vessel lurking in the depths of the cove. It was exciting and David made up his mind there would be no failure. He would find something.

They rounded into the cove, keeping close to the shore and against the dark background of the foliage. "Sir!" the Bos'n whispered excitedly. "There's a light or at least I saw a flicker just off our starboard forequarter. Look, there it is again!" he spoke, pointing.

"I see it, we're in luck. Best we put ashore but be very cautious as they probably have guards posted along the shore," David warned. He found it somewhat uncomfortable speaking to the man who only days ago had used his rattan on his bottom. He also knew that this man had spared him somewhat from the full force of his beating. David would speak to him later.

The boat scraped quietly onto the sandy shore and the crew concealed themselves in the foliage nearby.

David could not help but draw a parallel between this assignment and his rescue mission a few months before.

"Bos'n, space the men two meters apart, and any instructions will be passed man to man down the line. In another hour we'll have the moon to light our way."

The investigating party moved silently through the undergrowth towards the source of the light. As yet, they were unable to see even the barest outline of a ship.

"Hold up here," said David. "I'm smaller and I can move easier through the growth. If I'm not back in an hour, return to the boat and make your way to the *Halcyon*."

"Sir! Let me come with you, Harkness can take command," the Bos'n whispered as he moved after David. David nodded his head in agreement.

"Follow me," David responded. They crept away into the dark embraces of the forest. They had traveled for fifteen minutes when David held up his hand to halt. There were voices coming from a short distance ahead. The privateer crews were partying.

The Bos'n patted David on his shoulder to draw his attention to the outline of a large vessel. At first he thought it to be a sloop of war but, upon closer observation, he discovered it was a medium size frigate of French design. Her outline could barely be seen, but she was a large vessel.

"Sir, we must return and pass the information to the Captain," the Bos'n whispered.

"We can't, at least not until we have seen what we are up against on shore. We should determine how many crew man the vessel," David tried to sound authoritative. He knew the Bos'n was right. This was to have been an information gathering mission as opposed to an attack party.

David could not put aside the memory of his last success, and was torn between his assigned duty and the joy he derived from capturing an unattended enemy vessel.

"Return to the crew and bring the launch alongside the ship. I will meet you there. Watch for a waving lantern. I hope there is one available," David said as an afterthought.

"Sir! How can you even think about taking this vessel with so few men? There are only nine of us including you."

"We will have enough men to set enough sail to move her out. If I find it is impossible, I'll return with you to the *Halcyon*." As he said it, David wondered if this was the time for him to carry out his plan to escape, but was quickly reminded of his obligations to his two shipmates back aboard the *Halcyon*. He would not leave them to the ship's First Officer. *Never! Never!*

"Go quickly. Do as I say. I am going to swim out to the vessel," David ordered.

The distance was farther than his last swim and would require all his strength to make it. He would have to take his time and conserve his strength. He stripped off his clothing, realizing the added energy saved might make the difference between success or failure. As he stepped into the chilled water, he thought about his orders, but realized if he failed, he could always say it was part of his reconnoiter.

He had been swimming for almost ten minutes, and even though he had tried to conserve his energy, his desire to reach the vessel as quickly as possible was driving him on. He was exhausted but at the same time very excited. *If only his schoolmates could see him now.* He was nearing the ship when he thought he heard the dipping of oars. *How could my crew have arrived so fast?* he thought.

A boat coasted past him and bumped alongside the ship. He counted three men. Two on the oars and one on the tiller. From his position under the stern plates he could see three crewmen climbing down into the boat. It shoved off and there was a lot of laughter as David heard them passing a jug amongst them. The ladder was left dangling from the entry way. The boat was gone and he climbed the ladder to the deck. The stern lantern was still burning but, other than that, there were no lights showing. He felt awkward standing naked and shivering on this strange vessel.

He crept along side of the deck railing and quietly descended the stairs to the lower deck. It was here he could expect to find the guards. He made certain to orient himself so that he could make a hasty retreat if he was required to do so. He found no one, the ship appeared to be deserted, although he had seen three crewmen being placed aboard. They would be somewhere below. He climbed back to the deck. He heard the bumping of a boat alongside the hull. He stooped down, looking over the side. It was *Halcyon's* launch, and the crewmen were about to climb aboard when he heard someone approaching. He motioned to the crew to be silent and stay put.

He skirted the main mast to find the newcomer who had a bottle and was taking copious swigs of the contents. David reached up to the racks and removed a belaying pin. Holding it firmly, he crept along the railing until he was able to come up behind the unsuspecting crewman. He raised the belaying pin at the exact moment the man looked up. The man started to open his mouth to cry out but the belaying pin knocked him senseless. He fell to the deck where he would be attended to later.

David walked over to the side and motioned the crew aboard.

"Mr. Henry, there are two other guards aboard. I suspect they are asleep from the grog they've consumed. Seek them out as quickly as possible. Can we sail this ship out of here?" David asked. David knew most of the *Halcyon's* crew by their names.

"Why lad, I mean, Sir, if you can capture this vessel by yourself we can surely sail her out for you. Hadn't you best find some clothing to protect you from the chills?" the Bos'n asked awkwardly. David suddenly realized his nakedness and departed for the lower deck to find something to wear.

"All right me hearties, the lad has secured us this prize, so we can't let him down. Quietly now. Set the head sail and prepare the mainsail. I can't shout orders, you will have to watch what is going on and act accordingly. We want to have the ship headed out before the alarm is set. Mr. Stokes, this is going to be tricky. I want you to cut the anchor. I suggest you get started at it immediately. You can't use an axe, you'll have to hand cut it. Make certain you do not let go, until I give the signal. Once that anchor is let loose we are committed. There is always a chance the sails will not give us enough way to steer around. If that happens we'll be aground and dead meat for the privateers," the Bos'n warned his crew.

If anyone on shore had glanced over to the vessel they would have seen the foresail raising slowly up the stay. Six men were ready to drop the mainsail. When that dropped, the noise would be heard all over the bay.

David appeared on deck dressed in Midshipman garb. He had located the clothing in a trunk. Probably from some poor Middy before him. In any case, he felt better. He could only stand and watch as the Bos'n took control.

"Sir, we have a slight breeze coming with the dawn, would you kindly go forward and tell Stokes to cut her loose. It is now or never." He signaled the topmen to drop the main and at the same time the fors'l was slowly hoisted into position. There was still no cry from the shore. *So far so good.*

David ran forward and gave Stokes his instructions. His knife flashed several times and the great hawser tore loose and disappeared over the side. The vessel was now drifting across the cove. The little breeze there was seemed to be taking them broadside until slowly it picked up way and the rudder took hold. The Bos'n was at the helm himself. He handled the great wheel like he was spinning a delicate machine. He was feeling every move and each little pressure that was being brought to bear on the rudder. The pressure was increasing and he knew the ship was responding to her helm. Slowly she gained speed and turned outwards to the entrance. Still no shouts from ashore. It was obvious the pirate crews were too preoccupied to hear the ships dropping sails.

"Sir, I've attended to our inebriated friends. They're asleep in the brig. Won't they be surprised when they wake up with the grand daddy of all headaches?" Stokes laughed.

"Thank you Mr. Stokes. It would seem we may have been successful and nary a shot fired or a seaman lost." David was beside himself with excitement but tried to maintain an appearance of calm.

"Sir, best you get yourself some sleep while you can. We can handle the ship from here on. Her name is *Marquis de Charlois*. Young Sir, you have just captured a French frigate, albeit a small one," the Bos'n praised David.

"Sir, I intend to stay clear of the *Halcyon* until daybreak. Any sudden appearance of a French ship can only spell a fight with our own people. We'll hoist a white flag at first light then try to locate her," the Bos'n advised.

David didn't argue. Everything seemed to be going fine and the moon was slowly sinking below the horizon. The seamen had set the other sails and the ship was sailing well. The night being clear, there was no chance of a collision and perhaps they might even catch sight of their own vessel, *Halcyon*.

* * * *

"Sir! Sir! Wake up Sir. We're approaching the *Halcyon* and have identified ourselves. Come up lad and enjoy the fruits of your efforts. See, we are hove to and the *Halcyon* has a boat launched and it will be here in no time. Aren't you proud young Master?" the Bos'n shouted enthusiastically.

Coming on deck, David was greeted with a cry of "Bravo! Bravo! Mr. Clements!" David looked smart in his newly acquired Midshipman's uniform even though it was French.

Captain Fulton-Tate climbed up the side and virtually ran through the entry port. David saluted and approached the Captain.

"Sir, the crew and I wish to turn over the French Frigate *Marquis de Charlois.*"

The Captain looked about him with a look of complete disbelief. How could this young, completely inexperienced Midshipman have carried out such a coup?

"Thank you, Mr. Clements. I would appreciate a report of your investigations and the subsequent capture of this vessel at your earliest convenience."

The Captain, David, and the Bos'n were rowed back to the *Halcyon*, where an additional group of seamen had been selected to assist in crewing the prize. David tried to look away from the admiring crew as they went down the entry way.

"Hurrah! Hurrah!! Hurrah!!!" The cry went up from the crew of the *Halcyon* as David boarded.

Kenneth and Remus were at the entry port looking fondly at their friend. David wanted very much to talk to the two Midshipmen but knew it would have to wait until later. The First stood by himself on the quarter deck busying himself with the binnacle head. He realized that he would no longer have access to the Midshipmen now that the Earl had him at such a disadvantage and had established such a degree of credibility. The Master too had participated in the cheering.

"Quiet there! Quiet all of you! Bos'n take those men's names. I want quiet, we are still in search of the enemy!" the Captain roared, breaking his own rule of silence.

"Mr. Clements, may I ask you why you are on deck? I require your report as soon as possible and that means now," the Captain scolded David.

"Sir, the report is complete and in the hands of your clerk, Sir." David replied, not wanting to appear glib in front of the other men.

"Thank you Mr. Clements. I may wish to discuss the matter later," he said. "Mr. Wright, be so kind as to accompany me to my cabin and we will review the report together."

With the Senior Officers gone, David sought out Kenneth and Remus who had been waiting as well for this opportunity.

"We are very happy to see you David. And what a hero you are. We wondered if you would ever come back. It might have been the opportunity you had been waiting for. If you had gone, we would have understood," Remus ventured.

"I promised we would go together and so we will. Are you all right? Nothing serious occurred during my absence?" David questioned.

Kenneth looked away, gazing out towards the French Frigate.

"I was punished David. I had done nothing. He will find anything or any reason to punish me. We must leave as soon as possible. I can't suffer the man any longer," Kenneth concluded.

"Nor I, David. I was punished again. I can't stand the caning David. I can hardly stand I'm so bruised," Remus added.

"I've heard enough. I'm sorry about your punishments and we will take the first opportunity to leave this ship, I promise. I am sure my letters will finish him off once and for all," David replied, sympathetically.

The Captain took command of *de Charlois* himself while he placed the *Halcyon* under the command of the First. On hearing of this change of command, David approached the Captain.

"Sir, might I suggest you take two Mids with you, as you are short of Officers. After all, Sir, it is a larger vessel requiring more assistance," David practically begged.

He would have liked to have asked for his three friends but knew the ship only warranted two. His actions did not belie the fear he was experiencing in approaching the Captain this way. He felt, however, that he had earned the right to speak up.

"I'll consider your request Mr. Clements, but I cannot see that all three of the young Officers can be transferred. Leave it with me for now. Bye the bye, I must commend you on your initiative in the capture of the Frigate. The Duke should be most proud," the Captain said. This was the first time he had made any reference to the Earl's aristocratic heritage or of his heroic achievement.

It was time the two ships got underway and continued on with their assignment to search and identify. David was not afforded the opportunity of advising Remus and Kenneth of his request. He hoped and prayed the Captain would act on his suggestion. He must do everything in his power to remove the boys from Mr. Wright's perverse punishments.

The Captain addressed the crew. "You have been divided in order to crew the Frigate. I am taking direct command of the prize and it shall act as the flag ship. Mr. Wright will assume command of the *Halcyon.* I will be taking Mr. Clements and Mr. Tulliver with me. Let us get about the business at hand," he said, heading immediately for the entry port. David saw the distraught look on the remaining Midshipmen as the names were called out. There was nothing David could do at this time. Kenneth and Garreth walked to the stern looking out over the open sea. David could feel the sadness running through the minds of his friends.

As the new crew members were being embarked, David hastily ran to the stern. "Kenneth, I'm sorry. I promised you I would help you and I will. Watch for me. I'll be back, I promise. Please don't act hastily until I return." Kenneth could not hide the tears forming in his eyes. He and Remus were alone now with no friends to turn to. Their despair was overwhelming. David left before he, too, lost his composure.

CHAPTER FOURTEEN

Captured

The *Marquis de Charlois* sailed away to the northward, while *Halcyon* swung south and retraced her original course. This time she would be sailing between the islands of St. Vincent and Granada. Each of the large islands was surrounded by dozens of smaller, less known ones, each providing many little coves capable of hiding several fair sized vessels. These were ideal hiding places for the treacherous privateers who were lurking for unsuspecting merchant traders.

From the aft rail of *de Charlois*, David watched the tiny figure standing alone by the starboard railing on the *Halcyon.* He could imagine Kenneth's feeling of abandonment and hopelessness which plagued him every waking hour. He thought of the promise he had made to Kenneth and began searching his mind for a plan to rescue his friend while staying within Naval regulations.

The Earl's successful capture of the privateer sloop and the French Frigate had sparked in him a keen interest in the Navy. The adventure and excitement were almost overpowering as he thought of how he could manage the task at hand and still maintain his status within the Naval framework. David realized that he had deserved the horrible caning when he first came aboard the *Subdue*, but dealing with First Officer Wright and his particularly demeaning punishments was another matter. This would take a great deal of thought and planning. Remus, the new volunteer, would not be privy to his thoughts until he had formulated a strategy. He was still working out a plan.

Remus stood with him, looking towards Kenneth's small waving hand. Both knew what the other was thinking and they despaired for their friend. David made Remus pledge complete secrecy of anything that was said between them. Remus too, knew the great concern David had for his friend and how urgent it was that they act quickly. They were fearful of what Kenneth might do in his despair. David was appointed Senior Midshipman, while Remus assumed the duties of Junior Mid. Being a pressed colunteer Remusd has shown much promise and was classed officially as a Midshipman and sworn into the ship's compliment. Remus was assigned a day watch do his initial training. At thirteen Remus waa nearly as tall as the other midshipmen with a major fault of having the aristocratic air of the wealthy. The boy did not flaunt his strong build nor his apprent over-confident bearing. David wondered how he would act under the stresses of battle. He was also wondering, due to Remus's lack of experience, how much help he might be when called upon to act. David was going to need all the support he could get. He wished he could come up with a plan that would free them from the First Officer once and for all. He would have to wait and take advantage of each opportunity as it presented itself.

"Mr. Clements, a word please," Captain Willoughby called to David, as he was making his way forward to the gun section. "Since you are the most experienced and evidently the most resourceful member of my staff, I want you to repeat your investigation of the various coves nearby. Take the long boat along with eight crewmen and examine the various inlets. I might suggest you take extreme precautions. You might not be as lucky as on your last venture. The privateers hereabouts have been known to torture their prisoners, seeking information about our whereabouts in these waters. I shall take *de Charlois* into St. Vincent Channel. Might be an opportunity to catch one of the beggars returning." The Captain chuckled at the thought of more prizes.

David was fully rested from his last adventure, and was excited at the prospects of perhaps yet another capture. The Captain had advised him that his task was to only search out and not to play hero by engaging in any personal battles with the privateers.

There was still two hours until dark and once again the skies suggested a clear moonlit night in which to search the coves. With hardly a sound the searchers pulled away from *de Charlois* and rapidly made for the shelter of the coast. David spoke quietly to the Cox'n, more to ease his own tension than to pass on any relative information. The Bos'n, Rajah McLarity, had been promoted from the *Subdue* and took his new authority seriously. He was Irish for certain, with perhaps some East Indian blood. David wondered at the name Rajah, as he stood in the bow, his eyes playing back and forth over the coves.

The first searches proved fruitless and by midnight, David was wondering if the rest of the night would render the same results.

"Sir! I think the men should have a time to eat as the opportunity may not present itself later. The water here is quiet," the Bos'n observed.

"I would like to look into this next one and, if we see nothing, we will come ashore and have our supper. How are we provisioned?" David asked.

"Well, judging from the hungry looks of these swabbies, we should only have enough to last until tomorrow noon, Sir!" The Bos'n tried to lighten the somber mood with a bit of humor.

David was still not comfortable with the formal address and decided to risk a slackening of the tradition. "Mr. McLarity, while we are away from the ship, you may call me by my sir name.

I hope this is satisfactory. You and I have not worked together before and this being our first occasion, I thought it might be a more effective way to achieve our objective if we were less formal," David stated.

"If you feel better for it, your Grace, but I would be uncomfortable using this freedom. If it's all the same to you, I will hold to the traditional means of addressing my Officer," Mr. McLarity announced, turning away so as not to see David's eyes.

The cove proved to be as empty as the others. "Head in shore round that point," David ordered, pointing to the other side of the cove. They would be out of sight under some trees that spread their branches over the water, a likely place to conceal themselves while they ate.

David was having a hard time keeping his eyes from drooping every now and again as he sat with his back against a tree, eating his biscuit. His mind wandered to Kenneth and the *Halcyon. Where was she and what was happening to his friend?* He remembered his promise to Kenneth, and pondered how he was ever going to find an opportunity to keep it.

With the meal finished and the crew refreshed from the rest, the long boat was headed out of the cove for another patrol of the island inlets. They rounded the point behind which they had landed and were heading around the island when they discovered another inlet.

David determined that it was almost two islands, but for a narrow strip of land adjoining the two. There was enough growth of trees and shrubbery to prevent anyone seeing from one inlet to the other. That would suggest a narrow strip of land running between the two bodies of water. In order to search the cove it meant another hour of rowing. The men thought they needed a respite from their rowing as they were tiring quickly.

"Come about Mr. McLarity, and head back to our resting place. We will secure and hide our boat there and proceed by foot into the cove and through to the other side. It will save us a lot of time and the men will have a break in the routine," David ordered.

Mr. McLarity wondered how this young boy could have such a calculating mind as to be able to plan so well, and in spite of the assignment ahead of him, still take time to consider the welfare of the crew. He must only be twelve or thirteen. Proper hellion, he had heard.

The boat was beached and branches cut and placed to conceal it from any vessel approaching or entering the cove.

"Bos'n, all the men are to carry arms. We don't know what we shall discover on the other side," David ordered as they marched cautiously through the tall grasses growing along the shoreline. The bottom of the cove and the subsequent narrow strip of land would be approximately two miles or thereabout, although he couldn't be sure, but it wouldn't take long to cross.

* * * *

The *Halcyon,* in the meantime, continued to sail in and out of the channel islands, cautiously observing each one as they sailed past the entrances. So far they had seen nothing. Each cove had been completely deserted. Lieutenant Wright was hoping to have any opportunity to reestablish his position with the Admiral and perhaps have a permanent command. As First Officer of the *Subdue*, he had failed miserably and had received a severe reprimand for his handling of the privateer prizes. Most of that was thanks to that snot of a Midshipman Clements, who had been fortunate enough to have circumstances play in his favor. If it weren't for that child, he might well have been made a permanent Commander, what with the number of prizes they had brought in. Most had been of such value as to be immediately bought into the Navy. Well, he would make his mark on this cruise.

The constant sail handling was getting on everyone's nerves as the Commander shifted from one tack to the other. Second in command was Lt. Young. He was much older than most of the crew and had obviously been passed over several times for promotion. Mr. Wright wondered what Lt. Young had done to still be of such junior rank, as he seemed capable enough.

"Mr. Young, I want you to assemble a party to investigate the islands on the leeward side of these two islands. The *de Charlois* is investigating to the north and we'll pick up where they leave off," Commander Wright ordered.

Kenneth Walters had been close enough to hear the orders being given and approached the Senior Officer.

"Sir! I would very much like to join this party. I'm sure I could be of assistance and the experience would be good for me," Kenneth said, virtually begging. *Anything to get away from this ship and its perverted Commander*, he thought.

"Oh you would, would you? Like to run would you, Walters? How could I ever get along without my Senior Midshipman? You don't plan to leave us do you Walters?" the Commander laughed. "Hmmmmm, perhaps you might be able to participate. I might give you command of a second boat to investigate the windward coves. Do you think you're up to it?" the Commander asked.

"Thank you Sir. I'm sure I can handle it. I look forward to the opportunity, Sir," Kenneth replied, trying not to sound too enthusiastic.

"Then so be it. You will take command of the boat. I haven't anyone else to send, so you will have to do. I want you in my cabin as soon as your crew is assembled. I will brief you at that time."

Kenneth froze in his tracks when he heard the orders for his briefing. He was determined he was not going to be punished by the First Officer ever again and reminded the First od David's letter to the Admiralty and his Father Damned you hide you little snot. Following in thast brat Clemment's footsteps are we? Well we shall see. Now hear this. We are in very dangerous waters and privateers are everywhere. I hope they have the pleasure of seeing your puny body rot in hell" the First screamed.

The First Officer outlined the strategy Kenneth was to use in searching the coves. He assured him that they were in very dangerous waters. *Why wasn't he on deck? Why was there only one other Officer handling the ship?* Kenneth wondered. The briefing seemed to be over and it appeared he was going to be spared his punishment but the First had other plans. Kenneth's worst fears were about to become a reality.

* * * *

"May I go now? I must attend to my boatmen," Kenneth asked as he started dressing.

"Mr. Walters, the only word I have for you is this. If you try to run you will positively end your Naval career and what's more, I will have you shot on sight. And if you decide to leave us and are captured, I am sure you will be remember my warnings and forever be in my debt, won't you, Mr. Walters? You may carry on with your preparations for the search. We shall continue our little chat at a later time".

"Permission to embark Sir," Kenneth asked the First Officer, stifling back his tears.

"Bring all your men back with you Mr. Walters, we are going to be dreadfully short what with two boats on patrol," the First informed him.

* * * *

They turned around the nearest island out of sight of the *Halcyon*, and Kenneth heaved a sigh of relief. At least he was away from the boat forever if he had his way. He was not planning to return, even if it meant taking his own life.

It was his plan to carry out the patrol to the best of his ability, then give the Cox'n orders to return without him. It would be all over by the time the boat reached the *Halcyon*. He wondered where David was and how he was faring. He wanted desperately to contact his friend but knew this was an impossibility.

Midshipman Walters and his crew had been in and out of several coves but found no signs of privateers. He wanted to land but needed some excuse to make shore. They were gliding into a larger cove which was large enough to hide several ships, but on initial viewing the cove seemed to be empty. Kenneth's thoughts were interrupted by the sound of small arms and cannon fire. It seemed to be coming from inside the cove. *But that couldn't be,* he thought, *the cove was empty.* The explosions of cannon fire continued for some time while the patrol continued to the lower end of the cove.

By the time the search launch had reached the end of the cove the gunfire had stopped. "Sir, there is something strange about that gunfire. It sounded like it was coming from inside the cove but we've covered it all. I'd swear it was in there," the Cox'n ventured.

"I thought that too, but it's obvious there is nothing here. Pull to the shore and we'll take a short walk into the trees. Perhaps we'll climb that knoll over there and get a better view of the waters hereabouts. Post a guard by the boat and we'll have a look," Kenneth ordered.

The Earl, in the meantime, had also heard the cannon fire and along with three crewmen, climbed to the top of a small hill which overlooked the cove he had entered. The climb was a difficult one, and it took them several minutes before they achieved the top. The sight was magnificent, however, he thought his eyes were deceiving him when he looked in the opposite direction and saw another cove. He had been right. The island was held together by a narrow strip of land. He estimated it to be five cables. Not more.

"Sir, look, there are two ships sailing into the other cove. Good Mother, will you look at that! It's our *Halcyon* that's following the sloop. And that's not an ordinary sloop, it's a war vessel, or I'll be damned," the Cox'n observed. "Why would the *Halcyon* be sailing into this cove?"

"Look, her sails are holed. These two were in the combat that we heard. We had best get down and provide a welcoming committee for the ship. The *Halcyon* has captured the privateer no doubt," David said. "Let's hold fast here until we see what's taking place. There is nothing we can do and we're not attached to the *Halcyon*." *Thank God*, David thought to himself but quickly remembered Kenneth.

"David, er—, I mean, pardon me Sir, I never meant any disrespect but isn't that a long boat pulling across the cove to the *Halcyon*?" the seaman asked.

David could not fathom this latest occurrence. *Where had the long boat been? Probably ashore at the end of the cove. Who did it belong to?* David was racked with a thousand questions and no answers. He made the decision to hold fast in their present location. They could view everything from this vantage point. David wanted nothing to do with the *Halcyon*. She was commanded by his nemesis, Commander Wright.

As the long boat approached the sloop, small gunfire erupted and David could see men falling from the long boat. *Who was firing on a King's ship?* The long boat lost way and sat motionless in the water. There appeared to be no one aboard. A launch was making its way to the *Halcyon*. This must be the prize crew from the sloop making its way to the *Halcyon*. Three other boats were seen departing the *Halcyon*. She had dropped her anchor and was swinging around to face the entrance, as a fair wind made its way into the cove.

David watched as four boats departed the *Halcyon* and headed for the shore. It was then David saw the buildings. There seemed to be two of them, a quite large one and a smaller one. They were well hidden, deep in the strip of land dividing the two coves. The crewmen from David's boat looked on incredulously, as they witnessed the capture and imprisonment of their shipmates from the *Halcyon.*

Mr. Wright's inexperience had allowed her to be taken. *How stupid. How could she have been taken by a Sloop of War? How could that happen? The* Halcyon, *under proper command and circumstances, was large enough to take even the largest frigate however she was badly 'undermanned and commanded',* David thought. It occurred to him that the boats heading toward the shore could not possibly hold all of the crew, unless that was all that was left of them.

"Mr. McLarity, will you explain our situation to the men? Inform them that under no circumstances are they to leave sight of one another and above all – they are to remain silent. No guns are to be loaded until I give the word. There is some terrible mischief taking place here and we are privy to it. I intend to stay put until we know what is going on and what assistance we might provide our sister ship," David advised.

* * * *

On seeing the *Halcyon* entering the cove, Kenneth reasoned his ship would probably require additional hands and that perhaps there had been a change of the original plan with the ship showing up like this.

"Cox'n, under the present situation, I want you to take the long boat back and report to the Commander. He'll want to know what we've found. I shall not be going with you. I intend to investigate the other side of the island. I can be picked up at a later time," Kenneth said.

"Young Sir, I don't blame you one bit, nor do the other men, Sir. How you stood it so long we fail to fathom. Good luck, Sir. We'll leave you all the rations we have left. Perhaps we can make up a story about something befalling you," the Cox'n said sympathetically.

As the seamen departed they shook Kenneth's hand and wished him well. "We'd help you lad, but you know it would mean a mutiny, and we have kin elsewhere," they offered.

"Thank you all but it's my problem," he replied. Kenneth climbed the knoll that looked down into the cove. He watched as the longboat pulled away towards the *Halcyon* and was horrified to see his crewmen savagely destroyed by gunfire from the schooner. He rubbed his eyes to make certain he had not been deceived. He then saw the small boats leaving, filled with seamen from the *Halcyon*. At least it appeared they came off his ship. *What if he had not chosen this time to desert ship? What if he had been returning in the longboat? He would be dead, which would have been better than returning to the* Halcyon *and Lieutenant Wright.*

* * * *

In the meantime, David and his crew watched in horror at the scene below their vantage point. It was approaching dark and there was no way they could leave their hiding place, at least not until they had gathered more information about the demise of their sister ship.

"Cox'n, send someone to alert the guards at our boat that enemy is coming ashore. Thank goodness we did not put ashore in the low end. With nightfall, and our ideal observation post, we should be able to remain undetected. We might even—I shouldn't even think about it," David said, thinking about his last episode of cutting out a ship. Here he was again and in similar circumstances.

When darkness had completely engulfed them, they watched as fires appeared through the heavy forest below. The *Halcyon's* crew were being held prisoners down there somewhere. *Lieutenant Wright can 'rot in hell'*, David thought to himself. He would leave him there if they were occasioned to execute a rescue. *Maybe he could kill Wright himself.* The thought sent chills up his back as he remembered his treatment at the hands of Commander. *Rot in Hell*! kept nagging at David as he pondered their next move. He reflected back to the last rescue. He didn't have time to think about the danger he was in, he just acted instinctively. He wondered if he might do the same thing this time. He was frightened. He not only had his crew to think about but now he had the *Halcyon* and her crew.

In spite of his fright, there was a certain excitement as the adrenaline coursed through his veins. He was secretly savoring every moment. It was his twelve year old brain against the enemy. The privateers were more interested in celebrating their conquests than strategically planning for the future and the defense of their holdings. *They operated more by chance than by good management,* David concluded. This would be to his favor as it had been on the other occasion, at least he hoped so.

* * * *

Kenneth, upon seeing his crewmen mowed down and the capture of the *Halcyon,* decided he had made the right decision by leaving, at least he was still alive and free, while the others were dead or prisoners of the ruthless privateers. He still was unable to determine the chain of events which must have led to this state of affairs. His crew had hidden rations for him so he knew he would survive for a little while, but now there were other human beings on the island beside himself. He was of two minds as to what he should do. If he remained concealed he might never get off the island and would die of hunger. If he made his presence known to the privateers, he might well survive and wind up in a subordinate and perhaps more devastating role aboard one of their vessels. There was no entertaining the idea of trying to make contact with what was left of the *Halcyon's* crew. First, he would make his way quietly down the hill towards the camp and observe what was taking place. If he was quiet, it shouldn't be too hard to do. He was small and could crawl through the grasses as David had done on his rescue mission. He hadn't realized how hungry he was until now, so he made a detour to where the long boat had been beached. True to their word, the crew had left provisions for him hidden in the bushes just ahead of the keel marks of the long boat.

He could hear the noises from the camp and knew celebrations were taking place, so he would be able to get quite close without being detected. *They were probably all drunk by this time.* He made his way, crawling on his belly until he came upon the main path. Before crossing it, he looked both ways, then quickly dashed across. He was on his hands and knees when a pair of hands grabbed him around the waist and lifted him high off the ground.

"An English spy, are you now?" questioned this huge, half naked, black man. He was no native, judging from his English accent.

"What is a young Midshipman doing out here all by himself? Come and join the rest, we have to be hospitable you know," he laughed as he walked along, holding Kenneth under his arm. Kenneth was beside himself with fear. *What would they do with him?* He had heard that spies were shot or hung.

"Put me down!" he shouted. "I'm a King's officer and you'll hang for this," Kenneth attempted to bully his captor, who only laughed harder as he gave Kenneth a swat on his backside. They arrived at the cooking fire where a huge bullock was being roasted.

"Look what I found, Chiefy," he called. "Look what I found crawling about in the big black woods. Very dangerous wouldn't you say," the black man laughed again, still holding Kenneth under his arm. Kenneth kicked and squirmed trying to get away.

"Does he belong to this ship or is there another ship hereabouts?" shouted the man they called Chiefy. He was a dirty man who didn't appear to ever have washed in his life. His teeth were stained, what there was of them. He obviously was the authority in this camp. He was called "Chiefy Blackman" by some of the men.

"What have you to say, young Mr. Spy? Are there other ships hereabouts? Are you a member of this ship or from another?" he shouted directly into Kenneth's face. The man put him down, holding his arms behind his back. Kenneth looked around the campsite to see if the *Halcyon's* crew were imprisoned here. Finally his eyes came to rest on two men tied up on the far side of the camp fire. Second Lieutenant Wolsley and Midshipman Gerrard Garreth. They both appeared to have been beaten. Their heads lay slumped on their chests. Garreth was swinging his head from side to side as though trying to dispel the thoughts of his capture.

"Tie him up and we'll get to him after we've finished with these other two. I still think they have little nuggets of information they are holding back. Can't have that now can we little spy?" he smirked at Kenneth.

Kenneth lay flat on his belly with his legs and hands tied together at his back. There was no way he could ever consider getting free. His tears started running down his face into the dirt on which he was laying, making little pools of mud. So this was how he was to meet his end. He tried to reason that this was better than the *Halcyon.* Here he knew he was going to be killed and on the *Halcyon* he would die another sort of death at the hands of the First.

Several members of the privateer group stood in front of Lt. Wolsley and Gerrard as the two seemed to be regaining consciousness. Kenneth felt sadness for Gerrard.

"Now Mr. Naval Lieutenant, we must know about the Naval ships in this area. You are going to tell us and you are going to tell us now. We have picked up the small boy you employ as a spy, so don't try and cover up his existence." Kenneth felt Mr. Wolsley's eyes upon him and shrunk under their dreadful stare. He had seen those eyes many times before. How he hated those eyes and the man to whom they belonged.

The big man who had discovered him, stooped over as though he was trying to hear what Wolsley was telling him. The man glanced over at Kenneth who nearly collapsed as he imagined what the Officer was probably saying about him. He said a silent prayer to himself.

Finally the talking ended and Lt. Wolsley was brought to his feet and marched over to where Kenneth lay.

"Is this the one you call your orderly?" he asked. The Lieutenant just nodded his head. He whispered something into Blackman's ear that caused the privateer to smile as he stared at Kenneth. Kenneth cried openly as he tried to bolster his courage for what he thought was the inevitable.

The Officer was taken away and made to bend over, while the big man took a large pole and with what seemed like all his might, struck the Officer on his posterior literally sending him flying several feet away. The howling and screaming were horrifying. Again and again the pole struck until the Lieutenant lost consciousness. They left him tied on the ground. Next they went to Gerrard and asked him about the ships.

"I really don't know, Sir. We were the only one investigating the coves," he lied, trying to be convincing.

"How many ships were in the harbor at Guadalupe?" the Chief asked him.

"Sir, I never counted them but maybe four or five," he spoke through his weeping and mumbling.

"Four or five is it now? Well they can't be still holed up in Guadalupe, can they now young man? Can they?" he shouted into Gerrard's face.

"Do you see the bullock turning on the spit slowly cooking to a wonderfully delightful tenderness? How would you like to join the animal? I think that would loosen your tongue. Strip him and bring him here!"

The big man who seemed to be second in command, the one who had found Kenneth, was sharpening the end of a long, thin pole. "We'll have to skewer him first." Gerrard was stripped and stood naked, trembling near collapse.

"Sir, perhaps there were a few more in the harbor. Yes, I think there might have been twelve. Three ships of the line and five frigates and the rest were sloops of war," Gerrard bleated the secret information.

"Well now, where are they now? Your memory should delve even further into your brain because when that pole comes back it is going to be driven into your backside and up through your guts to protrude through your neck. You'll cook like the meat over there," the Chief threatened. Gerrard fainted. It was more than the fifteen year old could stand. He was going to die the most horrible of deaths. He awoke screaming that there were two ships patrolling the islands, *Halcyon* which had been captured and *de Charlois*.

"Where is *de Charlois*?" he asked.

"I don't know, Sir, please Sir, I don't want to die, I've told you everything you wanted to know," Gerrard cried, a babbling screaming mess.

"I think he might have one more piece of information we need. Carry on with the skewering. He'll talk as his guts slowly destroy themselves."

All the time Kenneth watched, petrified by what was taking place. Gerrard was made to kneel down on all fours and the black man appeared with a huge mallet which would be used to drive the skewer. Kenneth couldn't let Gerrard die in this horrible manner. The pointed end of the skewer, which looked needle sharp, was placed between Gerrard's buttocks. His screams could have been heard all the way to Guadalupe. Kenneth could do nothing but pray silently for the young Midshipman and try and create some sort of distraction.

"Sir! Sir! He doesn't know any more. I can give you the information you want. He is just new aboard and doesn't know anything but I do, and I'll tell you what you want to know," Kenneth shouted. The skewer was removed and Gerrard was hoisted to his feet.

All attention was now on the little Midshipman laying on the ground. He had difficulty raising his head in order to look at this captors.

"Your Officer likes you very much, and tells me we would like you too. Is that true, Midshipman who knows everything?" Blackman sneered. Kenneth was stripped and stood with his hands tied in front of him this time.

"Chiefy, since I found him – he's mine," the black man suggested. "I'll have the information we need by the time he and I have had our time together," he went on.

All this time the crew were sitting around laughing and drinking and they were now laying about, encouraging the activities. This didn't help matters with all that was going on. Kenneth knew he was going to die but made up his mind that he had planned on dying anyway and he would do it with dignity and not be a sniveling mess like Gerrard. It was easy for him to think that way. He hadn't been on his hands and knees with a skewer leveled at his backside like Gerrard had.

Through clenched teeth, Kenneth told the story of the two vessels scouting each of the many coves searching for the sloop. He told of the use of the small long boats to scout deep inside the coves. He said he wasn't aware where the other Naval ship had gone, but understood one was going northward and the other was to search the southernmost islands.

"Please, Sir, can you put me down now? I've given you what you wanted" he said.

The black man stood Kenneth in front of him. "I am giving everyone fair notice, this is my lad. I will be the only one to use him understand?" he informed all the others.

Blackman interrupted, "Remember, I'm still the Chief and what I say stands. If he is so good, then I will make the decision as to whether he belongs to you or not."

CHAPTER FIFTEEN

The Thrill of Adventure

David, in the meantime, while all this savagery was being carried out, decided to gather as much information as he could before he took any action. His crew, upon hearing the screams from inside the privateer's camp, grew impatient to get a rescue of some kind under way. It was almost more than he could do to restrain them, assuring them the same fate might befall them if they were overpowered, which in all likelihood they would because they were badly outnumbered.

"Raj, I want you and one other to find out where the crew are secured. I don't know how many survived. Perhaps they're all dead, who knows? The rest of you men, I want you to come with me back down to the bay. Raj, when you have the information, if you can find out, come down to the water's edge where we can formulate a plan. Judging from those screams we heard I hope and pray we are not too late.

Obviously they must be torturing the men. I will hopefully have devised a plan whereby we can rescue the crew and maybe even capture one of the vessels in which to make an escape."

David was thinking of his friend Kenneth. He wondered if he was among those still alive. *Who else, in all his life, had suffered as much as he had?*

"We'll have to take one of the boats from the privateers. I hope they don't mind," David joked. "I want you to row towards the mouth of the cove so that you are behind the *Halcyon*. You'll have to work fast as we only have a few hours of darkness left. Everything must be done and in place by daybreak," he ordered his Cox'n.

"Sir, what is your plan, perhaps we can be of more help to you if we had an idea what you had in mind?" the Cox'n questioned.

"I don't have a plan, at least not a complete one. It may change before I am through. Watch the stern windows for a light. Then you may come aboard. I'll have either distracted the guards or sent them off," David tried to sound confident but he really had no plan. It would have to be developed as circumstances presented themselves. He had no idea how many men might be guarding the *Halcyon*.

"Who is a good swimmer?" David asked.

"Sir, I am very good, been doing it all my life," a young man volunteered.

"Good, you'll come with me," David ordered.

"Away with you now Raj, and good luck, remember no sounds or we're doomed," David warned.

"What is your name," David asked the swimmer.

"I'm Stovel Sir, my mates call me Stovey," the crewman replied, embarrassed. He was not accustomed to talking to Officers in such a casual way, although talking to this boy seemed different. He didn't feel the least bit intimidated.

"Strip off Stovey," David ordered as he removed his own clothing. "We're going to swim to the privateer. She's the closer of the two and we're at the best point to reach her. "Follow me and be quiet or we'll give ourselves away," David warned.

Both naked bodies disappeared into the balmy tropical waters. Swimming was easy and both young man and boy took leisurely strokes to conserve energy. Now and again they could hear oars dipping in the water as the row boat made her way to its position near the *Halcyon.*

"I'm smaller and can hide better than you Stovey, but climb up with me as far as the chain plates. You'll have to wait for me there. You'll know when to come up," David encouraged the young seaman.

David disappeared over the railing and observed a guard standing by the wheel. He couldn't see any others. He had to somehow get him near the railing. He crawled back to where the seaman Stovel was waiting down the side, clinging to the chain plates.

"Stovey, I'm going to lure the guard over here, it will be up to you to do for him when I have him here," David announced.

Without waiting for a reply he crept slowly down the opposite direction from the quarter deck. Stovey, standing on his precarious perch on the plates, heard some severe sneezing coming from his right. David was making a noise trying to lure the guard to the rear of the ship.

"Who's there?" came a call from the guard. Another sneeze and the guard descended the stairs to the main deck.

He walked hesitantly, looking in either direction. "Anyone there? Come out you miserable bastards. I know it's you trying to put the wind up my sail. Ha! We'll see about that," he sounded unsure of himself and his haughty remarks were supposed to convince him he was not alone.

The guard proceeded along the port railing looking into the scuppers and occasionally over the side.

David saw the guard approaching the hiding Stovey. He had to distract him enough for the seaman to surprise the guard. He was just over the hiding place when David ran out and stood along side the mast. He was in the shadows but knew the guard could see him. He also knew the guard would be shaken and not so apt to start shooting or shouting when he found the boy standing there in front of him. The guard turned his back to Stovey and that was his undoing. With a gurgling sound he disappeared over the side and into the water leaving a trail of red as he floated away.

Stovey climbed aboard, wiping his knife blade and he and David departed to make a survey of the ship to determine if there were other guards on board sleeping. Their search proved fruitless.

"What now Davey?" the seaman asked, not noticing his failure to use the proper address of a Senior Officer. David ignored the omission, they had more important things to do.

"Stovey, light a lantern in the stern window and be quick about it, we need those men aboard as soon as we can," David ordered.

"Zoooks, but you're a cool one Sir! It's a privilege to be working with you," Stovel complimented, then departed down the stairs to the main cabin.

The rest of David's crew came aboard. "I cut the guard's throat I did," said Stovel to his mates.

"We know, we bumped into his corpse heading out of the cove. You do nice work Stovey," someone said sarcastically.

"Cox'n, can we get enough sail on this vessel with so few men?" David asked.

"Sir, I wouldn't attempt taking her out with the *Halcyon* ready to take chase," the Cox'n warned.

"You're right. Stovey, you and I have another swim to make. You feel up to it?" David asked. He knew the answer before it came.

"Cox'n, as quietly as you can, rig for sailing her out. When you see the *Halcyon's* fors'l pulled, you cut the anchor cable and point her out as fast as you can, but not before *Halcyon* shows positive signs that she is under control and turning toward the entrance."

"David, your friends wish you good luck and we know Stovey here will look after you," the Cox'n said affectionately. Without replying, David and Stovey slid down the plates into the water. The sides cut into David's legs but there was nothing he could do about it. It would have to wait. Their swim took them to the stern windows of *Halcyon* which were just above the water and easy to enter. David arrived puffing and snorting as Stovey, having found the stern window open, crawled in. He reached down and lifted David aboard. Quickly they darted about the lower part of the ship only to find they were alone. They recovered some clothing and dressed.

Motioning Stovey to stay behind, David climbed the companionway to the deck. From the sloop they had been unable to see any movement aboard the *Halcyon* but one could never be sure. It wouldn't do to have their plans foiled at this time. There was a slight sliver of dawn showing on the horizon. David realized he would have to act quickly in order to get the ships away.

"Stovey? Can we get the ship out of here?" David asked, hopefully.

"Davey, if you can cut the main anchor hawser, then I can get enough sail to at least get us some way and we can turn. You're so small I don't know how you can cut the cable. I'll come back and cut through it just enough to hold her, then when I give the word, you'll have to do the rest," he said his expression showing his concern.

"I can do that Stovey," David replied. David and Stovey made their way to the anchor hawser and Stovey started immediately to saw through it with his knife. David presumed it was the same one that had been used on the poor guard. *Too Bad,* he thought.

The hawser was cut to the proper depth, just enough to hold *Halcyon* from breaking free. "I'll go forward and get the fors'l and the jib set. When I haul the sail you cut the cable," Stovey said, disappearing into the dark. David hung back, examining the shoreline.

"Who's there? Who's on ship? Halt!" a voice ordered. David was taken completely by surprise and cursed himself for being so complacent. There had been a guard on the boat after all.

He crept alongside the rail until he saw the guard. He was holding a cutlass to the throat of Stovey who had been caught with his back to the assailant, entirely unaware that there was a person other than David aboard. He didn't fight, he would wait his time. In any case one thrust of the cutlass and he was done for anyway.

"What the hell you up to mate? How'd you get out here? Are you one of the crew? Were you left here as well?" the guard asked Stovey.

"That's right you dumb oaf, don't you know your orders? Can't remember them leaving us two aboard?" Stovey tried bluffing. He tried to avert his eyes so as not to show the action that was developing behind the guard.

"Well, I wish someone would have said you was aboard. Scared me half to death," he went on. At that moment David dropped a rope loop over the guard's head and shoulders and quickly darted around the bollard securing the guard with several loops of rope.

"Good lad, Davey. The bastard caught me flatfooted! I didn't know what to do. He'd a done me that's for sure, although I thought my bluff was working," Stovey remarked.

"Stovey, let's get out of here. We've no time to waste and the others will be getting impatient and may decide to slip their cable too soon," David said as he ran forward to the anchor cable.

As David was waiting for the signal from Stovey at the fors'l, he was wondering what action he might initiate to free the crew. He wasn't the least worried about the Officers for they deserved everything that could be given to them. He wondered who had done the screaming. It wasn't Kenneth, it was too deep for that.

The cables were parted and the two ships moved silently out of the cove. The wind seemed sufficient as it increased with the first light. It was coming from inside the cove, taking them away from danger. David felt his luck was still holding.

The ships slowly turned and ran with the slight breeze that was just enough to take the ships clear of the cove. Now all that was to be done was to rescue the crew but David had no idea, at this time, how to do that.

Now he was the Senior Officer in charge of a cutting out exercise with two vessels terribly undermanned and quite incapable of sailing anywhere. The sea was calm with just a slight ripple on the water. The wind continued taking the ships clear of the cove.

A row boat could have caught up to them. David was slowly formulating a plan. If he could take the ships into St. Vincent's Channel, he would more than likely meet up with *de Charlois*. They'd have enough men to properly man the two vessels.

The thrill and excitement was wearing off and exhaustion slowly overtook the Midshipman. The sloops slowly made their way around the point and out of sight of the camp. The privateers would be taken completely by surprise when they found their ships gone. Not only had they lost their prize but also their own vessel. *Serves them right*, thought David, *the privateers will get their justice once the Captain catches up to them.*

The ships closed to hailing distance and David suggested to Mr. McLarity that the remaining crew members should be divided evenly between the two vessels.

"I was about to suggest the same thing lad, I'll have a boat swung out and we'll do this right off," the Master hollered.

"Any plans Davey?" the Master yelled. It had become quite common for the crew to address the young Midshipman by his Christian name. They were very fond of the lad and would now have followed the youngster anywhere, their admiration was so deep.

"Mr. McLarity, I'm taking Stovey and will require the smallest boat we have," David yelled, squeaking sometimes in his falsetto shrill. Soon one of *Halcyon's* boats was coming alongside the privateer with additional crew.

"Proceed around the island to the other cove. Don't enter, just stand off the point. Watch for my signal, it will come from atop the hill which you can see from here."

"David, we can spare another man if you wish," the Master offered.

"Thank you, but the fewer the better on this mission," David replied.

Once again, in spite of his exhaustion, he was feeling the thrill of adventure which lay ahead. It would take them awhile to reach the point, unless they spotted *de Charlois* first.

"Get some rest Stovey, you'll need it before this night's done," David said, turning to find a quiet place on the deck. The sun was warming the deck planks and he was soon asleep.

* * * *

"Sir! Sir! It's getting quite dark and thought you should know we are cruising off the point. The Master wanted me to arouse you," the seaman said apologetically.

"Thank you, will there be a moon tonight?" David asked, rubbing his eyes.

"Just coming up, Sir, off the starboard bow. We'll be quite visible for anyone with a glass," the seaman ventured.

"Mr. McLarity, can you bring us closer without grounding us?" David asked.

"The charts show plenty of water hereabouts, Sir. I can bring you closer, I just have to watch the currents off the shoals," he informed.

"Stovey, are we ready to go? Bring some powder and two muskets. I want us to be landed as soon as we can," David said excitedly. "I only hope the winds stay down. We'll never be able to ride a storm, crewed as we are," David said to the Master.

His brief but sound sleep had refreshed him and he was ready to implement his plan. "We're all prepared, Sir, perhaps you forgot. You gave me the orders before you took your nap, Sir," the seaman replied with a little chuckle.

"Stovey, you don't have to come on this unless you want to. It was to be a voluntary venture," David said sheepishly.

"Davey, how can you keep your head above water without Stovey, huh?" the seaman blushed.

* * * *

Having hidden the boat under the cover of some hanging branches, they set out to climb the hill on the far side of the camp. David wondered why there was no sound coming from the camp as they surely must have discovered the vessels missing.

"Before we climb the hill Stovey, let's get closer to the camp. I'd like to know what's going on and what we are up against," David said, motioning Stovey to follow.

As they came closer to the camp they could hear shouting and much activity. Sounds like they've discovered the ships gone. Someone was trying to arouse them.

They crept around the perimeter of the camp looking for guards. There was one guard lounging by a small structure.

"Stovey! Do you see the guard? Look there's our crew," David spoke excitedly. Both had seen the men sitting under the roof of the open structure. They were seated back to back with a chain running down the middle, to which they appeared to be attached. The center chain was secured to two posts, one on either end. David counted forty-eight men. Surely there must be more, they couldn't all have been killed. David looked over the bedraggled prisoners, searching out his friend. The Midshipman was not among them.

David had a despairing thought as he pondered Kenneth's threat to desert.

Not here, Kenneth. Not here, David silently prayed.

"What's that terrible smell? Smells like something is burning," David said, drawing Stovey's attention to the odorous fumes drifting their way. They were unable to see the fire nor the position where they had first seen Lt. Wolsley and Garreth.

"Stovey, we have to get the men free. I wonder if that one guard has the keys to the locks?" David asked.

"No need to ask Sir, I'll have 'em loose in a jiffy," Stovey chuckled and was gone.

The alarm sounded that the ships were gone from the cove and everyone, with the exception of the guard who had been watching the prisoners, ran through the bushes that crossed the narrow strip of land separating the two coves.

"The keys, your Honor," Stovey mimicked, presenting the keys to David.

"I'm going to crawl down the center of the chain between the prisoners and unlock them. Make sure they follow you, and Stovey stay clear of the hill. They'll go up there to have a look for the ships," David warned. He crawled to the first prisoners, who almost panicked when they realized they were being released. David motioned them to be quiet and to slip away one by one into the bushes where they would find Stovey. Then they were to return to the long boat.

The task was tedious and awkward and took much longer than David expected. Some of the privateers were making their way back and he had to have all the prisoners away before they returned and discovered them gone. They would have little time to get to the boats and shove off. Those who lagged behind might have to be left and hide until another boat could fetch them later, after darkness. Because of the location of the prisoner's stockade, the privateers were unable to see the missing men when they arrived back in camp. They were excited and raving mad. They had been duped by the British. They were marooned with no help to call on. David could hear some of them speaking broken English which sounded more Spanish than anything else.

The last prisoners were set free and David followed them until they were out of sight and safe for the moment. He knew Stovey would be racing them towards the long boat. *Where was Kenneth? He had to be among the Officers. He wasn't with the prisoners.* David became worried about his dear friend.

David crept along the outside of the camp to where the trail wound its way through the bushes. He could hear the men returning and also heard a boy's voice yelling and screaming. *It didn't sound like Kenneth, it had to be the other Midshipman. Where had he been?*

David lay in wait, watching the privateers file past him only a few feet from his hiding place. A large sailor was carrying the screaming Kenneth under his arm. He looked to be badly bruised. Between his screaming and crying the boy was struggling to shake himself free. They had hurt him, David was sure of that.

When the last of the seamen filed past, he moved around to the other side of the camp where the Officers had been kept. The seamen were standing about watching the one, who appeared to be in charge, manhandling Kenneth.

"He needs a lesson in OUR Naval discipline," the leader shouted as he turned Kenneth over his knee and proceeded to beat him.

"I'm just softening your behind for the skewer, boy," the seaman screamed in his fury. David searched around but couldn't see any additional pirates. He knew there had to be others. They must be climbing the lookout hill.

David moved closer and gasped in horror as he looked at the smoldering, smoking fire-pit. There were two bodies hanging over the fire, like sides of beef, their arms and legs dangling into the hot embers. They had been skewered and roasted as David had heard them threatening. He had to pinch himself to prevent himself from screaming. He wanted to vomit.

The larger of the two corpses had to be Lieutenant Wolsley. The smaller one was the Midshipman Gerrard Garreth. David heard the leader threaten Kenneth with another thrashing if he did not tell how he got onto the island and what he was doing there.

"Cat got your tongue?" the leader shouted as he once again turned Kenneth over his knee and thrashed him mercilessly. The seamen were too excited and furious to enjoy the entertainment even though they relished seeing a member of the King's Navy being humiliated in such an intimidating and embarrassing way.

"Someone bring me one of those skewers. I've got him in a good position," the leader screamed out his orders. At that moment, Kenneth saw the fire pits and the hideous corpses.

"Please Sir! I don't have anything else to tell you. I've told you everything I know. I was patrolling with a contingent of seamen. We were working in and out of the coves. I was to await my parent ship *Halcyon* and then rejoin it with any information I had gathered." Kenneth sobbed. He remembered the number of times he had wanted to die, but not this way. He wondered how long it would take and how it would feel.

"Is that all? Where are the other ships? Where is the commander of your vessel the *Halcyon*, and are these the crew that came with you?" he asked.

"I sent them back telling them I was going to survey the island myself. They were to fetch me later. You murdered them," he answered more bravely than he felt.

"Well now, isn't this nice and kindly? You weren't going to do anything of the kind were you? You was deserting wasn't you? Now ain't that a good one. We got our own Middy to join up with us men. Where are the other ships and when are they due back?" the Privateer asked. Kenneth answered, trying to stop crying. He hated them seeing him like this. He was still sobbing, the fright showing on his face.

"Sir I don't know. I didn't return to the ship."

"You see that burnt meat over there? They didn't want to give me the correct information either. Do you know how painfully they died? Does the young Officer know what skewering is? Don't you know you will pray for death a thousand times before you finally expire over the flames? Do you know that Mr. Deserter? Bring me that skewer," he ordered as one of the seamen brought the pointed pole. The skewer looked like a large spear with the point razor sharp. It could penetrate an animal with minimal effort on the part of the hunter.

Kenneth's screams were terrifying and David knew he had only moments to act or Kenneth too would die this most horrible death.

"I'm here Davey." Stovey had returned and was laying beside him with two muskets at the ready. "Davey, I armed the men and they're making their way around the enclosure. We can take 'em easy," Stovey assured.

"Stovey, I'm not going to let Kenneth die. I swear I'm not." David took one of the loaded muskets from Stovey and crept closer. Kenneth was laying across the leader's knee who was taking short jabs at Kenneth's posterior with the skewer, drawing blood each time.

"Hurt a wee bit? You want to tell me where the ships are and when they'll be here? I'm just teasing you a bit to show you how sharp the point is, the next time it's going right up to your heart," the leader threatened, becoming impatient. Kenneth was screaming again as the point was being pressed between his buttocks.

He screamed, "David! David! Please help me David!" Kenneth's terrifying screams rang through the forest.

At that point David stood up in plain view and shouted, "I'm here Kenneth, I'm here."

A shot rang out and the leader dropped to the ground, releasing the screaming boy. The shot had struck right through his forehead. The privateers ran for cover and to find arms for themselves.

Stovey came racing up with four seamen behind him. "We'll make short work of these heathen Davey," he shouted, putting his musket into his belt.

David knelt, holding his friend. The sobbing Midshipman clung to David as though nothing could tear him away.

"It's alright now, Kenneth," David soothed. "You're safe now."

"I knew you would keep your promise Davey," Kenneth sobbed.

"You called my name. How did you know I was here?" David asked.

"I didn't know for certain, but you promised David, and I knew you wouldn't break your promise." The two boys sat, comforting each other.

"We have to find you some clothes," David said, leading Kenneth to the perimeter.

Several seamen ran past heading to where the last of the battle was taking place. David and Kenneth were about to climb down the embankment to the boat when Stovey shouted, "Davey, look out."

The two Midshipmen fell to the ground as a musket fired nearby from an unseen sniper. In the pathway where the two boys had been standing, Stovey lay, mortally wounded. He had thrown himself in the path of the shot, to save the young Earl.

David fell onto Stovey, weeping and begging God to save his friend.

"Oh Stovey, you didn't have to do that. You've already given so much already. Please Stovey don't die." The seaman opened his eyes and smiled at the Midshipman.

"Davey, I'd have fought to the death for you. It appears the only thing I had to give my Commanding Officer was my life and I'll do that gladly. Bless you wee laddie," Stovey closed his eyes and released his grip on David's hand. He turned to the crew who had gathered around.

"Carry on please, I want to be alone with my friend. I'll be down shortly. Tend to the Midshipman, please," David ordered.

"David, I'm staying with you. Remember we're in this together," Kenneth said, with tears running unashamedly down his cheeks.

David sat, holding Stovey's head in his arms and rocking as though in a lullaby, with tears running down his face. *For God and Country and for his friend,* David thought. The two boys comforted one another then slowly rose to their feet and made their way down to the launch.

Seaman Julius Stovel was laid in the bottom of the boat and it made its way to *Halcyon* which was now riding majestically at anchor. They had launched a boat to meet the heroes. The captured privateers were placed aboard and given the option of working or spending the rest of the voyage in the ship's brig. They would all be tried by Court later.

CHAPTER SIXTEEN

The Admiral's Delight

The arrival of the four ships in Guadalupe caused great excitement in the seaport. News of the extraordinary victory in the capture of the privateer's vessels and the destruction of their hiding place was cause for much celebration, especially for those merchants depending on shipping for their livelihood. The shipping commerce between England and her colonies had received a great boost, thanks to the efforts of one small Midshipman.

The two outstanding sloops of war were riding quietly at anchor as the shipping companies viewed them with much interest. They recalled being boarded by the two marauders over the past years. It wasn't the end of the piracy but it would certainly help having these two out of circulation in their regions of concern.

The welcome back on board *de Charlois* was marred by the sadness over the loss of so many of the crew. Both *Halcyon* and *de Charlois* had suffered many casualties during the cutting out expeditions and the recapture of the *Halcyon.* Both ships were undermanned and would require additional crewmen before setting sail again.

The Admiral was ecstatic over the surprise windfall of two excellent prizes and, of course, the substantial returns they would bring for both him and his Officers. His thoughts were constantly interrupted by his recollection of the rules of prize distribution. He recalled that if accompanying vessels were within sight of the subsequent captures, they were entitled to share the prize returns. He had carefully calculated what each of the prizes were worth, and how much the Navy was going to pay for them when he bought them into the fleet.

There was no question that the two vessels would be well received. He reasoned that, in spite of the fact the conquerors were members of a scouting party made up of crewmen from one of his ships, the ships themselves were not within sight of the action. This would take a great deal of thought, but it was a technicality that he thought worthy of attention. It might even result in his not having to share any of the prize money. Sir Charles Wellingham rubbed his hands in anticipation.

The bodies, or what remained of the Officer and Midshipman, were returned for proper burial with the Admiral in attendance. Commander Wright, who had been killed in his vessel's capture, was buried with honors for his heroic efforts while on patrol. Obviously all the details had not been released by the Admiral who didn't want any stains on his command. Stupidity and inexperience would appear as an embarrassment for him. He didn't lie, he just omitted a few details. The Commander was dead, why not let him die with honor? The only ones left to suffer would be his family.

High tribute was paid to the Second Lieutenant and the young Midshipman who, due to no error on their part, had died in a most cruel and hideous way for their country and would be duly honored and mentioned in the *GAZETTE*. This would be little consolation to their families in England.

Seaman Julius Stovel was buried at sea with full Naval honors, while Midshipmen Clements read the eulogy, weeping silently throughout. Stovey's shipmates had never really known the young seaman until now. He had been a man who enjoyed his own company and was alone most of the time. He was very efficient and knew his job well. His heroic act would be touted throughout the service for some time to come.

The Admiral, in his report, made particular mention of the two Midshipmen, especially Midshipman Clements, heir apparent to the House of Windsor. It was well known that the Duke was one of the richest and most powerful members of Parliament. There was no question the young Earl would receive wide acclaim for his resourcefulness, heroism, and devotion to duty.

As the Admiral sat reading through the Midshipmen files, he could hardly believe he was reading about the same lad who had come screaming and shouting aboard the *Subdue*. He read further of the gross abuse the boys had suffered aboard the ship under First Lt. Wright and the Senior Midshipman. It was enough to have destroyed any normal human being, let alone a twelve year old boy. He marveled at the other successes the Midshipman had achieved while securing the release of the prize, as well as the recapture of their own vessels entirely due to his initiative. The child was a born leader like his Father, the Admiral mused. Disciplining him the hard way had obviously been exactly what was required to turn the young man around and now he had a promising Naval Officer in the making.

He completed his report and sent it over to *de Charlois* along with other dispatches for England. The ship would be escorting a small convoy of merchantmen to England.

CHAPTER SEVENTEEN

The Convoy

Shepherding a group of sluggish merchantmen across the Atlantic was no easy chore, for they were always lagging behind and never in formation. The *de Charlois* had her work cut out for her and, at the rate they were moving, it would be many weeks before they made Portsmouth.

Midshipmen Clements and Walters were quick learners and the rules of the road at sea and other Naval training came easily. In their off watch hours, they were either sleeping or discussing plans for their arrival in England. On occasion, they would reflect back on the terrible experiences they had endured at the hands of Commander Wright and Senior Midshipman Breckenridge. There had been times when the Midshipmen felt they would never see their homes again.

David was making few plans, while Kenneth was almost beside himself with excitement as he conjured up the welcome he would be receiving from family and friends.

* * * *

Kenneth Walters was the youngest son of a dairy farmer who managed to support his family comfortably on a small holding in Devonshire. They were not Devonshire people by birth, they had settled in a family estate left to Kenneth's father.

Kenneth's school had recommended that the boy be sent to the Naval Academy for further training towards a career. He was bright and could hope for education and advancement within the service. His brothers remained on the farm helping their father.

It was with great joy and enthusiasm that the Walter's household was preparing for the arrival home of their Hero son. It would be a grand occasion. They had had no contact with him since his departure over a year ago, but the latest newspaper reports revealed the activities and successes he had enjoyed and where he had been.

* * * *

"Walters, signal the straggler, what's its name? Oh yes, the *Dartmouth*. Signal the bastard to either get into position or receive a shot across her bow," the Captain ordered as he paced back and forth. Each turn on the quarter deck saw him eyeing the vessels in his care through his telescope. He would curse the stragglers and laud the others.

Kenneth had matured in his Naval training and thinking. He thought as a seaman and, as such, felt he could share his opinions and concerns with his Captain as one of the ship's Officers.

"Sir, if I might suggest Sir, the *Dartmouth* has caused us no end of grief and doesn't seem to respond to our threats. May I hoist a signal inferring that an unidentified sail is reported? It might frighten him into rejoining the rest of the convoy if he thought there was a chance he would be left behind to face possible enemy capture," Kenneth said unabashedly.

He had never spoken to this Captain before and wondered if he should not have kept his mouth closed. After all, it wasn't his responsibility to offer suggestions. To his surprise the Captain stared at him and, after a moment said, "Damned smart thinking Walters! Damned smart. Hoist the signal if you will. We must watch for her reaction."

As the *de Charlois* was in the rear, it could be assumed that any sail coming up from astern would be observed by that vessel first. It became obvious that the other ships in the convoy, including the *Dartmouth*, altered course so as to be within easy protection of their escort. The ruse had worked and, perhaps as long as *de Charlois* stayed in the rear, the others would never know the truth.

Kenneth Walters had turned thirteen, but only shared the occasion with his fellow Midshipman David Clements. *No one else celebrated birthdays so why should he?* But he did confide in David that he was now a year older than his friend – which made him senior, not only in service, but in age.

"I'll be having my birthday after our arrival," David said, wondering what sort of welcome he would have. He was not looking forward to the return to Windsor Castle, nor for that matter, to his father.

"David, don't look so glum, you'll be well received by everyone, I'll be bound. You're a hero and there will be a huge welcome home for you," Kenneth tried reassuring the Earl.

"Kenneth, I don't want to go home. It took me a long time and considerable canings to make me realize what a proper snob and rotten person I was. I'm not that way any more. I love the excitement we've experienced and I'm sure that was all that was lacking in my former life. There was no challenge worthy of any effort on my part. I should have been caned many times before, but the rules governing the schools I attended would not allow the administration of corporal punishment to Royalty," David continued, explaining his views of himself and his new life.

"Kenneth, I belong here. I will make a good Officer and perhaps even another Nelson," David laughed.

"Some of the crew think you're Nelson already. They are always talking about you and the things you did. They treat you with more respect than even the Captain," he went on enthusiastically.

"I was very lucky and you are aware of that. If it hadn't been for all the help I had it would never have turned out the way it did. Two of our nemeses have had their just rewards and we won't have that to face us any longer. I was afraid you were going to do something dreadful and even end your life. I knew how miserable you felt. I might add, not as miserable as I felt when I had to leave you, while I was sent aboard the *de Charlois*. I prayed that you would read my mind and hold on. You did, Kenneth, and now we are together again," David confessed.

"You are my best friend and I will always respect you, not only for the things you achieved, but for saving my life," Kenneth said, wiping a small tear from his eye.

Six weeks later, the small convoy arrived off Portsmouth and the merchant vessels made their way to their separate anchorages while *de Charlois* anchored near the Admiral's ship *Subtle*. Anchors were let go, sails were furled and the Admiral requested the presence of the Captain aboard at his convenience. David and Kenneth did their watch inspections with a new spring in their steps. They were exuberant and could hardly maintain their excitement. After all, they were still young boys and they were coming home. *They were home.*

Walking down the deck past his gun crews, the crew members crowded towards David to shake his hand and to give him a word of their respect. David knew he would not be seeing many of these men again, but realized how attached he had become to them, even learning their names. Shouts went up from the crew as David and Kenneth stepped through the entry port into their quay boat.

"That's our Davey! God bless you lad. Hurrah! Hurrah!! Hurrah!!!" they shouted. David was embarrassed and found it difficult to hide his emotions. Seating himself in the boat, he was able to wipe his eyes with his sleeve. No one noticed, except Kenneth.

"See David, what did I tell you? You are a hero," Kenneth said, smiling at his friend.

The quay was packed with crowds wanting to get a glimpse of the Earl of Windsor, the hero of the *GAZETTE*. The chronicle had made capital with the story of the young Midshipman's heroism and achievements. The House of Lords made an observation that David was just what England needed. A young hero in which to focus their attentions, rather than on the many failures of the war.

"May I carry your valise m'lord?" the boatman asked. David was struggling with his bag but refused any assistance.

"I'll manage just fine thank you," he replied smiling. The two boys were received with much enthusiasm and they found it difficult to move until a squad of Marines took over escort duties of the two seamen.

"Kenneth, Kenneth Walters. Over here my boy. We're over here," shouted Kenneth's father.

"David, you must meet my parents," he said, drawing David by the arm through the Marine guards. After much hugging and hand shaking Kenneth said, "Mother, Father, this is the Earl of Windsor and my best friend."

"We are most honored your Lordship. The *GAZETTE* and the London Times have been full of your exploits for weeks. It was in the *GAZETTE* that we knew you were to arrive today. Your ship had been spotted yesterday and we knew it was true," Kenneth's father went on. The Midshipmen shook hands with Kenneth's family.

David caught a glimpse of his family's carriage trying to make its way through the crowd and quickly turned to Kenneth. "Kenneth, I can't return home, at least not yet. Would you feel it too great an imposition to have me as a guest? I would be no bother," David pleaded.

"M'lord, you're more than welcome. It is our great privilege to have you," Kenneth's mother replied.

"Can we leave now? I think it would help me no end to be free of these people as soon as possible," David asked, as he flung his bag onto the coach the Walters had borrowed. The boys jumped onto the back and were driven away. David watched Samuel, his father's personal secretary, trying to get his coach through the throngs. The noise was deafening and the cheering made it impossible to contact the young Earl.

The roads were dusty and the trip was very rough but both boys were happier than they could remember. They were happy to be back in England and on dry land.

CHAPTER EIGHTEEN

The Stowaway

The boys laughed and carried on as the carriage rocked and bumped over the rough back roads. They were completely oblivious to their uncomfortable positions in the boot of the coach. Kenneth's father had borrowed the carriage from a neighbor so that he could meet his son in style and transport him home. Although the coach had seating for four, the boys chose to ride on the freight platform at the rear of the carriage. Neither boy had much in the way of clothing or personal effects, so their luggage took up little room.

The coach finally came to a stop at the Redmond Inn where they would lunch and change horses. They still had another three hours of fast driving to get home before darkness set in.

The boys hardly spoke as they bumped along, choking on the dust but reveling in their new sense of freedom. It wasn't until the stop at the Inn that they entered into any conversation. Mrs. Walters asked the boys if they were hungry and, if so, they could enter the Inn and join the rest for a light repast before journeying on.

"M'lord, if I might be so bold, may I ask why you do not wish to return to your home? We have heard the news that the Duke has been invited to the palace to meet with His Royal Highness. Perhaps you are not aware of what kind of commotion and excitement you have caused across the country."

"I'm sure the Duke will be more than a little disturbed that you have chosen to come home with us," Kenneth's father added with a troubled look. The Earl's attitude of disinterest concerned Mr. Walters but he knew no satisfactory answer was forthcoming. The boy didn't want to talk about it.

"David, let's go in and eat. May we go in now Father?" Kenneth asked.

"Yes, by all means, but David, I mean your Lordship, you must be aware that people will be clambering to talk to you giving you no peace once they know you are here," Mr. Walters said.

"Mr. Walters, to you and your family I am David, that is all that is required. I must tell you, in a way of explanation, that my main reason for not wishing to return, at least at the present time, is I have changed and they – my Father, his family, and his friends –

remain the same. I am not the same person who left eight months ago. I'm sure no one will understand that and they will treat me as before, like a spoiled puppy. I can't endure that, and I'm sure it will take the family many months to get used to the idea that I am a King's Officer and not the terrible person they once knew. I'm certain it will all be for the best. It would be best if we didn't reveal my identity to anyone. Your neighbors are only expecting Kenneth and I will just be a friend who has come to visit. What could be simpler?" David offered enthusiastically.

Kenneth beamed at David and, looking at his father said," Father, David must be allowed to handle this matter in his own way. He is certainly capable of doing that, I can tell you. No one need know that he is the Earl. Let's allow him this time free from social demands, and besides we have things to do, right Davey?"

Mr. and Mrs. Walters were not used to this sort of informality and wondered what the neighbors would think if and when the news got out. It was difficult for them to entertain royalty, especially one of such fame, even though he was still just a young boy.

The meal served in the Inn was a pleasant one, however meager, but satisfying to everyone. The Walters had a table to themselves and no one seemed any the wiser as to the strange boy in their midst, although they were interested in talking to Kenneth. It seemed the entire countryside had heard about the Midshipman. There was much a do over Kenneth, who was questioned continually while they were eating. It wasn't long before the tavern was jammed to the doors with well wishers and inquisitive people, wanting to hear the stories of the conquests and prizes taken by the *Halcyon.*

THE GAZETTE had published the news, and the newspapers picked up on the information, and soon it was a full blown national event.

"Master Walters, did you know the Earl was aboard the ships? Did you have an opportunity to meet him? Hear tell he is another Nelson in the making. What was he like? A proper snob, I'll suggest," one farmer questioned.

"No doubt he had a cabin of his own, but how was it he was able to accomplish all those outstanding feats? Were you involved in any of them?" They kept on with their questions. It never occurred to anyone to ask who the handsome young stranger was.

Kenneth remained very modest as he related a few of the incidents, just to satisfy the crowds. Everyone hung on his words as he related the young Earl's cutting out performance, every now and again flicking a quick glance in David's direction. It was all he could do to keep from blurting out the identity of the boy who sat across from him. His father came to his rescue advising that the boys were tired from their journey and needed some privacy. The crowd seemed to appreciate what the young man had been through, and withdrew to allow them to eat in peace with several of the men acting as guards to ensure privacy.

The balance of the journey was as uncomfortable as the first part but still they didn't want to sit in the coach. When they arrived at the farmhouse, Kenneth's brothers were at the gate to meet them. They were excited to see their brother home again and wound up picking him up and bodily throwing him from one to the other. They were delighted.

David stood back while the homecoming welcome played out and everyone went into the house. David was introduced as a friend of Kenneth's who had come to spend some time with them. He was made very welcome and the brothers showed the boys to Kenneth's room. It had changed since Kenneth last slept there and had been enlarged. It had been a six foot by eight foot room with a little thatched bed in one corner. It was now twice that size with two beds and there was a window overlooking the barnyard. To David it was heaven.

"Mother?" Kenneth asked, "Do you have anything for us to wear? We can't wear these uniforms any longer, they are falling off us."

"It so happens that I have just finished some new clothes for you. They aren't really new, but I made them over and they are practically new. They'll be new for you boys in any case," Mrs. Walters laughed as she pointed to a pile of clothing on Kenneth's bed.

They quickly changed, turning their old clothes over to Mrs. Walters to wash and repair.

Mr. Walters sat on the front balcony smoking his pipe as he watched the two Midshipmen behaving like normal boys, unfettered by Navy rules and regulations. Here, they could act as they wished.

Each day they spent hours romping and playing in the grassy fields. They chased each other and were soundly trounced by the older boys. Claire Walters was nearly eighteen, while his other brother John was fifteen. They weren't all that much older than the young seamen. They might have seen sea duty had it not been they were required to work the farm. They were not allowed to be pressed for service.

After a hearty supper, the boys were too played out to continue and decided to retire early, at the family's orders, that is. Mr. Walters had obtained another mattress for the Earl to sleep on in Kenneth's room. He entered their room as the boys were getting ready for bed.

"David, I wish to tell you how proud and thrilled we are to have you here with us. Never in our lifetime would we have ever dreamed of such a thing happening. You are a fine young man, and a model and good friend for our Kenneth. I trust you will always remain close friends. David, we will do anything you wish in regards to your privacy, but I must say that it will only be a day or so before the newspapers are full of your disappearance. The people we met along our journey will be sure to give away the information about the stranger accompanying Kenneth. We will honor your wishes whatever they are," Kenneth's father said.

"Will you boys kneel by your beds as we offer a word of prayer for your safe return, and that He will protect you wherever you go?" Mr. Walters suggested. They were joined by the rest of the family. They knelt and as the words of prayer for the boys unfolded, both David and Kenneth had tears in their eyes. They could remember only too vividly their utmost despair of only a few months ago when they were ready to take their own lives in order to obtain their freedom.

The morning sun shone in on the two sleeping Midshipmen, and they would have stayed there all day had it not been for Claire and John pulling the two naked boys from their beds. They laughed and the rough housing started all over again.

"Get down here this minute all of you, breakfast is going to get cold," Mr. Walters yelled good naturedly.

Table grace was pronounced, this time by Claire, who spoke quietly and reverently about how he personally missed his "wee brother". David was moved by the closeness of the family and the love that each shared, one for the other. The outwards physical show of affection was something David had never experienced until now.

"More eggs, m'lord?" Mrs. Walters asked, suddenly realizing she had used the Earl's title by mistake.

"What did you call David, Mother?" John was quick to pick up on the slip.

"What do you mean? What are you talking about?" she said, trying to disregard John's observations.

"Mother, you called David m'lord like he was royalty or something. Oh Lord, Father!" John exclaimed realizing David's identity. "David, you're the Earl of Windsor! You're David Clements! Father, how could you not tell us?" Now both boys were pressing for an explanation.

"Claire and John, it was at my request that my identity be kept secret. You see, I did not want to return home to my family. I am happy here with you and with my best friend, your brother Kenneth. I hope you will forgive our little deception, it was not your parent's fault. I hope you will understand. You have enjoyed this very happy home and close relationship, while I have yet to experience it in my home. I have never had it until now, thanks to you all. I would be pleased if we could keep this quiet for the time being as I am afraid my whereabouts will be discovered soon enough but, in the time remaining, I want to share your life with you. I am David or Davey, whichever you prefer. I am not the Earl in this house."

The boys were still reeling from the revelation that David was the Earl.

"David, we even hustled you and Kenneth out of bed in a most undignified manner, will you forgive us?" they asked.

"If you had pulled Kenneth out and not me I would have been sorely disappointed. As it was, I can never remember a time when I was awakened in such a way. It was very funny," David laughed.

"Will you swim with us in the river, David?" John asked.

"I'd be delighted," came the reply from the Earl. With that the four boys headed for the river which ran lazily through the farm. David for once in his life, was truly at peace and happy.

He was not thinking of the ship nor the Officers, nor anyone for that matter, only what was happening to him here and now. He didn't want it to end.

Two days later, a messenger arrived from the Admiralty, with orders for Kenneth to report as soon as possible. The orders did not state any reason for the request.

"Kenneth, I hope this will not spell trouble for you in any way. I could never live with that," David exclaimed.

"I'll have to go David. It can't be orders to sail. The ship had only been up for the past three days, I was told it would be at least a week, or even more, before the ship was ready to sail again," Kenneth reasoned.

Kenneth departed for London, leaving David with the family. David was apprehensive as to Kenneth's summons to the Admiralty.

"The Admiral will see you Mr. Walters, make certain you follow protocol when speaking," the secretary advised, looking the boy up and down. He could never recall a Midshipman being summoned to the Admiralty before. He too wondered what it was all about.

"Your Lordship, may I present Midshipman Kenneth Walters of *HMS Halcyon*," the Lieutenant announced. Kenneth was shaking so badly he thought his legs would not hold him any longer.

"Mr. Walters is it? Ah yes my lad, I have heard great things about your initiative and heroism and devotion to duty. For those qualities you are being handsomely rewarded along with recognition for the above. You have the makings of a fine King's Officer, even at such a ripe old age of thirteen. There will be a ceremony honoring you and the Earl of Windsor, whenever he can be found. We suspect there may have been some foul play, due to the Earl's notoriety and position. He suddenly disappeared upon landing five days ago. Nothing has been heard or seen of him since. It would be a ghastly shame if some mishap has befallen the young man, especially in view of his achievements. He is just what our country needed. He may only be twelve years of age but, like yourself, the whole nation has been thrilled to hear about his exploits. Quite extraordinary," the Admiral went on.

"Now young man, I must ask you. Do you know where the Earl is at this very moment? It seems you were the last one to be seen talking to the young man. Did he tell you where he was going or anything else that might give us a clue as to where he is?" the Admiral asked.

Kenneth pondered the questions and could not see that a negative answer would be lying. He didn't know where the Earl was at that very moment nor what he was doing. David had not told him where he was going. He didn't want to provoke his Lordship with some curt reply, so he informed the Admiral that the Earl was last seen heading south in the farm country of Devonshire.

"Well, so much for that. You will be informed within the next day or so as to what your orders will be. You, of course, will be meeting his Royal Highness, an occasion every young man in England would wish to do. Make yourself available Mr. Walters. Lieutenant, make certain the Midshipman has a new uniform. That's all," the Admiral said, dismissing Kenneth. He wondered if the Admiral would remember their conversation later.

The newspaper headlines were full of the disappearance of the Earl. The Naval hero had disappeared without a trace and the entire country was searching for him. David was a national hero and the people were not about to have him snatched away from them.

The Duke was prepared to offer a reward for the young Earl, if he were returned safe and sound. People from all over the country were passing on bits of information about possible sightings of David.

The days went by and finally the day arrived for Kenneth to have an audience with His Highness. The King was enthralled with the idea that a young boy would be receiving his attention for honors and commendations. It had never occurred before, where a young boy had been so honored.

The Earl was, in fact, lounging lazily in the shade of a huge oak tree, with a piece of straw hanging from his mouth. Kenneth lay beside him begging the Earl to identify himself to the authorities and to the Admiral. David said he was enjoying himself too much to spoil it by returning home. He secretly wanted his family to give up searching for him. He actually didn't feel that way, he just wanted to be away from his past life and pass the time until the ship sailed again, in peace and quiet, and with his friend.

* * * *

"Mind your manners Kenneth. This isn't the Senior you're visiting today. I'll be thinking of you every minute and sympathizing with you, as you bow and courtesy and all the rest of that courtly behavior. I know what it's like Kenneth and it's false and hypocritical. You'll see right through it. I hope they give you a cross or something," David said, making a small cross sign on his chest.

The word was about, that there would be a small procession from the Abbey to the Palace, with the Officers of the victorious *Halcyon* riding in huge carriages, while the crowds would hail them as heroes. It was further rumored that they were gathering to honor the young Earl who, unbeknownst to them, would not be in the entourage. It had been agreed that the family would be allowed to journey to London to view the parade. After much discussion, David was talked into coming along.

Kenneth was dropped at the Admiralty, while the family delivered their coach and horses to the local livery a quarter of a mile away. The crowds were already gathering and the excitement was felt everywhere. Claire, David and John mingled amongst the people and were caught up in all the excitement and cheering.

The talk, as they walked along, centered on the young Earl. It was he they had come to cheer and pay honor to. David was embarrassed and wondered if he had done the right thing by remaining hidden. No one recognized him as he made his way through the crowds.

Kenneth and David had discussed the entire matter, and David had a difficult time to convince Kenneth that he was as much a part of the prize taking as he had been.

"David, you know that isn't true. It was you and you alone, who mastered the plan and its success. I feel like a hypocrite accepting these honors when you are the one to whom the honors should go," Kenneth lectured.

"Kenneth, please remember one thing. Do not, under any circumstances, give our secret away. If you value our friendship, do this for me," David asked.

"Look! Look! here they come," the crowds were surging forward. The Marine band was accompanying the procession playing their fifes and drums.

The coaches slowly made their way along the narrow streets lined with enthusiastic well wishers. They were shouting, "Hurrah for the Earl! Hurrah for the Earl! You'll get 'em Davey!"

The Admiral waved as he rode along. Kenneth was in the second coach along with Captain Fulton-Tate and the newly appointed First and Second Officers. He looked very small sitting amongst the other Officers. The crowds, upon seeing the small figure seated waving at everyone as he went by, shouted all the more.

"Hurrah for the Earl! Hurrah for Davey!" they pressed forward towards the coach. The Marines held them back.

David, in the meantime, was standing with Kenneth's family and they were waving at Kenneth, but Mrs. Walters was wiping her eyes as she rested her arms on David's shoulders. He looked up at her. There were tears in his eyes as he tried to hide his emotions.

The Admiral was aware of the crowds having mistaken Kenneth for the Earl, but was not about to create an embarrassing situation for either himself or the Navy. *Where was that boy and what had happened to him?* He was sure there would be more headlines, only this time announcing that the Earl had been found and had been presented to His Royal Highness. They were unaware that there were to have been two Midshipmen presented with honors.

* * * *

Life was slowly returning to normal at the Walter's farmhouse except for the many well wishers who came to pay respects.

Kenneth had had enough of it, and he and David went to great pains to escape and avoid the visitors.

Still, no one was aware of the true identity of the Walter's visitor.

Kenneth received his orders to report for sea duty. He was not being assigned to his old ship the *Halcyon* but to the frigate *Repulse*. He would be leaving in the morning. It was a surprise to both boys that he was being reassigned. A horrible thought occurred to David.

"Kenneth, your orders will not have anything to do with me. No one knows where I am and any orders would be sent to my father. Perhaps there won't be any orders as everyone thinks I'm still missing. How am I ever going to resolve this mess I've got myself into? I never thought about how I would receive orders," David questioned.

"David," Mrs. Walters interjected, "why not return with Kenneth as though you had received the same orders? After all it is quite possible you were both destined for the same vessel."

After a tearful farewell, the two Midshipmen departed for Portsmouth ready to commence their sea duties and full of apprehension for the future. David realized he was probably in serious trouble.

* * * *

"What ship?" the boatman asked as the two boys unloaded their belongings on the quay.

"*Repulse*", said Kenneth, trying to appear confident and look and act the part of a ship's Officer. Arriving at *Repulse*, David was exhibiting more self control in his behavior than Kenneth and with confidence, climbed the chains and stepped up through the entry port.

"Names?" a burly Officer greeted them. Neither boys were impressed by his appearance nor his attitude. This Officer could spell difficult times ahead.

"Midshipman Kenneth Walters," Kenneth answered.

"Midshipman David Clements," David replied, knowing that this could be the moment of truth and the end of his anonymity.

"Stow your belongings and report to the First Officer," the Lieutenant ordered. The two boys were more than happy to be excused and darted towards their berth below deck.

So far – so good, thought David, but it was only a matter of time before someone would realize who he was.

"Mr. Clements, are you aware the entire country has been searching for you? Where have you been and by whose orders are you reporting to this ship?" the First Officer questioned.

"Sir, I just presumed I would be assigned to the same ship as Mr. Walters. I had received no orders," David replied. He knew there were going to be serious consequences to his little escapade.

"I suppose, because you are the Earl, you think you are exempt from Naval discipline and orders, do you? As a matter of fact, Mr. Clements, you are not assigned to this ship. Collect your belongings and report to the Admiralty. I shall see you have an escort to assure you arrive, and Mr. Walters, we will want a full explanation as to your part in this folly. You may have enjoyed a moment of notoriety but you are now aboard the *HMS Repulse* and we do things differently from your last vessel," the First Officer continued. Kenneth tried to hide his disappointment.

David looked crestfallen but had expected trouble and was not surprised by his reception. The First Officer was not intimidated by the young Earl, nor in fact did he like him. He was giving David no quarter to explain.

David waved a farewell to Kenneth as he stepped down into the shore boat. The Third Officer was already in the boat, waiting to escort the Earl. David turned away from the Officer and boatman as he endeavored to hide his tears.

He was unable to formulate a plan by which he could satisfactorily explain his behavior without implicating Kenneth and his parents. He realized he had been foolish to have attempted such a deception and now it could cause serious trouble for his benefactors and his best friend.

"If it wasn't for the fact you are the Duke's son and your outstanding achievements aboard the *Halcyon*, you would receive the thrashing of your life! You think that because of your station in life you may disregard all rules and authority, do you?" The Admiral didn't wait for David to speak.

"Your Father is enroute as we speak, and will certainly have something to say about this incident. You realize you are still a King's Officer and as such you will be treated accordingly. You are to remain in detention until such time as we decide what we are to do with you, is that understood? I fail to understand how you could destroy the outstanding achievements you have had for a personal whim. You will remember that you are a ship's Officer first, and Earl of Windsor lastly. Your orders will be prepared in due course. Best of luck lad," the Admiral said, dismissing David and his escort with a smile.

CHAPTER NINETEEN

No Alternative

The escort took David to a remote part of the Admiralty building where he was placed in a room by himself. There was one window, which was barred, and which contained no glass. The weather was free to blow in at will.

The young Earl was exhausted by all the happenings of the day, but knew he couldn't sleep. Although the cot in the corner of the room looked inviting, he realized he must quickly formulate a plan. He didn't think there was a chance he could escape this place, but to sit and wait until his father arrived was worse than standing to the mast.

He was still pacing back and forth in his cell, when he heard some pebbles flying through the open window. He ran to the window, but there was no one in sight. He wondered if he had been imagining things. He was staring through the bars, when more pebbles struck him lightly on the face. A larger stone carried into the window, landed on the floor and rolled out through the barred door into the hallway. There was a note attached, and David realized he had to retrieve the note before the guards arrived for their cell check.

He struggled trying to reach the stone with its message. His fingers touched the note, but there didn't appear to be any way he could grip the stone. His arm was too short and there was no way he was going to reach the note.

He ran to the window. Perhaps another stone and message would come through but no one was in the yard. Whoever threw the stone, expected the Earl to have retrieved it and had departed.

The bars were so close together, he was having difficulty getting his arm through, so he removed his coat and shirt, and laying on the floor, stretched his bare arm through the bars until he could stretch no more. Still the stone remained only slightly out of reach. David reasoned that if his arm couldn't reach, then maybe his leg could. It was longer and if he removed his trousers and lay on the floor, he might just squeeze far enough to pull the elusive stone close enough to reach with his hand.

Lying on the floor and twisting and turning, he slowly rolled the stone close enough to pull it in with his hand. He was so excited to read the message he completely forgot his clothes.

He undid the cord which held the note to the stone, and read.

> *Your Lordship is in serious trouble, and your friends have rallied to your assistance. When the guards are changed at 5 AM tomorrow morning, you will be released. Follow the guard and obey his instructions to the letter. The plan is quite complicated and leaves no room for error. Good Luck. Hurrah Halcyon!*

David decided that if he were to be of any use to anyone, he must get some sleep. He lay on his cot wondering who specifically was going to secure his escape until he fell asleep.

He was aroused by someone gently shaking him awake. The door to his cell was open. He remembered his instructions and without a word, followed the guard through the door, down the hallway, and out into the fresh morning air. A light fog was sweeping in from the sea.

Four other seamen joined David as he followed close behind the guard. He recognized a few of the voices as being crew members from the *Halcyon.*

"Davey boy, did you think we would forget all you did for us? You saved our lives, and when we heard you were in trouble, the crew picked us to get you out. We're going to the quay, the *Repulse* is sailing at first light, you'll have to swim a short distance Davey, as we can only get so close without being detected. Kenneth will be waiting for you, and take you into hiding until the ship is well clear of the Nose. Can you do it Davey?" The Coxswain asked. He had been with David on his cutting out expedition.

"I can do it Jack," David said remembering the Cox'n's name.

"We figure once the ship is at sea, there is no way they can return you, and they certainly aren't going to do anything serious to a national hero. Good luck Davey. Remember, you don't know who helped you escape," Jack instructed.

The small boat shoved off from the quay and quietly made its way towards the *Repulse*. The oarsmen had wrapped their oarlocks with rags so as to eliminate any sounds. There was only the occasional dripping sound as the oars lifted out of the water.

The fog was quite heavy around the ship, which could easily have been missed had not the sounds of water lapping against her side given her position away. The boat swept quietly under the ships stern, and David slipped into the water without a sound. He swam only a few yards before his hands touched the sides. He pulled himself along until he found a rope dangling over the side. This was the work of other crewmen. David seized the rope and looked up to the anxious face of Kenneth. He pulled himself clear of the water and up the ship's side. There had been knots placed strategically along the rope's length to assist David with hand grips.

Reaching the deck, Kenneth threw a blanket over the dripping Earl, and hustled him below deck to the powder room. The powder boys looked on in utter amazement as they viewed the two boys preparing a hiding place. Kenneth had received their oath not to repeat the happenings of the night.

David had removed his wet clothing and was sitting on a locker with only the blanket to keep out the chill. One of the powder boys gave the Earl some hard biscuit and water, along with a piece of salted pork. David was famished and the food tasted like a feast.

Very few ever ventured into the powder locker, so the boys were left pretty much to themselves. When the ship went into action, the boys had more than they could handle to keep the guns fed. It was said the powder boys were ruffians off the streets of London, who were orphans or deserted, and as such, were expendable when it came to battle.

The boys were excited at having true royalty in their midst, and were hard put to know how to address the other boy whose station in life was so far beyond theirs. The degree of mystery and covertness surrounding the hiding of the Earl, added some thrill into their otherwise dull existence below deck. David remained successfully hidden for three days until on the third night, Kenneth advised that they were going on deck, where Kenneth was to stand watch.

"David, it will be up to you how you handle matters, but at least you will have been on a watch for half the day before someone recognizes you. I will try to do everything I can for you, but you know how my hands are tied. I know you'll come through this easily, David. I am your friend and I won't let anything happen to you," Kenneth spoke sincerely to his friend.

The time had arrived for David to confess and beard the lion, so to speak. He had already been working on a plan as to how he was going to explain his presence aboard. He paced back and forth, and on two occasions walked forward to the bows.

The morning was dark, and the threat of rain lingered in the air. They were bound for the Azores, and at this time there were no Naval detachments located there and no court-martial could be assembled. Whatever the consequences of his actions, they would have to be dealt with by the Captain. For better or worse.

Kenneth was relieved of his watch and went below by way of the forward deck. "The Captain's had his breakfast and will be on deck in a minute. Are you settled on a plan, Davey?" he asked.

"I'll manage Kenneth, and thank you for all your help," David replied as he started to make his way towards the quarter deck.

Walking forward, many crew members gazed in surprise as they recognized the young Earl. Many had been aboard the *Halcyon* and her prizes. They restrained themselves from breaking out in cheering. It was comforting to David who felt he was walking his last mile, to know there were men aboard who remembered him and how he had saved their lives.

CHAPTER TWENTY

The Punishment

David climbed the stairway to the quarter deck with his heart pounding so hard it almost took his breath away. This was it. This was the end of his career and his new life. He was afraid his legs were not going to hold him up – they were like sponges. He kept his eyes on the deck so the Captain could not see the teary glaze which threatened to blind him. He couldn't let anyone see this display of weakness.

"Sir. Midshipman David Clements reporting as requested, Sir." David spoke in a clear and confident voice, feeling far from any degree of assuredness. He was going to try his very best to make his case convincing and acceptable, in view of all the extenuating circumstances.

"What are you doing aboard my ship? How were you able to board this vessel undetected, and when did you come aboard? Who were your accomplices?

Speak up boy, I want answers and I want them now! Do you realize you can be hung for the felonies you've committed? Do you think that just because you have a nobleman's title you are above the law, and Naval discipline?" the Captain shouted, getting louder and louder with each beckoning question.

"You think your title places you above your fellow seamen? What right have you to involve others in your reckless and disorderly actions?" the Captain seemed to seethe, as he bellowed loud enough for the entire ship to hear. Every now and again, he would realize he was shouting and would quieted down to start his tirade over again. He was in a terrible position having to contend with, what he felt was a major political situation the Earl had foisted upon him.

"Mr. Clements, I want you to proceed to my cabin where you will dictate a full explanation of your behavior and your actions since leaving the *Halcyon.* I will make a decision what is to be done with you at that time," the Captain spat. He turned to bellow out another order.

"Mr. Carter, will you send a signal to be passed along to the merchantmen, for forwarding to any Naval vessel within sight. The Earl of Windsor is aboard *HMS Repulse* and I am proceeding on original orders," he dictated, as he paced back and forth.

* * * *

David's report read:

To: The Captain of HMS Emmejay

Re: Midshipman David Clements, Earl of Windsor

Sir before coming into the Navy, I had a rebellious life of misbehavior and overindulgence. I was expelled from every school of standing, until my Father would tolerate it no longer. I was kept at home where a private tutor endeavored to work with me. I knew more than he did, and the engagement was dissolved. My Father called me incorrigible, and indulged beyond redemption. His friend, the Admiral, agreed to an arrangement whereby I would be accepted into the Navy as a Midshipman. I knew Father was plotting something, so I badgered our man servant to tell me. He would not tell me of the plan to enroll me in the Midshipman's Program in the Navy. I was bodily transported before the Admiral who, being forewarned, threatened me with a caning if my manners did not improve. I was sure he would never allow any punishments nor ever touch royalty, so I thought I was safe.

I fought every inch of the way until I landed aboard the Subdue. She set sail before I was able to escape. In accordance with the Admiral's orders I was disciplined before the mast with twelve canings, this all occurring before I had been interviewed by the Captain. He was not the least bit impressed nor sympathetic of my behavior. I must admit now, I was most juvenile and rebellious, and deserved the discipline I was getting.

There was no support for me anywhere aboard the ship, and I knew for the first time in my life that I stood alone with no one to fend for me.

Before I reached the berth deck, I had received twelve more canings and was unable to stand. I was carried to the Mid's berth where I met Kenneth Walters, the Junior Midshipman. He was ordered not to speak with me, so my efforts to talk and order him about went on deaf ears. He was only doing his duty.

He did, however, warn me that if I continued in my rebellious ways, I was bound for more severe punishment, and that I might just as well go along with it, and perhaps get to like what I was doing. He was right, and I soon found I was mastering the Rules of the Road and Navigation without any trouble at all. The Master informed me, in the presence of the Captain, that I was his best student. Until that point, I had plans to disable the ship in anyway I could. The Master stopped me in time, or I might not be here now.

I was fortunate to have been able to use my brains and ingenuity accompanied by much good luck, in cutting out several prizes for the Navy. This must be on my records. There were eight vessels all told. I had never been happier than when I was living dangerously and pitting my brains against the enemy. I was happy to have been able to rescue my fellow seamen. We all became good friends.

Upon arrival in Portsmouth where the de Charlois was to be laid up for a week, Midshipman Walters and myself found ourselves free to do as we wished. Mr. Walter's parents were at the quay to meet him. The throngs of people had gathered to welcome the ship and its crew home, as the GAZETTE had marked us all as heroes, and wanted to wish us well.

We had a difficult time making our way to the Walter's carriage, but the crowd also prevented my Father's carriage from reaching us in time. They had not seen me, as I moved away through the crowds. I explained to Mr. Walters my reason for wishing to leave before my Father found me. It was at my request, that the Walter's family agreed to allow me to stay with Kenneth for the week.

They also agreed to keep my identity secret until such time as it was discovered. It was a very difficult time for everyone, and I now realize what a terrible imposition I had presented to the Walter's. They were entirely innocent of any wrong doing. Kenneth is my best friend. I had never had a friend before. I was treated with respect by them but also as one of the family. I was so engrossed in my own well being to have never thought of the consequences of my own selfish actions. I take full responsibility for those actions.

The ceremony at the Palace caused me further concern, as I realized the anguish I had put Kenneth through endeavoring to play his roll in my charade.

Kenneth received his orders to report to the Repulse. With my address unknown to the Admiralty, there were no orders for me. I once again prevailed on Kenneth to allow me to come aboard with him as another Midshipman and part of the crew. I was hoping we would be at sea before the deception was discovered.

Captain Youngman ordered me ashore under Naval Guard to ensure I was incarcerated in the Naval Goal, until such time as the Admiral could deal with my case. I was at my wit's end. I wanted more than anything to remain in the Navy and with my friend, and thoroughly detested the idea of returning to my previous life style of social engagements and hypocrisy. I couldn't stand that.

A guard released me early one night and told me I would be able to make my way to the ship. I was unaware how I was going to do this. I was assisted along my way, and a boat had been engaged to take me to the ship under cover of darkness and a low lying mist in the early morning hours.

I was able to climb aboard, as I had done other ships in the prize taking, and made my way to Midshipman Walter's berth. He gave me a change of clothing, and informed me I was on my own. In this regard, I also take full responsibility. My friend allowed me the opportunity of make my disclosure to the ship's Commander in my own time.

I was recognized by several members of the crew who had been with me on the Halcyon and the rescue mission. My life will never be the same. I am not the same person who was enlisted into the Kings service. I am a King's Officer and prepared to take such disciplinary measures as may be deemed fitting.

I have the honor to be, Sir, your obedient servant,

David Clements, Midshipman

* * * *

The Captain invited the Commander of the frigate *Essendeen to* dine with him along with the First Officer.

It was difficult for David to keep his eyes off the Officers and the youthful Midshipmen as they ate, savoring the feast prepared by the Captain's Cox'n. It was the first real meal David had enjoyed since leaving the Walter's home. In spite of his nervousness, he ate with much enthusiasm. The other Officers talked and discussed David's case as though he were not in attendance. He'd blush whenever some ingratiating remarks were made in his favor. The Midshipmen sat throughout the meal staring at David, making him even more uncomfortable. He realized he was in serious trouble and that frightened him.

"Gentlemen. I have asked you here tonight, to make a judgment, or should I say to help me make a judgment on Midshipman Clements. I cannot help but be impressed. You have all read his report, and no doubt have some recommendations to offer in the matter."

"Clearly the boy had disobeyed orders. He has escaped custody while in the care of the Admiral's secretary. He has unlawfully boarded a King's ship without authorization. He conspired to damage a King's ship. He insulted an Officer and heaven only knows how many other charges we could bring to bear, any of which could see him court-martialed and perhaps hung."

All the time the Captain was itemizing the charges that could be laid against him, David was fraught with a bout of trembling. Never before in his life had anything so moved him to respond in this manner.

"Captain, If I might make a suggestion," Commander Tate began. "We are not dealing with a hoodlum, a vagabond, an uneducated twit. The Midshipman has shown beyond any reasonable doubt, he is a talented young man. He has, in the carrying out of his duties, displayed outstanding acts of heroism. I cannot see how anyone could not take into consideration these factors on his behalf. Sir, you and I are of equal seniority, and it is not my intention to dispute any decision you may arrive at but may I suggest, Sir, that I would be more than happy to take the Midshipman into my crew. Sir, I would deem it an honor to have the Earl aboard *Emmejay*. He is the most Senior in both experience and time of enlistment. My compliment of young men is made up entirely of inexperienced, 'off the street' type boys, who could stand to have a role model to emulate." Commander Fulton-Tate of *Emmejay*, who had been giving his diatribe, sat down exhausted by his narrative on David's behalf.

"Sir, if I may offer an opinion, being as that is the reason for our gathering, I whole heartedly agree with the Commander. The Earl is not a treasonable lad, and it might have serious repercussions throughout the fleet if anything were to come of this. After all, the boy is a hero and in his Majesty's court as well," the First

Officer explained as he watched the Captain for signs of agreement.

"All you have said gentlemen, makes good sense. I did not feel that I could reach a positive decision myself, without first discussing the matter. You have confirmed my opinion, however, Mr. Clements, it must not be seen that the Navy abides disobedience, so it will be necessary for you to stand to the mast. You shall received six strokes of the cane, then you will be assigned to the *Emmejay* as Senior Midshipman. I trust you will not find me too harsh, and that the assignment will further your experience and develop you into a fine young Officer. The Navy is in sad need of upgradeable Officers. I'm sure you are one of them."

David stared at the deck, shifting from one foot to the other as the Captain gave him his orders. He dreaded the pain of the rattan on his backside, but he was fully reinstated and legally a King's Officer, and that was all that mattered.

It had been decided that in view of the position of the Senior Midshipman among his peers, the punishment should be carried out before he went aboard the *Emmejay*.

The Coxswain led David to the gun deck. The crew were drawn up to witness punishment, however there were no sad faces. Many grins and even some chuckling could be hear among the gather seamen.

David was bent over the gun's barrel, and in so doing the Cox'n whispered in David's ear.

"Davey lad, you'll not feel a thing, but you must show a little pain, for effect that is." The rattan swung six times and each time David groaned and twisted as he had done many times before only under much different circumstances. The crew was outright laughing at David's performance. The Captain turned away and joined the other Officers, who were wearing smiles as well. "Punishment carried out, Sir," the Coxswain shouted.

"Very good, Cox'n. Dismiss the crew and carry on with getting the *Emmejay's* boat away," the Captain ordered.

As David made his way towards the entry, many crewmen came forward to shake his hand or to just give him a pat on the back. David tried to look in pain, however he was unable to pull the charade off.

"Avast you men there, back to your stations," the First Officer threatened.

Kenneth stood by the entry port, with unrestrained tears rolling down his cheeks. "Goodbye your Lordship, and God Bless you Davey." With that, he put his arms around his friend and they hugged each other. He turned away before anyone could notice. Everyone noticed and witnessed the wiping of eyes.

David was overwhelmed by Kenneth's show of affection.

"I'll miss you too, Kenneth. We'll be together again sometime soon, I'm sure."

With that he jumped into the stern sheets of the boat and waved at the ship's crew. In spite of the orders the crew were waving their farewell to the Midshipman.

CHAPTER TWENTY-ONE

First Command

For the next three weeks, the young Midshipmen were engaged in lessons in seamanship, navigation, calculus, and drills with their respective gun crews. David quite enjoyed the challenge the studies presented, and out-performed his fellow classmates. He was finally learning the basics of seamanship which, up until now, had been just so much theory that other people performed.

In fact, the Midshipmen had performed so well, and the conditions were ideal, so the Captain decided that they should be allowed to swim off the ship along with many of the crew. The weather was treating them well with moderate winds and bright sunshine. This was exciting, and the Earl was in his glory diving from the rail and trying to keep up to the ship. A long boat was put over the side to assist any swimmers unable to keep up. It was a welcome relief from the many days of monotony when there was little to do, other than standing lookout and searching the sea for any shipping, friendly or otherwise.

The deck activities were halted when the Commander determined they were entering the privateer's areas of operation. The closer they got to the islands the more chance there was of encountering the renegades who plied the island waters for unsuspecting merchantmen. They often took the island passages to cut several days off their voyage.

David along with the other Midshipmen, grew excited at the thought of action and being able to put some of their learned skills into practice. Even the ship's crew were hoping for combat, knowing many might not survive the encounters. Anything would be better than the monotony of the present time.

The privateers operating in these waters were Spanish, or at least were supported with supplies and crews from Spain. It was also rumored that the Spanish had established outposts in amongst the islands in order the keep their own ships, as well as those of the privateers, supplied with arms and provisions. They were self sufficient, and would not require stores replenishment from the main ports. They could sustain themselves for months.

Britain had spent months searching out these supply bases, however none were ever discovered. Many Naval ships were assigned this tedious task of searching, when they were not required for escort duties to the many convoys traveling the trade routes.

Naval Headquarters was beginning to wonder if the stories about the supply bases weren't part of a giant deception to engage the Naval ships.

Ships for patrols and convoy duty were few and could hardly be spared for this fruitless search. They knew the privateers were somewhere in the islands, and needed to be rooted out, but the question was, where?

"Sail Ho'!" shouted the masthead lookout. "Deck there! Two sails on the horizon off starboard bow," he continued.

"Identify if you please?" roared the *Essendeen's* Commander.

"Signal *Emmejay* we wish to intercept," shouted the Commander.

"Ship's are sloops, Sir, flying no colors that I can see," reported the Masthead.

"They're running down on us, Sir," the masthead excitedly continued his commentary. "Signal from *Emmejay* – to *Essendeen*: 'Intercept strangers'," the Midshipman reported. "*Coaldale* is to stay with squadron, while *Emmejay* investigates another ship running to intercept the convoy."

The strange vessel from the South East hoisted her Spanish colors and turned toward *Emmejay*, intending to engage.

"Run out the guns, prepare for port broadside," shouted the First Officer. "Sir! This Spaniard is the largest frigate I have ever seen, short of being a ship of the line."

"You're correct Mr. Carlson. Double shot the forward guns, as we might not have another go at her," the Commander shouted.

There was no question the bigger ship was planning to broadside with the intention of boarding in a surprise maneuver.

The first guns were fired by the Spaniard, and even though the vessel was poorly handled, she scored several lucky hits with her salvo, disabling the *Emmejay's* rudder, which became completely unmanageable. *Emmejay's* Commander had held his fire too long.

At the same moment, the *Coaldale* signaled. "The Convoy is under attack and she is unable to protect the stragglers. The privateers were cutting them out," the signal read.

A signal from *Essendeen* advised their ship has been disabled and being boarded by privateers. That was the last signal from her.

The Spaniard swung into the *Emmejay* with a resounding crash, and at the same time took a full broadside. The Spaniards proceeded to board, after grappling hooks had been made secure. *"Emmejay* fire!" roared the Captain. The port guns fired and blasted the enemy at point blank range, destroying their first attempt to board.

The Spanish Captain was leading a second attempt to board *Emmejay*, when his foot slipped from under him, as he stepped on a loose belaying pin. Several of the Spanish Officers watched in horror as their Captain struggled to keep his balance. His efforts failed and he fell backwards and down between the ships. His screams were heard over the noise of the gun fire of the deck battle.

The *Emmejay's* damaged rudder, caused her to drift to starboard, kept her close to the *Jose Carlosa.* She was out of control. Commander Young raced to the sides with sword swinging, shouting, "Repel the bastards! *EMMEJAY* repel!"

The screams from high above the deck of a falling crewman shot by a stray musket ball, failed to reach the Captain as he battled beneath the tumbling seaman. The luckless seaman's body landed atop the dueling Commander crushing him against a splintered railing. He was impaled by the splinter, and screamed for the First officer.

"Mr. Carlson, what is the status of combat?" the Commander questioned between groans of his horrible pain.

"Sir! We've beaten them back, the Spaniard is ours. Their Captain died when he fell between the ships. Several of the *Jose Carlosa's* Officers were killed and the crew lost their taste for further battle. They hauled their colors. Congratulations Sir!," the First says, realizing his Captain was dying.

In a feeble voice he motioned the First Officer closer to whisper his last orders.

"You are now in charge Mr. Carlson. I have fought my last battle, I'm afraid. Have the Master and Midshipman Clements placed in command of the prize. It is imperative that you make up to the convoy," the Commander sighed and closed his eyes.

The two ships were still grappled together and the First Officer ordered the Master and David to take command of the *Jose Carlosa* and sail to join *Coaldale.*

"Mr. Clements. Get your command untangled from us, and under way immediately," the First Officer ordered.

David and the Master boarded the *Jose Carlosa*, the Master with sureness and confidence, and David with fear and uncertainty. To command a small sloop would have been enough of a challenge, let alone being placed in command of a frigate.

"Davey, you run the ship and I'll attend to the sailing of her," the Master shouted.

The prize crew were experienced and capable of handling the vessel well enough. The prisoners were split evenly between the two ships, and many were locked up below decks. Some volunteered for duty as *Jose Carlosa* commenced beating her way up to the convoy.

Cannon firing could be heard to the north and *Emmejay*, still making rudder repairs, signaled *Jose Carlosa* to assist *Coaldale* to ward off the pirate vessels. The Sloops had done their damage and had captured the merchantmen and the *Essendeen.* They did their work quickly and efficiently. They were too fast and disappeared behind the maze of islands.

*Coaldale sig*naled that she was unable to cover the whole convoy by herself, and one merchantmen had already been cut out and captured. So far, one merchantmen vessel and the *Essendeen* had been captured.

Coaldale's Commander made signal to *Jose Carlosa* advising that he was taking command of the larger vessel. The First Officer would take command of the *Jose Carlosa.* David heaved a large sigh of relief, at the same time, he felt some disappointment at having to relinquish his command.

The long boat carried him across to the *Coaldale* where he assumed Senior Midshipman's station. The realization that he was now on his own without the Master or his best friend Kenneth to help him, caused

David to question his own ability to assume his new roll. There was no other choice as he walked along the port railing observing the gun stations. It was different aboard the *Emmejay* – he knew most all the crew by their first names; here he was a stranger.

The crew had only heard of the young Earl, but now here he was in their midst and there was a sense of admiration, yet some mystery, around the boy Midshipman.

The *Emmejay's* rudder repairs were finally completed and she was ready to resume her duties. Her signalman bent on signals ordering *Jose Carlosa* to accompany remaining merchantmen to port, while *Coaldale* was instructed to pursue privateers and endeavor to locate the captured vessels.

Coaldale's First Officer had never held command of any vessel before, let alone one filled with enemy prisoners. His apprehension was obvious as he accepted his orders from *Emmejay*.

"How in Heaven's name are we going to be able to find these buggers amongst this maze of islands. What will we do if we find them? I don't know what I would do, if we met," he complains to David.

"Sir! There are no enemy vessels in sight, why not continue to the coast and investigate between the islands. I have had experience in searching and I'm sure we would be carrying out our orders that way," David offered the bewildered Officer.

"Damned good idea, that way. We might never have to engage them if we can't locate them. Is there a chance we might find them?" he asked.

"If they're as clever as they seem to be, we won't set eyes on them again," David assured. He couldn't help wondering what he and the rest of the crew had got themselves into. A Commander who was entirely incapable of commanding anything, least-wise to plot a course of action against an unseen enemy lurking in amongst the islands was a bit frightening to David.

He wondered if the island search was a good idea. *What would happen if they were taken by surprise and their ship lost? Anything could happen under this First Officers Command. Court-martial for everyone, including himself.*

Darkness found the *Coaldale* preparing to anchor in a protected location between two small islands. The Commander felt it would give them an advantage if they were to discover the enemy sloops.

"Mr. Clements, have you any plans for search?" the Commander asks.

"Sir. It might be of some advantage if I were to take a search party now, and search some of the smaller coves. If there are any fires burning, they should be easily spotted from the water," David suggested.

"Splendid idea. Take the Cox'n with you, and six of our best men. That should give you some backup in the event you encounter anything," he replied.

The long boat glided silently over the quiet waters, with only a slight disturbance from the oars dipping in unison. A small entrance way was discovered but only by the slightest chance.

David reasoned that the entrance was really too narrow for any vessel to pass through, but ordered the Cox'n to take a lead reading on the depth.

"Six fathoms, Sir," the man replied.

"It is enough, and could probably accept a vessel if it were sailed very well," David commented.

The boat glided through the entrance way and into a large deep cove. An excellent cove to hide ships. One would pass the cove without ever knowing it was there. There were no fires, at least that the seamen could see, and David decided to pull in towards the nearest shore just inside the entrance.

"Sir!" the Cox'n whispered excitedly, "There's a vessel approaching the entrance and it looks as though it plans to come through."

From their vantage point close to the shore, they were surprised to see one of the enemy sloops driving directly into the narrows. It was obvious they had been in there many times. They were trapped and there seemed to be no way out for the search team.

"Mr. Scott, move onto the shore and try whatever way you can to hide the boat before they discover us," David ordered the Cox'n.

"It's too late, Sir, they've spotted us. What do you intend we do now?"

The enemy sloop's launch headed towards David and his crew. He realized his crew did not stand a chance, and told them to escape into the woods. Muskets balls chased them as they retreated.

Dashing through the trees, they were able to elude the pursuers. David lead the crew until they discovered a narrow pathway. He could see ahead and noticed the path divided into two trails. One trail seemed to head towards the ridge, while the other headed inland.

"Mr. Scott, I can't really say what to do, but I'm going to climb to the top of the ridge. Perhaps I can get a better view of the overall lay of the land. You take the trail leading inland and keep out of the way. I'm sure they will not let us alone. I'll be able to follow your course from up there. If I'm not back in an hour, you come after me," David said, sounding more confident than he felt.

"Be careful Davey, your the only Middy we have," came the reply.

The climb to the top of the ridge was more difficult than David anticipated, as the scratches and bruises on his body attested. Making the top, he searched the area in all directions. To the south he saw another island a little larger than the one he was on, showing a large open cove. There was a sloop anchored there, but without a glass he was unable to determine its identity.

Judging from the sun, he figured he had been away more than an hour. The crew should be starting to make their way after him, and decided he must return before they started up the ridge. Gunshots could be heard far below, and he scanned the area for any signs of action. A break in the trees covering the trail the crew were traveling, revealed that his crew had been captured. They were being marched along the same trail by the Spaniards from the Sloop. Now he not only has his own life to protect, but also the lives of his captured crew. There was no reason for him to hasten down, as there was nothing he could do at the moment. He scanned the area to the north and discovered the enemy sloop riding at anchor in the cove they had uncovered.

There was also another larger vessel, which looked like the *Essendeen.* He sat down on a rock nursing his injuries, and contemplated his next course of action.

The best time for any surveillance at a closer range would have to be done after darkness. Another advantage would be his ability to spot any fires if there were any. That would indicate the location of the camp or supply base. He wondered about that. *Could this be one of the legendary supply bases? What a coup if he could somehow identify its location to the Admiralty.*

David was certain the crew would not have given his presence away to the privateers, so he decided to rest and regain his strength. Darkness would arrive in a hour or so he reckoned.

As he had hoped, a huge bonfire somewhere towards the center of the island revealed the camp. It was concealed by the trees during the day, but now the flames lit up the area and he was able to see the outline of buildings.

This must be the base camp, he thought.

David looked back towards the cove and discovered not two ship's lantern, but three. Perhaps it was the merchantmen that had been captured. What a find, if only there was something he could do. He wished there was some way he could get word to *Coaldale*. He was certain the *Coaldale's* First would not be anxious to find the enemy, let alone engage it. The man was a coward and a complete disaster to the Navy.

David wondered how his crew was faring, and if they were still alive. The Spaniards were bad enough, but not as bad as the privateers who had a vicious reputation for being cruel and torturing prisoners for information about shipping in the area. Having a

Naval crew in custody, would provide them several men from whom valuable information could be obtained. That worried David the most.

He decided it was dark enough and prepared to start down, but not before searching the area where the other sloop had been anchored. It was possible that she was the *Coaldale*, and if that was the case, it was his main task to get to her some way.

It was very difficult to see the other cove, but if there had been a ship's light, he would have been able to spot it. No light. David grew exasperated as he saw his only hope for rescue, gone.

He walked along the ridge traveling on a narrow path, leading in the opposite direction. As long as it ran along the top of the ridge, he would stay on it. The trail was overgrown with brush causing him to tear his clothing and suffer many scratches.

Traveling the path was getting to be an almost impossible task. It was so dark, and the many rock outcroppings caused him to lose his footing and tumble down the embankments. He virtually felt his way along, keeping in sight where he could, the enemy's camp.

It was David's hope that he would not be discovered, as his only weapon was his dirk, and that would count for nothing against swords or muskets. The trail leveled off somewhat, and he was able to make better time.

The clouds forming indicated rain, and from the sound of the increasing wind, the island was in for a blow. *That was all he needed – a rain storm. At least it would cover up any tracks he might be leaving.* He felt he must be directly above the camp, as the sounds of voices could be heard. His plan, although it wasn't all that well thought out, was to descend the ridge once he got past the camp. Perhaps he would be able to assist in freeing the crew as he had done on another occasion. Not likely he would be so lucky this time. There would be no moon tonight by which he might guide himself.

CHAPTER TWENTY-TWO

A Remarkable Event

The Midshipman continued his way along the ridge. One thing he was sure of was that it would lead to the far end of the island and would be closer to the location where he had last seen the sloop. He still hoped it was *Coaldale* or that she was still in the area.

Somehow he had missed the trail down the ridge which caused him to change his plans. *What if the ship was in a cove at the far side of this island? I would have all the help I needed and the sloop could close off any escape route. Wouldn't that be a remarkable event*? he thought to himself.

He was drenched to the skin and longed for some dry clothing. His bruises were aching so badly he took to stopping more frequently. He had just risen from one of his rest places when he felt himself being flung upwards into the sky. His small body was smashed against the pole that had sprung the snare trap around his ankle and he was now hanging upside down, flailing the air some thirty feet above the ground.

He had stepped into a snare, attached to a small tree designed to entrap a person of some weight. David was like a leaf in the wind flying high into the air. He was beside himself. The pole against which he was now resting had pounded his bruised ribs and the pain caused tears to mix with the rain dripping down his face. He was in utter despair. He thought how stupid he had been to be caught like this. He should have been more observant. How was that to be when he couldn't even see his hand in front of his face from the heavy downpour.

David grasped his dirk which was still fastened to his waist and dangled near his face. He managed to swing his body into a position where he could reach the rope. He was about to start cutting when he realized that when the rope was cut he would plummet to the ground and perhaps kill himself. The tree was like a spiked pole where the branches had been removed.

He determined that he would take hold of the tree with his free arm and cut through the rope with the other. When the rope was severed, he reasoned, he would drop the dirk and take hold of the tree with both arms, getting a foothold on one of the branch stems. He had never done any climbing before and wasn't sure what was involved in descending the tree. One things he was sure of, he had no other choice.

He realized he would have to act quickly if he wanted to get to the other end of the ridge before daylight. He had been awake now for over forty hours and was exhausted.

He swung his body towards the tree and took hold while cutting the rope. The weight of his body tumbled downward as he grappled to get his arms around the tree to slow his downward momentum. The short stub branches ripped his legs and body terribly. He couldn't help but scream from the pain. Each branch took another piece of his flesh with it until he finally reached the ground where he collapsed at the foot of the tree.

He lay weeping silently to himself as the pain tore at his very being. Never had he felt such anguish. His clothes had virtually been ripped apart by the protruding branches. Consciousness left him and it was sometime later that he recovered. It was all he could do to keep from fainting again as he examined the damage done to his body. The scratches on his chest and stomach were bad enough and more superficial, however the damage done to his inner thighs and lower body was very serious and he was bleeding profusely. He had to stop the bleeding as soon as he could. He also realized he hadn't eaten for some time.

He tried to sit up but the task was too much for him. He slowly forced himself up and took hold of the tree and pulled himself to his feet. He noticed his genitals had almost been ripped from his body and seemed to be hanging like entrails from his stomach. "Oh God please help me I can't just lay down and die, not here, not alone!" he cried in his agony.

Daylight was now showing above the ridge top as he slowly made his way along the trail. He took one of his socks and made a bandage of a kind to wrap around his injured parts. He wondered if he was going to die and what it would feel like. He wondered if he would still have this terrible pain. *Please let the Coaldale or Essendeen come to this island and find me*, he prayed silently to himself.

He didn't know how long he had been wandering until he heard voices. At this point he didn't care who it was as long as it was someone who might help him.

The bushes and trees suddenly opened up to the sky and he stumbled once more, falling down an embankment leading to the water's edge. He had finally reached the end of the island. That was the last he remembered until he felt his body being carried gently onto the deck of the *Coaldale*.

"Get that boy below and have the doctor attend to him immediately," the Commander ordered. It was the ship's Bos'n who discovered David's almost naked body lying in a clump of shrubs close to the water's edge.

"Davey, you're going to be fine. Just hang on for a little while longer and your pain will go," the Bos'n said, trying to comfort the boy. He hoped he sounded more convincing than he felt.

David awoke to find himself in the Commander's small cabin with the doctor hovering over him. "Sir, Sir! I must talk to the Commander," David begged.

"I'm here David," the Commander spoke quietly to the tattered little body laying on his cot. Tears were flowing down David's cheeks as he tried to keep himself from fainting again.

"Sir! The *Essendeen* and two merchantmen are in a narrow cove at the other end of this island. You can trap them inside if you make your way around and follow close to the shore. There is plenty of water even through the narrows. You'll need help, Sir!" David cried, laying back on his pillow and closing his eyes.

The Commander was moved by David's bravery and realized he had been derelict in his duty to support the boy. "Up anchor, Mr. Scott, we're going to cut the bastards off. Somewhere out amongst these islands the *Emmejay* must be searching for us," the Commander remarked.

The *Coaldale* skirted the shoreline following David's instructions.

"Sail Ho!" shouted a lookout.

"Where away?" the First inquired.

"Coming down on us fast, Sir, on the starboard quarter, looks like the *Emmejay*," he observed.

"We're in luck Number One. Between the two of us we should make this quite a show. Serves the bastards right," he shouted enthusiastically. He felt much more secure and confident now that there was another ship capable of taking command of the situation.

"Make signal to *Emmejay*. 'Closing in on privateer's entrance, require immediate assistance'."

"Signal from *Emmejay*. '*Jose Carlosa* should be arriving shortly. Secure cove entrance until they arrive'."

"*Jose Carlosa* in sight, Sir, should reach us in about an hour," the lookout shouted, trying to keep the excitement out of his voice.

Jose Carlosa received a signal from *Emmejay* to proceed into the cove with *Coaldale* following.

With two ships of His Majesty's Navy surging through the narrow entrance, the privateer lookouts fired shots to warn of the impending danger.

"We've got 'em dead to rights Mr. Carlson. Send a shore party using the Marines as the main front. We will board both the *Essendeen* and the privateer's sloop. I would like to see as little bloodshed as possible," the Commander announced, feeling confident he had won this battle.

Sporadic firing could be heard from the camp and the marines were able to make quick work of the encampment, having the element of surprise in their favor.

The *Essendeen* was now back under Naval control and the merchantmen and the privateer's sloop were placed under control of prize crews.

"Sir!" shouted the Cox'n as he climbed up the boarding ladder on the *Coaldale's* entry, "There is no sign of the leader. We've questioned all of these slimes and they claim he has bolted to the far end of the island. He must have a boat cached somewhere thereabouts."

"Blast and be damned! How are we going to know for sure if they are telling the truth or if the bastard isn't masquerading as one of them? How are the crewmen from the *Essendeen* who were captured? Can they shed any light on the identity of this chief of thieves?" the Commander asked, shaking his head in frustration.

"Sir, we have talked to each of the crew and they all say the leader is not among the captured privateers. Our man has given us the slip, it seems," the First advised the Commander.

The rain was getting heavier again and it appeared the storm would keep the ships in their quiet protected cove for at least another day or until the weather cleared enough for them to leave. The seas were raging across the entrance and would have created a major problem in negotiating the long narrow channel had they attempted to depart.

"You have the watch Mr. Carlson. I am going below to check on our young patient.

Lord, that boy was certainly mangled. He has more guts than anyone I have ever seen," the Commander said as he walked toward his quarters.

"Well Doctor Bosnoff, what do you say about the Midshipman? Will he recover? The First tells me the boy has a bad infection. Surely he doesn't need that on top of all the other damage he has sustained," the Commander remarked, trying to see past the doctor to look at David.

"I have given him a narcotic. He will sleep for some time I hope, otherwise his pain will be intolerable. I have tried to save his testicle but it is so badly damaged and so terribly infected that I cannot. I will have to remove it before it is too late. The young Earl has a good deal of strength but this battle he won't win, I'm afraid," the doctor said as he rolled the coverings from David's injured areas.

"Good God man, don't just stand there. Do what you have to do, you're not to let this boy die, do you hear me? You must save his life. Cut them both out if need be but you must save his life," the Commander spoke with a determined set to his jaw.

The storm abated and *Coaldale* with her prizes, sailed out to meet the *Emmejay*. She had been weathering the storm some fifteen miles away towards Guadalupe.

CHAPTER TWENTY-THREE

Painful Recovery

"How are you feeling young man? You have given us many anxious moments since we brought you aboard. You are lucky you didn't bleed to death. We were very concerned for your well being David, or should I say, your Lordship. I know you have not wished to use your title, but under the circumstance I feel you have sincerely earned the privilege of being addressed formally," Commander Francis Ball said. "Midshipman Clements you are a credit to your uniform and to the Navy. Your courage has been outstanding, particularly when we consider what you have already accomplished. The Admiral will certainly have something to say to you on our arrival. The doctor tells me he is going to let you up in a day or so, which means with good luck, you will be up and walking when we arrive in port," the Commander commented as he paced back and forth in his cabin.

David had been occupying the Commander's cot since he 'd been injured.

"I'm sorry to have caused you this disposition, Sir. It must have been very inconvenient for you. If I had been aware I surely would have protested," David apologized humbly. "Sir, may I ask you a question?" David asked looking away from the Commander, not wanting to display his embarrassment.

"Of course lad, of course."

"Sir. The doctor told me he had to operate on my organs removing some things. Sir, does that mean I will not be able to make babies?" David asked with all seriousness and looking deeply concerned.

The Commander laughed heartily at David's forthright question. He had not been prepared for this. *Why hadn't the doctor explained these things to David,* he thought.

"David the doctor removed the damaged and infected testicle. Luckily it was only one and you will certainly be able to make babies one day," he said chuckling.

"I'm very glad of that Sir, I should feel badly for the lady I may meet one day," he said with a mischievous look in his eyes. The Commander was convinced that David was truly recovering, when he was starting to display his old sense of humor.

The crew who knew David were allowed to come to the Commander's cabin to visit the young Earl. They had great admiration for the young boy whose courage and heroism saved many of them from certain death at the hands of their captors. Their joy knew no bounds. Some openly had tears in their eyes, as they looked at the pale and helpless Midshipman laying quietly on the cot. Through his pain, he still managed to smile and call each man by name as they paid their respects.

"David, what's this talk about you making babies?" the Cox'n asked. The men started to laugh and soon a grin appeared on his face.

"Laugh if you will, but you'll all be surprised one day when some waif calls me Papa," David quipped. They realized the young Earl was on his way to recovery.

The *Emmejay* was three days out from port, and David had been walking, although requiring a crutch to steady himself, for the past two days. Each day saw him improving, and his pain more tolerable. He was even weaning himself off the doctors potions. His legs and arms were healing to the point he suffered little discomfort, but his groin remained another matter.

The doctor had insisted he have someone with him when had to do his toilet. David chose his Cox'n, who was only too happy and willing to help his young friend during this period of his recuperation. As embarrassed as David was, he soon grew to accept his situation as being another phase of his life, one he would just as soon forget.

The day before entering port, David looked for the first time at his damaged organ, looking away in disgust at the sight of the heeling wound.

"David, you mustn't fret about it, it's a lot better now than it was a few days back – so it will mend and soon," the Cox'n assured him.

"Come on me lad, time to get your trousers on. It might be a little uncomfortable but you can't meet the Admiral without them," the Cox'n laughed. David laughed too at the thought of standing before the Admiral in just a flannel shirt and his bandaged appendage.

The dressing changes were an agonizingly painful experience, and David had to bite his lip to keep from screaming, but allowed his tears to flow freely in front of his friend.

"It's alright my little man, I've seen many men cry in my day, and they weren't nearly as brave about it as you've been."

David still walked with a noticeable stoop, but was no longer in need of his crutch. *I waddle like a duck*, he thought to himself.

"David. I'm glad to see you up and about. Are you ready to see the Admiral? He is making a special presentation to you today. I've been with him for the past several hours making my report and answering his questions about the taking of the prizes and recapturing *Essendeen.* He is most overjoyed at your accomplishments."

David bowed his head in embarrassment. He wished he could sit down some place. He was very tired and his bandages were very tight causing him a great deal of discomfort and nausea. He jokingly referred to his bandages as a huge diaper, and all he needed to make his appearance complete was a baby bottle. The crew was very ready to supply him with that, however their bottle contained everything but milk.

Even with the addition of humor to try and make him feel better, David didn't feel up to visiting the Admiral, especially with the impending boat trip to the Admiral's ship.

"Cox'n please take these damnable things off me?" he pleaded as he tried to unwrap the bandages. "I can't stand them any more! They're too hot and are chafing my skin terribly. Can't you find something a little less binding?" David complained, insisting he not be carried everywhere and allowed to go below under his own steam.

The Cox'n disappeared down the ladder before David started down, preparing to catch the boy if he stumbled. With much grunting and groaning, he finally made it to the bottom.

"Take this thing off me Jack! I'll not have it another minute—please?" he pleaded. The Cox'n removed the diaper, and examined David's injuries. With a sigh of relief, he told David things looked very good and healthy. The color was good indicating the absence of infection.

"Do I look funny with it gone Jack?" David asked.

"Davey lad. No one will ever suspect your impairment, although you might walk a little to starboard from now on," Jack joked. David laughed heartily, the first time anyone had heard the boy laugh for sometime.

The Cox'n obtained some bandages from the Orlop, as the doctor was elsewhere, and bandaged David expertly. Without the heavy padding from the diaper, he was able to negotiate much better. He could even put on his own trousers.

"Pretty soon you won't be needing me," Jack said sadly.

"Jack, I think after all we have been through together, I will always need you." David paused. "Jack. Will you try and discover where Kenneth Walters is? He should be aboard the *Emmejay*," David asked.

"Right you are me lad. Now let's see you climb those stairs and see how well you do on your own. I do believe you're standing straight for a change," Jack said following behind David as he climbed back the ladder.

The sunlight hit his eyes blinding him momentarily, almost causing him to lose his balance. He found he was able to walk with greater ease and very little pain. There had obviously been too much pressure on his wounds.

David managed to delay his visit to the Admiral, begging pain and exhaustion. The Commander too realized the discomfort of the young Midshipman, and also his reluctance to attend the Admiral's interview and presentation.

Two weeks of recuperating and David was performing minor duties and resumed his instruction classes. A Packet Vessel had arrived bringing David a letter from his Father, the Duke. The letter was full of admiration and anxiety his father was experiencing for him. Word had been received in London, of the young Earl's exploits, and the Duke was overwhelmed with a keen desire to see his son again and endeavor to heal the differences that existed between them.

It hardly seemed possible a year had gone by since the Duke had packed the young Earl off to the Navy. Crewmen had watched as he had to be bodily manhandled aboard his first shop, subjecting everyone to vicious accusations and threats. Even those seamen who had served on the *Subdue*, remembered the day when the Earl was first placed aboard. They remembered the canings and harsh treatment he had undergone during those first weeks of trying to tame the wild and infuriating boy. His past life as an Earl had spoiled him, and the adjustment to this new life, which was not of his choosing, had not been acceptable to David.

The transformation that had taken place in David's life was beyond his Father's fondest aspirations. It was obvious he had adapted to his Navy life, and had performed courageously and was making a name for himself. David was moved by his father's display of sentiment, but dreaded the prospects of returning to his former life. He vowed he would never return under those conditions. The Navy was his life and that was where he was going to stay. He was afraid his father might exert some pressure on the Admiralty, to have him returned.

David decided to write his father explaining the conditions under which he would consider returning for a visit. The letter, along with the Admiral's dispatches, left for England aboard one of the Company Trading vessels.

David could no longer delay the Admiral's request for an audience. He was so impatient, he decided to journey to the *Coaldale* to visit the Earl and make his long delayed presentation to the young man. He hadn't even met the boy, and from all he had heard from the Earl's first days aboard the *Subdue*, he was most anxious to meet the young man and see this remarkable transformation for himself.

The *Coaldale's* Commander and entire crew were drawn up to General Quarters to welcome the Admiral aboard.

After the final whistles had blown and the Admiral was safely through the entry port, Captain Ball introduced the ships Officers. David, along with two other Midshipmen, stood at attention waiting for their turn to be introduced. They were very uncomfortable and inclined to be jittery.

"Midshipman Clements, I am very pleased to finally get to meet you. You have made a name for yourself in the annals of Navy History. You no doubt know why I am here." The Admiral turns to the Captain and says, "Captain Ball will you give me the case I handed to you as we boarded please?"

The Commander obliged and surrendered the velvet case to the Admiral.

"Midshipman David Clements, Earl of Windsor, it gives me the greatest pleasure to present to you, on behalf of his Majesty King Edward the Third, the Silver Cross for Gallantry and Devotion to Duty, for having displayed great bravery, resourcefulness, and having no regard for your own safety, but only for those men under your command. You, young man, are a credit to the Navy and her long standing traditions of heroism." He then pinned the medal on David's breast pocket.

"I understand you are recovering from very serious injuries. I wish you full recovery," the Admiral said shaking David's hand.

"I'm sure you will be pleased to know that you are being returned to England and to your family for a well deserved leave, where you can rest and recuperate. I trust this meets with your satisfaction, your Lordship," said the Admiral using David's title for the first time.

"Sir. It is not my desire to return home at this time. I am sure the doctor will give me a clean bill of health and allow me to return to duty. I really wish to stay with my ship, Sir," David almost pleaded.

"Your Father will be most disappointed, I'm sure."

"I will return one day soon, but at this time my best rehabilitation will be amongst my friends."

"Very well Mr. Clements, if the doctor signs your clearance for a return to duty, then I will make out your orders."

The crew, who to this point had remained in awe of the pomp and ceremony that had taken place, broke into thunderous cheers and hurrahs on behalf of the Midshipman. The Commander had to use his bull horn to return order to the deck, dismissing the crew as the Admiral made his way to the entry port. He could not help but be overwhelmed by this spontaneous show of affection for the Junior Officer. He thought to himself, *And well they might!*

CHAPTER TWENTY-FOUR

The Discovery

True to his word, the Admiral, having examined the doctor's report on David's condition for active service, drafted orders for David to be transferred to the Sloop of War, *Robin.* The crew roster showed provision for thirty-two seamen, a Commander, two Lieutenants, and two Midshipmen. As it turned out, David was the only Midshipman available. The position provided an opportunity for David to study for Lieutenant's examinations. If he were successful, at the end of this tour of duty, he would be the youngest commissioned Officer in the Navy. The challenge in itself was enough for David to throw himself into his studies. David was impressed with his new ship but was disappointed at not being allowed to stay with his old ship.

His reputation preceded him, and he was welcomed aboard the *Robin* with much fan fare and a great deal of curiosity, which made David feel uneasy. He didn't like the undue attention he was being paid. It seemed that already he was a legend among the crews of the Caribbean Fleet.

Although he had made numerous esquires into Midshipman Kenneth Walter's whereabouts, he came up empty handed. He had received a letter from Mr. and Mrs. Walters, but their letter did not disclose Kenneth's whereabouts. They mentioned that they had not heard from him for several months, and presumed he was in some very far-off place. They were sad that he could not be with them to celebrate his birthday. There was no mention of any ship, in his last letter home.

David inquired of his new shipmates, if they had run into or had heard of his friend in their various voyages. The only word of encouragement came from a seaman whose ship had been blown by a major gale onto the rocks at Val Lapraisia, the very area they were patrolling.

There were Midshipmen aboard, but he didn't know their names, nor what happened to them. David remembered hearing about the incident, and that there were few survivors due to the strong current around the reef. Most would have been swept out to sea.

There were several islands in the area, but the reef itself was not a part of any chain of islands. It was located in the middle of a well-used shipping channel. David felt the chances of Kenneth being aboard the

Cynthia when she ran aground were very slim. He could be on any one of a number of ships in the southern fleet. It worried him just the same, and he longed to see his friend again.

The *Robin* was assigned scouting duties for the incoming convoys from England which were escorted by several frigates, or at least as many as could be spared. Frigates were in short supply, engaged in more demanding rolls in the Mediterranean Fleet.

The voyage so far had been uneventful, and David had many hours to himself whereby he could study. They failed to sight their convoy, even though they were at the exact location and at the right time to intercept the ships.

Lieutenant Bishop, the Commanding officer, was showing his concern as he paced back and forth on his tiny quarter deck. David was asked to plot their course over again, as though they were just starting out. It would be a good exercise for him, a chance to put some of his navigational training to work.

The Ship's Master, Mr. Cook, watched over David's shoulder as he plotted the *Robin's* course. He was delighted with the accuracy of David's work, nodding his head in approval at the various lines on the chart. Finally David concurred that they were where they should be. The Master agreed the work was accurate.

First Lieutenant Carl Westmont was second in Command. David thought him quite elderly for his position, and was not impressed. He wore a scowl on his face, never smiling, and usually kept to himself, eyeing the crew's performance. He didn't hesitate to suggest that the Master had provided help to the young Midshipman. It seemed that the First had failed his Lieutenant's exams many times before finally succeeding in scraping through. He was bitter at having been passed up for promotion. The Master informed David that the man didn't have the skills nor the brains to go any further. He expressed his view that the Navy should have terminated his services many years ago, and not kept the Officer around.

"Be wary of the man, Sir. There is something about him," the Master warned. David was still experiencing some weakness in his legs, especially when he would attempt to climb the shrouds to the lookout. After several tries and the disappointment of failure, he decided that exercise on the deck steps would strengthen his limbs. The crew would often see the boy climbing up and down the stairs into the late hours of the night. He was not required to stand night watches.

Commander Bishop decided that they would stay in the area for one more day, then head to the windward islands. Perhaps the convoy had been blown off course, or even intercepted by privateers. There could be any number of reasons for their delay. Bishop pondered the various options open to him, and decided that one more day then they would leave.

The weather turned sunny and very hot as they neared the islands, and the wind had died to nothing. The *Robin* lay becalmed, and time weighed heavy on the crew. It was boring. The crew could only exercise and do gun drills for so long. Tempers were wearing a little thin, so the Commander allowed the crew to dive off the railings and enjoy the cool tropical waters to cool them off. David, embarrassed at his still healing injuries, declined to join in as much as he would have treasured the relief of the cool water.

The *Robin's* Bos'n, a Swede by the name of Lars Janson, approached David timidly, hat in hand.

"Sir, if you would like to take a dip, I would be more than happy to assist you. I think the exercise in the water would be as good as the stair climbing, and I would be with you at all times," he said rather apologetically.

David looked at the young man, and after thinking about the man's offer, agreed to allow the boatswain to assist him. He wore his old uniform pants to hide his scars and with the aid of the boatswain, slipped over the side into the water.

At first he was afraid he would sink, his legs were not functioning as they should. The boatswain supported the boy as he began to swim short strokes. It was like a balm feeling the soothing water on his skin. He felt immediately refreshed.

The crew had encouraged David as he swam amongst them. He was feeling much better and very grateful to the Bos'n.

The swim lasted for about 20 minutes, then the Bos'n suggested David had been in long enough.

"Grab hold of my neck, Sir, and we'll climb the ladder together." David's weight was nothing for the Bos'n who with David clinging to his back, climbed up the side easily.

Towards evening, the wind had increased and was well placed to take them amongst the islands. Commander Bishop felt they would make landfall before it was too dark to navigate, especially in those dangerous shoaling waters.

The *Robin* sailed into a small inlet and dropped anchor close to shore. It was an ideal place to weather a storm no matter how severe or from which direction the wind was blowing.

It was nearly dark and the crew was standing by the railings observing the beautiful tropical growth and white sand. The First Officer was making his way towards David, when the Bos'n stopped beside him and the two made casual remarks about the scenery and the swim during the evening. David thanked Lars once again for his assistance.

"Sir, what is that object on the beach over there?" he pointed towards the shore. They looked, trying to make out the object.

"Looks like some part of a crate or wooden box of some kind," David remarked.

"It's washed up from some ship no doubt," Lars explained.

"I think we should report it and investigate, don't you Lars?" David suggested.

David approached the First who was also looking towards the beach. "Sir have you noticed that piece of wooden crating or wreckage over there?" he asked pointing to the shore.

"I've seen it. Do you think you are the only one who sees things," the First replied sarcastically.

"Do you think we should investigate it, Sir?" David asked.

"Off on another tangent, are we your Lordship? Looking for another medal are you, and at whose expense this time?" he spat.

David was taken aback by the hatred in his voice and the abruptness of the reply.

"I know all about you Midshipman Clements. Lieutenant Wright was one of my best friends until you destroyed his career," the First snarled angrily. "I don't forget my friends," he said as he walked away, leaving David perplexed and a little frightened by his exchange with the First.

Now he had something else to worry about. He remembered only too well Lieutenant Wright and the punishments he had suffered, and shivered at the recollection. He had hoped he would have been done with the memory, only to have it rear its ugly head again in the form of the First Officer. He had good reason to be wary of any friend of First Lieutenant Wright.

The next morning a boat was put over the side, with the First in charge and David accompanying the group. He wanted to walk on dry land again, but not with this man. The crew were happy to have the young Midshipman in their midst. Lars Janson, the Bos'n, asked to be assigned the boat, but the First refused to take him. Carl worried about this situation and saw that no good could come from it. He worried for David.

The boat ground up onto the sand as the crew jumped off into the shallow water. The First made his way to the object of their investigation. There was printing on the side of what appeared to be a shipping crate of some kind. Digging it out of the sand revealed that the box had been consigned to *HMS Cynthia*. So it was possible for survivors to have drifted to this island. Perhaps there were survivors here. David pointed this possibility to the First who admitted it could have happened, and a search should be made. The boat departed for the *Robin* in order to make up a search party and to advise the Commander.

* * * *

"Where is Mr. Clements?" the Commander asked.

"I gave him permission to stay and do some preliminary investigation, Sir. I approved, providing he stay within sight of the beaches," the First explained.

"Very well, organize a search party and get on with it. It shouldn't take too long to discover whether anyone has been living on the island or not," the Commander said.

* * * *

David walked with some difficulty along the beach. The soft sand was making it difficult to make any time and his strength was fast fading. He decided to move off the beach onto firmer ground while still being able to watch the beach.

The Commander, in his directions to the search crews, indicated where they were anchored in relation to the rest of the island. It was almost two miles across and three or four miles long. David had observed that this island looked very similar to the one where he had found the *Essendeen* and her crew. It looked like the letter "H" with two large inlets, one on each end, and a very narrow strip of land joining them. The water was deep in both inlets and the approaches were clear of shoals. David thought it would be an ideal place to hide a ship, for each bay had a little inlet within itself. It would be easy to slip into one of these coves and never be seen by another vessel anchored in the bay itself.

He heard the crews shouting his name and he returned their calls with his own soprano acknowledgment. He had walked far enough up the shore to be able to see into the first inlet. There was nothing. That was good news.

David waited while the First and several crew made their way to his position. "You take three men and work your way towards the center of the island. You should be able to see into the other bay from there. I'll take the rest and we'll search the island on this end. Send someone back to the boat if you find anything," the First ordered.

David was very tired but knew the exercise could only be helping his weak legs. In any case he would not have complained to the First regardless of how badly he felt.

"Sir, would you like to rest a while, while we search up ahead? There is a nice grassy knoll up there. You can see very well from there, and if we discover anything we'll come back and tell you," one of the crew suggested.

"I should be with you."

"Sir. You're tired and a few moments to recuperate will do you a world of good. We'll manage just fine, Sir," he said.

David reluctantly allowed the men to go on without him while he sat and rested. He watched them as they disappeared into the undergrowth, appearing and reappearing from time to time.

David waited for what he estimated to be several hours and thought it time his men should be returning. He decided to call out. His voice would carry for some distance he thought.

"Robins! Robins!" he shouted at the top of his voice. There was no reply. Once again he shouted. "Robins Robins!" but still no answer. *Surely they could have heard that.* He called several more times, his shrill voice ringing out over the island. Still nothing.

He started along the path taken by the search crew, perhaps they had found something and were making their way back to him. He felt there was no better way to make his position known, than by shouting periodically.

Robins Robins! Robins! "Kenneth! Kenneth!" *Robins! Robins! Robins* "Kenneth! Kenneth!" *What made me shout Kenneth's name? It just seemed to come out,* he thought.

"Robins! Robins!" he shouted again. He kept wailing until he came to a rise. If he could get to the top he would have a better command of the area. It was a clearing ideal for a lookout. He had seen just such a location before, where privateers and pirates could observe the island's approaches. He was certain the hill had been cleared of trees as a lookout.

"Robins! Robins!" he shouted once again.

"We're coming, Sir!" came a reply from some distance off. His crew must have been somewhere below his location. Finally, he saw them.

"Any signs of survivors or any signs of life?" David inquired.

"Sir. Someone has been on the island. The grass is trampled down in many places. Can't tell how many but I would say there had to be quite a few. We haven't found anything else," they explained.

"Do you think there is anyone on the island now?" David asked.

"It's hard to tell, Sir. It's possible, but where would they be? We've searched this end of the island," the Bos'n said.

"It's almost evening. We had best be returning. You go ahead, I'm going to go a little slower if you don't mind," David apologized.

"We'll stay with you, Sir, it ain't nothing extra to take our time," one of the men replied.

David stood up and cupping his hands to his mouth like a megaphone, shouted again. "Hello-o-o Hello-o! Anybody hear me? Hulloo! Kenneth!" he shouted.

"Begging your pardon Sir, but who is Kenneth you keep calling?" one asked.

"I don't know why I'm calling his name. I was rather hoping he might have survived the *Cynthia's* sinking. He is my dearest friend and we have served on several ships together," David explained.

The men were standing watching David, when a faint voice cried out from somewhere to their right.

"David. David," the voice sobbed but was too faint to tell from where it came.

"Kenneth! Kenneth! David shouted in a frenzy of excitement. His heart was beating like a drum. He knew what he had heard, but hardly believed his ears.

"Did you hear that?" he asked.

"Yes Sir, we heard right enough. Could that be your friend?" the Bos'n asked.

"It is him! We must find him. One of you return to the boat for help, and advise the First that we are searching for a survivor," David ordered.

"The rest of us will search. He has to be close."

"We must find him," David said, his voice quivering. There were tears forming in the corner of his eyes as he tried to hide his emotions.

"Kenneth! Kenneth! It's me Davey. Kenneth please speak again!" David shouted within the dense forest around him. The crew were moved by this show of deep concern on the part of the young Officer. David knew he had to find Kenneth before darkness set in and there was little time left.

David and the men spread out and worked their way down the slope and in the direction they had heard the voice.

"Sir! Sir! Come quick! I've found him," shouted an excited seaman. David pushed his way through the underbrush to discover a little shelter of trees and brush under which lay his friend.

"Oh Kenneth, I've found you," he said, as he knelt beside the frail withered body of Midshipman Kenneth Walters. He wept unashamedly as he cradled Kenneth in his arms.

"You're safe now Kenneth. You're going to be fine. I'm so glad we found you," David cried, tears rolling down his cheeks. The seamen looked the other way as not to cause the Midshipman any embarrassment. They were affected by the reunion of the two friends unfolding before them.

"We can't move him until we make a splint to secure his leg. I'm sure it is broken," David observed. Kenneth was so dehydrated he couldn't generated any tears. The look on his gaunt, scared little face told it all.

Kenneth was quickly returned to the *Robin*, where he was bathed and had his leg set. It was going to require a professional physician to set the damaged leg properly, it had started to heal in its twisted form.

The *Robin* made her way towards the nearest port, where Kenneth would receive better medical care. He was in very bad condition and everyone wondered if the young Midshipman would survive. Obviously there hadn't been any food available and with a broken leg and in his weakened condition, he would not have been able to search for any.

The Commander allowed David to stay by Kenneth's side almost continually, having respect for David's deep concern. He thought the young boy had little chance of survival, he was so emaciated.

Little by little Kenneth took water. Color was slowly returning to parts of his face and hands. Fresh fruits were squeezed into his mouth. Most of the time he was unable to remain conscious and would drift in and out of a deep sleep. David was fearful he might not awaken and begged Kenneth to hold on.

"Kenneth you can't leave me now," David begged. "Please Kenneth. Please?" he cried.

"Sail Ho!" shouted the lookout.

"What vessel?" shouted the Commander.

"She's the *Metropolis*, Sir," came the reply.

"Signal her that we require medical assistance. Matter of life or death," the order came.

Two hours later, the *Metropolis's* doctor was hoisted aboard. His first glance at the Midshipman was one of shock and disbelief that the boy was still alive. He was nothing but skin and bones.

"Doctor. You must do everything you can to save him. He is my best friend and we found him so he could live, not so he would die," David said with deep concern and emotion. The Commander introduce David to the Doctor.

"Doctor, this is His Lordship, The Earl of Windsor, no doubt you have already heard of him," the Commander claimed.

"Well – Your Lordship, seeing as it is you who make this request, I will do the best I can. Your friend must be special. Oh by the way, I have orders to examine you as well young man," the doctor said reaching to shake David's hand.

The two vessels sailed together for the next two days, until the doctor felt Kenneth was out of danger. It would take time, and much healing, but he had rebroken the leg and reset it properly. Kenneth would survive. David was ecstatic with the news, and shared the prognosis with Kenneth, who was now awake and eating little amounts of fruit and biscuit.

"Sir, I have been ordered to stay aboard your vessel until you reach port. The Captain of the *Metropolis* has instructed me to stay and tend the boy. You are to make all possible speed to port and the home fleet is expecting your early return. By the way, the convoy you were to meet, finally made it to port. They were beset by privateers, and only by hiding amongst the islands were they able to reform and reach port. All together good news all around," the Doctor said.

Until now Kenneth had not spoken a word. The doctor wondered how the boy had found the strength to cry out at David's call. It saved his life.

David found it hard to look at his friend without weeping. He had great love for Kenneth, and would gladly have given his own life to save him.

"David you came. I prayed you would come. I knew you would come. I heard you call my name and I thought I was dreaming. I thought I had died and that God was taking me to heaven allowing me to hear your voice. Thank you Davey." Tears now streamed down Kenneth's face.

The two boys hugged and wept at their happy reunion.

Kenneth's progress was quite amazing considering his condition over the last week. He was able to walk even though his leg was splinted. His appetite had returned and it appeared that almost everything he ate converted itself into muscle and weight. The fact he was with David made his recovery much more tolerable.

By the time their ship arrived in port, both Midshipmen were excited with the prospects of going ashore, and Kenneth, although hobbling still, was getting around quite well.

Shore leave was granted to the Officers, who were already lined up for the ship's launch to take them ashore. Although Kenneth favored his leg it was healing rapidly, and the doctor had seen no reason to hold the Midshipman back from shore leave. He felt the break from ship life would be good for him.

CHAPTER TWENTY-FIVE

The Powder Boy

The two Midshipmen enjoyed their time ashore and stayed clear of all things Navy. They were enjoying being boys for a change. Kenneth was almost back to his normal self.

David was ordered to his new appointment, while Kenneth was ordered to remain a few more weeks until he was fully recovered. Kenneth begged to be allowed to return to sea, but was told that even if he did return, he would be on a different ship than David. The boys lamented their position, and decided there was no other way. Perhaps in the near future, David could exert some influence in order to be shipmates again. David realized, contrary to Kenneth's belief, that the additional time for recuperating would do Kenneth a wealth of good.

David's ship was making several short sorties into the islands searching, as always, for the elusive privateers. It seemed they were for ever cutting a ship, usually a straggler, out of a convoy and escaping into the protection of the hundreds of little coves located amongst the islands.

On each occasion of his return to port, David made his way hastily to visit his friend. The two boys would have tales to share and were happiest when they could be together.

Kenneth presented David with a number of letters and copies of the Navy *GAZETTE* directly from England by way of a Navy Frigate.

David read through his mail, which included one from his father advising that he would be enroute by the time the letter reached David. David didn't know whether to ask for a posting to sea, or wait it out and come face to face with his father. It bothered him just the same. He knew why his father was coming and it troubled him.

"David—you should be happy your father is coming all this way to see you. After all it's been over a year now since you last met. Surely things will have changed between you. You aren't the same person you were when you first came to sea. You've changed. I should think any Father would be more than a little proud to have you as their son," Kenneth went on.

"I guess there isn't much I can do about it, and you're right, I might just as well face him here as in my home in England. In any case you will be with me." David said nudging Kenneth. Kenneth nudged him back, and it was obvious the young boy was now his old self again. His ordeal had not left him scarred nor bitter from his experience.

"David—here we are again on page twelve of the *GAZETTE*. 'His Majesty is proud to announce the awarding of the King's Medal for Outstanding Bravery and Devotion to Duty, to his Lordship, the Earl of Windsor, Midshipman David Clements, and to Midshipman Kenneth Walters. Both officers are stationed with the Caribbean Fleet'."

"Look David, here is another one about you and me. It's about the rescue. About how you found me. And tons of things about how I survived in the face of wild animals and hunger. They certainly don't half doll it up – I never saw a wild animal all the time I was on the island. Look here again, we are receiving commendations. Where do we wear those, on our britches?"

Kenneth laughed. There was no question the two Officers were receiving a great deal of notoriety over their past achievements, in particular the young Earl. David shrugged off the compliments.

David had just arrived from his last short tour, and had gone immediately to the rooming house where Kenneth was being attended to. They decided to take a stroll down to the beach and see what was going on in the harbor. Kenneth was being re-assigned to a new ship. They were hoping their postings might bring them together again on the same ship.

Knowing the Navy, anything that made sense and sounded logical was to be ignored. The service would search for the illogical and perform it with the greatest success.

Kenneth nearly stumbled over the little crumpled form sitting on the stairway down to the wharfs. It was a young boy almost the same age as the two Midshipmen, and he had his head buried deep in his arms weeping away to himself, his body shaking with his sobs.

"Here boy, what can be so terrible to make you this sad and uncomfortable. Are you ill?" Kenneth asked. The boy raised his tearful face to look at the Midshipmen.

"I can't go back aboard, Sir. I just can't," he wept unabashedly.

"Are you a Midshipman serving here?" David asked.

"I'm a powder boy aboard the *Lancaster*," he answered.

"How old are you and what's your name?" Kenneth asked.

"I'm twelve and my name is Jonathan Walters," he sobbed.

"Your name is what?" Kenneth interrupted while the boy cowered away from the two Officers, as they looked at each other in disbelief. The boy had Kenneth's same last name.

"My name is Jonathan Walters. I'm a powder boy aboard the *Lancaster*," he informed them again.

"Did you say Walters?" Kenneth asked incredulously.

"I am Kenneth Walters. Perhaps we are related in some way. Isn't this a coincidence?

Jonathan, this is David Clements – we are Midshipmen." He was hoping to calm the boy enough to discover the problem which seemed so heavy on the youngster's heart.

"Now, what's the matter? You can tell us Jonathan. We are King's Officers, but what has happened that is so terrible that you have deserted your ship. Surely you know the consequences," Kenneth stated.

The boy broke into uncontrollable bouts of sobbing at the mention of King's Officers.

"It's okay, Jonathan. We shan't harm you. Now tell us what happened so we can help."

"I couldn't stand the goings on and the flogging's, Sir. I couldn't stay on the ship any longer," the boy wept.

"What's so terrible about that? I know it isn't pleasant at times, but we all go through tough times, what's the trouble?" asked David.

"I can't tell you. I would be flogged to death. Might be best for me if I were," he continued weeping. "Officer's aren't supposed to tell lies, but they do, and you will surely inform on my behavior that's certain," Jonathan sobbed.

"Jonathan, we promise not to inform on you if you'll only tell us what's wrong!" declared David.

Jonathan looked first at Kenneth then stared in disbelief at David, realizing that this was the Earl of Windsor, the boy who all the stories of the sea were about.

"Go on now! Go away. I know you're ship's Officers by the way you tell stories," Jonathan replied looking sadly at each in turn.

"Jonathan, as an Officer and a gentleman, I am telling you the truth. We are who we say we are and would like to help you if we can," David replied. David and Kenneth sat down beside the weeping boy, one on each side. David gently put his arm around Jonathan's shoulders.

"No one can help me not even you, your Lordship. I deserted ship when we reached port.

I will be hunted down and if they don't hang me from the yards, then they'll flog me to pieces and feed my body to the sharks. I couldn't stay any longer. Some of the other boys were going to come with me, along with the junior Midshipman, but they were too frightened of the consequences if they were caught and returned. They decided to stay and suffer," he moaned.

"Suffer what Jonathan? What did you have to suffer? Everyone suffers a little working below decks from time to time. Were you flogged? What do you mean suffer?" David prompted.

"Some of the officers treat us like animals and even worse," Jonathan had stopped his weeping as he sat more comfortably between the young Officers. "I shouldn't be sitting beside you I'm not worthy of being in your company," Jonathan shifted uncomfortably.

"Who is your Captain Jonathan? Who are the Officers?" David asked.

"The Captain is Sir James Crohn. Spends all his time in his cabin drunk, I've been told, Sir. Then there is First Officer Breckenridge," Jonathan started to sob again.

"Stop right there. Did you say Breckenridge, a young man with mean brown eyes and bushy eyebrows, rather tall and skinny?" David asked knowing full well what was coming.

"Yes Sir, that's him, and it's him what will do for me," he sobbed.

"Jonathan. Did the Officer ever have you to his cabin? Does he do things to you?" David knew the answer before the young boy answered.

"How did you know, Sir? Please – I never told you that," Jonathan begged.

"Go on," David encouraged, "tell us what *exactly* has happened."

"Mostly it's the Midshipmen that go to his cabin and also the cabin of the Second Lieutenant. Those two Officers come down to the powder room and do us right there. We just wait our turn. I can't stand it any more. The others can't either, but they know the consequences for informing. I don't care any more. I just hid in the jetty boat. No one saw me leave, I'm sure. But they'll find I'm missing. None of us were allowed to leave ship, not even the Midshipmen," Jonathan completed his tale of horror.

"Sounds all too familiar!" Kenneth mused.

"How did you know what they did?" Jonathan asked.

"We were once shipmates of that Officer. We were abused in the same way. He would make up false charges against David and me so as he could have us whipped in front of the crew. We know him all too well. We thought he was being court-martialed out of the service. How it is he is still here and an Officer of a vessel I cannot imagine," Kenneth said.

"Come with us Jonathan, we're going to take care of you. No more trouble for you lad," David tried to sound official.

They took Jonathan to the rooming house where Kenneth had spent weeks recuperating. They cleaned him up with a bath and some better clothes. When he was washed and tidied up he was a pleasant enough looking boy, however skinny. When the three boys had eaten a hearty meal, Kenneth wanted to know about Jonathan's family.

"Jonathan -where are you parents? How did you come to be conscripted by the press gangs?" Kenneth asked.

"I have no parents. They were stricken with the plague and died while I was away at school. With no money, I was forced to leave school and live off the streets. I can read and write for a fact, Sir. Any boys who could not prove they had legitimate guardians, were pressed," he said.

Kenneth and David exchanged glances, knowing they could think of a way out of this situation for Jonathan.

"What is going to become of me? I don't think you can help me without endangering yourselves. Just leave me be and I'll make out some way. Maybe escape into the islands somewhere," Jonathan was looking sad again.

The three boys talked into the late hours of the night of what they were going to do. It was decided that Kenneth was going to claim Jonathan as his brother, and that he had been assigned to the *Lancaster* as a Naval informant. No one could prove otherwise way down there in the Caribbean.

"My father is due to arrive any day, so I am relieved of any duty that will take me away. We'll work out a plan. We must stop Breckenridge once and for all, but Jonathan, we're going to need your help. Will you help us and tell a court what you know? We'll be right by your side all the time. We too will back up your story, then maybe the others will come forward and we can have those Officers stopped for good," David suggested.

"Why do you want to help me? I'm only going to cause you grief and a lot of trouble." Jonathan stopped, realizing how pathetic he sounded. "It isn't that I'm not grateful, it's just no one has ever stood up for me before. I just don't know how to act in front of you," Jonathan apologized.

They were sitting on the edge of the bed and David put his arm around Jonathan's shoulder once more. This started him weeping again. "I've never had any friends before, only those who wanted to hurt me," Jonathan continued his tale of hopelessness.

David decided that he was going to the Admiral and lay formal charges against the First Officer Breckenridge and Lieutenant Feebe, the Second. He realized it might be difficult getting the Admiral to believe him, but he knew he had to do something.

The three boys discussed what had to be said to the Admiral. David figured he was the one to go aboard the *Lancaster,* make contact with the other powder boys and the Midshipmen, and convince them they had to support Jonathan's story, even testify at a court-martial if necessary.

"David, that's going to be very difficult getting aboard that ship and talking to the boys. What if you're caught? What will you say?" Kenneth asked with deep concern for his friend.

"We have no other choice. If we don't do it now we may never have another chance. In a few days we might be miles away at sea. It has to be done now. What about Jonathan? We can't desert him now, remember – he's you're brother."

Jonathan looked at the Midshipmen with despair reflecting in his eyes. "Things can't be much worse for me your Lordship, I'm willing to help anyway you want me to. I'm going to be done-in one way or another," Jonathan assured sadly.

"Jonathan will you come with me to the *Lancaster*? You can help me find my way around and the other boys know you. That will be a great help," David said with enthusiasm.

"Sure, I can do that," Jonathan replied.

Jonathan's offer of help was just what David needed. Now he could get on with the rescue.

"Kenneth, we're going to have to take the boys off the *Lancaster*. They won't be safe anywhere once Breckenridge knows they're missing. He'll be desperate to find them. Have any of you an idea as to how we can do this? How many boys all together?" David asked.

"I think there were ten, your Lordship," Jonathan replied, his East London accent making it difficult to understand. It made Kenneth laugh.

"Stop calling me that. My name is David and I am your friend."

The supper bell rang in the rooming house and the three boys headed down to the dining room. David's heart nearly stopped when he notice two Naval Officers sitting at a table by themselves.

"Jonathan when we pass their table I want you to walk straight, no slouching – and salute them as I do. No mistakes now, your life depends on it," David instructed the shaking powder boy.

The two Officers glanced at the approaching Midshipmen and returned their salutes.

"Hold on there young gentlemen. Don't I recognize you from some where?" he said, a quizzical look on his face, trying to remember. David's heart was drumming his chest apart. He decided he had to play the charade out or end everything here and now for Jonathan.

"Sir, I am Midshipman David Clements of *HMS Halcyon* and this is Midshipman Kenneth Walters, just rescued from the island of Suiga off the Frigate *Cynthia*, and this is Midshipman Jonathan Walters, Kenneth's brother from the same ship, Sir," David spoke with as much assurance as he could muster.

"Excellent. Excellent. And congratulations to you young gentlemen. You are a credit to the Navy. Your father is the Duke of Windsor? Ah yes, now it comes back to me. You're the Earl who has made quite a name for himself. Best of luck and a pleasure meeting you. Carry on gentlemen," the two Captains continued their talking occasionally glancing in the direction of the boys.

Jonathan had stopped his shaking and was playing his roll like a proper gentleman, watching the Midshipman as to how they ate and what utensils they used. He even attempted to disguise his accent. Kenneth remarked what a fine job his new brother was doing of it.

"The Lancaster may be sailing anytime now, and we had better make our plans to do something tonight. First we must get a boat large enough to take all the boys off," David schemed.

"How can we do that David? It would have to be bigger than a ship's launch, and where would we find one anyway? Anything else will be too big for us to row," Kenneth ventured.

"The minute we finish supper let's go to the waterfront, and remember, we have to stay clear of the boat sentries. I don't know how we are ever going to be able to launch one of the long boats," Kenneth said doubtfully.

"There is a small dingy drawn up a short way down the landing from the ship's boat. I could take us over to the ship," Jonathan offered.

"Well we can't do anything until the Officers leave, then we'll get out of here and start to work. We'll have to plan as we go. Who all is aboard, Jonathan?" David questioned.

"Well, just like always, they let the crew ashore and make a junior Officer stay on duty, along with the Midshipmen until everyone returns, sometimes not until early in the morning. Then the powder boys like me, who are always locked up in the powder room until the Officers come back, are let out just like dogs. They are just making sure we don't high tail it when they're away. Just like me." Jonathan said.

"Do you know where the keys are kept for the powder room?" Kenneth asked.

"Well they should be hanging on a hook just atop the door. I watched the gunners hanging them up and dropping them sometimes."

"The Officers are coming this way. Watch me for signals, "David said.

The two Officers stopped by the table, turning their attention to David.

"Mighty proud to have met you, your Lordship, and the very best on your future endeavors. Remember me to your father. I'm Sir James Crohn of the Frigate Lancaster. Met your Father at a court-martial on one occasion. Very fine gentleman if I might say so. Well, we must be off. Once again good luck gentlemen," he said, and with that they departed.

David looked over at Jonathan who was looking very pale. "Jonathan stop shaking. He didn't know you from a hole in the wall. But it is important that you remember him, because we'll be seeing him at Lt. Breckenridge's court-martial within the next several days I expect," David said confidently.

"I'll bet you wet yourself when he said he was Captain of the *Lancaster*," Kenneth said jokingly to Jonathan.

"Oh I heard of him before, although I never set eyes on him while aboard," Jonathan commented sadly.

"Come on brother smile. It's going to be all right," Kenneth said, smiling at Jonathan.

CHAPTER TWENTY-SIX

The Liberation

The three boys waited in their room until darkness set in. It was a difficult time for Jonathan as he thought about returning to the ship where he had suffered so terribly. David and Kenneth had convinced him that in order to develop a case against the two Officers, they would require the testimonies of the other powder boys and the remaining Midshipmen. Jonathan wondered how he was going to convince the boys to desert their ship. That would be a task, as he had tried before when he had first planned to leave, and none of the boys had the courage to leave with him. They knew only too well the horrible consequences that lay ahead for them. Terrible floggings and an eventual hanging would be in order so as to establish an example for other would-be deserters.

The three made their way down a back road that lead to the wharfs. Fortunately for them the street was empty and they were able to make their way to the small boat undetected. David had made the plan and had discussed it several times with his two mates. Jonathan was still frightened but said he would take the word of the Earl that no harm would come to him if they were caught. David had made the promise knowing full well he would have little or no more power over the Admiralty, or its course of justice than any other seaman. Treachery was treachery regardless of who was involved.

"The boat's alongside the dock. It should be easy to launch the dingy, but I wished we could have taken the larger boat. We'll need the room if we're going to take the boys off," Jonathan said pointing in the direction of the other boat.

They crept quietly around the stern of the seaboat and found the dingy as Jonathan had said. David looked around searching for any sign of guards protecting the boats.

"Davey, we're going to need more space. Do you think we might find another boat if we were to row along the shore a bit? I could even run along the beach and locate one and make a signal to come and fetch it," Kenneth volunteered. David was happy to see his friend back in his happy state again after what he had been through.

"Good plan, Jonathan, and I'll launch the dingy and row along the shore as well. It's really quite dark now, we might not be able to see your signal," David said looking towards the *Lancaster*. She was anchored just off the shore line towards the bay entrance. The boys realized they would have a fair pull to get over to her. It was even going to be more difficult when they had to keep quiet in their approach. The darkness would be a blessing in the long run.

David and Jonathan quietly launched the dingy and commenced rowing parallel to the shoreline. They could barely make out Kenneth as he trotted along keeping pace with them. He would disappear from their view dodging behind small buildings or trees.

They hadn't gone very far when they heard a whistle.

"That's Kenneth," Jonathan said.

"Maybe he's found a cutter or something."

"We're going ashore. Pull harder Jon but keep your oars from splashing the water," David scolded.

"Yes Sir!" Jon replied obediently paying attention to his stroke. The dingy drifted quietly to the shore and the outline of a larger boat floating at anchor came into view. Kenneth was standing in the stern sheets of the larger boat preparing to take the dingy alongside.

"Davey, we'll tow the dingy and row the cutter," Kenneth offered.

The transfer to the larger boat was made with great care and the anchor was cut loose. The boys rowed towards the *Lancaster*.

"I know we have been over the plan many times but it is important that there is no fouling up in our attempt to board unseen. Jon, be as quick as you can in releasing the boys from the powder room, then don't do anything else other than get them aboard the cutter. Nothing! Do you understand how important it is?" David said going over this part of the plan again. He realized how frightened Jonathan was of being aboard his horror ship again.

"You can count on me Davey, 'm naught to let you down," he replied trying to sound confident.

"Remember, lads, it will be over in a few moments if we each follow the plan," David tried to reassure them.

With the dingy in tow, the cutter came up under the stern windows of the *Lancaster*, which towered over the small boats. There was a light in the aft cabin, but Jon said it was probably empty as he knew the Officers were ashore. Lanterns were on just as a guide to the other ship's at anchor. They all had lamps burning steadily, giving the boys her exact location.

Jon untied the dingy and quietly pulled the boat hand over hand along the side of the *Lancaster* to her bows, always looking up at the decks for any sign of lookouts. He felt very uneasy being this close to his old ship and considered what would happen to him if he were caught. He knew he would not see the light of another day.

In the meantime David climbed up the main entry hatchway searching for signs of guards. He gave a sigh of relief as he found no one. He was worried about Jon but at this point there was nothing he could do to help him. He was on his own to affect the release of the powder boys. His entry was over the rail using a ship's rope to haul himself aboard.

Kenneth performed the same maneuver with the larger boat as he hand-over-handed the cutter boat alongside the ship's counter, until he was under the stern windows. He secured the boat to the ship and climbed aboard crawling on his hands and knees to peer into the cabin. One of the windows was open and he hoped the cabin was empty so that no one had heard the slight bump as he tied up.

David had made his way along the starboard side working his way close to the ship. He hoped Kenneth had the boat secured under the stern panes. He climbed down and walked forward to where the Midshipmen's berth would be located. He wondered how he was going to talk the young Officers into deserting and wondered if his personal guarantee of safety and immunity from their charges would be enough. David tried to shut out the memory of tales he had heard where irrational Captains, flogged the men until they were red and bleeding then strung them up the main yard for all to see. Usually the poor souls were dead before the rope was attached. He shook himself as he approached the room. Quietly he turned the corner and found two boys huddled together on one berth. They stared in disbelief as David made signs for them to be still and quiet. The boys were speechless as they looked aghast at the young Midshipman and listened to his plan for their escape.

"Sir, Mr. Breckenridge is aboard. He is in the Captain's cabin with Charles and Griffin," they informed David whispering the information through their tears.

David wanted to scream when he heard that his nemesis was aboard and still engaged in his filthy practice. It made him all the more determined to bring Lt. Breckenridge and his Second Lieutenant to justice.

"Gentleman. I am going to secure your release, but you must obey every word I tell you – to the letter. I'm a Midshipman like yourselves and I've come to help you."

"How did you get aboard, and how are you going to get us off the ship?" one of the shaking Midshipmen asked.

"Krikey! You're not David Clements are you? You're the Earl of Windsor?" Roberts said incredulously, his eyes reflecting his complete shock.

"How did you ever guess that? I was going to tell you but thought you might not believe me," David said. "Yes, I am the Earl, but just call me David. We can't talk anymore, just make your way down the starboard side where you'll find a dingy tied up towards the bow. The powder boys are being evacuated as we speak. Join them in the boat and then move back down towards the stern. Midshipman Kenneth Walters and myself will join you in another boat. We will have to be very quiet as there will be all hell to pay when the First finds out you have escaped the ship."

The Midshipmen were shaking their heads in acknowledgment of David's instructions.

"Where will Charles and Griffin go?" asked David.

"Usually they come back to the berth, Sir," Roberts said.

"How long have they been gone?" David asked.

"They should be back anytime now, depends on what the First decides he's going to do with them. They're being punished, you know. Anyway, now that we know you are with us Davey," Roberts said awkwardly as he momentarily forgot who he was talking to, "can we be of any help? We finally made up our minds to leave after Walters deserted. The First still doesn't know he's gone," Roberts exclaimed.

"We have to upset the First's plans. Were you two to be next?" David asked.

"It all depends on whether the First wants us. He'll tell Griffin and Charles to inform us if we're to get our punishment," another Midshipmen named Scott volunteered.

"Sounds like the same Breckenridge I know and hate," said David.

"David we are doomed whether we stay or desert. No one would believe us if we tell, but they'll have to listen to you, Sir," Scott said almost happily.

"Does the First usually lock the door to the cabin," David asked.

"If he is alone aboard then he doesn't lock it, only when there are others aboard," Scott answered.

"Who is releasing the powder boys?" another one asked.

"Midshipman Jonathan Walters," David said watching the surprised look on their faces.

"Sir, are you telling us that Walters is an Officer like ourselves? Well, will you believe that now? No wonder he had the nerve and pluck to try something like this! Why didn't he tell us this before?" Roberts said, grinning nervously at Scott and then at David.

"Alright away with you. There is no turning back now. We have this man dead to rights and he'll be hung for his deeds," David advised as he ordered them away.

David, alone once again and feeling a kind of warmth of excitement surging through his body, made his way to the entry port where the dingy was secured. He cautiously pulled himself along the ships counter until he was beneath the ships stern windows.

Kenneth was busy making his way towards the Captain's cabin. He could hear voices as he listened outside the door and heard one of the Midshipmen begging to be released from his punishment this one time. He was telling the First that he was feeling very ill.

"You haven't even begun to feel ill my boy. I don't know why I bother with you anymore. From now on you'll feel the rattan on your backside, no more favors from the First do you hear?" he snarled at the boy.

David found it hard working against the current as he grappled his way under the windows. Peering in, he was filled with such anger he could hardly hold back a scream as he observed the scene taking place in the cabin. If he'd had a musket he'd would have sent a ball through the First's head. David was fuming. He knew he had to wait until Kenneth made his entrance into the cabin.

Kenneth pushed open the cabin door. The Officer was incapable of action and stood staring in complete disbelief as he recognized the Midshipman.

"Well, Mr. Breckenridge we meet again. I see you are still up to our old filthy tricks at the expense of innocent Midshipmen and powder boys. Sir, you have had you're last occasion to punish these innocent Officers. I am sure you will be hung for your deeds," Kenneth said, enjoying watching the First Officer fluster and fume as he tried to put on his britches, at the same time making towards the cabin door.

"You! I heard you were dead. How did you get aboard? You'll never get off this ship, my boy, and I will make you pay for all the humiliation you've put me through. It was a good thing for me and a bad one for you, that I had friends in high places or I might have suffered even worse." He made a dash for Kenneth and the doorway. At the same moment David swung open the windows and motioned the two Midshipmen to escape. They were so frightened and bewildered that for a moment they had lost all sense of what was taking place.

The First ran at the door waving his sword. Kenneth shut the door just as the First was about to pass through. He crashed into the door, and for the moment had forgotten his two victims who were now safely out of the ship and into the boat.

He had not noticed David.

Kenneth turned the key locking the First in the cabin. It was then the First frantically realized that his victims had escaped. He looked out searching for his escapees but his vision was marred by the light of the cabin. The thought of what was transpiring was driving him insane as he ran back and slashed at the door with his sword.

He climbed out onto the combing and was making his way along the stern windows, when Kenneth, hearing no sound, realized the First was attempting to escape. He opened the door and rushed in pushing out on one of the windows behind which the First was standing. He lost his hold and fell into the water. Kenneth knew he would have no trouble getting back aboard but at least it would give he and the others time to make their way to shore. There was no question in his mind about the turmoil the desertion would create, and to what ends the Officer would go to locate and silence the Midshipmen. He also knew his life depended on immediate action.

The dingy pulled alongside the entry port, and Kenneth swung down into the stern sheets as the boat made its way to shore. They reached the shore about the same time and the boys stood quietly waiting for instructions. They were still bewildered and confused by all that had taken place.

Kenneth motioned for the boys to follow him and made signs to keep quiet. They were to stay close together for fear of getting lost. They made their way to the rear of the rooming house where they found Mrs. Cassidy, the landlady, waiting. She rushed the boys into the house.

David had already made arrangements with Mrs. Cassidy for the boys to be hidden and fed. She despised the way the Navy treated the young boys and was more than willing to be a part of bringing the Officers to justice. David wondered, as he ran with the rest, what she would say when she finally heard the whole sordid story.

Mrs. Cassidy now had nine young boys to attend to and feed instead of her original two. For the present, the boys were safe, but she and David knew that it would not be long before a full scale search was underway and they would be discovered.

CHAPTER TWENTY-SEVEN

The Note

Three hectic days went by and the searchers could be heard knocking on doors and marching up and down the streets in their efforts to locate the deserters. The boys were plainly frightened, but after Mrs. Cassidy's kindly care and the many good meals they had received, they were feeling more at ease. The powder boys were uncomfortable being in such close relationship with the young Midshipmen, but none more than Jonathan Walters. The others considered him a bit of a hero, and held him in new respect. David had forewarned Jon of his new status and he was to play the roll as he had been instructed. No one would ever know that Jonathan was not a truly qualified Midshipman. He was wearing a smile for the first time since being kidnapped, as David referred to Jon being pressed into the service against his will and being a child. There would be difficult times ahead for the boys.

"We are safe for the moment, but now Kenneth has to get to the Admiral with his accusations. It is he who will be presenting the statement and the charges. You will all be witnesses if and when we have to produce evidence. You must trust me when I tell you, things are going to work out to your benefit. Mr. Breckenridge will no longer figure in your lives. You will be free of him once and for all. But you must trust me. You are not to show yourselves outside this house until I call you. Kenneth will keep us posted as to what is transpiring. We must get a court-martial organized against Breckenridge and Feebe," David instructed.

Twice the searchers inquired of Mrs. Cassidy whether she had seen any wayward waifs wandering the village. The second time they insisted in searching the house against her will. She had thought that the house might be searched, so she had prepared a hiding place she was certain they would not find.

Kenneth and David spent much time together planning how Kenneth was going to get to the Admiral. They had written a lengthy statement concerning the behavior of the Officers and about the punishment Kenneth was subjected to while a Midshipman on their ship. It was a damning statement which had to be delivered to the Admiral at all cost, otherwise all would be lost. Kenneth might even wind up being imprisoned. David remained with the boys not wanting to be discovered before the proper time. He wanted to be, along with the others, the damning witness to convict the Officer.

"I hear the Admiral will be the guest of honor at a gala banquet in the village at the Governor's mansion tomorrow evening," Mrs. Cassidy announced. "That might be a good time to get your statement to the Admiral without any risks at all. Having to get yourselves out to the Admiral's ship would certainly have been a risky state of affairs, I'm thinking."

"All we have to do is get the statement to the Admiral or his Flag Captain and let him do the rest. It should be easy to find someone going to the reception who will be willing to take the envelope to the Admiral, thus reducing the risk to anyone. I really was worried about you taking it, Kenneth," David said, deep in thought.

"Jonathan. Rather than risk Kenneth being recognized, you will deliver the statement. The chance of meeting any of your Officers is pretty slim and—"

Scott interrupted. "David let me go. I am the oldest and I'm a Senior, just in case any of the Officers get carried away with their authority. I think it is putting the others at risk when it will be relatively easy for me, and beside I can write, in case I have to."

The boys looked at each other in approval, all except David.

"Someone will surely recognize a Midshipman, but they'll not soon recall the lowly powder boy like Jonathan," he paused.

"I didn't mean that quite the way it sounded Jonathan, but none of your Officers are going to expect you to be here on shore, unless they discover your gone," David pointed out.

The logic of David's statement seemed to make sense, and once again Jonathan was elected to carry the envelope to the reception. The plan seemed a good one. One more day and the message would be in the Admiral's hands.

They all wondered, *What then*? It would be anyone's guess.

That evening the boys were in their rooms waiting for the call to supper. The relationship between the boys was extraordinary as the Midshipmen, even though they were Officers, treated the powder boys as equals – calling them by their first names, and frolicking on the beds like any youngsters might do. They seemed happy, something they had not experienced for a long time. David tussled among them like the others.

Each night the boys would ask David to relate the stories of some of his adventures. They were especially excited at the telling of David's close encounter with death through his injuries. Mrs. Cassidy would sit on the bedside as well, listening to the tales. She was flabbergasted at what the young men had to endure at the hands of the unscrupulous Officers, including the beatings and sexual abuse.

Their eyes opened wide as they noticed the terrible scars on David's legs, as he was preparing for bed one evening. Unembarrassed, he showed them the whole wound area. They held their breath in awe realizing the heroism of the young Earl they were now calling their friend. Kenneth related other adventures of David's achievements. David countered by relating some of the acts of heroism on Kenneth's part.

"Jonathan, er—I mean Sir, it must seem to you that we were frightened and weak when we allowed you to take off without us joining you. I guess we were too scared of the consequences and didn't think you would make it. You know you would be dead by now and there would have been nothing we could have done to help you," Midshipman Charles apologized.

"We didn't know you were a Midshipman. Were you acting as a spy on the powder room? What were you doing there?"

Jonathan looked at David, and was relieved when David answered for him.

"Jon can't answer your questions at the moment, you just have to trust us that everything is fine now. None of you have been spied upon, and you have nothing to fear from Jonathan's experience with you."

"What an amazing undertaking. I've never heard of such a thing being done before. What a way to learn what's happening aboard the ship. A spy I think they call you Jon," Charles volunteered.

The others laughed, all except Jonathan who sat looking uncomfortable and saying very little. David was pleased at Jon's behavior. He was certain Jonathan Walters would make a good Midshipman. Kenneth usually sat beside Jon as brothers might be expected to do. Each of the boys had heard tales of two notorious Midshipmen from talk aboard ship from the crew. They felt very honored and knew they were in good hands.

"Supper's on the table you ragamuffins," Mrs. Cassidy called up the stairs.

"Coming Mother," the boys replied in unison, teasing her. She laughed. She enjoyed looking after the 'tykes' as she called them. Business had been slow and there had not been many guests. This lull in her otherwise monotonous life was a cherished one she would always remember. The four day stay of the young men had drawn them very close. No one had ever Mothered them the way Mrs. Cassidy had. The most responsive to her nurturing were the young powder boys. They were classed as expendable, as often they were killed in fires or explosions during battle. The youngest was twelve, that was Jonathan, the next two were just thirteen, and Paul, the oldest powder boy was fourteen.

Paul and Kurt, from the powder room, were the first down and were seated at the table waiting for the others when the parlor room door burst open and a Naval officer and a crewman entered the room.

"Mrs. Cassidy," they called, looking at the two boys.

"You've claimed not to have seen or heard of any of the deserters from the *Lancaster.* Then who are these two?" The boys tried not to show their fear and tried to act unconcerned. Mrs. Cassidy rushed in and asked why they were intruding in her dining parlor.

"Your a rooming house ain't ya Ma'am? Well, we've come for a meal. Why don't you introduce us to the young gentlemen," the Officer said sarcastically.

"These are my two nephews from up island. They have been me with me for the past week or so, and are returning tomorrow. What seems to be your concern here?" she asked contemptuously.

"What's your names?" the Officer asked.

"Paul Dumas," Paul answered, catching himself as he was about to say Sir.

"I'm Kurt Dumas," Kurt replied nervously as he chose to be Paul's brother at the last moment.

"Have you been out and about? Have you heard of the deserters? Have you seen any of these waifs who are going to be whipped until they are raw, then hung by their scrawny little necks until they choke to death?" the Officer replied trying to unnerve the boys. He didn't know how close they were to breaking and making a run for it. Mrs. Cassidy kept shaking her head at them behind the Officer's back.

"We've been searched and had Officers in here every day for the past four days asking. I haven't seen anything nor have the boys. They would have told me had they encountered the deserters," she scolded.

"Best you keep these two in doors until they are ready to depart, otherwise they might be picked up and shipped aboard one of our ships," the Officer said as he turned to leave.

"My best to the Admiral. Tell him I have some real good food for him when he is next ashore," Mrs. Cassidy called after them.

It was several minutes before David and the others came down to the dining room. They had been shocked at what they overheard down below, as they hid away in their secret place in the attic.

Nothing was said as the boys sat down to the table.

Jonathan had overheard the Navy men talking to Paul and Kurt, and was shaking as he ate his meal. He knew he would be leaving on his all important mission right after the meal and wondered if he would be able to carry it through.

It was dark when Jonathan departed with the well wishes of his friends.

"We'll be waiting for you, Sir," Kurt said, trying to sound encouraging.

"I've just had an idea. I want you, Paul, to follow Jon and keep us informed of his progress. We must know if something goes wrong," David ordered.

Paul looked a bit startled at first, then he patted Jon on the back and said, "Come on Sir, mustn't keep the Admiral waiting." The boys knew the risks involved and silently prayed that they would be successful.

The boys left the rooming house and followed the lanes to the Governor's estate, where Paul hid in the surrounding bush watching Jon make his way to the front steps. The visiting ship's Officers were entering the reception in groups, depending on the seniority of the ships they were serving on.

Jonathan approached one of the Officers, who quickly dismissed him as a beggar child, and told him to get away from the steps. Jon dug in his coat for the envelope and told the Officer that the envelope was very important and should be delivered to the Admiral right away.

"What business would you be having with the Admiral? Now be off or someone will paddle your behind."

"Please, Sir, I have orders to give this to the Admiral. It is a matter of great importance," Jon persisted.

"Oh give it to me. I'll see if the Admiral is aware of any messages coming to him. Now away with you."

Several officers had heard the boy's insistence on having the envelope delivered – one of which was Lt. Feebe, the Second Officer from the *Lancaster*.

"Seize that boy. He is a deserter from my ship," he shouted to the other Officers who quickly restrained the struggling Jonathan. His life was over and there was no one to come to his aid. He looked around to see if Paul was nearby. He knew if Paul saw what had occurred, then the boys would be aware of his plight.

The commotion on the steps caused the guests to gather at the door to see what was happening. Jon continued to struggle in the hands of the Second Officer. The Admiral questioned the Officers as to what the ruckus was about, and was told about the deserter being captured.

"Attend to the lad and let's get on with the festivities," he said holding Jon's envelope in his hand. He noted the neat and precise handwriting on the envelope and determined it might be important. He opened the all important document and read the contents. He grew red in his face and he flustered about searching for his Flag Captain. He handed the document over and paced back and forth in front of the large window overlooking the front steps. He saw the struggling boy in the hands of the Second Officer Feebe and then Lt. Breckenridge appeared on the scene.

The Admiral watched as the Lieutenant struck the young boy across the face knocking him to the ground. Jonathan sat on the rocky ground holding his swollen cheek and weeping quietly to himself. He realized he had been discovered and the end was near for him.

The Flag Captain joined the Admiral at the window.

"Sir. It would appear we have a terrible scandal surrounding the fleet here in St. Vincent," he said.

"Yes indeed we do," the Admiral conceded.

"Captain Carter. Who is that Officer taking the boy away? Have the boy brought to the Governor's office along with the officer who seems to have taken charge of the boy."

"Yes Sir. A very prudent move, if I might be so bold, Sir."

The Admiral motioned the Governor away from his lady friends and whispered in his ear. "Mr. Kenworthy, I would like the use of your office for a few moments. A matter of some urgency has arisen demanding my immediate attention and some privacy. I trust this won't inconvenience you too much," the

Admiral questioned knowing the answer would be a positive one.

"Do have another claret, Admiral, before you take on your heavy responsibilities. I should think a little liquid reinforcement might be just the thing at this moment," the Governor said holding a goblet towards the Admiral.

"Yes. Yes. Sometimes these things can become quite nasty – if you get my drift," the Admiral said almost swallowing the entire beverage in one gulp. He was anxious to get to the bottom of the terrible accusations in the statement of charge he had just received. How dare anyone make such statements against a King's Officer! There would have to be a very good reason for such a ruse.

Paul observed Jonathan's apprehension, and quickly ran back to the rooming house where the other boys were in hiding.

"David!" he shouted. "Mr. Feebe recognized Jonathan, and I think he is being sent back to the ship. I ran as fast as I could when I saw what was happening. Perhaps we can do something to stop it," the excited youngster panted.

"Did the Admiral get the envelope, can you tell us that?" David pressed for an answer.

"I think so, David. Another Officer, who went in before Feebe, took the envelope from Jon, but he didn't seem very happy about it. I heard Jon telling him the message was a matter of life and death," Paul reported.

"That may be absolutely true. I must figure away how to tell if the Admiral received the statement. Paul, I want you to go back to where you were and keep an eye out for anything going on. Chris, you and I will try to get a look inside through the windows. The building isn't a very high one, in fact the windows are almost at the ground level. Look into any window with a light. I am going to join you in the search. Kenneth I want you to stay here with the boys. If the First spots you, you're in for it. You won't stand a chance. The rest of you stay put with Mrs. Cassidy regardless of what might happen to us. She will see you are not harmed," David told the remaining boys. There were groans of why they had to stay and why couldn't they get into the fray. David assured them they would have plenty of opportunity for that very soon.

The guards seemed to be gathered at the front entrance to the Governor's mansion, as though they had caught the only person they had been looking for. It made it easy for David and Chris to make their way from window to window. Several of the rooms were showing no light at all, so they passed them by.

Chris was making his way along the back side of the building when he caught a glimpse of the First Officer standing in front of the Admiral, who was seated. He still had a drink in his hand and sat fidgeting in his chair. Jonathan was seated on a lounge beside Capt. Carter, the Admirals' Flag Officer. The window was swung open and Chris, laying on his stomach, was able to hear everything that was being said. Chris was startled when David suddenly appeared at his side. He had never heard the Earl approach. David laid a finger to his lip motioning for nothing to be said. He was now in a position to hear as well.

"Boy! Are you the complainant in this damning report? This Officer tells me you are a powder boy aboard the *Lancaster*, is that correct?" the Admiral asked getting up from his seat and standing directly in front of Jonathan.

David had coached Jonathan as to exactly what he had to say if he were caught, and began by advising the Admiral that he was not a powder boy, but in fact, he was Midshipman Jonathan Walters, brother to Kenneth Walters of the *Halcyon*. The First looked incredulously at the young boy and stood for several seconds before he was able to speak.

"Sir. This young deserter is lying through his little teeth. He is a lowly powder boy. I know where he was working. It is from that post that he deserted. He has a reputation for lying, Sir. The little bastard!" the First went on trying to convince the Admiral.

"Who ever you are, I hope you realize the very difficult position you are in. Your Senior Officers have made statements to the fact you are a trouble maker and a deserter, and because of that, you have made up this preposterous tale of wrong doing on the part of the Officers. What do you say to that? How is it, if you are a Midshipman, that you were serving in the powder room in the first place," he continued his questioning feeling uneasy, and not really knowing who was telling the truth. The story seemed too fantastic for a child to have dreamed it up.

Jonathan stood up and stared directly into the Admirals eyes, and with a slight tear in each eye and holding his face where he had been hit, replied, "Sir, rumors had spread throughout several of the ships in the fleet that Mr. Breckenridge and his Second Officer Mr. Feebe, were engaged in terrible abuse of the young men of the ship. It was my assignment to obtain information regarding the rumors to see if they were founded. The Officer particularly enjoyed punishing the powder boys, so that is where I started. The Midshipmen were also punished in the First's cabin but, like all the rest, were too frightened to expose the Officers for fear the Captain would not believe them, and charge them with contempt of authority and even mutiny. Their punishment would be devastating and certainly would end their careers," Jonathan completed his report, and the Admiral compared the statement with the note he had received.

"Young man, you are in very serious trouble unless you have evidence to support these horrific accusations. Can you provide witnesses who will testify at a court-martial, that they were molested and beaten by the Officers? It appears the young men in question have told you they would not come forward, so it becomes your word against two respectable Officers." The Admiral looked at his Flag Captain and quickly looked towards Lieutenant Breckenridge. The Officer was squirming and sweating in his chair before the Admiral. He had to maintain his innocence and destroy Jonathan's statement. He was certain the other boys were too frightened to say a word. He had warned them already of the consequences of terrible floggings and for Jonathan, the hangman's noose.

"Sir, I suggest this is all a prefabrication of terrible untruths, and I shall take responsibility for this deserter to ensure such a thing never occurs again," the First added almost pleading. He made a move in Jonathan's direction. Jonathan looked around for some means of escape realizing the odds were heavy against him.

"Sir, let me call a guard and we'll be done with this charade," the First announced.

"Mr. Breckenridge, I cannot entirely ignore this terribly damning piece of information without looking into it a bit further. If the lad's story is true and he is who he claims to be, then I shall not be responsible for interfering with justice or the Admiralty's investigations," the Admiral explained, uncomfortably wringing his hands as he paced back and forth. He knew he couldn't take the chance of failing to act on the report.

"Mr. Carter what is your opinion of the matter? Should we release this Midshipman, if he is a

Midshipman, to the Lieutenant, or shall we detain the boy ourselves and determine whether we have sufficient evidence to establish a court-martial."

"Surely a board could be set up to make inquiries into the matter, Sir," Captain Carter offered. He had a distinct dislike for the *Lancaster's* First.

"Yes. Yes. Perhaps you are right. I dread the thought of this matter getting to a court-martial. What a damning blotch on the Fleet's records and of these two Officers. Their careers would be ruined and they would suffer terrible humiliation, if the inquiry does not show evidence for a court-martial," the Admiral noted, as he paced back and forth with his hands clasping and unclasping behind his back.

"Sir, there is no question of the validity of these accusations. They are charges made up in retaliation for the punishment this boy has brought upon himself," Breckenridge was fighting for his life. "We have no record of his being a Midshipman, and certainly not in a position of an informant. We would have been told if such were the case," he continued.

"Why so, Sir? If it is you, then there would be no point in this boy working under cover, so to speak. I feel that forming the board of inquiry will work better for you and Mr. Feebe. If the board exonerates you and the Lieutenant, there will be no shadow over your reputation. It will be best for all concerned. In the mean time, Mr. Carter, have Mr. Walters confined aboard my ship until such time as we clear this mess up. He is not be to held as prisoner and can have free access to the ship's facilities."

"Mr. Walters, if you should attempt to leave the ship, no matter what the circumstances, you will be deemed guilty of desertion and I need not remind you of the consequences," the Admiral warned.

"Mr. Carter, now is as good a time as any to gather three or four of the Fleet's Officers and have them investigate the charges, and let's be done with this horrible mess."

"I'm returning to my ship Sir, I would be happy to drop this Officer at your vessel on my way," Breckenridge offered as he attempted one last plea.

"Thank you, but no. I would prefer you to stay clear of the boy until this is over. Is that clear?" The Admiral stared at the First Officer.

"Yes Sir, I was only trying to be of some assistance. This investigation will prove that this boy has contrived this fairy tale to discredit me and I'll be happy to see it end. Thank you Sir," he said as he left the interview.

"Goodnight gentlemen, and enjoy the rest of the festivities," the Admiral said, dismissing the group and motioning for Jonathan to remain.

"Young man, you will return to my barge and locate yourselves with the Midshipmen aboard.

They'll see you're looked after," the Admiral said kindly, waving him towards Captain Carter.

"Take the boy and see he is not in contact with anyone between now and when he arrives on board."

David and Chris were shocked yet relieved. Several times when the First was attempting to get his hands on Jonathan, they were afraid the Admiral would allow it. In any case, their plans were now under way and it was now up to them to establish a strategy.

Upon returning to the rooming house, they told all they had heard and Mrs. Cassidy agreed everyone of them were going to have to be most careful. Mr. Breckenridge would be desperate and would stop at nothing to ensure their silence.

CHAPTER TWENTY-EIGHT

Deserters

The search for the missing Midshipmen and the three powder boys had gone on for almost a week and there was still no sign of their whereabouts. Lieutenant Breckenridge was beside himself with concern, for if these deserters were to make an appearance at the inquiry, he would be doomed. He had assigned several seamen to personally search for the boys, and every lead had wound up at a dead end, that is, all except the report of Mrs. Cassidy's two nephews. Perhaps they were truly her relatives or perchance they might be some of the powder boys. It was worth any effort to find out for himself.

He ordered his second Lieutenant to disguise himself as a civilian, and make a surprise visit to Mrs. Cassidy's rooming house. Mrs. Cassidy answered the door herself, and was asked if she had a room for the night. He had been aboard the ocean packet and wanted a night ashore before departing for Panama.

Mrs. Cassidy looked the young man up and down and decided that, perhaps, there was nothing to fear. He looked innocent enough, but one could never be too sure. She didn't want anything to happen to her charges.

"I understand from one of the ship's Officers, that you are enjoying the visit of your young nephews. That must be a pleasant time for you and the boys." Mr. Feebe remarked nonchalantly.

"Oh yes, they are darlin's, and it was pleasant indeed to have them here," she said.

"You mean they have departed already?" Mr. Feebe sounded disappointed.

"Oh yes they've left for up country again. Can't tell when I'll see the young rascals again," she replied wondering at the young man's interest in her guests.

"Mrs. Cassidy, there's a wagon drawn up at the front gate," Scott yelled from upstairs not realizing that there was company below talking to Mrs. Cassidy. He bounded down the stairs only to draw himself up short letting out a small scream as he realized who was standing in the hall way.

"Well! Well now, Mr. Scott I believe it is? We have been searching everywhere for you, young man. You have had us all worried that something might have happened to you," Mr. Feebe said with a look of triumph on his face.

"I think it is time that you and I return to the ship along with the rest of the Midshipmen, whom I presume are sheltered in this rooming house. I suggest you not make a scene, or I shall have the shore patrol manhandle you and the others back to the ship. Mrs. Cassidy, do you know the penalty for harboring deserters from Naval ships? You will surely suffer dearly for your maternal leanings," Feebe snarled.

"Fetch all the others. My patience is running thin," he shouted.

"Mr. Feebe, Sir, there is only myself and Mr. Woodward here. We have not seen the others, nor did we know they had come ashore," Scott lied with as much conviction as he could muster.

"Madam you have lied to me about your nephews! I will call the ship's patrol and we will search your house. I suggest you turn over the runaways to me now!"

"Scott is quite right. He and one other boy were the only two who have been here. They were the two boys I claimed as my nephews. I didn't know they had run off. They just told me they were given permission to come ashore. That's the truth. Search the house if you will, but you'll not find another soul here," Mrs. Cassidy said convincingly.

"Well that may well be, but by the time we finish with these two, I am sure they will be able to shed some light on the whereabouts of the others," the Lieutenant said.

"You two come with me," he had taken his pistol from his belt and was waving it menacingly towards the two distraught boys.

"What will become of them, Sir? They're just wee mites, I'm sure they meant no harm," Mrs. Cassidy pleaded.

"They are deserters from a King's Ship, and as such they will be dealt with accordingly," the Lieutenant said as he marched the boys out into the street, seemingly satisfied that Mrs. Cassidy had told the truth. Two seamen who had been waiting in a wagon outside the house came forward to take charge of the luckless young boys.

David and Kenneth had overheard the entire conversation from their hiding place and Kenneth whispered, "We can't let them take them back to the ship Davey. They'll be killed for sure. Mr. Feebe and the Second can't let them free to testify or answer any questions. He has to do away with them." The other boys were hiding in the small nook in the upstairs attic and nodded in agreement.

"We have to get them free somehow Davey, Sir," young Kurt Smith said almost in tears. He knew full well what lay ahead of the boys if they were taken back aboard the *Lancaster*. Beatings and other measures to get from them the whereabouts of the others. Mr. Feebe looked all over the dock area for the First Officer, but was informed he had already returned to the ship. He had been feeling ill. Mr. Feebe hadn't been feeling so well either, at least until now, and he knew he had the way by which he could discover the other boys.

"We have to create a diversion of some kind. We must get to the shore right away, but I don't want to be seen yet. Kenneth you take the boys and get down to the boat before they leave and do whatever you can to cause a ruckus. I'll do my part at this end, trust me," the Earl said ordering the others on their way.

"You men watch these two with your lives while I go and inform the Captain of our good fortune," Feebe ordered the two guards. "He will have to be informed before I can take them back to the ship," Mr. Feebe advised as he headed back into the Governor's mansion.

David saw the Lieutenant re-enter the building and immediately headed towards the shore and the ship's boat. He could barely see the outlines of the seamen and the two boys, but enough to know they were not being injured or mistreated.

Hiding by the supply dock, he discovered several kegs of gunpowder. He rolled one off the dock and onto the ground, breaking the keg open and spilling the powder onto the beach. David lit a slow match and threw it at the powder as he scrambled for safety behind the dock. The blast created a huge flare and the two seamen were distracted away from their charges, long enough for Kenneth and the others to scramble away to safety and away from the docks.

"Kenneth keep going into the hills. I'll make contact with you as soon as I can with food and whatever else I can find. Don't come to the village under any circumstances – no matter what you hear. I'll be fine. The rest of you get a move on! Sharply now!" David ordered.

"Davey please take care, you're also in danger if they discover you are here," Kenneth said concerned for his friend's safety. Kenneth knew full well what would happen if either Breckenridge or Mr. Feebe caught them. They would die, but not before they had been made to tell where the remaining deserters were. Kenneth had cause to be frightened.

David waited until well after midnight and the streets were deserted. He made his way to the rear entrance of the rooming house, crawling cautiously lest a guard had been posted outside to wait for the possible return of the boys.

The entrance was locked as he had feared it would be, so he made his way to the drain pipe on the corner of the house. He knew it ran past the room where he and the others had been lodged. Climbing as quietly as he could, he reached the window and opened the louvered window coverings. He slipped inside and made his way to Mrs. Cassidy's room.

"Oh dear me! Oh dear boy, where have you been and what have they done to the others? I've been laying awake fretting something terrible. How did you get in? I locked every door just in case one of the guards tried to enter. They were there until just about a half hour ago. I don't think they'll be back but you can't take a chance Davey son. Let me get you something to eat – you must starved."

"Mrs. Cassidy, thank you for all you have done for us. I shan't ever forget your kindness. I must have some food for the boys until the appropriate time for them to make an appearance. They are hiding in the hills overlooking the town. They'll be able to see anyone approaching. I think they'll be safe there for the time being. Maybe a blanket or two to keep warm at the night," David asked.

"Of course laddie, of course, and I'll see you have food every day. I'll make a little stash nearby where you won't have to come near to the house. Let me know if there is anything you need, or want me to do," Mrs. Cassidy said, putting her arms around the Earl.

"Oh, I'm so sorry your Lordship, I got a little carried away with myself," she said feeling embarrassed at having taken such liberties.

"Mrs. Cassidy, you have no need to apologize," David replied as he hugged Mrs. Cassidy.

CHAPTER TWENTY-NINE

The Rescue

The explosion created the diversion David was seeking; however, the two guards quickly came to their senses and realized what was happening. The guards ran to the boat where they had left the young Midshipmen, to find them gone. The ruse had worked and the guards now were going to have to answer to the First and to Lt. Feebe.

Lt. Feebe had heard the explosion and quickly darted off the front steps of the mansion in time to spot Midshipman Remus Tulliver making a hasty retreat. He had been hiding and listening beneath the Admiral's window, having overheard the conversation within the Governors' office. Little did Remus realize he was running right into Mr. Feebe.

"Well now, what have we here? MrTulliver having a nightly stroll before beddy-bye are we?" he said sarcastically as he took a firm hold on the young boy.

"You're not going anywhere tonight, my young friend, but to the *Lancaster* where you and I have some talking to do. Perhaps we can loosen your tongue before the night is through, unless that is, you want to tell me now where the other deserters are? It would go well with you, Mr. Garrith, if you cooperate, otherwise, you will never forget this night mark my words," the Second Lieutenant threatened.

David in the meantime, had taken advantage of the diversion to whisk Kenneth away and into a hiding place where they would not be found. It was an old fisherman's shed, and it would do until they could get away to Mrs. Cassidy's.

They waited for about an hour until the festivities at the mansion had come to an end, and the ship's boat had returned to the ship. The shoreline appeared to be deserted when David and Kenneth left the shed. They made their way back to the house undetected.

Mrs. Cassidy was so happy to see the boys she wept openly as she hugged them to her ample bosom.

"Ah laddies, I felt I had let you down and caused them reason to do great harm to you. I can't tell you how happy I am at seeing you. Remus was hiding near the mansion endeavoring to discover what was going on. He probably heard the explosion and took off for the dock hoping he would be in time to help you. He is with you isn't he?" she asked looking past the two boys.

"We've not seen him Mrs. Cassidy. Why would he leave when we gave orders for him to stay regardless of what was happening? Oh My God! If he has been taken by Mr. Feebe, then Heaven help him," Kenneth said shaking from the realization of what lay ahead for Remus.

"I must find out what has happened David. I will go and see if I can gather any information," Kenneth said heading to the door.

"I'll go with you. It may mean we will have to go back out to the ship."

The other boys had gathered around and were listening to what was going on. They wanted to come but David was firm when he ordered, "None of you. I mean no one, is to set foot out into the street – regardless. Remus disobeyed my orders – now who knows what has happened to him. If we are taken, then you are on your own. Mrs Cassidy will see to you and perhaps you can start a new life for yourselves. But once again under no circumstances are you to leave this house. Is that understood?"

David thought it might be wise to see if there was any activity at the mansion before going any further. The Governor was engaged in a heated conversation with the *Lancaster's* Captain. It appeared the Captain and the Admiral's Flag Captain were going to spend the night ashore as guests of the Governor.

Breckenridge and Mr. Feebe would be the lone Officers on duty aboard the *Lancaster*.

"David we must find a boat or Remus will die. I know what those two will do to him once they get him alone. They'll make him tell where we are, that's a certainty," Kenneth said.

"I agree and I know just where to find a boat. The fisherman's shed has a punt. It will hold the two of us and will be easier to handle," David said, as he took off on the run to the shed they had vacated only a short time before.

The boat was launched quietly and the boys made their way to the *Lancaster*. They were able to make their way, unobserved, to the stern windows where they had rescued the Midshipmen.

"It worked once Kenneth. The Officers must be on deck, otherwise they would have placed a watch aboard. They were pretty certain they were not going to be disturbed," Kenneth observed. He was trembling both from the cold and from the fear that was deep within him as he recalled the rescue.

Both boys were hauled up short in their tracks as they were shaken by the piercing scream of a young boy. It was Remus. Like their last visit, they had climbed aboard through the stern windows. They knew the Captain was ashore and his cabin was empty.

"Davey, that's Remus, we must do something before they kill him," Kenneth sobbed.

"Up on deck and not a sound." David searched through the Captains desk and the only weapon he could find was a Midshipman dirk. He shoved it in his belt and as he was leaving the cabin when another scream rented the night. David wondered where the rest of the crew were and why they wouldn't come to the aid of the young boy.

"Kenneth I don't want them to recognize me yet. You will have to do as I say, and between us, I think we can stop these maniacs," David ordered.

They climbed the companionway ladder to the deck, quickly darting in behind some rope coils. They found the Midshipman naked, tied to a grating as Mr Feebe administered a ship's short paddle against Remus's buttocks and back. He was bleeding and screaming.

"Well you little snot, you're going to tell me sooner of later or there won't be a piece of flesh left on your scrawny little bottom. Now once again I will ask you, where are the Midshipmen hiding? Who is with them? Tell me!" he shouted as he delivered another stroke using all of his strength behind the blow. Remus lost consciousness and lay still. It was all David could do to restrain Kenneth who was all for tackling Mr Feebe himself.

Where was Mr Breckenridge? the boys wondered, only to see him standing by the rail with a bottle in his hand. He was obviously drinking himself into oblivion trying to escape the predicament he was in, and at the same time enjoying the agony of the young Midshipman.

David made his way to the seamen's section below deck and rounded up the Bos'n and the Cox'n, both who David had met before. They recognized David.

"Sir, there was naught we could do for the lad," they apologized.

"Sir. What are you doing aboard? If they find you you're a goner," the Bos'n offered.

"We are not going to allow Remus to take another stroke. Do you understand me? I found the key to the arms case. I want the two of you to get a musket each and make your way on deck. I want one round fired, on my command, alongside Mr Feebe. Don't strike him. Don't let either Officer see you. Mr. Kennedy, you will securely tie the hands of both Officers, and deliver them to the cage. Threaten them if you must, but try not to let them see your faces. Wear a covering of some kind. It should be easy as you're only dealing with one man. Breckenridge is too drunk to offer any resistance."

The three men made their way along the deck until they were almost behind Feebe. He was getting ready to administer additional blows to the whimpering young Midshipman now that he had regained consciousness.

"For the last time Tulliver, speak up or so help me I'll shove this handle up your rear into your rotten little heart. Do you hear me? Now once more, where are they?" he screamed at the battered boy.

David nodded and the shot rang out. Mr. Feebe stopped, his arm raised to deliver the blow. He knew the shot had been close but had no idea where it came from.

The moment's hesitation was all that was needed for the two crewmen to secure both Officers and then deliver them to the cage where they were locked in.

"All secure from our end, Sir, they are none the wiser as we never spoke to either one. They are sure some scared," the Bos'n chuckled.

"You know, Sir, we could be classed as mutineers for what we done tonight."

"How can they accuse you when they don't know who you are. You have rendered the Navy a service. I will need you when the time is right and the hearings get underway, to testify to what you saw here tonight. You need not have to implicate yourselves in the shooting," David said.

Kenneth had cut Remus free and was soothing the crying boys pain as he slowly dressed.

"I just wanted to save you, Kenneth," Remus sobbed, his body racked with the utter pain of his mutilated back and posterior.

They carried Remus to the Captain's Cabin where they quickly found the doctor's supplies in the Orlop and placed temporary bandages on the boy. They decided that Mrs Cassidy could better mend the lad.

The trip to shore was an agonizing one for the three boys, as they made their way to the house. They carried Remus, and when Mrs. Cassidy saw the damaged and cruelly beaten youngster she broke down in tears. She regained herself and quickly had the boys bring him to her room where she bathed and salved his wounds. She fed him a bowl of chicken broth and comforted him throughout the night. Both Kenneth and David kept a sharp lookout for unexpected visitors. In the morning Gerard, still in pain, felt slightly better and related his tale to the others. Each one thought of themselves being in Gerard Garrith's position and what they would have done under the circumstances.

"I would never have told Davey," he sobbed again.

"I know you wouldn't have broken, Gerard. I'll see that you're beating was not in vain, I assure you," David said.

CHAPTER THIRTY

The Court Martial

"Gentlemen. I have established this court-martial based on the results of an inquiry I authorized a few days ago. Because of the seriousness of the allegation against two ships Officers of *HMS Lancaster*, I have decided that a court-martial is the only way we can put the matter at rest, save the Navy irreparable damage here in the South, and remove the blemish of reputation presently experienced by the two Officers under question." Admiral Sir Charles Willingham continued reading from notes laying before him.

"You all recall I received a most distressing document which purported to be a true statement, under oath, by Midshipman Jonathan Walters, attached to the afore-mentioned vessel the *Lancaster*. I have it on good authority that the Midshipman was ordered aboard the vessel as a powder boy without the Captain nor any of his Officers having any knowledge of the posting. Furthermore, the document goes on to say that Mr. Walters' orders were to infiltrate, if you will, the powder room to determine if there was any undue punishment or wrong doing against several of the powder boys. Examples suggested are most distressing but I must read them just the same."

"That the Officers, with the exception of the *Lancaster's* Captain, did fabricate misdemeanors against several of the boys in order to provide—hrmmmmph—provide sexual favors, in order to escape severe punishment and canings. It seems that word was somehow passed to the Naval authorities and Mr. Walters was assigned to the powder room as a powder boy to verify the mistreatment of the boys. I must tell you that none of my staff were aware of the elicit deception, but we can certainly understand the need for secrecy. The report goes on to tell of specific abuses by the boys including dates and punishments." Several of the Officers were shifting uncomfortably in their seats as they realized it could have been any of them who had been subjected to the Naval deception.

"You have all read the charges against First Officer Breckenridge and Second Officer Feebe. It has been decided that both men shall be examined together as the offenses were jointly undertaken by the Officers. I realize none of the charges have been substantiated, and there is some doubt they ever will, however to clear the matter and remove all tarnish from the two highly respected Officers, we will precede," the Admiral said taking a drink from his water glass. He was perspiring and the beads of perspiration were dripping from his chin.

"The Midshipman known to the *Lancaster's* crew as Jonathan Walters, powder boy, has sworn a statement alleging Mr. Wright, on several occasions, did invent bogus charges of misbehavior and insubordination, for which he was caned and placed in a cell without food. He further states that he would be allowed to rejoin the others and escape further canings, if he would agree to provide his body for acts of sexual gratification."

There was an uneasy mumbling from the gathered Officers as they listened to the outrageous charges.

A young naval Lieutenant was appointed as defense attorney to represent Jonathan, and went about his duties with obvious reluctance. His client was not going to get away with this, and would suffer even worse punishment if by some horrendous error he could not substantiate his claims.

"Midshipman Walters also states that all the boys in the powder room were so abused, as were several Midshipman amongst the ships Officers. He also states that the threats of horrible punishments kept the boys from making formal complaints to the *Lancaster's* Captain James Crohn." This brought another stir from the gathered Officers.

With the reading of the charges out of the way, the Admiral decided that a lunch break was in order, and that Midshipman Walters was to be held *incommunicado*. No one was to be allowed to talk to him. David, Kenneth, and the others had put together their story and rehearsed their statements so often, it would be very difficult for anyone to break their spirit, although each one was petrified – especially at the sight of the two Officers. David had given his instructions and now came the time for the acid test. The first witness was to be Jonathan himself. David wished he could speak to him, to offer his own personal support. Jonathan would have the most difficult part in the court-martial because he was prefabricating his position. He would be lying under oath. He determined it was for the good of the others and the two Officers were to be punished.

"This court is now in session. Sir Charles Willingham presiding. All rise," the court clerk announced. He was the Admiral's ships recorder.

"Will First Lt. Breckenridge and Second Officer Lt. Feebe please rise and make yourselves known to the court?" The two Officers reluctantly stood gazing around the courtroom for anyone who would offer support, and also searching out the Midshipman.

"Will Midshipman Jonathan Walters please stand and make yourself known to the court?"

Jonathan stood looking neither to the right or left but staring straight at the Admiral. David concluded the boy was playing his part well, however it was plain to see he was shaking and having a hard time controlling his speech.

"Mr. Walters, these are most unusual circumstances and probably rank amongst the first such cases where the claimant is a King's Officer, performing Naval duties while operating undercover. Most unusual indeed. You have made some serious allegations against two very highly respected Officers. I trust you have witnesses who will attest to and support the charges?" the Admiral stated.

"Yes Sir I have."

"The two Officers have stated in their own defense that it is you who deserted the ship while in port, that it was you who took it upon himself to trump up these ridiculous charges because of the punishment meted out to you for your deplorable conduct. I don't expect you to reply," the Admiral said looking at the *Lancaster's* Captain sitting beside him.

"The court calls Jonathan Walters to testify," the clerk said. By this time Jonathan was having second thoughts as to whether or not he was going to be able to carry the charade off.

Lt. Banner, the Officer assigned to Mr. Breckenridge and Mr. Feebe, walked across the room and stood in front of Jonathan endeavoring to upset him. David had told him this would happen and he was to look over the Lieutenant's shoulder at something over the Admiral's head.

"You claim to be a Midshipman assigned to the *Lancaster* to carry out some covert mission against the ship's company, am I correct"? he asked smirking at the rest of the court.

"Yes Sir."

"Who made this assignment and when?" he asked.

"Sir, William Lord Duffey – Chief of Naval affairs, Sir, on July 3rd of this year, Sir," Jonathan stated.

The Officers in the court were obviously impressed and quite taken aback by such an appointment. It was obvious Lt. Banner was feeling like he wanted to throw up, as he realized he might had bitten off more than he could chew. Failure winning this case could see his career ruined.

"Do you have any documentation of this appointment?"

"I was ordered to retain no identification for obvious reasons, Sir."

"Carry on Lieutenant – get on with the questioning we haven't all day," the Admiral urged.

"You came aboard the *Lancaster* posing as one of her powder boys, and assigned to the powder locker. Did you at any time discuss with the powder boys why you were there or what you were intending on doing? I'll put that another way. Did you at any time suggest or even hint that they were being abused or unduly punished? How did these allegations come to your attention? Did the boys complain or inform you of their punishments?" Banner questioned.

"Not at first, Sir. I found the Officers were very hard to please and were inclined to pick on certain of the boys time and time again. I wondered why. I also observed their physical appearance when they returned from their punishment. Some could hardly walk, and cried openly. Some carried huge bruises on their hind ends and back. It was only then that I asked why they were being punished. None would talk to me about it. I was still an outsider as far as they were concerned."

"That's quite a story. Exactly as we thought. These young hooligans are just trying to retaliate against the Officers who were only performing their duty by disciplining them," Banner went on.

"How did you find out about these abuses? No doubt the boys opened up finally to anyone who would go along with their absurd tale?" Banner asked.

Jonathan paused as he remembered the first time he had been punished.

"Mr. Feebe sent me to the gun deck to check on sand bags. Mr. Breckenridge noticed what I was doing and asked me why I was on deck. I explained I was following orders. He asked Mr. Feebe, who denied having given me the order. I was ordered to be whipped as punishment for disobedience. None of the others in the powder room asked me anything nor even spoke. This was the first time I had experienced the trumped up punishment."

"Refrain from assuming the charges were 'trumped up'. That is only your opinion," Mr. Banner smirked as he felt he had chalked one up for his clients.

"If no one talked to you, how is it that you have gathered this so called, concrete evidence, that they also experienced the same treatment – justified or otherwise?" Banner came on again staring directly into Jonathan's face only inches away.

"Powder boys are required to stay below deck unless authorized otherwise, or if there is an eminent battle approaching. Midshipman Roberts came to the powder room ordering me to report to Mr. Breckenridge in his cabin. I was hesitant at first because I knew it could be a hoax just to get me punished again. Mr. Roberts seemed to have been crying."

"Hold it right there. You don't know anything of the kind, so why make such remarks? All presumptions on your part. Sir, this is ample evidence that the boy Walters was about to disobey another order by his own admittance," Banner said, addressing the Admiral.

"Sir, I just wondered that's all. I didn't want to have another beating," Jonathan said. He was getting tired and hated having Mr. Banner breathing his smelly breath in his face.

"I presume you decided you had best take the chance and report to the First Officer. Isn't it true that when you saw the Officer he informed you that ship's crew were to obey orders without question and was just trying to help you? Is that not right and you turned on him with these lies?" Banner walked back to his seat.

"Is that true boy? Did Mr. Wright say those words to you?" the Admiral asked.

"Yes Sir, he did."

"There we are again, Sir. The little liar can't even keep his story straight!" Banner shouted.

Lt. Filmore stood up for the first time, beginning to wonder if perhaps there was truth to the boy's story and if he was on the winning side. It would certainly further his career to be successful in the courtroom. He would give it his best effort.

"Mr. Walters. Did anything else occur after you had been warned?"

"Yes Sir. He instructed me to take my clothes off, or I would be beaten as soon as I left his cabin. I obeyed and undressed."

"Are you saying you were naked?" Filmore questioned looking at the Admirals table. "Yes Sir."

"Why were you asked to undress? Did you know why?" Filmore asked.

"Sir!" Banner was on his feet again. "It is just hearsay. We don't have any proof that Mr. Wright gave any such order," Banner said getting red in the face.

"Mr. Wright will have his chance to testify in this matter," stated the Admiral. "Continue, Mr. Walters."

"He told me that if I did as I was told, I would not receive any more punishments and I could consider what he was going to do to me as punishment. I would not suffer or be bruised."

"Lies! Lies! Sir. We cannot listen to this! It ridicules the court," Banner shouted.

"Sit down, Mr. Banner. I will be the judge of what is contempt and what is not. Is that clear?" the Admiral warned.

"What was the punishment?" asked the Admiral looking very uncomfortable.

"He made me bend over his Sea Chest and then he entered me, Sir." Jonathan was starting to feel uneasy, and wished he could cry.

"Objection! His word against the Officers," bellowed Banner.

"It is just one witnesses testimony, Mr. Banner. The court will decide as to the allowability of the remark," the Admiral intervened.

"Do you know the meaning of buggery?" Filmore asked.

"Yes Sir. It is when someone does something bad to another person," Jonathan stated pointing to his rear end.

The court stirred at the revulsion of the boy's statement. *How could a twelve year old boy make up such a tale*? they wondered.

"Then what happened?" Filmore asked.

"Sir, I must protest. I am assured by Lt. Breckenridge that he did indeed have the boy strip but for the purposed of administering a paddling," Banner snorted, looking at the two accused Officers. He was not happy with the way things were going. Jonathan was not breaking under his pressure.

"Sit down, Mr. Banner!" the Admiral warned, slamming his hand against the desk. "You're clients will get their chance to tell their side of the story."

"Continue Jonathan," Lt. Filmore prompted.

"When he was finished he told me that if I wanted to stay in his good grace, and if I wanted to have the odd favor like extra rations, I was to take this new kind of punishment whenever he called me."

"How do you know other's were punished in this same manner?" asked Filmore.

"We all knew what was going to happen when one of us was called to the First's cabin."

"Stop it right there! You have no idea why the others went to the cabin. You told us yourself you never questioned or solicited any information from the boys," Banner shouted.

"Mr. Banner, I'm warning you for the last time! You had your chance to question the boy, now sit down and control yourself! Be quiet before I hold you in contempt!" barked the Admiral.

"Sir. After one of my sessions with Mr. Feebe, in the First's cabin, Mr. Breckenridge came in and did it to me, too. I was hurting terribly and wanted to scream, but I didn't. When I returned to the powder room the others asked me why I wasn't crying. They always came back crying. I told them it would take more than those two to make me cry."

"Did you ever cry?"

"Yes Sir, all the time after the others were asleep."

"You stated that the Midshipmen were involved in the same punishment. How do you know that?" Mr. Filmore asked.

"I had not been punished for over a week, when I was ordered by Mr. Feebe to the First's cabin. I had thought I had been lucky until then. When I arrived at the cabin, the door was slightly open and I heard a boy crying. I opened the door ever so slightly, and there was Mr. Feebe punishing Mr. Griffin. He was the youngest of the Midshipmen. I stepped back out of the way not wanting to be caught. Then I heard the paddle and the Midshipman was punished again for not having taken his punishment like a man. I heard the conversation, Sir," there was no turning back for Jonathan now. He knew if Mr. Breckenridge and Mr. Feebe were found not guilty, he would be hung for desertion and many other charges.

It was three o'clock and the Admiral complained that he had had enough of this very difficult and distasteful case for the day and adjourned the court. He ordered the prosecution to have ready additional witnesses if any were forth coming.

"Gentlemen, I forbid any Officer from having conversation with the Midshipman Jonathan Walters between hearings, is that clear?" the Admiral ordered, leaving the ship's cabin. It was hot and stuffy and everyone was happy to be free of the stuffy quarters where the court-martial was being conducted.

CHAPTER THIRTY-ONE

The Witness

"Are you telling me that both Mr. Breckenridge and Mr. Feebe were found aboard ship locked in the restraining cage? That is an absolute act of mutiny! Whoever is responsible will surely pay for this act of treachery," the Admiral said to his Flag Captain after being informed of the news.

"What in heaven's name is going on around here. Charges of abuse of powder boys and now this act of mutiny. I want answers, Captain, and I want them immediately," the Admiral shouted as he paced back and forth.

"Now we have this damnable court-martial. I wished I was anywhere but in this damnable command. A Command from Hell, I calls it," the Admiral continued to rave.

Jonathan sat in his room watching the door for word that he was to come for his breakfast. He was being well treated and this made him feel uneasy. He was not used to being treated as an Officer. He hoped David knew what he was doing. He thought of the relationship that had developed between himself and Kenneth. He wondered if it would ever be that he would one day be Kenneth's brother for real. So far the act was going well, and with each day passing he was feeling more certain of himself. He was distracted from his thoughts by a tapping on the window. It was Kenneth. He rushed to the window but couldn't get it unlocked. Kenneth had a message pressed up against the glass. Jonathan was so happy to see Kenneth he nearly cried. Kenneth too was happy to see his new brother.

> *Jonathan—Midshipman Charles is going to come forward as a witness right after you begin. The devil's teeth will break loose after that. Be prepared for whatever takes place and don't be afraid.*
>
> *You are winning,*
> *David*

Jonathan smiled as Kenneth waved good-bye and was gone.

* * * *

"All Rise! Admiral Sir Charles Willingham convening," the clerk shouted.

"Gentlemen, it has come to my attention that two Officers of the *Lancaster* were captured and placed in the ship's brig last night until they were found this early morning. Mutiny is afoot here and I shall get to the bottom of it. I have little doubt that the deserting Midshipmen and powder boys are responsible, heaven knows how they were able to carry out the deed," the Admiral stated, wiping his brow which was already wet from the heat.

"Sir," said Lt. Banner, "all we have heard so far is a lot of trumped up charges against two outstanding Officers, from only the mouth of a supposed spy from the Admiralty, and a boy at that. I would like to have all these charges and allegations dropped. The scandal and rumors are afoot which, I might suggest Sir, do not help our reputation in these waters. Furthermore, where are the other witnesses? Too frightened to come forth because of their lies, and because there are none? No one has seen the deserters except for this misfit posing as a Midshipman and one other.

Can they be produced? And if not, I wish to call for a dismissal of all charges," Lt. Banner addressed the Court in his most sarcastic yet eloquent manner.

"Lt. Filmore, what say you to the comments and the request by Lt. Banner?" the Admiral asked.

Jonathan looked around the cabin for Paul Charles who was going to testify, but couldn't spot him. This worried him terribly, but he worried more at the thought of the two Officers being present when other witnesses were going to testify.

"Sir Charles, I wish to introduce Midshipman Paul Charles of *HMS Lancaster*, Senior Midshipman. He will testify that he too had been abused and punished on false charges," Lt. Filmore announced to the shocked court. Everyone strained to get a view of the new witness.

Paul walked from the cabin door to the front where he stood erect, facing the Admiral. He was a good looking seventeen year-old and carried himself with confidence. He was sworn in by the secretary to tell the truth.

"Mr. Charles, you have taken a sworn oath that you are telling the truth when you say that you were mistreated by both of the Officers under investigation. Is that correct? And if so tell us in your own words the various occasions of such abuse," Filmore asked.

"Yes Sir. I was charged by Mr. Breckenridge for failing to carry out my duties as an Officer in the instruction of the Midshipmen. They were new and the systems were strange to them. They had trouble grasping the instruction. I was ordered to stand for punishment which was to be a caning. The crew will verify they witnessed my embarrassment and humiliation. Two Junior Midshipmen tried to come to my defense by informing the First that it was their fault in not having studied hard enough. They too were ordered to be caned for insubordination. Griffin and Scott were the other two. They took their punishment very badly."

"I was a few minutes late in my watch relief and I was ordered to be punished by caning. The First told me that I could escape the caning if I would attend him in his cabin. The punishment would be less humiliating and less painful. I reported to his cabin where he ordered me to undress and he did it to me. Mr. Feebe walked in to the cabin without knocking and was invited by Mr. Wright to punish me as well. There were several other occasions, Sir. I didn't mind so much for myself as I was older, but when the younger Midshipmen were punished in the same way, I couldn't bear it, but had no one to turn to," Paul Charles continued his damning testimony wiping his eyes.

"This went on for several months, with very few canings taking place but many of the other punishments. I was surprised one day when I was bringing a message to the First Officer to find Jonathan Walters coming out of the cabin. He wouldn't tell me what was wrong. It was then I found out that all the boys aboard were being punished by either one or both of the Officers."

"Jonathan came to me one day and said that he could not bear it any longer. We were going to be in port in a day or so, and he asked if we should get together and approach the Captain. Jonathan had no experience in such matters, at least so I thought, otherwise he wouldn't have made such a suggestion. I knew there was no way the Captain would side against his Officers, especially from the word of a Midshipman. We were without help, until the day following our arrival in port when we heard that Jonathan was missing."

"Two days later, Jonathan and another Midshipman came aboard and convinced us to join them in escaping the ship. We were afraid to, but what else were we to do? We couldn't continue being punished almost every day for things we had not done, and in such a way."

"We, along with the powder boys, escaped in two boats provided by Jonathan and his aide. We hid and hoped we could last until the ship set sail without us. We avoided the searching guards. We knew our lives would be worthless if we were caught, and we talked about killing ourselves rather than endure the two Officers treatment."

"Midshipman Charles, were you aware that Jonathan Walters was also a Midshipman and doing covert spying aboard *Lancaster*?" Banner asked.

"No Sir, he never mentioned it to me. I never found out until later."

"Where are the others, and are they willing to verify your accusations?" the Admiral asked in a kinder tone.

"They will testify, Sir, and are prepared to make themselves available if they are given protection from the two Officers or other crew members," Paul stated. He had come this far and there was no turning back now. He might die for the things he had just said.

"Sir! It is apparent there is a conspiracy amongst the Midshipmen and powder boys of the *Lancaster* to assassinate my clients," Mr. Banner said shaking. He was having a hard time with some of the details of the accusations.

"Mr. Banner. As I've told you before, the two Officers will have their opportunity to reply to the charges. I think we have heard enough for this morning. Break for lunch. We'll get back at one o'clock," the Admiral stated stretching himself as he whispered into his Flag Captains ear.

"I hate to say this without prejudice, but I'm inclined to believe the boys and their allegations. It appears we may have two scoundrels in our midst, but I defer judgment until we have heard from the other witnesses. I am appalled at the thought of what this will do to the Fleet's reputation," the Admiral whispered.

"Terrible business, Sir, terrible business," the Flag Captain commented.

CHAPTER THIRTY-TWO

Sir David

Jonathan paced the floor of the holding room wondering if he had spelled out clearly the terms of the witness protection plan David had worked out for the boys. He was afraid the Admiral might not have agreed to the terms of the testimonies. He had not actually heard the Admiral agree.

He wished he could talk to Paul Charles, but they were being held in separate rooms. He also wished he could talk to David and Kenneth. Talking to them and hearing their reassurance would help him in these very trying moments. He wondered whether he was going to be able to hold on, especially when the two Officers started to question him. That would be coming up after lunch. He was sure the two were all fired up and furious with what had taken place the night before. He wondered how it was that David and Kenneth were able to accomplish all they did and in such a short time? It was obvious they had to have had help from some members of the crew. He wondered who would have come to his rescue? He also worried about Remus's injuries at the hands of Mr. Feebe. Those two Officers deserved everything the court-martial could give them. They were evil and should not be allowed to live. He would be glad when all of this was behind him. He even dreamed of being able to continue his role as a Midshipman and really be a brother to Kenneth.

Jonathan recalled the first time he had met Kenneth and David. He remembered how they had taken him under their wings, provided food, a home, new clothes, and best of all their friendship. He recalled Mrs. Cassidy's motherly ministrations in caring for him as she had all the boys. He remembered how frightened he was when David outlined the plan for him to become a Midshipman, and he was certain he would never be able to fill the roll of an Officer. David had assured him that he made a fine Officer and was even surprised himself at how well he did. He particularly liked his attachment to Kenneth Walters who bore the same last name. Jonathan Walters and Kenneth Walters suddenly became brothers to all who knew them. Who was there to question the charade? David had certainly worked out a good plan to convince the court that he was indeed an Officer, having been sent to determine whether the mistreatment of the ship's boys was correct. No one could dispute his claim, thank goodness, at least not yet, and certainly not here.

A knock came at his door.

"Yes Sir?" Jonathan answered in a shaky voice. He had come to be suspect of everyone.

"Sir. You are to come for your meal after which I am to escort you to the court," the guard announced.

"Aren't you from the *Lancaster*? I know you don't I?" Jonathan asked trembling a bit as he wondered if the seaman was one of Lt. Breckenridge's men.

"Who assigned you the duty of escorting me to breakfast?" Jonathan asked fearing for his safety. He had been told to suspect everyone.

"Sir, it was the Admiral himself, Sir, he ain't takin' no chances of anyone meddling with you or Mr. Charles. The crew is right behind you, Mr. Walters. Bless you lad – you have more courage than all of us put together. We had no idea who you were. Our hats are off to you. Got a bit of news I'm sure you will wish to hear."

"The packet arrived this last evening bringing mail and news. The *GAZETTE* announced that his Majesty himself is placing a bloody Knighthood on his Lordship David Clements, the Earl. I don't figure anyone is surprised, eh? He will be the youngest ever to be Knighted. The paper says he was getting it for what he done in these here islands. I guess you know him. I hear tell he must be some kind of a miracle boy or something," the seamen said as he unlocked Jonathan's door and led him out into the hallway.

"What's your name please?" Jonathan asked.

"It's Farrel, Sir. Jimmy Farrel. I am chief gunner's mate on the *Lancaster*. I'm sorry, Sir, if I ordered you around when you were in the powder room, I had no idea who you was," he apologized.

"Jimmy it is alright and is forgotten. You were only doing your duty. At least you never hurt us," Jonathan said reassuringly.

"Thank you, Sir. I'll bet you wished the Earl was here during all of this. Seems no one has heard from him for some time now. They suspect he was ordered to sail on the *Margueta*. Even your brother doesn't know where he is," the guard Farrel said.

Jonathan was escorted to dinner by the guard. They seated him at a table with Paul, and the two boys leaned together in a quick conversation with a barely audible whisper to each other.

"Jonathan," said Paul, "are you alright? They are certainly treating us well. I haven't eaten this well since I left Mrs. Cassidy's home, and even then it wasn't this good. I don't think I'm supposed to talk to you, or you to me, but I just wondered if you had heard about Davey?" he said.

"Yes I've heard. It is indeed fantastic news. Davey deserves it, but I'll wager he won't be liking it,"

Jonathan answered, turning his attention back to the feast on his plate.

CHAPTER THIRTY-THREE

Midshipman Jonathan Walters

"Gentlemen, please rise. This court is now in session, with Admiral Sir Charles Willingham presiding." The clerk of the court was following procedures laid down for civil court cases, and Admiral Willingham obviously didn't approve, and let it be known in no uncertain terms.

"This is not a court in England, this is a Naval court-martial in the Caribbean," the Admiral admonished.

David, in hiding with the other Midshipmen and the powder boys, decided it would be too dangerous for the boys to appear before the court. He felt there would be retaliation against them for testifying against a fellow ships Officer, guilty or not. David was also concerned as to whether the boys would stand up to the cross examination of Lt. Banner. There was no question about the tack Banner was taking. He wanted to prove that the boys were trying to seek revenge against the Officers who had just been doing their duty in disciplining the boys for insubordination and other offenses. This was their way of getting even.

David was getting all his information from Jimmy the guard, who attended the court and would pass messages to David through Bos'n McClarity of the *Lancaster*. He was well informed and was laying his plan accordingly. Up until now, it appeared the Admiral and of course the other Officers, were leaning towards believing the boys' side of the story.

"I have a copy of the ship's log just presented to me, and it truly indicates that the boys had committed the offenses for which they were being punished. It is signed by the Captain himself," Lt. Banner said smugly.

"This only goes to substantiate the two Officers accused so unjustly, were only carrying out their duties in an official way. These two have conspired to bring false evidence to this Court. Why are there only the two of them? Where are the supposed others? I suggest, gentlemen, that the other boys are hiding, not from fear of the ships Officers, but by the coercion exerted by these two hooligans!" he completed his tirade grasping desperately at any opportunity to discredit the Midshipmen.

"Mr. Filmore, what say you to these counter charges? I am beginning to tire of all this testimony and wonder at the validity of their charges. How they could concoct a story so bizarre and terrible, I'll never know. We will take a recess for tea, then we'll continue. I would suggest Mr. Filmore, that you bring additional evidence forward or your two young men could be in very serious trouble, and the charges against the two Officers might well be dropped. It is, after all, two very junior Officer's words against two senior Officers," the Admiral warned impatiently.

"Sir, I have no further witnesses at this time. My case lies entirely on the testimony, under oath, of these two Officers and the findings of the Admiralty's own appointee," Mr. Filmore conceded.

"I'll not go over the statements made before our adjournment, you all will recall my remarks pertaining to Lt. Filmore's proposal, and he freely admits he has no further witnesses to call. I suggest then, there is no need to waste any more of this Court's time. If there are no further submissions, then I will discuss the case and will render a verdict immediately after the luncheon period."

Kenneth was starting to worry. Up until now it appeared they were winning and they were believed. He wondered what plan David might have in mind, and when it would be implemented? Kenneth was frightened.

Suddenly there was a commotion outside the cabin door and the guards were shouting and obviously holding back some intruders. Everyone in the court turned their eyes towards the door and were only able to hear a boys voice.

"Stand away, do you hear? Stand back I say!" David's voice rang out over the commotion. The guards stood back in dismay and awe at the young Midshipman. They had heard of the Earl's exploits and now here he was demanding entrance to the court-martial.

David entered the great cabin, followed by the Midshipmen and the powder boys. He walked between the chairs to stand before the Admiral, feeling quite sure of himself and committed to see it through.

"Sir. You called for further evidence regarding the disposition of the case against Mr. Breckenridge and Mr. Feebe. These fellows with me are prepared to cooberate the testimonies given by the two Midshipmen Charles and Walters. And Sir, if that is not sufficient, then I too will testify as to the abuse these Officers administered to all the ships boys including myself," David said looking the Admiral straight in the eye. The Court nearly collapsed at the news and of David's bold entrance.

"Sir David, we have not heard from you nor known of your whereabouts for sometime. I am greatly surprised and quite astonished that you have made an appearance at this time. I presume from your sudden arrival in this court that you have something to say pertaining to this court. Do you wish to make a statement, Sir David?" the Admiral questioned hesitantly, not sure which direction the Court was taking.

"I do, Sir. You may swear me in if you wish, however, I too wish to testify against the two Officers confirming my own personal abuse at the hands of the accused," David announced much to the excitement of his friends.

The Admiral spoke haltingly, choosing his words carefully. "The Court need not hear any further evidence. Your word is your bond, Sir David. This is certainly a fine way to perform your first act as a Knight of the Realm. My hearty congratulations on your appointment! I cannot recall anyone in history so young being Knighted. A great honor indeed," The Admiral continued uncomfortably, trying to form his next statement.

"In view of this overwhelming evidence against the Officers, without going into each individual boy's experience at their hands, I instruct the Court to find the Officers guilty. Sentencing will take place after lunch at 1400 hours," he concluded.

David made his way towards Kenneth, Jonathan, and Paul – each shaking hands with one another, trying to display professionalism and to hide their joy and excitement.

"Jonathan. You, my young friend, will now have to carry on in the roll we have placed you in. Both Kenneth and Paul feel that you have the brains and the skill to carry out your duties as a Midshipman." Jonathan smiled and could not hide the tears forming in his eyes.

"Sir David, you will join my staff and I at luncheon?" the Admiral prompted.

"Sir, if it is your pleasure, I would suggest that all the young men who have suffered so terribly at the hands of those two villains, be invited to attend. They have been through a great ordeal, not knowing if they were going to live or die. I would be most grateful for your act of hospitality," David nodded towards the other boys.

"Why certainly, Sir David. I would be honored to have all of you dine with me." He paused, "You have become such a fine young gentleman! I am sure your Father would be very proud of your performance and bravery today," the Admiral waved the boys into the cabin which had been cleared away and the tables reset for the meal.

CHAPTER THIRTY-FOUR

The Feast

The Admiral announced at the luncheon how delighted he was with the behavior and good manners of his guests, causing smiles to appear on the young faces.

"Sir. On behalf of myself, the other Midshipmen, and the powder boys, I would like to thank you for the sumptuous meal, the likes of which we have not seen for some time. We also wish to apologize for the embarrassment our actions may have caused the Navy and especially the Caribbean fleet. It was not our intentions to do so, but we had reached a point in our lives where death was welcomed rather than feared. His Lordship, the Earl of Windsor, and my best friend, showed us the way to overcome our fears and to remain faithful to the service while seeking justice. We owe him our lives." Kenneth finished his heartfelt expression of gratitude and resumed his seat.

"Well said, Mr. Walters. Indeed well said. My sentiments entirely. Perhaps all of this tragic nonsense will be a reminder to others who decide to prey on helpless young men in the service. I had thought of completing the Court this afternoon; however, The Duke of Windsor is arriving later today and I think it would be most fitting to have him in attendance to see justice at work within the Navy, and also to see his son as a fine Officer and a gentleman, who on many occasions, endangered his own life for the sake of those who depended on him."

The words shook David as he realized the time had come for he and his father to reconcile their differences once and for all. Kenneth and David exchanged looks.

The Admiral's Flag Captain stood. "With the Admiral's concurrence, I would like to propose a toast to Midshipman Sir David Clements, Earl of Windsor on behalf of us all," he said raising his glass. The guests stood and raised their glasses to the Earl who hung his head in sincere embarrassment. He did not enjoy the notoriety.

"Thank you very much. I do not deserve your compliments, as I was only doing my duty, as were all of us. May I propose a toast to our host, Admiral Sir Charles Willingham, with many thanks." Everyone stood and clinked their glasses. "Finally, I would like to propose a toast to my cohorts in all these adventures." Everyone chuckled. "The brothers, Kenneth and Jonathan Walters – my very best friends and accomplices. They are truly heroes," David concluded as he resumed his seat.

The Flag Captain suggested that the dining group be dismissed, and stood up to indicate luncheon was over. The guests filed out onto a bright shiny deck, where many of the crew stood about waiting to catch glimpses of the Midshipmen.

"Hurrah! Hurrah for the Lads!"

* * * *

The powder boys were reassigned to other vessels of the fleet, and reluctantly and emotionally said their good-byes to the Midshipmen who had saved their lives.

The *Lancaster* was put under the command of a new post Commander and given an entirely new slate of Officers.

CHAPTER THIRTY-FIVE

The Duke

The Admiral's Flag Captain paced back and forth in the *Emmejay's* main cabin impatiently awaiting the Earl's arrival.

"Drat the young people. They have no sense of time or responsibilities, it seems," he said to the ship's Commander.

David and Jonathan had been posted to serve on the *Emmejay* on her return convoy escort to England. The frigate had been in Guadalupe now for a fortnight and the crew was anxious to leave the heat of the Caribbean behind. Midshipman Kenneth Walters was assigned to the *Robin* as senior Midshipman and would also be on escort duties to the same convoy. David had asked that Jonathan Walters be assigned to the same ship as he as a personal favor. David had set his mind on making a Midshipman out of Jonathan no matter what. Having him aboard the same ship would help in his task. Jonathan was never happier, and performed his new duties flawlessly.

David arrived at the Captain's cabin knocking on the door.

"Enter," came the voice from within.

"Midshipman Clements reporting as ordered, Sir," David said, saluting and standing at attention.

"At ease David, er—I mean your Lordship. I bring a message from the Admiral requesting that you, along with Kenneth and Jonathan Walters, attend him in the Governor's residence this evening at 5 o'clock. Be on time. The Admiral felt that a special welcome should be provided for the arrival of the Duke of Windsor this afternoon. He felt certain you would appreciate seeing your father again. Be on time David, er—Clements, the Admiral does not appreciate tardiness," the Flag Captain ordered, dismissing the Midshipman with the nod of his head.

* * * *

"Pardon me, Sir," David said addressing the Master, "the time for me to meet again with my Father has arrived, and I do not know how I'm going to handle it. Have you any thoughts on the matter, Sir?" David asked.

"Davey—You are going to see a much different man from the one you knew when you departed England over a year ago. You have matured, you are a very experience and decorated Naval officer, and your Father will see someone he hardly knows. It will be up to you how you make your reunion – a pleasant occasion or an unpleasant continuation of your past differences. David, he is your Father, and he may not have changed on the outside, but I'm sure he has certainly changed on the inside. Give him some time to show you. Provide him with the opportunity he so much wishes for. Deep down laddie, I know you feel the same way but are afraid of what lies ahead for you both," the old Master said placing a hand on the Midshipman's shoulder.

"You must also remember that you have another family which loves you as well – the Walters. You have become very dear to them, especially since you saved Kenneth's life. I know you expect nothing, but nonetheless, how does anyone repay someone for the life of their child?" David shook hands with the Master and left to attend to the preparations for the reception. His thoughts were on what the Master had said to him. He trusted his friend and knew that he was right. The task still lay ahead and he wished he was in a scouting assignment rather than this pomp and circumstance situation.

Kenneth and Jonathan were busy putting their few possessions together for their departure to their assigned vessels. They were discussing the fact that the Admiral would be looking for someone to commend for both their actions, but they knew he would not discover who instigated the undercover investigation. It had been obvious to everyone they talked to that Jonathan would be highly regarded and complimented for his acts of heroism while suffering at the hands of the tyrants while he was supposedly carrying out his assignment aboard the *Lancaster*.

"Do you think I will be able to fill my roll as a Midshipman, Kenneth? I feel like I am pretending and that like a dream, I will wake up and find that it was just that. A dream. How are we going to explain things to your mother and father who do not know anything of me, let alone accept me as a member of the family?" he lamented sadly.

"Jonathan you are already accepted by your new family. They know all about you by now, and probably read about you in the *GAZETTE*. I must admit though, I wonder what the Admiral will say about Midshipman Jonathan Walters? Probably he will never realize the deception, your being a spy and all. I heard the Navy had received many letters from parents commending the service on its efforts to protect the young seamen aboard the ships."

"Jonathan—let me tell you something – you are my brother. We are both Midshipmen in his Majesty's Navy. You will conduct yourself as we have shown you. You will not, at any time, consider yourself less. I'm sure your new Mother and Father are very proud of their new son. I am proud of all you have been through Jonathan," Kenneth said embracing his new brother.

David arrived at the same moment, and could not help but feel an emotional tug at his heart at the happy show of affection. Both boys greeted David with a similar embrace.

"We must leave immediately for the reception. I was warned that we must be on time. We will go together, and Kenneth and Jonathan, I want you with me when I greet the Duke," David asked.

"He might just as well meet all his sons," David said trying to make light of his forthcoming ordeal. He had made up his mind that under no conditions was he returning to the family and the roll he would be required to play in it. He did not wish to be the Earl of Windsor. He was a King's Officer in the Royal Navy and had earned the right to be there.

CHAPTER THIRTY-SIX

The Reception

The three Midshipmen were sitting in an anti-room being briefed by the Flag Captain as to the protocol to be used at the reception.

"The Duke may be your Father, Mr. Clements, but he is still a representative of the King, and you are just an ordinary Midshipman serving in the Navy. Now then, the Admiral will be standing at the front of the dining hall in front of the head table. I will be standing at the end of the table with the three of you on my right. Mr. Clements, you will stand beside me, Mr. Walters you will be next to Clements, and Mr. Spy, you will stand next your brother," he said sarcastically enjoying the opportunity to order the Earl about and take a dig at Jonathan.

"The Duke will enter the dining room accompanied by several of His Majesty's dignitary's and representatives. There will be a reception line, through which he will pass, on his way to the Admiral's position. You will not look anywhere but straight ahead, do you understand me? If the Duke should speak with you, you will address him with 'Your Lordship'. You may speak freely, bearing in mind you are representing the Navy and are speaking to nobility."

David was shaking as he and the Midshipmen followed the Flag Captain into the dining room to take up their assigned positions. The moment they made their appearance, there was a tremendous round of applause and cries of "Hurrah!" from the gathered elite of Gaudalupe and many Naval guests who had been invited. The Admiral's entourage was completely overwhelmed by this spontaneous show of welcome and affection for the young Midshipmen. No more than the Flag Captain, who was almost beside himself that the protocol he had so carefully laid out for the ceremony had collapsed and he had no idea what to do about it.

With a great deal of uncertainty, he took his position, while the young Earl and two Walters formed beside him. They couldn't help but smile at the reception they were being afforded and were unsure what to do. They knew there could be no response, so they stood stiffly at attention. A trumpet blazed and the guests were shown through the main entrance. The Duke shook hands and greeted the various dignitaries as he walked the long distance to the front table all the while glancing towards the front to where he knew his son was standing.

David wanted to glance at the entering members of his father's reception committee, but knew he could not do so without being noticed. Kenneth was shaking as badly as David, knowing exactly how his friend was feeling and wondered how their reunion would go. Jonathan, on the other hand, was a perfect example of confidence and control as he watched the Duke nearing the front. After all, he had never met the Duke or any other members of nobility, so what was there to be afraid of?

The Flag Captain moved behind the Midshipmen to greet and salute the Duke, then turning around, he introduced the Admiral Sir Charles Willingham.

"A special thrill it is your Lordship to have you join us like this," the Admiral gushed.

The Flag Officer proceeded to introduce Jonathan Walters as the Naval Intelligence Officer who was responsible for uncovering evidence in the court-martial. Jonathan stretched his hand out to be warmly received by the Duke who congratulated him on his bravery.

"Your work of intelligence is most commendable in spite of your young age. I believe this to be the first occasion when such services have been initiated and with such a successful conclusion. It is no wonder your parents are so proud of you and your brother," the Duke remarked.

Jonathan was very moved and blushed at the compliment, wanting desperately to cry. He hoped the tear that had formed in the corner of his eye would go unnoticed. He longed to look at Kenneth and David.

"Your Lordship, this is Midshipman Kenneth Walters, often mentioned in the *GAZETTE* for his deeds of heroism."

"I am happy to meet you again, Kenneth. You have made quite a name for yourself, you and your brother. I might add, I have had several interesting and pleasant visits with your parents. They have every right to be proud of their sons. Your country, too, is very proud of you," the Duke concluded, as though he was reluctant to move to the next introduction.

"Your Lordship, Sir David Clements – Midshipman," the Flag introduced David. David stared straight ahead not daring to look into the eyes of his Father who he knew was focused on him. David responded formally to his Father's outstretched hand trying desperately to hide the tears that were forming.

"David, my son, you have distinguished yourself admirably and there are no words to describe how very proud I am of you, as indeed is your country and the Navy."

"Thank you, Sir," David replied, trying to maintain his composure and preventing the Duke from noticing the glistening in his eyes. David felt Kenneth's finger touch his own in a reassuring way.

The Duke took his place at the head of the table, along with the Governor of the Island and other dignitaries. The Midshipmen were ushered to a table at the rear of the dining hall, behind the ship's and other Military Officers. David was relieved that he would not be close to his father although he wanted desperately to converse with him, but not under these circumstances.

David was no longer upset or angry with his father, he was more frightened of having to lose his new life in the Navy and having to resume the life of a nobleman.

I can never go back to that, he thought.

Kenneth read his thoughts and gave him a gentle nudge. Jonathan who was seated across from David, caught the movement and smiled. The Midshipmen of the *Lancaster* were also among those Officers sitting close to them. They would all be seeing one another tomorrow in court for the sentencing of Breckenridge and Feebe.

"This court is now in session, Sir Charles Willoughby presiding. All rise," the Clerk ordered. The Duke had been ushered to a seat beside the Admiral and watched as the proceedings got under way. The accused Officers were brought in and stood facing the Admiral. Two swords laying on the table were pointed at each of the defendants, who had no doubt as to the outcome of the verdict. Both had been informed that hanging would be too good for them.

"Lt. Breckenridge, I have been led to believe that you started your career of these despicable acts while serving under First Officer Wright, now deceased. You were grossly misguided in your part in these affairs, however that was of your own choosing, and now you will pay for your misdeeds. Having been found guilty, you will be discharged from the service with dishonor, and will spend the rest of your natural days on the penal island of Australia." Breckenridge turned pale, crumpled to the deck, and had to be bodily removed from the court.

Lt. Feebe knew his fate would be similar to that of Breckenridge and shook as he prepared himself for a his punishment.

"Lt. Feebe you are being dishonorably discharged and will serve 10 years in a prison. You will further experience a flogging in the number of thirty-six strokes for each year of your sentence. You may well wish you were dead. If anyone has anything further to add to these proceedings, please let them be heard or I shall declare this court adjourned," the Admiral said as he began to stand.

The Midshipmen looked at one another smiling, for they had won and would no longer suffer under the two tyrants.

"Sir, if I may," the Duke stood up and faced the rank of young Midshipmen seated before him. He was having difficulty composing himself and often was forced to wipe the corner of his eyes.

"I am pleased that our justice system, whether it be in the services of the Navy or on the land, serves us well. I detest the actions of the two Officers, and my heart goes out to my son and the young men who suffered at the hands of these Officers." He wiped his eyes again. "It is not difficult to realize their anguish with no one to turn to. May we never see the likes of this again. Thank you, Sir Charles, for your forthright dealing of this matter. I shall see to it that His Majesty is made aware of your actions," the Duke said resuming his seat. David and his Father stared at each other until the court was dismissed and they were ushered onto deck.

The Officers who had served on the court-martial were rowed back to their respective vessels, which made immediate preparations for final departure. David and Jonathan were amongst the first to return to the *Emmejay* after having said their farewells to Kenneth. They knew it would only be a few weeks before they would all be together again.

CHAPTER THIRTY-SEVEN

Old Terros

David and Jonathan were standing at the entrance way as the Officers and senior crew members were coming aboard. The Bos'n came out of the line and approached the two Midshipmen.

"Sir, I heard there were people looking for you ashore. I told them you had already returned to ship and would not be returning ashore as the ship was sailing at sunrise," he said, doffing his cap.

"David—er, Sir. It was your Father looking for you. I am sorry I get carried away sometimes and I forget to pay my proper respects," Jonathan said apologizing for his familiarity.

"When you and I are alone Jonathan, calling me David will be fine," David smiled. He was happy at how quickly the boy was adjusting to life as an Officer rather than a lowly powder boy. He wondered if the ruse regarding Jonathan being a spy for the Naval Chief and a Midshipman would ever be discovered. He reasoned that most Officers would accept the story as fact, not wanting to question their peers, or being thought stupid for not knowing what was going on in their own commands. Others would be rushing forth to take credit for the idea of an undercover agency. David was pleased that Jonathan was taking advantage of the opportunity presented him and not letting him down.

"Well, if it isn't the scalawag himself, Sir David. How are you Davey and how did you make out with your Father? I'm sure t'was an ordeal and that's not half," the Master joked. He was still David's father image and mentor.

"It went better than I thought, although neither of us had more than a word together. Just as well, but I did feel a bit of sadness for him. I am his only heir, and I guess my actions could have been warmer. I will make it up to him one day, all things being as they should be and I am still alive," the young Earl answered.

David had coached Jonathan on every aspect of standing a watch. Up until now, the Midshipman was only allowed to stand a watch while in port, and this was his first official watch.

David was certain the boy would manage. He had adapted well to his new roll as an Officer and realized he must learn to accept the responsibilities that went with it. Jonathan was bright and would have no problem learning.

The following morning, the ship raised anchor and slowly made her way out of the harbor on a slight easterly breeze. Not the best for making a dignified departure. Sails flapped and men cursed, as the *Emmejay* gingerly threaded her way through the anchored ships. The convoy had gathered the previous evening and were all on station when the *Emmejay, Lancaster,* and the sloop of war, *Robin*, arrived to begin their escort duties. It would be a long voyage and they would still be in danger until they headed out into the Atlantic. They had several hundred islands to negotiate yet, if they intended keeping to the sheltered inland waters.

Jonathan and David spent some time imagining what Kenneth would be doing at any given moment, and both expressed their deep feeling of loneliness for their friend.

"Do you really think Kenneth wants me as his brother? After all we really don't know who I am do we?" Jonathan asked.

"Jonathan, I get quite annoyed when you keep bringing it up. I know you feel you are in a dream, but it has actually happened and I am just as sure that Kenneth's parents are going to accept you as their son. After all, you are a Walters you know," David smiled as he assured the boy once again.

"Considering all we have been through, we cannot let anything change between us and our friendship. Until I met Kenneth, I never had a friend, let alone anyone I could confide in. I have never been happier than when I am in his company and now Jonathan, in yours," David said smiling happily at the Midshipman. David's kind warm words brought a smile and a small tear to the boy's eyes.

"One problem though as I see it, you are really much too handsome to be a Walters family remember," David joked. Jonathan's face went sad for a moment until he realized David was joshing him a bit, and he broke into a bout of laughter.

"Best not say that in front of Kenneth," Jonathan chuckled.

The weather continued bright and very warm, and the convoy was keeping up however slowly and on station. Now and again they could see the *Robin* darting in and out of the stragglers and then disappearing behind some of the islands. The *Emmejay* plowed on relentlessly, leading her flock and maintaining a constant vigil for any strange shipping activity.

The convoy had now reached their turning point where they would be leaving the islands and heading into the open Atlantic and ultimately home. They were well up the American coast and the French would not suspect them to be so far north. The route would be a much longer voyage but a safer one, especially when one realized how much havoc the French raiders had created for the British convoys.

David wondered what his father was doing at the time. He could see the *Corsair*, the packet vessel his father was traveling on, two miles astern. The farther north they went, the heavier the seas and the winds strummed mightily upon the shrouds and stays of the ships as they plowed through the deep troughs.

All ships seemed to be maintaining station in spite of the bad weather, at least all except the *Robin*.

"We should have spotted the *Robin* by now Sir," David remarked to the First Officer.

"You're right, Mr Clements, and that is what has been bothering me. The islands are some fifteen miles astern, so she should have broken out and on her way to join us by now," the First added, taking the telescope from David and searching the rear of the convoy. The *Corsair* was one of the last vessels in the convoy and would be the first to signal their sighting of the *Robin* but still no flags.

"Two sails Ho! On the Port Quarter!" the lookout shouted from atop the nest.

"What ships if you please?" the First shouted.

"Can't tell, but I think one is the *Corsair.* The other is approaching from the west of her. Most likely the *Robin*," the look out replied.

"Better damned well be the *Robin* or the Captain will have their heads for dinner," the First commented. The entire quarter deck were now focused on the horizon where they expected the ships to appear.

"Sail Ho!" the lookout announced.

"Where away, where away?" the Commander shouted through his bull horn.

"She appears to be on the same course as the other two vessels, but closing on them fast," came the lookout's reply.

"Signal all vessels that I want identification of those ships approaching the *Corsair*," the Commander shouted to the signal Midshipman. Luckily it wasn't Jonathan. He was learning quickly, but not so as to be up to read them all so soon.

"I don't like this one bit! I think something is afoul back there and I intend to come about," the Commander informed the First.

"Prepare to come about and we'll run down on them. Signal the convoy to follow the *Lancaster*. We will rejoin as soon as we have straightened out these tag alongs," he said.

The crew scurried about their duties securing lines that would enable the huge vessel to turn on her heels and return to close the other vessels to the south. The sails and yards snapped and banged as they took up their new wind direction. It was ear shattering, but the wind was now on their stern quarter. Their closing speed would be much greater.

The *Emmejay* was burying her bows in huge waves as her stern was lifted high by the following seas, causing Officers and crew alike to run for shelter avoiding the huge spumes of water cascading down on them.

"Hello deck. Sir, it looks as though there is a strange vessel – like a small frigate overtaking the *Corsair*, and breaking from one of those islands is the *Robin*. They appear to be on a course to intercept," the lookout shouted.

The *Emmejay* was close enough now to be able to see the sails of the other vessels. The Commander, with telescope in hand, climbed the starboard shrouds heading for the nest. He had to see for himself. There was no question in his mind that the *Robin* would be no match for the stranger, and could be snuffed out like a mouse to an eagle.

"She is the French frigate *Bonaventure*. Make signal to *Robin* to disengage. They are not to intercept," the Commander shouted to the deck.

"Great Scott! The *Corsair* is firing her port gun. The other vessel is returning fire and they must almost be on a collision course. What in the damnable hell is *Robin* doing? She is heading down towards the enemy, putting herself between the *Corsair* and the privateer. Did *Robin* acknowledge?" the Commander shouted to the deck as he slid down the rat lines.

"No sir. They are hardly in sight, Sir," the Midshipman shouted. David and Jonathan stood watching, waiting for the Commander to give the order to stand to the guns. Jonathan was shaking from the excitement as he and David awaited orders.

"Robin is firing as she is running down. She has put herself between the *Corsair* and the other ship," the lookout repeated his information. The *Emmejay* was close enough to see what was taking place and it was obvious the privateer had spotted her as she bore down on them.

In the meantime the *Robin* was firing her starboard guns into the bow of the attacker. The privateer decided to call off the engagement but not before cutting towards the *Robin* and colliding amidships, crushing her under her bows.

"David's heart stopped as he watched the tangled mess that was once the *Robin* and the privateer endeavoring to untangle themselves. The privateer was unable to get free and the *Emmejay* drove down onto them less that three cables away.

"Fire as your guns bear, I want that ship! Prepare to board when we come around, there is not a second to spare. Watch for *Robin's* crew in the water!" the Commander ordered.

The *Robin* capsized and rolled under the larger ship until she broke her back and drifted alongside. David's concern for Kenneth knew no bounds as he tried to keep his mind on the gun crew under his command. They were not firing as they were on the opposite side of the engagement. He could only watch and hopefully pray for his friend.

The *Emmejay* swung around and smashed into the side of the privateer. There was no battle. The privateer could go nowhere with the wreckage of the *Robin* still attached. David was ordered to stand down his gun crew and board and secure the enemy crew.

"Jonathan, search the water for Kenneth," David shouted. He was torn between carrying out his orders to secure the prisoners and searching for Kenneth.

"I have to see to the prisoners, please find him," David pleaded. Jonathan's first show of emotion came in the form of tears that were blinding him from viewing the wreckage clearly.

I must take myself in hand, he thought. He would not be able to help Kenneth this way.

"I see him! I see Him!" Jonathan shouted as he dove over the ship's side into the floating wreckage. Kenneth was swimming towards Jonathan when from atop the privateer, a splinter from a yard slammed down into the water where he was swimming.

"Kenneth! Kenneth!" Jonathan screamed as he looked around him for help. He dove under the spar and was almost swept under by the forward momentum of the ships and the huge entanglement of ropes and other gear. He found Kenneth again and pulled him to the surface. There was large gash on the side of his neck. Jonathan steadied himself on a floating spar while he ripped Kenneth's shirt to make a bandage in an attempt to stop the bleeding. He fought to keep Kenneth's head above the water as two seamen from the *Emmejay* swam to assist him.

The *Emmejay* was alongside the swimmers and ropes were quickly sent over the side. Other *Robin* survivors were being helped aboard. Jonathan was literally thrown to the waiting hands on the deck while the two swimmers gently handed Kenneth to those on the deck. The bandage about his neck was soaking red with blood. Jonathan knelt beside Kenneth, tears streaming down his cheeks as he screamed for someone to help. Several crew were standing about the Midshipman when the Commander, followed by the ship's doctor, shouted for them to get back to their stations.

"Step aside Mr. Walters and let the doctor through. You cannot help your brother." It was at that point the Commander saw the crumpled body of Kenneth laying just inside the entry port. He knelt down beside him as the doctor gravely shook his head.

"I'm afraid we have lost the lad. He lost too much blood to survive. The shock alone would have killed him," the doctor stated sadly.

"I'm sorry, lad, there was nothing anyone could have done," the doctor said slowly standing and patting Jonathan on the shoulder.

David, who had been completing his duties aboard the privateer, jumped to the *Emmejay's* deck and ran to where the men were gathered. Jonathan was cradling Kenneth's head in his lap and weeping openly, rocking slowly back and forth. He stared at David as though willing him to save their friend.

The Commander put his hand on David's shoulder in an attempt to comfort the Earl. David could not control his emotions and tears rolled down his cheeks onto his best friend.

"Back to your work everyone, we will split the crew and take the prize to join the rest of the squadron. We are too far north to think of returning to port. Mr. Carruthers, you, Mr. Clements, and Mr. Walters will take over the prize. Please make preparations for the Midshipman's burial," the Commander ordered, leaving immediately for his cabin. He was visibly moved by the tragic scene that had unfolded aboard his ship. He realized the closeness of the three boys and it touched his heart. He decided that removing the lads from the *Emmejay* would be the best thing for the boy's welfare under the circumstances.

The Master gently lifted Jonathan from the body of his brother.

"Come, laddies. It is time to leave Kenneth to his Maker, and for us to make him proud that we knew him. David my heart goes out to you, laddie. If there was anyway I could bring him back I would gladly give my life to do so. Jonathan, your brother is very proud of your actions and of you. He will always be with you, son," the old Master consoled, as he led the boys away.

Kenneth's body was removed and prepared for burial. Many men had died in the engagement, but only Kenneth's body had been retrieved.

"Sir David—" the Master said using the Earl's formal title. "Would you care to speak over Kenneth before he is committed? I can arrange it I'm sure," he offered as he and the Midshipmen walked to the forward deck.

"I hope I will be up to it, Sir," David replied, the tears still coursing their way down his cheeks. David made no attempt to hide his sorrow. He may have been a Knight of the Realm, a King's Officer, and young man about to take official duties as an Officer aboard a King's prize, but he was still a boy and his heart was tearing it's way out of his body. He had never known such heartfelt sorrow or sadness in his life. It was beyond comprehension.

Their walk forward was met with words of encouragement and sympathy from various members of the crew who had know the boys over the past year.

"Mr. Clements, I have taken the liberty of having the Midshipman's body placed aboard the prize where you and the lad's brother may bury him in private. We must part and rejoin the convoy and continue as quickly as possible. My heartfelt condolences," the Commander offered. David thanked the Commander and saluted as he and Jonathan followed Mr. Carruthers to the prize. To their new ship.

The ships parted, and the *Emmejay* was soon beating to join the convoy. The prize followed quickly on her heels. She was a lively frigate of French design but was slightly smaller than the *Emmejay*.

* * * *

The burial ceremony was underway with the crew members gathered to honor the death of a shipmate. David walked slowly and stood beside the body of his friend.

"Dear Lord, I do not know why you have taken my best friend from me, or why Jonathan must suffer at this loss, but I know it is part of your overall plan. But for you I would have perished a thousand times over. But for you I would never have had a friend in the world. But for you I would not have a family. Jonathan and I grieve for our brother, his parents, and for ourselves. I know your spirit will always be with us Kenneth. I will require your strength, and the knowledge you will always be with me in my heart to continue to guide me. Goodbye dearest friend." David sobbed openly, nodded, and Kenneth's body slid down the plank and into the depths. The crew departed most with tears in their weather beaten eyes at David's heart wrenching eulogy.

Jonathan and David talked for a time, then returned to the quarter deck to assume their duties. This would be an entirely new commission for the young Midshipmen, and they would need to work in order to help them recover from their terrible loss.

The convoy made good speed and a month later was approaching England and their home port of Portsmouth. Jonathan and David talked at great length about how they were going to handle themselves when it came time to meet the Walters family, their family.

"David, how will we ever tell them of Kenneth? What if they will hate me and blame me? What if they do not want me as their son?" Jonathan questioned over and over again hoping and seeking for David's reassurance.

"Jonathan, they will know. We will not have to tell them – they will know. Kenneth told me his mother knew every time he was in danger and prayed for him. They will know, and we must do everything to make it easier for them. Jonathan, you are their son now, I can promise you that. You and I both have a family. It is important that we conduct ourselves as Officers and try to control our feelings. What am I saying? I am going to breakdown and cry forever," David said tears forming once again, his voice quivering with each word.

"I loved him too, you know," Jonathan said looking deep into David's saddened face.

* * * *

When a prize is sailed into the harbor, the entire town turns out to welcome the crews and see for themselves the captured vessel, and this day was no exception. The Naval ships anchored, and it was in short order that the bum boats were striking out to the ships to ferry the Officers and whatever crew were allowed ashore.

The Midshipmen waited as long as they could before disembarking into the boats. David carried Kenneth's few personal possessions in a small satchel as they climbed up the stairs to the shore. The crowds poured in around the young men, most recognizing the Earl. Some members of the crew of the *Emmejay* assisted the young men to move through the anxious and happy crowds. David spotted the coach and Mr. Walters standing on the upper deck waving frantically to get their attention. He waved, and with Jonathan in tow, made his way to the coach. Mrs. Walters stood by the coach as her husband and their sons rushed to David.

Mr. Walters stopped short of the boys as he realized his son was not with them. The sadness told the story as he looked into David's tear filled eyes. Jonathan hung back not knowing what to do or say. He wanted to run and never look back, his grief was so overwhelming. To look at Kenneth's family standing speechless, as Mr. Walters came and took David's hand and turned to Jonathan.

"Welcome home, my son."

Mrs. Walters was drying the tears in her eyes as the boys came to the coach and embraced her. She took her handkerchief and dabbed the tears from Jonathan's cheeks. She held his face in her hands.

"Welcome home Jonathan. We have waited a long time for you to arrive. Your brother spoke so highly of you that we felt your presence miles away. David. Dear Sweet David. Come, we will go home now and seek comfort from the Lord. Into the coach all of you," Mrs. Walters ordered.

The trip to the horse change and rest haven was a quiet one, with hardly a word being spoken. Mr. Walters was sitting with the coachman, while Kenneth's younger brothers rode on the luggage rack. The same luggage rack David and Kenneth had ridden on in a previous happy time.

"Welcome home, Jonathan Walters, your parents will be thrilled at your return, and Sir David, you won't fool us this time, we know you now and of your exploits. It is indeed happy we are to be honored by your presence at our lowly Inn. Mr. and Mrs. Walters and boys, news travels fast and we are saddened at the loss of wee Kenneth. He gave his life for his country and will be long remembered here," the Inn Keeper spoke as he greeted the passengers.

The family and David acknowledged the sincere words of the Inn Keeper and were ready for the refreshments that were served. It was obvious there had been special preparations made for their arrival. There were many towns folk gathered outside talking quietly amongst themselves. They too seemed to be sharing the family's grief.

Mrs. Walters could not take her eyes off her new son. He was handsome and his bright blue eyes, reddened by tears, were like windows to his bright mind and to his soul. She thought, *How very much like Kenneth he is.*

CHAPTER THIRTY-EIGHT

Another Prize

The newspapers carried the story of the *Robin's* demise and the subsequent capture of the enemy frigate. An article appeared on the front page of the *GAZETTE*.

Local family loses son in courageous attempt to save the merchant ship, 'Island Packet', which was carrying among its passengers, the Duke of Windsor. The Duke's Son, Sir David Clements, was serving aboard the Naval Vessel, 'Emmejay', which ultimately captured the privateer frigate and brought the prize to England. A sad memorial to those who mourn the dead and injured.

Mrs. Walters seemed to be coping better than the others as she went about her household duties, busying herself to block out her grief. She spent considerable time with Jonathan asking about his family and where he came from. Jonathan was provided with some new clothing that had been purchased for Kenneth. She always saw to it that Kenneth had a new outfit on his return so he could shed his Naval uniform for a short time and return to normal life.

Jonathan and David shared a bed, and both would eventually begin talking about Kenneth between bouts of tears. It had been three weeks since Kenneth's passing but their grief remained.

"Jonathan, do you know what happened out there when the *Robin* sank?" David asked.

"I know one thing for certain, David, the *Robin* sacrificed herself for the *Island Packet* and your Father. It was obvious that was her intention," he said looking at David for a reaction.

"You are right, of course, that is exactly what happened. My father owes his life to the *Robin* and to Kenneth. At one time I would have thought it a most unfair trade. My Father is aching terribly over my plight and I wish I could perhaps restore our relationship. I think he has grown up and matured as a Father, as I think I have as his son," David explained.

"Go to sleep my boys. It is long days you are having and you need your sleep. Who knows when you will be given your sea orders," Mrs. Walters said, as she sat on the edge of the bed beside Jonathan. She took his face in her hands and kissed his forehead.

"Kenneth chose his new brother well, Jonathan. You are a credit to us all and to the Navy," she said. Jonathan hugged her trying not to cry anymore. He was exhausted from all the tears he had shed. He had never known such a deep sense of belonging. Thanks to David and Kenneth, he had come a long way. He knew his life would be very different from what he was used to and he liked it very much.

"As for you, your Royal Highness, my little Davey, you will always be my son. My spirit and Kenneth's will follow you no matter where you go or what you do. You have two guardian angels to watch over you. Tomorrow your Father will arrive and I expect you to be charitable towards him and open your heart as I know you are able. The past is past Davey. What is done is done, and we must now turn to the future for what lies ahead. David, there is only unhappiness in store for you if you do not forgive. I have loved you as I have all my sons. You belong to us, and I will never desert you, nor will any of your family. Give your Father a chance to make amends for things of the past, Davey, show him that you are a mature young man capable of stretching out your hand to him. It has not been easy for your Father, knowing how you felt about him. He seeks your forgiveness, Davey, and I expect nothing less from you. Do you hear me David?" Mrs. Walters said, taking David into her arms. Words failed David as he hung his head on Mrs. Walter's shoulder, weeping silently remembering his lost friend and thinking about his Father. She was indeed the Mother he never had. She strengthened him and he resolved to let the past fall away, although the thoughts of meeting the Duke frightened him even more than battle.

The family was up early, completing the preparations for the arrival of the Duke. Neighbors for miles around had come to pay their respects to the grieving parents and to the Earl. David had begged the Walters family not to use his title at anytime, and they were used to calling him Davey as their brother had.

The Duke's coach arrived at noon, and the family were gathered on the front drive to welcome David's father. Mrs. Walters stood between David and Jonathan, her arms over their shoulders offering them her strength, while Mr. Walters and the other sons stood immediately behind their mother.

The Duke climbed down from the coach hesitantly, not knowing what he should do. It was like meeting a stranger, someone he hardly knew. David was new. He had changed and the Duke, more than anyone else, was aware of it. Mrs. Walters stepped forward, curtsied, and took the Duke's hand.

"Mrs. Walters, please accept my humblest condolences over the loss of your very brave son. I indeed owe my life to him and the other members of the *Robin's* crew," the Duke said, as he bowed kissing her hand.

She presented Jonathan to the Duke, who grasped his hand tightly, and patted the boy's shoulder.

"It is a great pleasure and honor to meet you again, Jonathan," he said, and with tears in his eyes trying not to let it be seen, he turned to his son.

"David. I am happy to welcome you home safely. I wish to express my deepest and sincere sympathy to you over the loss of your friend. I know how it feels to have lost someone you love so much." The Duke held out his hand and David stepped forward and embraced his father. They stood together oblivious of those around them as tears were wept in complete disregard for the attending family and friends. The Duke stepped back and looked David in the face, his hands resting on David's shoulders.

"Well, young man, you have brought great honor and respect to the house of Windsor. I can only hope that the Windsor name can live up to your expectations of it. The King himself has sent his condolences, and Kenneth is to be honored at a special ceremony where he will be awarded the Kings Cross for Gallantry. Little reward for the ultimate sacrifice. David, I know also the sacrifice the *Robin* made to save the *Island Packet*."

"I do not expect you to return to Windsor, however, I do wish to extend an invitation to you and your family, to visit our home any time they choose." He looked around at the Walters and exclaimed, "You are all welcome at anytime. Please consider it your home as well." He turned to Mrs. Walters and took her by the hands.

"Mrs. Walters. My heartfelt thanks for all you have done for David. He is a man for it all. You are the Mother he never knew. I should dearly have liked to have met Kenneth again. It surely took a special boy to befriend my son so closely."

"And to you 'Mr. Spy', Jonathan Walters, the King has also some special awards for your outstanding service." He smiled at Jonathan's awkwardness.

"May I sit and join you for a short time?" the Duke asked. "I have many things to discuss with you all, and especially my son, who I feel is now back in my life."

"We are deeply honored, your Grace," Mr. Walters offered, as he guided the family to the rear of the yard. The yard where David, Kenneth, and his brothers frolicked so many months ago.

"Your Lordship, thank you for your kind words. I know you are speaking from your heart, and we appreciate your concern for us. It will take time to heal the sorrow we feel at Kenneth's loss. We all loved our young sailor. I feel Kenneth is with us at this very moment in Jonathan." She struggled to hold back her tears. David and Jonathan, as though of like minds, walked beside her, holding her hands.

The rest of the afternoon was of stories of Naval battles and of heroic deeds as quoted in the *GAZETTE*. All Naval happenings were always written up in the *GAZETTE*, including the latest happenings to the *Emmejay* and the Earl of Windsor. As much as the authorities tried to squash the stories of the young spy working within the Internal Affairs Department of the Navy, the word was out, and the outstanding performance of the young man was mentioned in the communication.

The Naval paper went on to praise the Walter's family for having two outstanding Midshipmen who performed above and beyond what was required of Officers so young.

Orders arrived three days later ordering David and Jonathan to appear before a Royal Awards Ceremony. The orders were not received too enthusiastically; however, the second order assigning both Midshipmen to the *Emmejay* was a delight, and they were only too happy to be getting away from all the pomp and fuss. They regretted having to leave their family, but duty called and it would be good to resume their responsibilities aboard their old ship. They knew they would have to contend with all of the old memories as well.

* * * *

"Midshipman Sir David Clements, Earl of Windsor, it is my pleasure to present you with the King's Cross for Outstanding Gallantry and

Performance of Duty," the King said as he presented the medal and shook David's hand.

"Midshipman Jonathan Walters. I am delighted to present you with the Medal of St. George, and also the King's Cross for Outstanding Gallantry in the line of duty."

Jonathan's face remained beet red as he tried to avoid all the well wishers and those who had come to get a glimpse of Britain's youngest undercover agent. David's father mingled freely in the crowd of dignitaries and boasted of his son's achievements.

"Mrs. Walters, I would like you to accept this medal on behalf of your son, Midshipman Kenneth Walters. I am proud to present this posthumous King's Cross for Bravery and Devotion to Duty in memory of a fine example of Britain's young Navy men."

The ceremonies were concluded and the boys were only too happy to take their leave. David's father came to visit one more time and Father and son talked long into the evening.

* * * *

"Boys, it is time for bed and prayers. You have to leave early in the morning. Your Father will be up to take you. I will be busy here," Mrs. Walters ordered her brood. David knew Mrs. Walters could not stand to watch he and Jonathan depart, and chose to stay home where she could busy herself with other matters. Her heart would be with her boys and her Kenneth.

The following morning saw the family enroute to the docks amid cheers and shouts of good wishes to the boys. They stood awkwardly at the dockside with their packs ready to descend the stairs to the awaiting tender. David's Father arrived as though on cue and shook his son's hand.

"Davey, you have made us all so very proud, words cannot convey the feeling I have for you at this time. God speed and return home soon," the Duke said, then turned to Jonathan.

"And you, too, Master Walters, 'Mr. Spy', if I may make light of this happening. Come home safely both of you."

The Duke stood aside as Mr. Walters approached and hugged each boy in turn, trying to keep the tears from showing, all the while smiling at David.

"I will always find it very difficult to allow my boys to depart for the seas. I truly cannot help myself. I love you both so much and expect you to look out for each other as Kenneth was want you to do. Bless you my sons," Mr. Walters said, as he turned away allowing the boys to descend. The gathered onlookers were moved and some wept openly, as the boys waved their good-byes and descended the stairs to the waiting tender.

"Hold on there. Hold on there, I say," a voice shouted over the noisy crowd of well wishers. A man in the uniform of the King's guards was making his way to the steps, waving a document of some sort in his hand.

"Midshipman Walters Sir, I have a change of orders for you. Please come up where I might deliver them to you in person," the guardsman shouted. David and Jonathan looked at each other and both climbed the stairway to the quay. The crowd was moving in closer so as to pick up any morsels of information regarding the change of events.

The Duke and Mr. Walters, hearing the commotion, returned to discover what all was taking place. David and Jonathan were talking to the Guardsman when their fathers came forward.

"What seems to be the matter David? What's going on here?" the Duke asked.

David was peering over Jonathan's shoulder reading the orders Jonathan had just been handed. Mr. Walters stood beside his son, waiting to hear what was transpiring.

Jonathan looked bewildered and questioningly at David. "Father, I have been ordered to Naval Headquarters. I am to see Lord Aubrey," Jonathan said, turning to Mr. Walters.

David reread the orders and spoke to his father about the contents. There was no explanation, just the change of orders. He was informed he would not be sailing on the *Emmejay* as originally ordered. David looked shocked as many things ran through his mind regarding why Jonathan had been summoned to Admiralty House.

Had someone discovered the truth about Jonathan? Was he appearing before the Admiral to divulge his true identity? All these questions ran through David's mind as he thought of what Jonathan must be feeling and thinking.

"Jonathan, I am sure it is going to be fine. I feel certain this has nothing to do with other matters. I haven't the foggiest notion what can be afoot, but I am sure you will hold your head high and proudly – regardless. You have a large family who are behind you in everything you do, so don't be upset. We will be apart for awhile but our courses will cross again soon I am sure," David said reassuring Jonathan. "You are Midshipman Jonathan Walters, an Officer in His Majesty's Navy. Never forget that, regardless of anything else." David was trying, with great difficulty, to keep his eyes dry. He didn't want to lose another friend. Jonathan too was trying to keep from shaking, and stood beside his father as though drawing strength from him. He and David shook hands and briefly embraced, neither boy concerned about the onlookers who were still gathered.

The guard advised Jonathan that he had been assigned the duty of accompanying him to Naval Headquarters. Mr. Walters was told that he could accompany Jonathan, as he didn't expect the meeting would be a long one and that he would be able to return home. The Duke realized he would not get any additional information from the guard and ordered his carriage to take him to Sussex Street. He would talk to the Prime Minister directly. He gave Jonathan a reassuring pat on the shoulder and shook his hand.

"I won't be far away Jonathan. I will find out what it is all about. Mr. Walters, I will get to the bottom of this matter and advise you directly," the Duke informed them.

He waved one last good-bye to his son standing in the stern sheets of the departing tender. He knew the anguish David must be feeling not knowing why the change in orders and not having Jonathan as a shipmate.

CHAPTER THIRTY-NINE

The Assignment

Jonathan and his father were shown into a large anti-room where clerks and other Naval personnel were either waiting for an audience with the Admiral, or performing duties within the office. The guard, who had accompanied the Midshipman, spoke briefly to the Lieutenant who was obviously in charge of the Admiralty office.

Officers were pacing the floor, while others sat pensively staring at documents or reading the *GAZETTE*. It was a busy place. The Officers looked at Jonathan wondering what earthly business could this young Midshipman have with the Admiral.

There were no vacant spaces on the wooden benches lining the walls, so Jonathan and his father stood by the front entranceway waiting for instructions. Jonathan felt some comfort as he looked up and moved against his father. The uncertainty of his future and many other dreadful things were going through his mind, preventing Jonathan from relaxing. The threat prevailed that he might lose all that he had gained including his new mother and father and his best friend, the Earl.

He had been through many difficult times in his young life but this seemed to be one of the most stressful he could remember. He wished that he and his Father could just leave, but then the Navy would call that desertion.

"Midshipman Walters, the Admiral will see you now," the Lieutenant called. The room became filled with noisy jabbering Officers wanting to know what could be so important that a young Midshipman would take priority over them, some of which were Flag Officers and Captains. Jonathan felt completely intimidated as he followed the Officer into the large office. The Admiral sat in an overstuffed chair, which gave him a position of looking down on his visitors. It was even more so for Jonathan who stood alone in front of the Lord Master himself.

"Midshipman Jonathan Walters, Sir," the Lieutenant announced. Jonathan remembered to salute smartly and wait to be seated.

"Ah yes, come in young man and you may be seated. Take that chair over by the window and I will join you," the Admiral said as he moved his bulk from his desk chair to another plush chair opposite Jonathan.

"I am sorry to have to change your orders Mr. Walters, I think I will call you Jonathan. Something terrible has happened and I am going to have to call on your services to investigate. Let me tell you what it is you are to do. I will give you your written orders when we are finished." Jonathan heaved a huge sigh of relief as he realized he was not being questioned about his true identity. He moved to the edge of his seat so as not to miss a single word of the conversation.

"Young man, I did not have the opportunity to meet you at your investiture, but I have read and heard of your exploits, along with the Earl of Windsor, and I am greatly impressed. It does truly bother me that we must involve anyone so young. However, your experience seems to indicate you are quite capable of handling yourself and the matters we have at hand. You are probably the only one who will be the least suspected."

"I realize in your line of service, you have been in several theaters of operations, however I do not believe you have been involved with the Mediterranean Fleet. I will explain what has developed in that area and why we require you to move into that location. Gibraltar to be exact."

The Admiral continued, with a distressed expression upon his face as he glanced around the room, assuring himself they were alone. "We have reports that some of our vessels have been put into Gibraltar with crew so undernourished and virtually starving they could not perform their duties. Walking skeletons so to speak. Ships logs show no such problems, but we have it on good authority that Marines have had to intervene to maintain order aboard two of our frigates – the *Courageous*, under the command of Captain Roger Smeel, and the *Endeavor*, commanded by Captain Joseph Kleeprite. Both Officers have unblemished records. They are attached to Rear Admiral Sir Charles Tupper. This is not the first such reporting to come to our attention. Starving men will do most anything to keep alive. It is said that stores have been broken into regardless of the serious consequences. Crew have been hung or severely punished. Several have died from starvation and their beatings. Everyone we interview regarding the troubles are close-mouthed about everything. The ship's Officers have been threatened with contempt charges if they fail to identify the problems. Close knit squadron to be sure. There is something tragically wrong and as there is no Officer who will come forth and as we cannot even question the crew, we plan to insert you into the crew of the *Courageous*. Fortunately, you are not known in those waters and as this has just been brought to our attention, we felt we should act on it immediately before anyone becomes the wiser. I don't think there is any threat to your safety, Jonathan, but we have established a contact Officer in Gibraltar who will provide you with whatever support you may require. He'll keep us informed of anything you might uncover. We must act promptly as you know that Mutiny is a terrible thing. A huge festering wound ready to erupt and destroy. I hope you are able to handle this affair as successfully as you handled the *Lancaster* shame," the Admiral said. Jonathan wished he felt as sure of himself as the Admiral seemed to be.

"Sir?" Jonathan asked, "Will you give me the name of my contact Officer I am to meet?"

"I cannot do that at the moment, Jonathan, however he will make himself known to you at an appropriate time."

"I have had your orders written in such a way that no one will be able to identify you. We have masked a story for you which you will use when taking your duties on board *Courageous*. It will not be particularly easy for you, young man, but then you are accustomed to living below standards in your role as a powder boy, eh? Perhaps you will find untapped sources of information from that quarter." The Admiral stood, extending his hand to Jonathan.

"The best of luck to you, boy, and we trust this venture will be successful. Here are your orders. Do not open them in the presence of anyone, not even my own staff or anyone of higher rank." With that, the Admiral handed Jonathan a sealed envelope, which Jonathan promptly placed in the breast pocket of his coat.

The Admiral summoned his Lieutenant to enter and usher Jonathan into the anti-room. It was not until Jonathan entered the anti-room that the waiting Officers noticed the ribbon of the King's Cross on his uniform, and became aware of the importance of the

Midshipman and who he really was. They stood agog, wondering what had transpired in the Admiral's office with the young notorious member of the Navy. The guard, who had been waiting patiently for Jonathan to reappear, had obviously been instructed to whisk the Midshipman out of the Admiralty offices before he could be questioned by any of the inquisitive Officers.

Jonathan went to his father holding his hand out to shake but changed his mind. He was overcome with happiness at now having someone to come home to and who cared what happened to him. He held his arms out to be embraced. His smile left no doubt in his father's mind that all was well as they bade farewell. Jonathan, still looking back at his parent, walked with the guard.

He followed the guard down the long staircase and through the main hallway to a waiting carriage. He was dying for the opportunity to open his orders, but had been instructed they not be opened until he was well away from the offices and alone. Jonathan eyed the guard carefully and decided he would wait until he was alone before he opened his orders. The excitement was overpowering as the Midshipman felt the bulky package inside his jacket.

"Do we have much further to go?" he asked.

"Not far now. I was instructed to bring you to Chatham, the port chandlery. Can't imagine why they would want you let out in this part of the port. A mite dangerous sometimes. Officers are not welcome, that's a certainty," the guard replied looking out the windows at the passing warehouses.

"Can I ask you what is so damnably important that you rate a special carriage with escort? Who are you anyway?" the guard looked questioningly at Jonathan.

"I'm just a Junior Officer. I am to receive orders from the main chandlery office, that's all I know," Jonathan answered. He didn't want this conversation to proceed any further. The carriage ride continued until he felt the driver pull up on the horses.

"All right Mr. Walters, here we are and out you get. Good luck and remember what I said about being careful," the guard warned again.

The carriage drew away leaving Jonathan alone outside the large warehouse. He could see *Courageous* swinging gently at her anchorage. She was a beautiful ship and looked to be fresh with new paint, making her appear like she was new right out of Chatham Yard. He also observed that she was larger than most frigates, and he counted the gun ports on each side, confirming his observations. He reasoned she would carry a crew of at least 240 men and boys, including the Marines. He felt a degree of pride in knowing he was being attached to this great ship.

"Hold up there boy. What is you business at Chatham? Don't you know how dangerous it is for a young man like you to be wandering about the yards unescorted? To what ship are you attached and why is it you are here in this area? Speak up lad, or I'll report you to your Captain," the gruff old man took hold of Jonathan by his jacket collar.

"Sir, I was ordered here. I have no idea why I am here I have not read my orders as yet," Jonathan explained trying to release himself from the old man's grip.

"And where might these orders be may I ask?"

"They are still sealed in my inner pocket. I am to open them in private when I arrived here."

"Well then, let's get them open and see what this is all about, eh?" the man ordered.

"I am not allowed to open them in the presence of anyone," Jonathan said, gripping his jacket tighter about him.

"You may rest assured that I am a man to be trusted as I also act as Constable and Stores Advisor here at the port. My name is Joseph Blount, and everyone hereabouts knows not to fool with me," he said reaching for Jonathan and his sealed orders.

He seized Jonathan about the neck and removed the pouch from his inner pocket and commenced removing the seal.

Jonathan was frantic and demanded the envelope be returned to him immediately. This only got him a cuff on the side of the head knocking him to the ground.

"Something special to be in these orders is there?" he grumbled as he read the orders.

"There ain't nothing in this package but your orders to report to *Courageous*. Why would the Admiral be involved in a gutter snipe of a Midshipman like you that he would give you special orders?"

"Well, Mr. Walters welcome to the *Courageous*, a great ship, but you'll rue the day you ever heard of her – you and the rest of the crew aboard."

Mr. Blount gave the orders back to Jonathan and instructed him where he might catch a ride on one of the hoys moving supplies to the ship.

Jonathan made his way to the loading docks and watched while huge stores were being assigned to the *Courageous* and loaded onto the waiting barges. He noted the huge crates and barrels stacked along the dock marked for his ship. Two barges were loading the supplies and were just about ready to pull away for the *Courageous*. Jonathan approached the barge man if he might be ferried to the ship.

"That barge over there is for your ship, this one ain't going there," the bargeman advised. Jonathan wondered where this barge was going, as it was loaded with supplies from the stockpiles designated for *Courageous*.

Well, this is something to remember, Jonathan thought. He wondered at the Admiral's words and felt that this was somehow part of the problem. He climbed up on top of the supplies and opened his orders. Sure enough the orders simply ordered him to report aboard. There had to be more. He turned the papers over several times examining them for any other notes or messages. The paper felt extremely heavy for regular dispatch paper. Examining the paper closer, he noted a small piece of the paper edge had split and appeared as though two sheets of paper had been pasted together. He slowly pulled the sheets apart, glancing over his shoulder every now and again to make certain he was alone. No one would be able to read over his shoulder, sitting on top of the supplies as he was.

> *A precautionary measure, Mr. Walters, in the event someone became too inquisitive about your orders. If you are reading this, then you have discovered our scheme to keep the information contained here-in, secret. Read them then destroy them. Your contact in Gibraltar is a man called Kipp. That is all you need to know at the present time, other than keeping your eyes and ears open. You may pass on any information you might find important to Mr. Kipp. You are one of four Midshipmen aboard Courageous and unfortunately the youngest and most junior. I am sure you will handle yourself in an appropriate manner.*
>
> *Signed simply,*
> *Vincent*

Jonathan took the two papers one of which he rewrapped in its pouch. This was the document ordering him to the ship. The other he determined he would have to disposed of some way or another time. He couldn't have the paper discovered floating in the harbor.

"Midshipman Jonathan Walters reporting for duty, Sir," he addressed the Officer of the watch.

"Your orders, Mr. Walters," he asked. Jonathan reached into his pocket and produced the envelope containing his orders. The Officer scanned the paper and ordered him to follow one of the waiting Midshipmen to his berth. One, who appeared the older of the three Midshipmen, stepped forward and motioned for Jonathan to follow him. The eyes of the other Officers and Midshipmen followed Jonathan's retreating figure. He could feel their eyes upon him and he had a feeling that they suspected him of something. He couldn't quite put his finger on it, but as he followed the Senior forward to the Midshipmen's berths, he realized he was just imagining things. He hoped his appearance or attitude wasn't giving him away. He wondered how he would handle that if such were the case.

"What ship you from Walters?" the Senior asked bluntly.

"The *Lancaster*,—er—I mean the *Emmejay*, Sir," he said realizing he was not supposed to mention

Lancaster at any time. This was going to be harder than he realized, trying to remember what he said and who he said it to. *I could easily trip myself up or get caught if I'm not careful*, he thought to himself.

"What do you know about *Lancaster*?" the Senior asked staring Jonathan down.

"Nothing, Sir, only that she is attached to the Caribbean Fleet, Sir," he replied, sensing the burning eyes of the Midshipman drilling into him.

"Why then did you say the *Lancaster*? Of the hundreds of ships why did you say the *Lancaster*?" he persisted.

"No reason, Sir. I heard the name mentioned aboard the packet I traveled from London on. I never heard why they were talking about her, just heard her name, that's all," Jonathan said nonchalantly, hoping he had dispelled any further questioning. He knew he had to be convincing and stared directly at the Midshipman eye to eye.

The Senior looked back at him, then shrugged his shoulders and continued, "I am the Senior on this ship and you will answer to me. Cause any problems for me and the other Mids and you'll be very sorry. Do you understand Midshipman Walters?" he smirked as he departed the berths. "Oh yes, report to Midshipman Roberts when you have stowed your gear."

Jonathan startled at the name Roberts. Surely it wasn't the same Midshipman from *Lancaster*, the one he helped rescue. He climbed the stairs to the deck and found himself surrounded by the other Mids. His heart nearly stopped as he recognized Chris Roberts. Chris also recognized Jonathan but covered the moment by ordering Jonathan to follow him to the forward anchor windlass.

"You trollops get about your business! You'll have plenty to do before we sail – now away at it," the First Officer shouted at the Midshipmen.

Looking about to see if anyone was within earshot, Chris whispered, "Jonathan what are you doing aboard the *Courageous*? I never thought I would ever see you again. I have to tell you it is with a great deal of joy I welcome you! Jonathan, I think I know why you are here. I swear I shall never disclose your identity to anyone." Chris pretended to be busy while talking and make it appear as he was instructing Jonathan in rules of the ship. "I have only been aboard two months, and already I can tell you there is good reason to hate this ship. That's why I know, Jonathan, and if I can ever be of any assistance to you, you have only but ask. You saved my life.

You, Davey, and Kenneth," Chris said as he made some minor adjustments to the blocks hanging from the mast ring.

Jonathan breathed a sigh of relief. "Chris you do not know how happy I am to see a friendly face. I sense things are not right aboard this ship just by the feel of her. I beg you never to show any signs of recognition or over-familiarity. These people will be on their guard, I assure you. Any outward sign of trouble means the end not only for me but, perhaps even you, my friend. If there truly is any wrong doing aboard this ship, then you can be sure their cover-ups will be well planned out. Is it general knowledge you are from the *Lancaster*?" Jonathan asked.

"Yes Sir, it is. They often ply me with questions. I have tried to make out that I had little to do with any of it until the mess was over with. I don't think they accept that explanation. I can't figure out why they would suspect me of being involved, but then anyone on the *Lancaster* was involved, especially us. By the way, Jonathan, you will learn, as I have, to hate the senior Midshipman Albrecht. Hans is a German and a hate filled person. Watch him Jonathan." Chris looked over his shoulder to see if anyone was watching. "I have to go now. Pull three crewmen from the forward guns and have them assist you sorting these new blocks by size. They are too heavy for you, Jonathan. I was saddened by the news of Kenneth's passing. He was my friend, too. Can you tell me where Davey is?" Chris asked, as he made to depart.

"He's aboard *Emmejay*.

"I hear rumors than *Emmejay* is joining the Mediterranean Fleet. She will be Sir Charles Tupper's flag ship," Chris advised excitedly. Jonathan could hardly believe the news and prayed that it was true.

Someone began approaching the boys from behind.

"Well, Mr. Junior Midshipman—whatever your name is, ain't you about to make some orders boy?" one burly seaman said sarcastically.

"My name is Jonathan Walters."

"You going to take my name and write me up for somethin'?" he continued, hate written all over his face. "In case you're thinkin' about it, my name's Paxton. P-A-X-T-O-N."

Two other seamen joined their mate looking defiantly at Jonathan.

"It was not my intention to issue any orders. I was about to ask for some assistance in lifting these heavy blocks. I am afraid I'm too small and you could probably lift me and those blocks all together," Jonathan smiled, hoping they would accept his explanation.

They stared at the boy, and walked over to where the blocks had been laid out, and began lifting them to their allotted positions on the mast ring and on the shroud plates. Jonathan smiled as he attempted to lift one of the smaller blocks. The burly seaman picked the block and Jonathan up and set them on the gunwale. Jonathan was embarrassed and looked about to see if any of the Officers had seen the action. To his relief, the Officers were aft and had not observed.

"Don't ever do that again Paxton. You will get us both punished. Please, I want to be friends, not a bully."

Paxton paused wondering if he had heard correctly. *This is an Officer talking, and one of the new Midshipmen at that?* He'd never been treated kindly by an Officer before.

"Yes Sir!" Paxton replied. "My sincere regrets at my behavior. I just thought you was just like all the others. We ain't used to being treated special like. Some of us will do anything to get off this ship. Sir, watch yourself. The others will not take kindly to anyone who jaws with the likes of us," Paxton turned and continued moving the blocks.

"Thank you Paxton," Jonathan said, walking aft to the quarter deck, his assignment completed. He was more perplexed now than ever. The men appeared to be melnourished and close to starving and they hated the ship. He had an ill feeling about the ship and her Officers he had met so far. There was trouble here and the Admiral had been right to suspect so. He would have to be doubly careful.

CHAPTER FORTY

Mister Spy

"Mr. Walters!" the Senior shouted. "Get down below and assist the Purser. He has an inventory to carry out and it has to be done immediately, and no lolly-gagging, you mind?"

"Yes Sir," Jonathan answered, realizing he had just been afforded an opportunity to observe first hand what was taking place with the ship's supplies. He had been aboard five hours and was getting hungry. He was hoping the watch change would take place soon and he would be allowed to eat.

He went below and made his way towards the forward storage holds. "About time someone came to give me a hand. Took your sweet, bloody time getting here, I'll wager," the Purser scolded, as he handed Jonathan a stores list for checking.

"You just write if you can, what I tells you, and no mistaken what you write or I'll paddle your backside understand?" he ordered.

Jonathan took the sheets, and with the pen in one hand, he set the ink jar down on a crate.

The Purser continued his counting and occasionally looked at Jonathan to make certain he was noting his counts.

"Dried apples," he called, "seven and a half head." Jonathan was surprised at the count as he counted only four.

"Sir should that not be four?" he asked.

The Purser walked over to Jonathan pretending to look at the inventory sheets, and without warning, fisted Jonathan on the side of the head which laid him on the deck.

"Now my lad, let that be a lesson to yee. You mind what I tell you and nothing more. You write and I count, do I make myself clear? Next time I'll have you up to the mast and see how that feels. A mite more painful than the belt I just give yah," he warned as he walked back to continue his counting.

Jonathan now knew how the stores were being counted, and how they were made to read the same as what was laid aboard from the warehouse. The ship was selling off stores before they were even loaded.

That would mean that the ship would be short provisions for the next cruise. The men would be on short rations almost immediately. Here was a blatant act of sabotage, and it was exactly as the Admiral had suggested. Now that he knew how it was being done, he had to somehow get word to his contact as quickly as possible before the ship set sail. He wiped the blood from his cut lip on his sleeve and continued writing as more and more miscounts were reported as inventory.

"Well my lad, you do neat work, and very clean at that. Keep it up and you might become an Officer one day. Try another stunt like you tried to pull earlier with me, and you'll rue the day you ever met Joel Krippet, you hear?" he warned, taking the inventory count from Jonathan and leaving the hold.

Jonathan could only report on those miscounts he had written and wondered how much more had been done before he came on the scene. He also wondered at the deep trouble he was finding himself in. He had not met his contact person, so had no idea who to look for or even where. He was on board now, and there was no way he was going to be able to leave.

Even if I did know who I am to contact, how would I ever get word off the boat? What if I were caught? He put the thought out of his mind and climbed the stairs to the deck.

"Mr. Walters, you are to accompany the Purser ashore on the next tender. He will have orders for you," Chris ordered, not showing any signs of recognition. This was as they had arranged their relationship.

Jonathan realized that he had to pen a note of some kind for someone. This would be his only opportunity to get any word ashore. He heard the ship was pulling anchor at noon. In two hours, he would be away. He dare not desert even if he had the opportunity. He knew the Admiral could only help him if he were there in person.

The Purser ordered Jonathan to get the inventory listings and pen, and meet him at the entry port. Jonathan went down the stairs and entered the Captains quarters after knocking and making certain the Captain was not in there. He retrieved the lists and pen and searched frantically for something on which he could write a message.

What am I going to say? he questioned himself. He decided he would have to leave a scrolled message on a crate. Very few could read, so he felt it would probably go unnoticed by the rank and file stevedores loading and unloading ships.

The Purser, along with several seamen including Paxton, were rowed across to the warehouse jetty. They were required to assist in moving supplies and ammunition which included armament, mainly cannon balls and powder. Jonathan accompanied the Purser as they walked between huge bins containing the ammunition from the warehouse's magazine. Once again he was surprised to see that the entire supply was labeled for the *Courageous*; however, the Purser only took half of the allotment. The seamen did not seem to take notice, or if they did, made no mention. The Purser would have seen they were harshly dealt with.

Paxton asked if the entire supply was to be loaded, and was told they were loaded and this was for their next trip. The seamen had loaded all there was to be loaded and were climbing aboard the cargo barge. Jonathan looked at Paxton, who winked and turn away quickly.

Could Paxton be my contact? he wondered. *Surely not.*

As they were rowing away, Jonathan watched as a dray wagon and a team of horses pulled up to the supply bins and commenced loading supplies and armament from the *Courageous'* supplies. He noticed, also, that Paxton too was watching the shore activities. He would never be able to approach Paxton. He would simply have to bide his time until he was contacted. Those were the Admiral's orders, but he took some consolation in knowing, or rather hoping, he was not alone. Two days later, the *Courageous* was making good headway along the night towards the open waters of the Mediterranean. The moderate winds were warm and sailing was pleasant. Jonathan was assigned to the First Officer's watch along with another Midshipman. He thanked his lucky stars he had studied the signals, under David's tutoring, and had become quite adept at reading and sending messages.

"You had best watch yourself, Mr. Walters. The First is a very intolerant Officer who does not accept slip shod work. Keep on top of your assignments and you might survive, become sloppy and you will soon regret it," the older boy commented, providing a warning for Jonathan. The boy was about three years older, maybe sixteen or seventeen. He was tall and lanky with a face full of pimples.

"How long have you been on *Courageous*?" Jonathan asked.

"None of your bloody business, and I would suggest you not ask questions about anyone or anything," the Midshipman said, walking off. Jonathan wished he could be on a watch with Chris, at least he would have someone to converse with.

He was getting hungry and wondered when he would be called to mess. No one else seemed to be moving and his watch was almost finished. He decided he could last a while longer.

The watch changed and he watched the other Officers and the Midshipman to see what they would do and decided to follow suit. The Midshipman returned to his berth and Jonathan followed. Chris was not there, having reported for the next watch.

It wasn't long before a seaman came to their berth and handed each a piece of biscuit and a cup of water. Jonathan looked to see if there was more coming and then savagely began devouring his biscuit.

So this is what is happening, he thought. The men were on half rations and even less, and were expected to survive and fight on an empty stomach. No wonder the crew looked so thin and motley. *'Dangerous grounds for a mutiny'*, he remembered, the Admiral's words ringing in his ears. He wished he could write some of his observations down on a slate or somewhere, as he might not remember them all when they were needed. *How am I ever going to survive this? How long will the Admiral going to make me suffer in this investigation?*

He was passing by the open skylight of the Captain's cabin and overheard him complaining, "I wish there was more gun powder for my customers, and why isn't my meal on time?" *So*, David thought, *the Captain was sure eating well enough.*

Three weeks went by and conditions were slowly worsening. He was feeling ill and even faint at times. He drank as much water as he could, but the biscuits just swelled in his belly making him suffer from stomach cramps. He noticed he was not the only one who was suffering.

The punishment list was a lengthy one and growing each day as men faltered in the performance of their work. They were weak from hunger. Jonathan found it was all he could do to keep from falling asleep while on watch he was so hungry and tired, a result of the slow starvation. He decided to have a look at the stores hold himself to see how much had been depleted since their departure.

He pondered what punishment he might suffer at the hands of the Purser if he found him searching. He would be accused of stealing and that could mean hanging or at the least a terrible beating. He had to have some idea, so when his watch changed, instead of returning to his berth, he walked past his berth and proceeded towards the water barrels and the food stores. He was surprised to see the stores were almost depleted. He also noticed several of the boxes had been opened and left in that condition. Someone had been pilfering stores.

He made a hasty retreat away from the hold and to his berth. He lay awake for sometime, trying to wish away his hunger and get his mind off of food by wondering where David was at this moment. *Perhaps he was even in the Mediterranean already.*

His thoughts turned to home and his new parents, and he smiled in spite of his hunger at the thought that he belonged to someone who cared for him. Perhaps that was the only hope he would have to sustain him on this mission.

"Sail Ho!" the look-out cried, and everyone looked toward the direction he was pointing. From the deck there was nothing to see, but the Second Officer was sent aloft to identify the sighting.

"A Spaniard, Sir—small frigate I would say," the Second Officer confirmed as he slithered down the rat lines to the deck. "He isn't changing course, Sir. I suspect he is going to seek us out by the course he is steering," he volunteered.

Jonathan heard the call to battle stations, and hurriedly rushed to the deck. The Spaniard was closer and he could see her gun ports open. There was going to be a battle and he was afraid.

"Starboard battery ready," the First Officer shouted, as the gun crews loaded and made ready their guns. The powder boys staggered under their heavy loads as they carried powder below decks to the guns, while some were required to sand the decks behind each gun in order to prevent fires. He couldn't help but remember his days in the powder room. He could sympathize with the boys and wondered if they were as hungry as he. He reflected on how it was that he was here in the first place.

Oh yes, he was an undercover agent for the Admiralty, he remembered, his thoughts growing dimmer as the hunger became only a slight tightness in his belly.

CHAPTER FORTY-ONE

The Battle

Jonathan stared at the oncoming Frigate as she jockeyed for the wind gauge. As inexperienced as he was, he could tell the enemy vessel was going to take the advantage and *Courageous* was going to have a major battle on her hands, in spite of the fact she was the larger of the two vessels.

He watched the powder boys struggling with their heavy bags of powder. This was the first time he had seen them above decks as they were always kept below decks. *How he had hated that existence,* he thought, remembering his time in the powder room. The boys were skin and bone. He knew he had lost weight on the meager rations he had been on, and it was apparent these youngsters were in deplorable shape and much worse off than himself. He turned his back on the scene as the Bos'n's rattan struck one of the stumbling boys. Everyone aboard seemed to be living in fear of the vicious and cruel Bos'n.

The first shells to be fired came from the *LaCorosa*. She was bearing down on the *Courageous* as she moved to bring her guns to bear. As *Courageous* turned, so turned the *LaCorosa*, as she out maneuvered the British vessel. The First Officer was screaming for the Bos'n to get his men working faster or he would hang every last one of them. The men, as far as Jonathan could see, were almost on their last legs. They were as bad off as the powder boys and the tasks of manhandling the heaving lines was more than they were able to do.

The yards were slow in coming around, and the *Courageous* was taking hits into her stern with several rounds making it through the sails, potting them with huge black scars. Luckily, there was not sufficient wind to rent the sails into shreds, so the ship was able to maintain control, albeit unable to turn inside the enemy.

The enemy frigate reversed course and suddenly came up from astern, and as her guns came to bear on the *Courageous'* starboard stern quarter, they fired and pounded the British guns before they could fire. Minor explosions were occurring as fires set off bags of powder. The starboard guns began firing as the enemy vessel came alongside, destroying everything in their path. Jonathan was on the port side, supposedly in control of the forward guns, and the stench of gun powder was nauseating. He heard men screaming and running in all directions. Everything was in complete disarray as the Captain stood by the opposite railing of the ship, screaming orders to his First Officer.

"What in God's Truth are these men doing? Why are they floundering? We are going to be blasted out of the water if we can't control these men," he shouted. With that, he and the First Officer ran down to the deck waving their swords threatening the men with death. Men were falling everywhere. Grape shot at such close quarters was tearing the *Courageous* to pieces before she could do any real damage to the *LaCorosa.* The enemy vessel stayed on the starboard side inching closer for a boarding.

The two ships crashed together and the Captain screamed for the men to ward off the attackers. It was obvious from where Jonathan stood, his ship was lost. The only fighting was being done by the Officers, until finally they were dispatched by the overwhelming enemy seamen. Jonathan stood with his dirk in his hand, knowing he stood no chance at all against the boarders. He looked to the quarter deck for a sign of surrender but none was forthcoming. The Captain and most of the Officers were dead. He could taste the bitter salt from his tears as he knew he was about to die, and there was nothing he could do stop it.

The enemy Officers came aboard to access their prize and determine what to do with the prisoners. Jonathan was now a prisoner of war, and he had heard the Spaniards hardly ever took any prisoners. He was summoned to the forward gun position where several of the seamen were cowering. The men were physically too weak to have done anything to protect themselves.

"You!—Yes you, young Officer. Come this way if you please," a young Officer beckoned him to follow, his heavy Spanish accent made his attempt at English only partially understandable. Jonathan stepped over fallen shipmates, Midshipmen, and powder boys alike. He felt he was about to be sick. Body parts lay everywhere. Men were moaning and writhing in pain waiting for help. There would be no need for a doctor. Each was heaved overboard. Regardless of the injured or dying, everyone was forced over the side with a gaping cutlass wound to add to their indignity.

"How long have you been at sea? Where did you sail from? How many ships?" the Officer questioned.

"We have been out three weeks, Sir." He thought being respectful might keep him and some of the others alive. He wasn't prepared to antagonize his captors. "We departed Gibraltar alone," he said. He was not going to tell them anything more than what they specifically asked for.

"You tell untruths," the Officer shouted into Jonathan's face, as he smashed his hand across Jonathan's mouth, sending him sprawling to the deck. "We have examined the ship and its stores and there is nothing left. Your stores are depleted. Gone. You have also been in battle, no? Your powder is almost gone, no? What is your reasoning for these lies,

Senor? You have been to sea for many months, judging from your supplies. Now are you going to tell the truth or shall we cut off your fingers one at a time, eh?"

With that he struck Jonathan another blow with the back of his hand, knocking him down once again. He was lifted to his feet only to be punched again sending him to the deck. Two sound kicks to his stomach left Jonathan gasping for air. He was certain he was going to die. He looked around but there were none of his crew to be seen. He was once again raised from the deck and found his feet being tied together. The rope tied to his feet, he was thrown over the lower yard arm and found himself swinging upside down, ten feet off the deck. The blood was rushing to his head and his eyes started to see red. He knew he was going to lose consciousness.

"You want to tell the truth little big man, eh? You can swing there until there is no life in your lying little body! So? What shall it be?" the Officer shouted up to him. That was the last voice he heard as he lost consciousness.

He remembered nothing after that until he awoke to find himself laying on the deck near the bow. It was dark and he could hear the waves breaking against the ship. Everything seemed very quiet and as much as he wanted to shift his position, he realized any moment might attract attention and produce more beatings. His despair knew no bounds as he quietly wept to himself. *Oh David. Kenneth. I need you and I cannot do this mission by myself. I am afraid, please, Davey?* He cried silently. He prayed. His body was so racked with pain and his position so cramped he lost consciousness again.

He was awakened by the sounds of shouting. It was coming from the lookout. Looking down the deck toward to the helm, he could see the Officers pointing and shouting orders. Judging from the rushing around him and the rolling out of guns, he was certain the ship was about to enter battle of some kind. He prayed it would be a British ship and wondered if it could be the *Emmejay*.

He lay crumpled in a small ball not wanting to attract any undue attention, and became aware of another dilemma. He had to urinate so badly his bladder was pounding, creating terrible agony. When he saw the gun crews were engrossed in priming their canon, he raised himself on one elbow stretching his cramped legs, and drained himself into the scuppers. He could breath easier now that the pain had left him.

The shouting continued and he heard the guns on the opposite side open fire. More firing, and he saw yards crash down onto the deck inches away from him. He wanted desperately to look, and gradually raised himself to look over the combing. He was nearly overcome by his sobbing as he realized a British Ship was attacking them. It was obvious from the crashing and screaming of injured men, that the British vessel was getting the better of the engagement and was doing much damage to the Spaniard. Jonathan wondered how much longer he had to live. It was ironic to think that, with all he had been through, he would die from the guns of his own Navy.

It was obvious to Jonathan that the Spaniard was very undermanned, having had to supply a prize crew for the *Courageous*. He wondered whether Chris had survived, and where he could be. The British Frigate was now a cables length away and preparing for boarding. The canon on the port side had ceased firing. Most of the canons were laying on their sides being overturned by the British onslaught. Groaning wounded were everywhere. Jonathan cried openly when he saw an Officer lowering the Spanish Flag at the stern. They were surrendering, and the ship that was overwhelming them, was indeed the *Emmejay*.

He would be seeing David soon, and he wiped away his tears, not wanting his friend to see him sniveling like a whipped puppy. He tried to raise himself but found he could not. His legs would not straighten. He sat with his back to the combing, awaiting someone to come.

* * * *

"David!" he called. "David I'm here, Sir," Jonathan shouted not really knowing what he was shouting for. He awoke in the Midshipman's berth with the doctor and the Earl standing anxiously over him.

"Jonathan. Whatever has happened to you? I can hardly believe it is you! I didn't know you were in the Mediterranean. You are so thin Jonathan! Have you not been eating well?"

"They were not feeding us very much aboard the Courageous, David. I am so weak I can hardly talk," Jonathan said with a barely audible voice.

"I am sorry I am asking so many questions, but the Captain asked me to talk to you. He will be here shortly. We have captured the Spaniard and you are safe now, my brother," David comforted, hiding a little quiver in his voice as he held back his boyish tears. "I am so thankful that the Spaniards didn't kill you when they captured your ship. I don't know what I'd do if I lost you, too."

"When I found you, I feared you were good as dead. I could not have endured that. It would have been too much. Everything will now be all right Jonathan. You sleep now and I will join you after the Captain has been down," David said getting up to go. "I am so thankful you are going to be well again."

"David will you ask the Captain if I can see his clerk? I have a report I must make immediately. Please, David?" Jonathan asked.

"Jonathan. Were you on special assignment?" David asked. He didn't wait for an answer but departed up the steps to the quarter-deck.

"Sir! Midshipman Walters has need for a clerk to pen a report. He seemed adamant about his request. He has been sadly neglected, Sir. He was starved near to death I am afraid," David reported.

Jonathan dictated his report with only he and the clerk present. Every now and again the clerk would pause and gasp, accentuating some remark Jonathan made. He would stare at Jonathan then resume the report.

"You must not divulge the contents of this report to anyone," Jonathan advised. "The Captain will not ask you about it, I'm sure. This is to be delivered to the Admiral of the Mediterranean fleet as soon as possible. Great care must be taken to protect the contents of this report, as you can well understand."

Jonathan was given special attention as were several of the surviving *Courageous* crew. The malnourishment the men had suffered was very evident to everyone.

Two weeks later, the *Emmejay* rolled quietly in the harbor surrounded by Naval vessels of every description. Jonathan was almost completely healed and was slowly regaining his lost weight. David commented that he was looking like his old, ugly self again. He was happy to see his friend was on the mend. The Captain thought it would do Jonathan good to stand a watch now that he was getting better. It would take his mind off himself. He had also arranged for the report to be delivered by his First Officer's hand to the Admiral.

"Mr. Clements, would you be so kind as to accompany Mr. Walters to Headquarters? Sir Jonas Philby wishes to speak with Jonathan. No doubt regarding his report," the Captain ordered David.

* * * *

"Sir Jonas. Midshipmen Sir David Clements and Midshipman Jonathan Walters are here at your request," the Admiral's flag Lieutenant announced.

"Sit down gentlemen. Sir David, I asked you to come with your friend to make him feel more comfortable. Jonathan, I received your report and words fail me at this time. I found it difficult to imagine that this occurred, but it all falls into place. We are, at the present time, or at least within a week, rounding up the depot crew and everyone else connected with this deplorable mess. Lucky for the Captain and his First Officer they died in battle. Saves the Navy it's reputation and the expense of a court-martial. I was forewarned in a letter from Sir Charles, that I was not to ask questions other than to read the report. That I have done, but by tarnation, I am inquisitive just the same. Your are being reassigned to the *Emmejay*. I wish you the best of luck Mr. Walters, and congratulations on your splendid performance. I'm sure the Admiral will have something more concrete for you on your return to England. Oh yes, the *Emmejay* is returning to England."

David and Jonathan held their exuberance until they were outside the Admiralty Office before they let out their hoop for joy. They suddenly remembered they were King's Officers and straightened up as they walked back to their waiting carriage. Mr. and Mrs. Walters would be proud of their boys had they been there. They knew, though, that she would be holding them soon.

CHAPTER FORTY-TWO

The Homecoming

The *Emmejay* plowed her way northward through moderate seas and at certain times, more than enough fog appeared to set the lookouts on double duty. They knew French patrols would surely be searching for any kind of shipping making its way north to England.

Three weeks later, the Midshipmen were finding it difficult to contain their excitement as they knew that in three days, they should be sighting Portsmouth. David stood his regular watch while Jonathan was allowed to recuperate on double rations. He was almost fully recovered and his confidence was slowly returning. He was feeling more like a King's Officer when the seaman would salute as they passed by, or nod their heads smiling.

The trip across the channel was uneventful, with the exception of a single sighting, which was of no bother to them.

David and Jonathan imagined what was taking place ashore after reports that their ship had been sighted in Portsmouth. The Walter's family would be preparing a homecoming feast, and would be getting the carriage prepared for the journey to meet the ship. David did not think his Father would have received the news as yet, so it would be several days before they were reunited. He wondered how things might have changed at the House of Windsor and if Samuel would still be employed there. Because of the fact he had treated the old man so terribly, he wanted to make amends and put things right with the Butler.

Bos'n's pipes trilled their various signals as the sails were secured and the anchor was let away. Ships of war always attracted huge crowds along the quay to watch the returning sailors.

* * * *

David and Jonathan bade their farewell to the ship's Officers and were allowed to go ashore. The bum boat rowed by two young ladies, made it's way slowly across the bay, much too slow to David's liking. He could hardly sit still. Jonathan tugged at his coat sleeve more than once to remind him he was still a King's Officer. The ladies smiled at the two boys, having known beforehand who their famous passengers were going to be.

The boys climbed the steps to the landing, carrying their own bags, and were greeted unceremoniously by a warm-hearted embrace and a kiss on the cheek from Mrs. Walters, their new mother. At least David considered her his mother, since he'd never really had one before she came along.

People gathered about the landing sailors, laughing and shouting and expressing their joy at getting to see the heroes up close. The Walters family hustled them along to the carriage, allowing them to receive the welcome from their adoring and grateful well-wishers along the way.

Mrs. Walters was somewhat taken aback at the thin appearance of Jonathan and remarked so. He advised her that he was unable to explain at the moment and his mother did not pursue the questioning, knowing her son had been on special assignment.

The Walters' carriage was loaded with luggage, much more than just the Midshipmen's gear. Mrs. Walters informed David that the family had been invited to bring David home when he arrived, and the family would be the guests of the Duke and the young Earl at the House of Windsor. They were all very excited and looking forward to the experience. David was excited as well, but he was feeling more than apprehensive about returning to his home after almost two years.

The House of Windsor was the scene of major celebrations and partying as the Walters family and the young Earl arrived at the front gates. The carriage made its way to the front steps where the Duke and the entire household staff were gathered as a welcoming committee. David caught the tear in the corner of his Father's eyes as he approached him ascending the steps. David moved immediately to his side, allowing his Father to embrace him. David then shook hands with all of the household staff, including Samuel, begging their forgiveness for his former incorrigible ways.

The gates of the estate had been opened to allow neighbors and families to join in the homecoming as well. It was indeed a very special occasion and the celebrating went on into the late evening and early morning hours. There was much laughing and singing and dancing, and the Midshipmen were receiving more attention than they'd ever had in their lives.

David and Jonathan were very tired, but extremely happy to be home again, even for a short time. An opportunity finally presented itself for the boys to remove themselves from the festivities and locate a secluded corner of the garden under a grove of large oak trees. They stretched out on the luscious lawn, staring up at the stars on the clear, cool night.

"David, I wish Kenneth was here with us right now to share this time together. That would make me so happy." Jonathan breathed out a deep sigh as he spoke.

"Oh, I think he probably is with us, Jonathan. Somewhere up there, I know he's looking down on us and smiling."

"Yes, I suppose he probably is. You know, I never, ever dreamed my life would turn out this way." Jonathan said. "Since coming to know you and Kenneth, I've gained a family and real brothers. I always thought a life like this was only for other people, not for me. I guess dreams really do come true, though, don't they brother?" Jonathan turned and looked at David with a sheepish smile and a glistening in his eye.

"I think you're right, little brother. I think you're absolutely right."

Their hands came together and squeezed tightly as they looked back up into the night sky, the tears in their eyes sparkling from the light of the moon and stars.

* * * *

Mrs. Walters, looking around for the boys, found them outstretched on the lawn, sleeping peacefully after their long day. She kissed them both gently and said a little prayer to thank God for bringing her boys home safely to her once again. She knew with all her heart that she was truly blessed to have this newfound family.

For now, the life of sea duties and sea adventures would be left behind on the *Emmejay*, if even for a very short time.

ABOUT THE AUTHOR

Douglas Hargreaves was Born in Winnipeg, Manitoba Canada in 1925. He spent the first 10 years of his life there, later moving to Alberta. He lived in the area for several years then joined the Royal Canadian Airforce in 1943. He served a tour of operation with an RAF Bomber group, completing his tour of 35 operational missions over enemy territory. He returned to Canada and later obtained a job flying locally out of Pine Falls Manitoba. He then moved into to Northern Canada and became a part time Hudson's Bay Post employee and Bush pilot serving North Saskatchewan. He is married with two sons and their families. He has written many articles and short stories. His first published novel was *The Cowboy* now in its third printing followed by its sequel *From Cowboys to Cockpits* in its second printing.

The books, although fiction, are based on the many interesting experiences and adventures of the author as a young boy growing up in the foothills of Alberta, and his experiences while in the services and in Northern Canada.

The author resides in Abbotsford, British Columbia, but spends much of his time in Blaine, WA with his wife on their sailboat into the Georgia Straits.